MYSTICS

MYSTICS

The Third Book in the Punanai Series

David James Elliott

IGUANA

Publisher: Cheryl Hawley
Editor: Amanda Feeney
Cover design: David Russell

ISBN 978-1-77180-685-5 (paperback)
ISBN 978-1-77180-684-8 (epub)

This is an original print edition of *Mystics*.

Other Books in the
Five-Book Punanai Series

Most people manage the inevitable carnage of their middle years with the same efficacy that a four-year-old brings to running away from home.

Chapter 1

March in Toronto gets on your nerves and up your nose the way the odour of fish in an apartment hallway does. You feel the same contempt for it that you have for your overcoat and the hot, heavy rubber you're forced to wear on your feet. You cheered when winter was served eviction papers, but still, it lingers, hiding in the parking garage, sitting on a milk crate behind a pillar, in a torn T-shirt with a shotgun at the ready, certain one more victim can be found.

The guys at Punanai had been on edge. You could see it in the classroom. The way they raked their hair with their fingers. The elaborate doodles. The catatonic stares. This latest snowfall was a godsend. The young guys had it cleared away in an hour and were happily leaning on their shovels enjoying a smoke before class.

From his office window, Mike Sage took in the view as he placed his suit coat on the back of a chair and loosened his tie. A patch of devasted grass in shades of grey and brown had stolen out from underneath the frozen snowdrifts churned up by the plow. Madison Avenue resembled a pretzel covered in coarse salt, a world sick of winter, aching for spring.

Mike watched as a rope line of children from the daycare passed in front of the centre on their way to the park, struggling to move in their thick parkas and boots along the uneven sidewalk, young seals navigating an ice flow. They filled the street with new life and energy. The time scale was different at the daycare, but the process was the same in every institution. Move them along.

An image of Channing Hart handcuffed to his peers and shuffling off the prison bus ruined the moment. Could Hart navigate prison without Sean Miller at his side? Mike shook his head. Best not to worry about the departed. He still had a house full of live ones. Lots of crazy kids who didn't know how to make a bed, and Jacob Hutton, who just might be the most annoying client of all time.

Punanai House was the only building on the street with bare cement and interlocking pavement all free from ice and snow. With thirty young men in its care, there was always someone who could battle winter with a broom. The footing everywhere else on Madison Avenue followed slush-filled corridors worn down by the feet of passersby and the wheels of buggies.

Inside the house, the grand stairwell groaned under the weight of ascending scholars. It was the beginning of the morning session. Mike did a walk-through of the house, herding the reluctant before him as efficiently as a corgi driving sheep. He paused as he entered the coffee corner and looked through the glass window to check on his boss. Doug Moore was happily absorbed in reading the weekend report.

Mike stuck his head into Doug's office. "I need to leave early today."

The great stone face wondered why Mike was hiding behind the door, half in and half out of the office. The body language suggested he was unsure of his ground. Then it came to him. Mike wasn't wearing his tie. Doug fixed his friend with a stare. "I pay you to be here, not elsewhere."

A quirky smile crossed Mike's handsome face. "This is work, kind of. You remember the neat freak?"

Doug leaned back in his dark leather swivel chair and cupped his hands behind his head. "The guy that Paul calls Mr. Clean?"

Mike nodded, trying to keep the good feeling going. "That's the guy. He got up halfway through his interview and started dusting. Anyway, he's gone walkabout and his mother wants me to check on him. Kaiser's going off shift at three. I want to take him with me."

Doug leaned forward and rested his forearms on the armrests as he adjusted his position. "You're a bona fide tough guy. Since when you need a bodyguard?"

Mike leaned his shoulder onto the door, confirming not only the absence of a tie but the additional sin of no suit coat. "He used to be a cop, remember? And he's a little touchy about his privacy. I'm not afraid of him, but I'm not going to get myself dusted doing a favour. I need someone for him to gun down. Reg suggested I take Kaiser."

Doug had to smile. *Why can't he keep his tie on? Everyone else does.* "Is this how you plan to deal with staff issues when they fire me? Lead troublemakers into ambushes?"

Mike looked as if he was mulling it over. "Well, I wouldn't make it a policy exactly, but yeah, falling off ladders, mysterious fires, and the occasional disappearance all get the job done and..." he said with considerable emphasis, "all of them are cheaper than long-term disability."

Doug happily returned to the reports and was once again finding his stride when he heard the ring from his private line.

Interruptions ... interruptions ... interruptions.

The voice on the other end was a welcome intrusion, the former face of the franchise. "Bob Bourns! What the hell are you doing off the golf course? It's ten a.m. You should be starting the back nine."

The voice dripped petulance in a comic vein. "The world can be a very unfair place."

Doug missed Bob's endless ability to have fun. "What are you doing back in Toronto when it's snowing?"

Bob sighed theatrically. "I came in to do some legal stuff and got involved with a family about their young fella. It's a peculiar situation. I was wondering if I could play the old-boy card and bring the erring tyke in for an assessment this afternoon."

Doug didn't care if he brought the kid or not. He wanted to see his old friend. "We always have room for a paying customer. Let me get the particulars."

***

Bob hung up the phone and looked over his shoulder, keeping a wary eye on his hosts from his perch in the dining room. The Canons were sitting in their beautiful living room, enjoying a cup of fair-trade coffee. Bob sighed. Doug wanted the particulars about this bunch, but perhaps the right word was *peculiars*. This family portrait was off.

Bob wondered how it must feel to rest your cup of Kicking Horse on the Bösendorfer while you admired the purported Vermeer — the one that Grandma Ames claimed she picked up at a garage sale in 1932 for six dollars — all the while chatting with mommy about how she planned to decorate the premier's office come the fall.

Bob had done a lot of interventions in his time at Punanai, but never in a room this well decorated. The guest of honour didn't even have the decency to be hungover like a rat. Lou Canon was sitting upright in a straight-backed chair. He was clean-shaven, wearing a sports coat, and looking every inch the gentleman. No shakes, no sweats, no insane lies or denials. In fact, he looked as healthy as a horse. A young man of twenty-five, just out of college.

A badger couldn't get to the bottom of this, Bob thought as he watched the bizarre family process continue to play out. He glanced across the room. Lou's fiancée, Lori, was playing the piano as if this was a social occasion. The rubber crocodile that Lou never let out of his sight was sitting on the end table beside his cup and saucer. Lou and Croc went everywhere together, and, if Lou was to be believed, they passed their time discussing classic films and stock market plays. But that was only the first piece of gravel Bob bit down on in this bowl of chowder.

Lou's progenitors sat opposite him on the couch. The paterfamilias of the Canon clan exuded the faint whiff of fraud. For a man in public life, it was bad enough to have a son who was a drunk. But if that sort of thing could be properly managed, it might actually garner a clever politician some sympathy and support, especially if he could blame his child's failings on the badly thought-out educational system imposed on the province by the current liberal government and position himself as the epitome of long-suffering parental providence.

It was a worse fate to be blessed with delusional progeny who spoke to make-believe friends, because that pointed to weakness in the breeding stock. The ruling class-in-waiting needed to make a better showing than that with the constituents.

But what would the voters make of a politician whose son had outperformed the leading market indicators for six years in a row — the first of which was in a bear market. It screamed corruption and insider trading.

Could that be what this was about? Perceptions?

Lou had listened politely to what his parents had to say, had answered Bob's questions honestly, and had been gracious. But now, if his furrowing brow was to be believed, his temper was beginning to chafe.

The senior Canons should have let Bob do the talking. At one point, about an hour ago, he'd made a very compelling case for looking into the role that drugs and alcohol were playing in Lou's health.

Because of his long experience, Bob had had the good sense to shut up after he'd made his point, a potent strategy not shared by Kay and Thomas Cannon. They kept blathering on about the upcoming campaign and how much it was going to mean to the family and the province of Ontario for Thomas to be re-elected with a majority. Then there was the upcoming wedding! She felt overwhelmed and he unappreciated.

Lou was giving way to their provocation — his sang-froid not unlike the surface of a frozen lake that was being undercut by a fast-moving stream, one that polished the lake's opaque surface into a transparency that could no longer bear any weight.

He leaned forward suddenly. "I'm nowhere near bad enough to have to go to Punanai House. Do you even know what Punanai means!" He looked first at his mother and then his father with a look of triumph. "Well, do you?"

There was a profound silence as they looked at each other helplessly. Lou smirked at the backfooted pair. "I thought as much."

Lori left the piano and walked behind Lou's chair. Her hands lightly touched her fiancé's shoulders and gave him an encouraging little tap. "Well, I'm interested. What does it mean?"

There was another prolonged silence as Kay and Thomas exchanged furtive looks. They dared not admit that they didn't know. They lived by lawyers' rules. To be mistaken in a single fact implied that your argument was not to be relied upon. They were prepared to brazen this moment out in silence if they could and to shout and pound the table if it came to that.

Lori noted their distress and enthusiastically doubled down. "Well, what does it mean?"

Lou sat straighter. It was time to spray-paint the word *fake* on this latest garage-sale masterpiece. The name of the place was a gift.

"It's slang," he said, lowering his voice to a conspiratorial tone. "Jamaican slang. Don't make me say more. It's rude."

Lori looked up from the pamphlet Bob had given her with a puzzled look on her face. "It can't be all that bad, it's on all their literature."

Kay snickered. The general sense of the word had penetrated the country club. Her patrician good looks and grooming amplified the meaning of her glance, which seemed to say, *You had better have more than that.*

Lou, brightening in mock acquiescence, said. "Oh well then, if it's on their literature!" He got to his feet and retrieved Croc from the coffee table, suggesting that he was about to decamp. "This is as bad as Life Skills."

Kay smiled at her son in a way that said, *Be a good boy and put down the crocodile.*

Lou took Lori's hand in his and looked theatrically into her eyes. "'I am one whose bones are broken to pieces through the taunting of his enemies.'"

Lori looked at him quizzically. She didn't recognize the reference. She'd google it later. Dramatic utterance was a game they both loved.

As Bob lingered in the dining room, he had a wonderful view of the backyard. A side door opened and a black Labrador was given his freedom. He tore across the fresh fall of snow with a look of joy on his face. Bob could've watched him all day, but he had duties. His thoughts landed on his host.

Thomas Canon had made millions bullying people. He was the putative minster of health in the provincial opposition's shadow cabinet. If two more ridings changed hands, the government would fall and Thomas would become the morning-line favourite to inherit that cabinet post at the very least.

But his ambition went further. He wanted the premier's office. And his boss, the oversexed, scandal-plagued leader of the opposition, was slated for demolition at the next party conference. His personal failings were all that stood between the party and a throne speech. With him out of the way, good things were certain to happen. Happily, his tearful farewell speech was scheduled to take place one week after the next round of by-elections in April.

The polls supported these ambitions. His political stars were aligned. All that Thomas had to do was camouflage a few small blemishes (keep Lou out of sight), avoid a major gaff (such as getting caught in a hot tub with a woman named on a deportation order, as his feckless leader had done), and wait for the whole thing to fall into his lap.

All of this was top of mind for him as he turned to his son. "The doctors can't do their work unless you cooperate. They don't know if you're crazy because you take this crap, or crazy and take this crap for kicks. They have to see you clean and sober before they can decide."

Lou regarded his parents with suspicion. "There's a good reason they can't come up with a diagnosis. I'm fine the way I am. There's nothing wrong with me! 'I am as God made me. Day and night I taste only tears, while they steadily belittle me, saying where is your God?'"

"Where in the world did you hear that?" asked Lori with a look of sly admiration on her face.

"Hard to remember, but psalm where."

Kay and Thomas looked accusingly at each other. Dramatic utterance always reduced them to impotence.

Lori picked up a passing cat and settled it on her lap as she took a seat beside Lou. Her long, graceful fingers went to work on the feline's lucky neck muscles. "Whenever we get somewhere painful, I always try and get the logic of the choices straight. It helps me make up my mind," she said.

Kay and Thomas scowled. "Lou, what your dad says has some merit. You've been experiencing all kinds of wild daydreams, and sometimes you see, hear, and smell things that aren't there."

Lou's tone was respectful. "You don't experience them, but that doesn't mean they're not real."

Lori nodded and moved on to her next point. "I believe what you say, because you don't lie about important things. But the point remains, alcohol could be at the bottom of this."

He danced a little with his reply. "Or cream cheese, or chocolate, or pet dander."

"Or tumours, or infections, or trauma," thundered Kay. "What we're talking about here is a process of elimination."

Thomas was done. "It's more a process of shutting your mouth and doing as you're told." He rose to his feet to signal that the matter was resolved.

Lori was annoyed. She wasn't going to let the Right Honourable get away with that. She glanced over at Lou, who was desperately trying to make a pun out of heir apparent and errors of the parent.

She went back to scratching the cat as she smiled sweetly at her future father-in-law. "It's not hard to see why the voters love you…"

That earned her a frown from Kay and a dismissive pulse of air from the minister-in-waiting, who crossed the room and took up a new station looking out the window with his hands clasped behind his back in the classic fed-up posture. Her marriage to Lou was supposed to put a stop to all his foolishness, and now here she was fanning the flames, taking his side, in this madness, in an election year! She didn't even vote for the party last time. Lori was a bellwether riding consistently polling the wrong way.

It was a shame. She and Lou made a lovely couple. Both were tall and thin and elegant. Lori always looked vaguely the part of a budding movie starlet, one whose face you recognized but whose name you couldn't bring to mind, always well dressed and groomed in her casual but stylish way. The voters would eat her up.

Lou's outward appearance pegged him as an aristocrat, but that was far from being the whole story. He had a long, serious face that shone inquisitive as well as handsome. There were hints of rebellion and adolescent sloppiness too — and then there was Croc.

Croc had shown up at the dinner table the year Lou entered puberty. A phase of development apparently without end. He gave Kay the creeps and made Thomas impotent with fury. When Thomas locked Croc in his desk drawer, twelve-year-old Lou held the Vermeer over the roaring fireplace until the hostages could be exchanged.

Lori was enjoying the impasse. "If you don't think you have a problem with alcohol, then why don't you allow the people at Punanai to have a look at you?"

Lou put down his coffee cup. He'd known for months that he was going to spend some time at Punanai. His half-hearted protests were disinformation mixed in with a good measure of pest control.

The physical structure of the treatment centre had been a part of his consciousness for weeks. He could've walked the halls blindfolded. And he was curious to see the layout of the building and put a few names to the faces he'd been seeing. But this was the stuff that a long exposure to the supernatural had taught him to keep to himself.

Knowing the general shape of the future was dangerous if it gave you a sense of control. Thomas ached to know and control the future, and to further this end, he commissioned a new poll once every three weeks that he paid for out of his own pocket. He need not have bothered. Lou knew what was in store for him.

Lou had been trying to put a healthy distance between himself and his parents since early adolescence. Even his impending marriage to Lori had not changed the way they treated him. He lovingly referred to the chronic problem as the crusades. He was Jerusalem, and his parents were ideologically bent, slightly heavy-handed fundamentalists, trying to change him from what he was into what they thought he should be.

Unlike Lori, they'd never developed a taste for the ice wine of Lou's essence. When this latest attempt failed to produce a wholesale change in him for the better, they would simply come up with something new, likely something one of them would find in *Psychology Today*.

Lou frowned. "I'm fine. There's nothing wrong with me. I might be odd, but I'm never boring. And sure, I take a little drink, but I never order Chablis with breakfast."

Thomas missed the inference and turned away from the window in fury. "What has that got to do with anything?"

Lori was ready to go home but she soldiered on. "Oh look," she said brightly. "Bob's off the phone. Let's see what he has to say."

Bob had been watching them kick the conversational football around while he was on the phone. He didn't care much for the way these people spoke to each other. But his tone didn't give that away. He wondered what was really going on as he looked around the room. There was a vase of beautiful flowers decorating the big mahogany table by the front window, but all he could smell was something sour. His con light was burning bright. For a split second he wondered if he was being punked.

"I've spoken with my friend Doug. He runs the treatment centre I used to work at. I told him a little bit about you, and he suggested that we come in and have a talk this afternoon."

They all looked at him as if he were trying to sell them life insurance. He gave them his trademark pause and smile. "I can drive you over there and then bring you back."

Thomas clapped his hands together. This was progress; now he could get back to work on something important.

Bob knew from the look on Lou's face that this wasn't settled. He twitched his moustache and tested the waters. "Are we all in agreement?"

Kay looked forlorn in her green knee-length dress as she fingered a long run of pearls. "When can they get him in?"

Lou recognized this bluff of pretending the matter had been settled. The idea was to push him into a car while he was still sputtering. He turned to Lori and whispered, "This has been their plan all along. With me out of the house, they can invite the bridge club over." He dropped his voice. "They play strip Chicago!"

Lori whispered "*Incroyable*" into the cat's ear.

Lou's hand came up to cover his mouth. "It's why I freak when I see a deck of cards."

Lori's head went back as she guffawed. She loved Lou Canon.

Kay hated Lori's laughter. It meant that she was still on Lou's side. "What was that ... dear?"

Lou waved his hand in a dismissive way. "We were just picking seats for the ride over."

Chapter 2

Kaiser's Toyota was a wonder of the world. The vehicle had been gifted to him when Uncle Oren went into the Granite Glen Nursing Home. It was the only car Oren had ever owned. He bought it to impress a comely widow. The fastidious old bachelor seldom drove, but he vacuumed the car once a week, as he did everything else that he owned. In the decade that followed, he put eleven thousand kilometres on the odometer. He was a terrible driver and the car was marked with the paint of his victims.

When Kaiser asked where he took the car for servicing, his uncle simply shrugged. So Kaiser took it back to the dealership where it had been purchased and watched in fascination as one technician after another joined the crowd around the service bay computer, all talking at once and pointing at the screen. The car had never been in for service. As far as they could tell, everything, including the oil, was exactly as it had been when it left the showroom.

Kaiser had them do an oil change and made an appointment for a much larger service, but he didn't follow through. When the warning lights started to flash on and off, Kaiser took the view that there was nothing to be done but run the car until it gave up the ghost. He hoped that what the wreckers would give him on that inevitable day would cover the cost of the tow truck and a cab ride home.

Mike was enjoying the drive. The car smelled of new leather. He believed Kaiser when he told him that the reason the lights on the dashboard kept coming off and on was a fault in the sensor and that the car was otherwise in racing shape. That made sense. A vehicle this clean must be in apple pie order, even if the dents said otherwise. Mike micromanaged them through rush hour and a series of side streets until they arrived at their destination. "Here's the building on the right. Pull in there."

Kaiser edged the venerable Toyota into the narrow visitors' parking spot. The car continued to run very roughly for thirty seconds after it was switched off. Kaiser pretended that this was the first time it had happened. He cultivated the image of a highflyer, with Rockefeller looks and Roosevelt wealth and taste. Oren's Toyota let him down badly on both counts. But it only needed to survive until the end of March. In Lakefield he wouldn't need a car.

They made their way across the parking lot and entered through the rear door — the one that boasted the garbage bins and recycling containers. In spite of the cold, there was a scent of decay in the air. As Kaiser looked around, he realized where they were for the first time. "That's your building across the way, isn't it?"

Mike nodded as he held the door open for Kaiser. "Yeah, it's all managed by the same company."

They made their way to the lower level and walked down a long, deeply carpeted hallway until they came to the only door in the building that boasted a mailbox. Mike knocked on the super's door. A distracted man in grey coveralls appeared with a sandwich in his hand. He looked dirty and tired. He obviously wanted the intruders to know he had his hands full.

"Perry, we're going upstairs to check on Fred Grant."

Perry wasn't a volunteer. "Off you go then."

"His mother's worried about him. He hasn't answered the phone in three days."

The grubby man had an intuitive flash. "Does he drink vodka?"

Kaiser was intrigued by the question and shouldered Mike to the side. "Why do you ask?"

Perry gave them a knowing look. "Someone's been drinking Prince Igor with both hands."

"Any way to tell who it is?"

"Nope. The stuff ends up in the blue box. I separate the bottles and take them back for the refund."

Mike was trying to get back in charge. "I don't suppose we could get you to tag along. I don't know this guy very well and it'd be good to have you do the introductions — and be a witness."

Perry thought about what he'd heard for a minute. "This could be bad. We've had bugs, but Grant wouldn't let us spray his unit. Said he didn't have any."

He closed the door behind him and led the way to the elevator as he finished his sandwich. They went up two floors, and the little man led them to the apartment they wanted. He looked at Mike as if to say, *It's all up to you now.*

Mike knocked very softly and waited for a response. Nothing stirred from inside. He knocked louder.

"Fred, it's Mike Sage. Are you there?"

Dark thoughts and feelings of foreboding began to take root in the trio's imaginations. This could be awful. Mike patted down his pockets, looking for the keys.

"Fred, your mom is worried about you," Mike called through the door. He knocked louder still. Even a deep sleeper would've heard him pounding. As if to confirm this, an old woman in a housecoat stuck her head out of her door to watch what was happening.

Kaiser fanned their unspoken fear by putting his handkerchief over his nose. "Do you smell that?"

"Huh," Mike said as he instinctively took a step back. He looked over at Kaiser who had a smug look on his face. He gave him a shove and returned to the vexing problem of the lock. He got the door open a crack only to be confronted with a chain. He searched the ring of keys in his palm until he found a small one that looked right. The chain gave way, but this was still someone else's place and he didn't feel right about barging in. The chain meant that someone was here. He stuck his head inside and called out again. "Fred, are you in here?"

Kaiser bulled his way past Mike and strode into the apartment. "Are you sure this is the right place?"

"The key fits."

Perry followed them cautiously and stopped in his tracks. He was confused. "When he moves out, I'm taking this unit."

Kaiser walked around the well-lit living room, taking in the new surroundings. "Is he selling? All it needs is a pie baking in the oven." He ran his finger across the top of the wall unit. There was no sign of dust. Uncle Oren would have been in awe. *Nobody's place looks this good when they're on a binge. Not even Mr. Clean.*

Mike shared his wonder. "Maybe his mom is wrong. I was expecting pizza boxes and a dead cat."

Perry called from the far room. "Here he is."

They followed Perry's voice into the den. The little man was opening a window. A large man with powerful shoulders and arms was face down on the floor. Mike took a short sharp breath. "Oh shit, is he dead?"

Kaiser knelt by the man's side, feeling for a pulse. "Dead drunk." He rolled the man onto his side into the recovery position. "Smells like a bottle of hand sanitizer." He held up a half empty pint bottle of Prince Igor.

Mike poked his nose into the kitchen cupboards looking for prescription drugs and intoxicants. What he found were perfectly lined-up canned goods. *This guy could work for Sobeys.*

Kaiser tapped Fred on the temple with his finger, which generally caused enough discomfort to wake a deep sleeper, but not someone who was in a coma. "Fred, can you hear me? Do you want to buy a Mexican time-share?"

Mike came out of the bathroom with three bottles of pills, sat down at the kitchen table, and started to count them out. "This is all stuff for his heart, and if the dates on the vials are right, he's been taking this stuff the way he should be."

"Does it say to wash it down with vodka, comrade?"

Mike looked at the forlorn man on the floor. He felt a moment of compassion. *You know exactly how many steps it is to the front door, don't you?*

Kaiser was back in charge. "We need to get this guy to detox. He's gonna have a seizure. Perry, is this guy well off?"

Perry nodded sagely. "He's got a civil service pension. He's fixed up real good. Gets four cheques a month."

"Good," said Kaiser. "Then he's going by ambulance. I don't want him barfing in my car."

Perry's brow furrowed. "What if he doesn't want to go?"

Kaiser felt an evil spirit move him. "I'll ask him." He picked up the unconscious man and put him in a sitting position. "Fred, do you want to go to detox?"

Kaiser gently moved Fred's head up and down as if he was nodding in agreement. "What's that..." he said. He leaned into the man's space, pretending to hear a dying utterance. After a second, he returned the man to the floor. "He says he wants to go to Toronto East because it's closer to the library."

Perry shook his head. This was disrespectful. Fred was a cop. "Are you guys nuts?"

Kaiser continued patting Fred down, looking for drugs. He tossed a small spray bottle of disinfectant he found on the floor and then reached into the other sweater pocket. "Whoops," he said as he brought out a compact pistol. He expertly jettisoned the clip and emptied the chamber. "Safety's off."

This guy is ready to rock and roll. But on who?

***

The ambulance arrived quietly. There was no need for a siren. The paramedics accessed Fred's file en route. This was almost certainly going to end with them being ordered off the premises by an irate inebriate. The paperwork generated would be a marvel of clarity and a gem of brevity. An A.M.A. (against medical advice) would be tersely followed by a D.N.T. (did not transport) — an outcome common on tosspot calls.

Mike met them in the lobby and brought them upstairs. It was a tight fit in the elevator with the two big attendants and the gurney. The old woman down the hall was getting an eyeful. She had gotten dressed and done something with her hair.

Kaiser met the medics at the door. "I need you to have a look at this guy."

Mike was a little surprised to find himself again supplanted by his wheel man. He took a seat on the sofa to watch the fun. *Why does Kaiser have the wind up?*

The paramedics asked the stupidest question they could manage, to communicate their displeasure at being spoken to as if they were idiots. "Is that him over there?"

Kaiser was fully immersed in his new role and missed the inference.

"Yes, I have his medication here, it was in the bathroom. We counted the pills. He appears to be taking them the way he's supposed to."

The paramedics exchanged a look. Their gentle rebuff hadn't worked. They took it up a step.

"Are you a relative?" The older of the two had begun to wonder if Kaiser was sober. The younger wondered who Kaiser was trying to impress.

"No." Kaiser looked over at Mike for help. "We work at a treatment centre." He nodded toward Fred. "The super says he's been drinking a quart of vodka every day for at least a month."

The attendants exchanged a professional look that said *busybody* and moved past Kaiser into the living room. "Okay, let us do our stuff."

Mike got up from the sofa and whispered in Kaiser's ear. "Why don't you go over there and show them how to do it?"

At that moment, the police arrived. Kaiser bristled when he saw them. He saw a chance for a little more payback. "Officer, I have a ticklish situation here."

The cop was all ears. "This man is a retired Toronto policeman. We need to get him to detox. But here's the bigger problem. When we found him on the floor, we frisked him for drugs and found a pistol."

"Where is it now?"

"I put it in his sock drawer."

"I hope he has a permit."

"Anyone who drinks as much as our friend Mr. Grant here has no business having a pistol. Why do you fellows run around with guns anyway? Don't you get enough of that at work?"

The officer looked Kaiser up and down, trying to place him. *This guy's been in handcuffs.* He strode past him. "I'll handle this."

Kaiser smiled. That was only a field goal, but it felt good to score even three points on these bastards. How he hated cops.

Chapter 3

While Lori and Lou gathered up their things, Thomas and Kay cornered Bob in the alcove. He was watching the maid play with the dog in the bright sunshine. The inner courtyard was surrounded on all sides by windows and open to the sky. Beds of flowers formed a perfect oval around a snow-covered yard that was large enough for a game of croquet in the summer.

"What do you think, Bob?" Thomas asked.

"I wish I could still have as much fun as your dog's having."

"About Lou," Thomas said. "Will they take him? Can they fix him?"

What a pair. Their lips were drawn and their eyes half closed. He'd seen this look a thousand times — in a hotel room that smelled of cigars or when a garment comes back from the dry cleaners with a ragged edge. It suggested mild disdain.

Bob gave it to them straight up. "Why is this *your* problem?"

They were taken aback, but they put on their lawyer faces. "He's our son. We love him."

Bob kept his voice low. "If there's a substance abuse problem, it's in its infancy."

Kay wasn't having that. "He does crazy ridiculous things… It has to be the booze."

Bob shook his head. "No. He doesn't drink enough at any one sitting and he goes for long periods of time without drinking."

Thomas looked stern. "What else could it be?"

Bob looked back at the garden and the happy dog and wondered why the maid was doing the honours. *Is that how Lou grew up?*

"Let's start at the beginning. What made you think he's a drunk?"

The Canons looked blankly at each other. They were far past this point. Pliable opinion had coalesced into hard fact. Kay spoke for both of them, and it cost her something to say, "He's odd…"

Bob cocked his head. "He's young."

Thomas amplified their shared discomfort. "He doesn't want to work."

Bob was surprised by that. "He told me he makes his money day trading."

Kay now looked ashamed and tried to hide it by looking away. "That's not work. It's gambling. It can't last."

Thomas put his arm around his wife. "He has no friends."

This didn't jibe with what he'd observed of the bright and personable young man. "What about Lori?"

They exchanged a look that said *can we tell him*. Kay sighed and Thomas shook his head. "We had great hopes for her, but now she's as bad as he is."

Kay ran her fingers through her hair. "We've tried everything with him. The right schools. Tutors. We even enrolled him in Life Skills, you know, that program for young people. But he stopped going."

Bob thought about deconstructing Life Skills for them. He was old-school and took a dim view of coddling addicts and alcoholics. But the model was increasingly in favour with public funders. He could cut his thumb on this and make trouble for Doug if he wasn't careful. *These two have a horse in that race. Are they using Lou as a test case? Is that what I'm smelling?*

Thomas let his anger notch up a rung. "He needs to straighten up. I can't run this province if I can't manage my own family. The voters aren't fools." He pointed his finger at Bob. "Your job is to get this boy out of the swamp he's stuck in. Lose the crocodile, wipe the smirk off his face, and bring him back with a proper attitude, a suit and tie that match, and a new briefcase."

Kay chimed in. "Lots of our colleagues insist we should be mothballing treatment centres. They think they're a waste of the taxpayers' money. This is your chance to prove them wrong and show the world that you deserve public funding."

Bob was horrified. "Don't put that on me. I'm not convinced they can help Lou. I don't think he's an alcoholic. I'm doing this as a favour to you. This would be a very poor basis on which to decide what to do about treatment facilities."

***

Greg Bass was a rock-and-roller with a wife and two coming-of-age boys. But the music didn't pay the bills. Punanai was his straight job. He was always well dressed in expensive suits that he wonderfully undercut with long, blond hair that said *no* to convention. To get to the bottom of Greg, you had to see him at the top of his game fronting his band, Pataphysics, on a Saturday night.

This month, Greg was doing initial interviews. His task was to assess people and direct them to an appropriate agency. Some of the other counsellors felt abandoned when they had to do this chore. They missed the camaraderie of the counsellors' office, where five bodies were always competing for three desks. They complained that it took them out of the rhythm of the house. Greg didn't look at it that way. He had an uncanny ability to read people, which suited him perfectly for this task, and he enjoyed putting some distance between himself and the rest of the pack. He'd brought along his Les Paul and used the time between calls to work out new arrangements for the band. But there was no time for that today. Mike had summoned him in for an assessment. The crowded office suited his mood.

Reg made his way painfully into the office, supporting his weight on two canes. Handsome, with a full head of hair and thick muscles through his chest and shoulders, he looked every one of his lived years plus a decade. He sat down on the edge of Mike's desk. "There's a man sitting in the waiting room with a brown paper bag glued to his face."

"That's Mr. Zeld," Mike said as he handed Reg a manila file. "He's here to see you."

Reg got a playful look on his face. "This is Gluey!"

Mike smiled. "He makes an appointment for assessment every week but never shows up."

Reg closed the file. "Well, you'll never be able to say that about him again." He slid off the desk and limped to the door. Through the window he could see the unfortunate man attempting to pull the paper bag off his cheek. "How are we going to help this guy? I tried to speak with him on the way in. He's fried."

Mike made a face as he joined Reg at the door to have a look at Mr. Zeld. His appearance spoke volumes: drastically underweight with dark circles under his eyes and a skin colour that screamed ill health.

"Well, we could start by getting some solvent to remove that brown paper bag from his face."

Reg brightened. "He'd be down with that."

Greg looked up from the sheet music he was sight reading. "No, let's not."

"Don't complain, Reg, you're getting the easy one," Mike said.

"Well, if Gluey is the easy one, tell me about the hard one."

Mike handed Lou Canon's file to Greg. "This one comes with a crocodile."

"That beats a paper bag glued to your face."

Reg didn't miss a beat. "I thought paper covers croc."

Mike had to smile. "You know me. I don't tell you what to think about clients before you see them. But this time, well, this is the guy Bob brought in. He gave me the lookout sign."

Greg put down the music and began leafing through the file. His eyes went straight to Bob's summary. "What is 'unwanted clairvoyance'?"

Reg gave Greg a little punch in the shoulder. "Don't pretend you don't know."

Mike made his way back to his desk. "Bob told me Mr. Canon uses substances to turn off the voices."

Greg and Reg exchanged a glance.

"Voices…" they said in unison.

"Look," said Mike. "I'm just an incredibly good-looking guy in a designer suit whose mother owns the company, but let me tell you what I really think, because I know you want to hear this. Spring break is just around the corner. This is a dump job."

Mike picked up his ruler and started to tap it on his palm. "Rich families who want to have a happy holiday dropping their defective brats off for servicing. The BMWs slow down outside the centre, and the maid and butler roll the young darling out onto the sidewalk with the certified cheque safety pinned to his shirt." He shook his head.

Reg thrust his file toward Greg.

"Trade you…"

"No way."

Chapter 4

Greg looked through the window into the interview room. Lou Canon was sitting in the swivel chair, admiring the spider plant that Reg had brought from home to decorate the otherwise bare and uninteresting room. A handsome rubber reptile had taken up a position on the desk facing Lou. There was a touch of the gargoyle about him.

As Greg entered and took his seat, he caught a movement out of the corner of his eye. He could've sworn the crocodile swished his tail. He put it down to a curiosity of the light. Putting the figure on the table was an obvious provocation. "What's with the crocodile?" he said.

Lou didn't bat an eye. "This is my colleague, Croc. He came along today to help me make up my mind about this place."

Greg was struggling to keep up appearances. He didn't want a prolonged silence to give away how ill prepared this last comment made him feel. He said the first thing that came to mind. "He's missing a piece of his tail."

"It's the women in his life."

Greg made a great show of getting comfortable in his chair. He needed time to compose himself. He was fighting an urge to giggle. He took pains to lay out his pen and the paperwork Lou had completed. When he was finished, he felt more settled. He hoped his face was radiating goodwill and acceptance and not the turmoil he was feeling. *Why do I have the yips?*

"So…" he said, drawing out the vowel sound, "what brings you guys in to see us today?" He tapped his finger on the manila file. "According to this, it's not addiction."

Lou sighed and pointed his thumb at Croc. "We lost an argument we should have won." He looked over at Greg, trolling for a reaction. "Mommy and Daddy think I'm nuts."

"Are you?"

"Different. Not nuts."

"Different but not nuts is a compelling diagnosis."

Lou smiled and leaned back in his chair. "Croc and I were hoping we'd get you."

Greg's con light flashed on with this attempt at the familiar. "But we've never met before."

Lou brightened. "What an odd thing to say to a clairvoyant."

He was hoping for a laugh from Greg. When he didn't get one, a look of disappointment stole across his face. He tried a different tack — a little fib to grease the wheels. "We hoped you were someone we could talk to. That you might be a fit."

Here it comes. "For what?"

"An unusual situation…" His voice climbed one octave.

Greg badly wanted to pick up Croc and lock him in the desk drawer. Instead, he cleared his throat. "You've listed clairvoyance as a medical condition."

Lou leaned back in his chair and began to rock. The chair squeaked, and the squeak combined with Lou's grin asked *Are we really doing this?*

"Croc's idea. My parents are certain that my clairvoyance is a delusion. They want me to stop using alcohol and drugs so I can be 'properly assessed' by a psychiatrist." He shook his head playfully and then spun around in his chair a few times. He put his foot down to stop the rotation and then leaned into Greg's space. "A doctor who will then give me lots of drugs I don't need or want."

This guy is gonna have an answer for everything.

A frontal assault on defences this well prepared couldn't possibly succeed. Greg leaned back in his chair, hoping to strike the posture of two friends getting caught up in a coffee shop. "You remind me of a girl I dated. She was empathic. She did therapeutic touch. Believed anything could be cured by prayer and physical contact. My point is that she gave off this wonderful energy. I could tell she was inside a room before I opened the door. It was weird. I never understood what was going on with her."

Lou looked supremely disinterested. There was a long silence as Greg considered the possibility that his anecdote had sunk the interview. He sat up in his chair and tugged at his tie. "Is that what this is about? Are you pumping out some kind of energy?"

Lou looked over at Croc as if to ask for permission before he answered for both of them. "Are you a scientist?"

Greg said the first thing that entered his mind. "Hell no. I'm a skeptic."

"Define *skeptic*."

Greg thought about the question for a second before he responded. "I don't take things at face value. I make up my own mind."

"How are you different from a cynic?"

"I don't know. I'm not smart enough to know the difference."

Lou punched his next question, hoping to sound confident and in control. "Have you already made up your mind about me?"

Greg's stratagem had worked. He'd knocked on the front door of the fortress and had been invited inside. "I think you're messing with me. I think you're trying to make up your mind whether or not you can trust me. Don't stop — I'm enjoying the ride."

Lou's face betrayed him.

Greg made an adjustment. "Does the crocodile play guitar or is he just another pretty face?"

Lou feigned annoyance. "Can't you be serious for a minute?"

Greg shook his head. "Can I hold him?"

"No."

"Why?"

"He'll bite you."

Greg laughed. "Okay, you got me there. Let's quit the clowning. Why are you here?"

Lou blew out a breath and tried to focus. "I really am clairvoyant. I'm a frigging X-file. I see things. I hear things. I know things I couldn't possibly know. When I try to talk to people about this, I see their faces change. They think I'm crazy or trying to con them."

He looked at Greg again, searching for his reaction. He expected to see the same look of disbelief that the doctors had. It was easier for them to land on crazy than to take an unprecedented step into the unknown. But no, that wasn't it, at least not yet. Greg still looked calm and interested.

Greg had spoken the truth to those near and dear to him more than once only to see a look of horror steal across their faces. Things that can only be learned through experience are impossible to teach. Not everyone knows that. You can't tell how something tastes by just shaking the box it comes in and reading the ingredients.

Lou took a breath. *Is he really going to listen to me?* "I drink and take drugs because, when I do, it stops the racket in my head for a few hours. I can be myself. No insights, sensations, or premonitions. Only silence."

Greg was struggling to find a place to land the plane. There was no box on the checklist for this. He went for the easiest piece. "Are you telling the truth about how much you drink?"

"Two drinks a day."

"We double what the client reports."

"What I put down is what I drink. Am I an alcoholic? I've never even considered the possibility. I don't even have a beer gut."

"You drink a lot for a social drinker, but not enough to be an alcoholic. How much pot do you smoke?"

Greg's lack of concern on this usually thorny issue encouraged Lou. "I smoke pot when I have to hang around with my parents and their friends. They'll only give me two small G and Ts when Lori and I visit. The pot helps stretch the drinks out and make the conversation bearable."

Is that what his parents are basing this on? "I thought you only drank beer."

"Mommy says beer is low class."

"So the booze and dope put the family on mute. What does the reptile do?"

Lou's smile outdid the Cheshire cat's. "He advises me on my investments."

Greg tilted his head and smiled as he looked up from his notepad. "Does your fiancée get headaches, psychosomatic pains, and occasional episodes of hysterical blindness?"

Lou smiled this time. Bullshit had been called. But were they getting on friendly terms? Greg's face was hard to read. He was always frowning as he fingered his guitar in Lou's premonitions. He was different in three dimensions. The rock-and-roll hairstyle clashed with his blue pinstripes in the same way that the wise-guy comments did with the job title on his business card.

Where does this guy fit? Is he playing dumb with me? Lou could hear surf washing ashore and smell salt water in the room. Greg seemed the most likely source. *Does this guy do a little business on the side?*

Greg spoke into the lengthening silence. "Mr. Canon, dealing with you is like dealing with one of my schizophrenic clients."

"How flattering," he said as he picked up Croc and held him close, as if he were in danger. "I mean for both of us."

Greg persevered. "Schizophrenics have their own perspective on reality. They make sense of the world in a unique way. Sometimes they have to tamp down their perceptions to avoid being overwhelmed by unwanted sensory information. That's the part that made me think of you."

Lou still wanted to play. "So, you think I'm schizophrenic?"

"If you were, the doctors would've found you out years ago."

"So why did you bring that up?"

"We need to talk about Croc."

Lou feigned shock. "While he's in the room?"

"Bob says you and Croc are inseparable."

Lou was beaming. "He never leaves my side. He'll get into trouble if I'm not around."

Greg made an unnecessary note on the file to give himself time to think. "We can live with that."

Lou was surprised, bordering on disappointed, that Greg wasn't lecturing him about being an adult, behaving himself, or some other thing he had no interest in doing. That was invariably how these interviews ended — that or with a grim-faced clinician furiously scribbling notes on a pad.

All of this whet Lou's curiosity further. *He has to be where the salt air is coming from.* "Are you really okay with Croc, or are you playing with me?"

Greg sounded as matter of fact as he could under the circumstances. He was very good at propagating a line of malarkey for a good cause. He was still determined to get to the bottom of this, if, in fact, a bottom existed. He was certain that Croc was an active complication, an all-purpose tool, something to keep boarding parties from attaching grappling hooks to Lou's superstructure.

"Well, my boss is going to make a fuss about Croc, but he won't really be angry and the world won't end. We can get you in here tomorrow. The guys are going to think you're odd for carting Croc around with you … and they're going to make fun of you, at least at first, but you must be used to that…" Greg heard a silver dollar hit the bottom of an empty tin bucket. *And besides, keeping people at bay, well, that's the point, isn't it? But why?*

Lou sensed Greg's growing awareness and showed his head without fully coming out from behind his cover. "Do you believe I'm clairvoyant?"

Greg pursed his lips and blew out a long, steady stream of air. "You're asking me for an opinion about something I don't know anything about. I haven't seen you do anything out of the ordinary. In fact, in your interview with Bob, it sounded as if you hated being clairvoyant. That surprised me. It's a gift, isn't it?"

Lou looked fully engaged for the first time. His brow thickened with lines that didn't belong on his youthful face. "It's a double-edged sword."

"Aren't all swords double-edged?"

Lou returned Croc to his resting place on the table. "In the ancient world, the double-edged sword was — what's that, Croc? Yes, it was cutting-edge technology. The first two-edged swords were huge. The problem with a two-edged sword is that it cuts both ways. A guy standing behind or beside the sword wielder was frequently killed by the backswing of the weapon."

Lou got to his feet and swung an imaginary sword. "Clairvoyance presents the same difficulty. Most people want to know what the future holds for them. But only until they find out. Then they want to change it." He checked for Greg's reaction. "The world is full of spiritual beings. They go about their mysterious business without most of us ever noticing."

Bingo bango bongo loony. Greg's face was passive, but his right knee was more forthcoming. It began to bounce without him noticing it — but Lou did.

Lou stayed on his feet and put his hands on the back of his chair. "When I find myself in the future, things take on a clarity they never have here. I feel at peace. I see the turmoil that's going on all around me, but it's as if I'm in a bubble. I don't know if I change the future by looking at it or if it changes me. I wonder sometimes if me being there causes things to happen that otherwise wouldn't. I can never work that part out. What I do know is that it's a real trip to find yourself in the light." Lou made his way to the window and looked quietly out into the street for several minutes.

When he returned to his seat, he looked Greg straight in the eye. But it wasn't a challenge. If Greg had the calling, if the salt smell was coming from him, this would be enough to flush him from his cover. If not, the interview would end in a flurry of scribbling.

Lou continued in a lower voice. "Other times, when the dark forces predominate, it's creepy. I hate it when that happens. It's hard to see a bad outcome coming for someone. Knowing it's going to happen and being powerless to stop it…"

On the face of it, this was crazy. Therein lay the problem. "You know," Greg said very softly, "if you said that to a psychiatrist, he'd put you down as a loony. You'd get the look."

"You know about the look?"

"Oh yeah. Back in the day, yeah, I got the look."

"Stink eye. That's what Lori calls it. Oh what the hell, I shaved and came all the way down here. While you were talking, it all came clear to me. I know how this bit ends. That's the annoying thing. I see the future, but not all of it. I know what happens in a general way, but never what it means. I have to stick around if I want to know the whole story…"

Greg ached to have his guitar in hand. *That's enough to explain any failures…*

Lou had the expression politicians get when they realize that the microphone is still on. Greg had made him feel safe, or maybe it was something about this place. He'd told Lori as much as he dared, but not all of it. He couldn't take a chance of alienating her. She was far too important to him. Telling his truth, owning what he knew for the first time, had swept his decks with dopamine. He was ankle deep in the stuff and feeling a preacher's high.

"I see images, I hear voices, and sometimes even bits and pieces of conversations. But it's only a preview. I know when and where something is going to happen, but never why." The energy was visible in his eyes. "Prophets always have the big picture. They know why things happen and what they mean. With me, it's different. There's always something I didn't see coming that makes a huge difference in the end."

Greg was feeling a burn. He was comfortable playing a hand of *just supposing* with a con man. But had that game given way to something more complicated? He imagined himself explaining to the coroner why he had invited a delusional man to stand a little closer to the precipice. *Time to end this conversation.* "Is there any point in lying to a clairvoyant?"

"It's an uphill battle. But you've pulled it off."

Greg knew he had to meet intimacy with intimacy here. He deliberately mirrored Lou's body position with his own and adopted a conspiratorial tone. "I'm only clairvoyant on the one subject. I know how addictions work and all too frequently how they end. My job is to help people by knowing things. The theory is simple. People get into trouble with substances because they don't have a spiritual life. When you don't believe in anything, you drift from thing to thing. Excitement gives way to boredom and despair time and again."

Lou's head went down. He didn't want to hear this. The hounds were straining at the leash, howling to be let loose, aching to be baying at the cornered prey. But the fox they scented was long gone.

"It's more complicated than that," Greg said, becoming more animated. "Without an adequate spiritual life, people experience existence as empty, painful, meaningless. When they use a substance or an activity to medicate these uncomfortable feelings, it feels spiritual to them. Special and powerful and full of meaning. It's not the real thing, but it's close enough to fool them, to satisfy them in the short term."

Lou looked up at him with a glint of sorrow. *Ah, Greg, you were doing so well.*

Greg mistook the inference for resignation. "After a while, they only feel alive when they drink. The honeymoon period of their addiction is usually the best two years of their lives. Alcoholics and drug addicts always describe their first experience with their drug as if they'd fallen in love."

Lou's disappointment found its way fully to the surface. "The first time I drank, I barfed."

Greg soldiered on. "Most kids overdose or underdose the first time. I'm talking about the first time they get the right amount down the hatch and it works its magic. People describe the feeling as sudden and wonderful. A spotlight illuminating them on a stage. Life changes in that moment — they feel immortal."

Croc and Lou exchanged a look. *People do that? That's nuts.*

Greg couldn't stop. "But then, to keep the party going, they need more of the drug. Over time they build tolerance, and their occasional dalliances become a habit. Then they begin to crave the substance, first psychologically and then physically. Once that happens, the solution to their spiritual problem becomes the cause of their spiritual demise. They're caught in a never-ending cycle of wanting and dissatisfaction. Not unlike your double-edged sword. The thing you want leaves you feeling empty and disappointed."

Croc looked into the fire in Greg's eyes.

"When they're detoxed, they feel even worse. Most clients describe getting sober after years of use as devastating. They feel like animals waiting for the slaughter — vulnerable, miserable, frightened. They hate reality. The world is again empty, painful, and meaningless. Mr. Canon, is this familiar?"

Lou was disappointed. He'd experienced a moment of hope only to see that hope ticketed, towed, and impounded. He adopted the tone he reserved for his parents and their henchmen. "Who the hell are you to say I don't have a spiritual life? I'm drowning in the shit!" The anger showed at last. "What I'm looking for is the off switch!"

Greg played the last card in his hand. "And that's what the alcohol does?"

Lou was now fully engaged. Greg had put on the mantle of all those flat-footed healers who had gone wrong before. All their mistakes, their superior attitudes, their stupidity and arrogance and posturing were his to wear now.

Lou looked Greg straight in the eye with a powerful gaze. "Yes, that's what turns it off. When I'm buzzed a little, I can ignore it all."

Greg leaned back in his chair. *Man, there must be a million scientists in the world salivating over you.* Then it became clear to him. *This is where Croc comes in, isn't it?* He had a reframing moment. The nonsense wasn't nonsense anymore. It served a very practical purpose.

"Mr. Canon, how is coming in here going to help you?"

"I don't know. I thought we were connecting there for a minute until you went nuts."

Greg couldn't give an inch. "You said you know how this segment ends. Make me a believer. Tell me what's going to happen when I go in to see my boss."

"You mean your bosses — you forgot Mike and Bob."

"Parlour tricks or genuine second sight?"

"Go talk to your bosses. Whatever they decide, I'll do it."

Greg shook his head. "We won't accept you on that basis. You have to tell us that you want to do this. That you see some value in it. Maybe even that it gives you some hope."

"You're talking as if you were already inside my head! How about you be the seer and tell me, do you think I'm tracking?"

Greg leaned forward in his chair. "If drinking alcohol stops your visions and brings you some peace, then why would you quit?" He let that sit between them for a moment before continuing. "But if there's something wrong with you, other than an addiction, and the doctors need to have you detoxed before they do their work, well then, we can accommodate you — but do you really need a treatment centre if you're only having two drinks a day? You see how this is a weak point in your argument…"

Lou laid off his fastball and delivered an off-speed change of pace. "Something good is going to come out of this. I can feel it in my gut."

The ploy worked. Greg understood and accepted intuition. It was how he made important decisions. He was never going to buy second sight. Why would he? It never happened to him. The subtle shift in meaning from supernatural to intuitive made Greg feel grounded enough to broker a deal. *This is his way of walking back the crazy talk. There's a problem after all*, Greg thought.

"Here's your first assignment. Go outside and talk with the guys. Ask them if this is a safe place and if what we do here is working for them. Can you do that for me?"

Lou gave Croc the high sign as he gathered him up from the table and made his way to the door. *It won't matter shit if you can't resist the temptation to reduce everything I've ever been or experienced to a single word,* Lou thought bitterly.

Chapter 5

It took the better part of an hour for the two old ghosts to make their way to the third-floor landing of the Beta Psi sorority house. They were in a mood. The space was illuminated only by light from the street that passed through an opaque window. The two ghosts walked right past Walter and plopped themselves down on the cane chairs by the window to catch their breath.

"Is that horrible smell coming from Walter?" John asked.

"The cat box, I think."

John followed his nose. "The butts in the ashtray are smouldering." He considered stubbing out the blaze but thought better of it.

"They don't let them smoke in their rooms."

Peter and John stared at Walter's back, hoping for inspiration to strike, wondering how they were going to move the old spook. Walter had taken up a position on the staircase that offered him a commanding view of the shower room below. The tuxedo he'd been buried in gave him the appearance of a well-loved maître d'. He'd been there for months, rocking back and forth, pulling on the banister with a wild, fearful look in his eyes.

Peter felt sick at heart to see his old kick in these circumstances. Back in the day, it was night after night of live theatre, concert halls, the opera, and the ballet. A never-ending cycle of the best seats in the house and a free pass backstage to the dressing rooms. No impresario could ever dream of the unfettered access that Walter had to the arts.

"Maybe we shouldn't do this. Look at him. What is throwing him into the light going to accomplish?" Peter asked.

John gave him a sharp clout on the ear. "Grab him."

Peter gently put his arms around Walter's waist while John aggressively tried to get him in a headlock. They struggled for five minutes, but the old bastard would not move. His eyes were demonic with pain, anger, and frustration. This was a face out of place on Walter. He resembled a frightened infant.

Peter flung himself into a chair, huffing and puffing. Moving objects in the material world was bloody hard work. Manhandling another ghost took less effort, but it was still more than he could manage.

"We need to come up with another plan, John. This is not working."

John was surprised by Walter's tenacity. This kind of strenuous work was bad news for a ghost, it burned energy that couldn't be replaced. Peter and John were still cognizant of this fact, whereas poor Walter was spending the last of his strength without understanding what he was doing.

"I wish there was some way to light a fire under him; something that would move the old bastard along."

Peter thought about Barry striking the match on the subway platform and shuddered. All it took was a spark to immolate a ghost.

John was playing with Walter's fingers, wiggling them to try to make one of them come loose. "We could cut the banister and carry him out that way."

Peter sighed. "What are we going to do? Look at his eyes — not an ounce of sense left in them. This is what happens at the end — the final marriage of hangover and migraine."

John was looking around for something he could use as a lever. "I can see why exorcists have such a hard time with poltergeists. There's nothing left to work with. I don't think they talk them into going — I think they wear them out."

Peter rose to his full height and began to rock back and forth as he spoke. "Maybe our pushing him and pulling him is the wrong thing. He only has enough smarts to take the contrary. What would happen if we put a bag over his head?"

"He would probably think someone turned out the lights."

Peter walked back over to where Walter had attached himself to the hall banister. From there, he could see all the comings and goings of the young sorority girls in the house. This was now Walter's whole life: rocking back and forth and watching the young women come and go. What a comedown.

Peter grasped the rail with his left hand and tapped his index finger on his chin. "We need to return to first principles here, John. How is it that we move?"

John turned his back and made a face. "I wait for someone to announce they're going somewhere, and then I grab them by the scruff of the neck."

"And why is that, John?"

The thin ghost's eyes rolled back in his head, but his tone did not betray his irritation. "It takes no energy."

"Quite right. And so having said all that, what have we learned?" asked Peter, still striking a dramatic pose.

John was able to refine, Nothing, you lout. This is a stupid plan. If we keep this up much longer, all three of us will be stuck here as clueless as dying flies on a strip of adhesive *into the more tractable, "What I want to know is this — why is Walter hanging on to the railing? What would be lost if he let go?"*

"He's hanging on to avoid being sucked up into the light. And he wants to stay here, watching the girls. He probably thinks he's backstage at some theatre."

"He should have made his last stand at the strip club."

"Don't you see, John? He's terrified of the light. It's going to take him away from what he thinks he wants. He's a piece of lint clinging to the couch, avoiding the vacuum cleaner, and if we're not careful, the same thing is going to happen to us." Peter added a "naff" softly but with feeling.

Inspiration showed on the thin poser's face as he parodied his fat colleague's recent rhetorical flourish with a little chin tapping of his own.

"The light can scoop him any time it wants to." John rested his right elbow on his left wrist and let his index finger find its way to the side of his nose. A top hat would have been an invaluable aid. "How stimulating can it be standing in a hallway for eternity, rocking and moaning and making things go bump in the night? He must be bored out of what's left of his mind. Here's my thought — since we can't reason with him, or even try and deceive him with words, I think we should try to lure him away."

The fat ghost was intrigued. "What could we use as bait?"

John walked behind Walter and beat a drum pattern on the top of his head as he spoke. "I wonder if Walter remembers that we can't eat, drink, or smoke anymore? I recall you saying that he was a smoker…"

Peter didn't like John taking liberties with Walter. "What evil thing is in your heart?"

"This," said John, striding across the landing to pick up a coffee cup that had been left on the windowsill. He threw it at Peter, who put up his hand to

protect his face. But without enough time to focus his thoughts and energy, the cup passed through his fingers and crashed onto the staircase below.

Peter was incensed.

A young woman in a towel came out of the bathroom to investigate. Seeing the broken cup shards on the stairs, she yelled down the hall. "Dandruff, bad cat!"

When he saw her, Walter's feet began to move spasmodically; he was practically dancing.

"I guess that amounts to a big afternoon around here," said John with a broad grin.

Peter's face went red with shame as he pushed past John and down the stairs.

"Where do you think you're going?"

"Anywhere but here!"

Chapter 6

Things kept coming in and out of focus for Fred Grant. He was aware of pins and needles in his hand and stiffness in his hip, but then the darkness returned. The sensation of being lifted onto the gurney made his head swim, but only for a second and then it too was smoothed over. He floated through a memory, something one of the detectives had said about a guy who drove his car into a sinkhole gushing like a geyser from a broken water main. An alcoholic in a blackout has a lot in common with a demented man driving the streetcar. If nothing complicated comes up, he can handle it. But if someone steps onto the tracks in front of him, well, they've pushed all their chips into the centre of the table.

The paramedics detected an arrhythmia. They packed Fred up and took him to St. Joe's, where they whisked him through the emergency room and parked him in the critical care unit. The doctors went to work. They got his heart settled down, but they were concerned about his blood pressure and terrified that he was going to have an alcoholic seizure. They gave him a big intramuscular dose of chlordiazepoxide and sent him off to the detox unit for observation. They applied linen restraints to his hands as a precaution; he could easily injure someone without meaning to.

Fred saw only a few frames of this documentary. There was the sensation of being wrapped in a blanket and the bump of one bad wheel as he progressed through miles of corridors. One eye opened long enough to sense the light before the blind was pulled down with finality…

I want to go home.

***

Mike walked toward Lois Grant with a pathetic cup of ersatz coffee from the mean-spirited machine in the hospital lobby. The hot liquid burned as he shifted the thin plastic cup from hand to hand. Lois received it with a smile and didn't seem to notice the heat. Her fingers were long and elegant. It was hard to believe that such a petite woman could have given birth to a brute the size of Fred. She had short grey hair and straight teeth that were stained around the edges from tea. A looker in her day, she'd gently settled into a comfortable and poised retirement. She was a creature at peace with herself and intently interested in the world around her.

Today she looked frightened in the gold track suit she'd thrown on in haste. The news had shaken her. This was a situation she never imagined finding herself in with any of her children, but least of all with Fred. He was the responsible one — always cleaning up messes, both in the family and in his work as a policeman. He'd always been focused, in control. How had things ended up here?

Mike felt comfortable with her. "It's good you called me when you did."

Lois took a sip from the cup and made a face.

"This poor thing needs something…"

"More sugar?"

"No, it's the coffee that's missing."

Mike had to smile. "Tell me about Fred. What made you worried?"

She looked into her coffee cup, hoping that the answer might be found there. "He always answers his phone…" She put the cup down with a look that suggested that she might not take it up again. "He's always taken care of me. I'm glad I can be here for him now." She looked up at Mike. "Is he going to be all right?"

"Oh yeah, they know what to do. But something's going to have to be done about his drinking."

"Are you certain this is down to the drink?"

Mike frowned and pursed his lips.

She rose to the bait. "I could always tell when he'd taken something. There's a smell. But it wasn't only on his breath. It got into his skin. He reminded me of those people on the subway who reek of garlic. I could smell it when he walked into the room." She reflected for a moment before going deeper. "But more than that, there was a tone that got into his voice. Well, no, maybe tone isn't the right word. But there's a sorrow that I hear in his voice and sometimes a sadness in his eyes. But I only ever see it for a second."

Mike encouraged her to continue with a look and a nod of his head. Even so, it took a minute. She took up the coffee cup again, took a small sip, and put in back on the floor.

"Fred is private. I could never get to the bottom with him. When he was young, he'd get a tormented look on his face. If I pressed him, he'd look surprised and smile, always a smile, and he'd say, 'I'm fine,' always 'I'm fine.' Even as a baby, he never cried."

Mike was picking up a familiar scent — the vapour that hovers over the groan that fills the room when a stillborn truth finally wrenches free. "Tell me about the sadness."

Lois put her head down and lowered her voice to a whisper. She looked the portrait of grief, her words coming at a price. "He had to go to hospital three times for … moods. But it was only when horrible things happened. The first time was in high school, when his friend Marvin died. The second was when his marriage ended. And the third, when he got crushed in the car crash." She looked uncomfortable. She picked up the coffee cup and got to her feet. "He's had a lot of bad luck."

Talking about the past was dangerous. The past held a malevolent power that only a fool would provoke. Mike sat stone-faced while the gears in his head sprang to life. *Oh, Freddy, how did you put the one person on the planet who knows you best and loves you the most off the scent? But maybe the how is not as interesting as the why?*

Her mood brightened as she landed on a positive. "Let me tell you something. A couple of times he felt bad for some of the street kids he met on the job. He would bring them home with him, and I'd give them a meal. He knew he wasn't supposed to, but he couldn't help himself. He was that way with animals too when he was a boy, always bringing home a stray."

"How did that work out?"

Lois made a face. "It never did. Something would go missing. It always hurt him deeply when they left that way."

Mike's gut told him that guilt was at the bottom of Fred's problems. But about what? All he had so far was a hunch. But at least now the pistol and bottle of disinfectant spray made sense. One for the bad guys and the other for the shame.

***

Greg retreated to the reading room on the second floor. He would have it all to himself for a glorious hour. He chose one of the red-striped club chairs and put his feet up on the coffee table. His new desert boots looked rad with his pinstripes. The combination had earned a considerable frown from Doug.

The afternoon sun was restoring hope that winter might soon give way. He fingered his beloved Gibson Les Paul while he tried to make sense of his trip down the rabbit hole with Lou. His notes resembled a hastily scrawled musical score. Could this most challenging of rock operas be adapted to a new venue?

How would it feel to experience the world the way Lou described it? He mindlessly turned one of the tuning keys until the string went slack. *What would a ghost want with a human being anyway? What possible use could we be?* He tightened the string, producing a comic sound that suited his mood.

Greg had nothing in the way of second sight. His intuitive powers were formidable, but his insights were not mysterious. Intuition was all about picking up on subtle clues. The way people walked, talked, held their bodies, kept fit or not, dressed — it all spoke volumes about them.

As Lou described it, the supernatural was a collage of images and voices. Greg wondered if they sounded male and female, articulate or desperate, good, evil, all of them pressing their way to the front of the line, talking over each other or shouting for attention. He kicked off his desert boots. *Could they be as annoying as those two women on the subway this morning, barking at each other about their grandchildren?*

He did the scale in F-sharp as he considered these possibilities.

Lou said he always knew where and when something was going to happen, but never what it meant or how it was going to turn out. Were the apparitions aware that they were being seen and overheard, or were they going about their business, oblivious to Lou's presence? As unaware of him as the living were of them. There was a lovely symmetry to that thought.

These hallucinations — there, he'd finally used the word — didn't sound as if they were coming from drug use. It was possible that Lou was taking a new designer drug that was causing these specific delusions, but they were unlike anything Greg had ever come across before.

This boy's take on reality is unique. But it's not supernatural. Something is busted in his brain pan and he needs to be someplace far more sophisticated than Punanai.

Chapter 7

Fred woke up with a scalding headache. He felt dehydrated in spite of the intravenous fluids, and he had a blazing desire to urinate. The diuretics were working their magic. He couldn't work out where he was. His hands were tied and there were tubes everywhere.

"I need to piss."

He was surprised when a voice responded and set about releasing his hands and giving him a plastic bottle. There was no time for introductions. He set to work and marvelled at the volume he produced. He damn near filled the whole bottle. It was hard to keep his hands steady. He looked around for someplace to put the jug down, and he felt dirty not being able to wash his hands.

He was covered in perspiration and his muscles were twitching. His heart rate was elevated and his blood pressure through the roof. Into that fog and confusion, he said the truest thing to ever pass through his lips. "I want to go home."

"Not a good idea," said a voice through the blur. "You seem a little agitated, Mr. Grant. Why don't you lie back down and let me have a look at you."

Fred was ready to kick ass. "Who are you? I can't lie here on this ... this filthy bed. It smells of vomit. And the lights don't work. They keep flashing on and off. Where's my stuff? I'm leaving."

"Okay, but first, sit up for me and let me take your blood pressure again."

The world skidded to a stop and reversed its orbit when Fred sat up. He was reminded of the experience of being walloped good in the boxing ring. Muscles and joints would not make sense of each other. He felt as if he'd jumped from a high tower and was in midflight. He grabbed the rail on the bed, which stopped the sensation of falling for a moment.

The nurse moved in close to take his pressure. Her hair smelled faintly of spice and ocean air. Fred felt the cuff constrict on his arm and that brought him back into the room.

"Have you been taking your medication?"

"Yes, I'm very organized that way."

"You're sweating a lot and your hands are cold and shaky. Did you eat something today?"

Fred couldn't process either *did you eat* or *today*. "Everything burns when I swallow. Look, I gotta go."

She couldn't get a reading with him squirming. "Hang on a second. Don't run off with the cuff still on your arm. They'll make me pay for it."

Fred had to smile. He hadn't talked to anyone outside his own head in a while. He could tell the nurse had never been in the back seat of a unit. He felt bad about talking to her roughly.

He was drawn back inside himself. He had the oddest sensations, funny tingles in the small of his back and hard little sores on the roof of his mouth. Touching them with his tongue made them burn. *It's all these drugs they've pumped into me. These filthy, clinging tubes. Why can't they leave me alone?*

Fred had spent half his career hanging around hospitals, waiting for something bad to happen. What he wanted, and what he knew was going to fix this little problem, was a drink. "I'm going."

"You've been here for four days. Will two more minutes matter?"

"Four days!"

Fred fell backwards onto the gurney. *Four days. Oh God, how did this happen?*

"Your friends brought you in. Remember? They came with you in the ambulance."

Not even the phrase *you have cancer* could've shaken Fred up more. *Friends? What friends?* Ex-coppers can go bad, but they can't embarrass the force. Those are the rules. That's why he drank alone. The idea that other people had found him in the middle of a blackout and taken him to hospital was disturbing. What else did they know about him? He felt a wave of fear displace the nausea. "You have me confused with someone else."

She started to pump up the pressure. Fred hated the sound.

"I'm going home! Where's my stuff?"

The nurse tried to gently push him back down onto the bed, but it was hopeless. He outweighed her by one hundred pounds. Even at sixty, he was an imposing figure: a yard thick through the chest with forearms to match and neck muscles that bulged when he was annoyed.

What he needed was his armchair and a tall, cool drink of vodka. He recalled placing a quart in the freezer for this very eventuality. All he had to do was get from where he was to where he wanted to be. He unwrapped the Velcro from around his arm.

The nurse could see the call signs going the wrong way. She tried bluffing him. "You used to be a cop. You know how this works." As she left the room to summon some help, she played her last card. "Don't embarrass yourself in front of your colleagues."

Watch me, young lady, and I'll show you how this is done. He looked at the needle in the back of his hand and hoped that it pulled straight out. It did. Halfway home already. He struggled to his feet and looked around the room until he found his clothes and his shoes piled neatly on the chair. He grabbed the rail of the bed to steady himself. The world appeared darker and narrower to him now. It possessed a sinister consciousness that was aware of him. He could feel its predator eyes even if he couldn't hear it draw a breath. He drew in a deep breath of his own and flexed the muscles in his arms and legs to get the blood flowing.

The simple act of putting on his pants confounded him. He lost his balance and fell. Cursing, he got to his feet, and it was only then that he realized that he was still wearing a hospital gown. Suddenly he hated it worse than any rash on his skin. Hated it the way he hated … well, there was no time to think about that now. He tore the gown as he tried to take it off and threw it with disgust into the corner. Everything was in the wrong place. It took all his concentration to do even the simplest thing. It felt like he was trying to run with his legs entangled in the bed clothes. He stopped and bent over. He started gulping air. He couldn't catch his breath. When he straightened up, he saw stars.

If I've been here for four days. I need a drink right now.

There was a funny sound coming from the hall, a low-pitched hum. Before he could work out where the sound was coming from, it vanished. He sensed that something awful was about to happen. His eyes were giving him trouble too. The lights kept dimming and brightening. *Bloody fluorescents! All the more reason to get out of this godforsaken place.*

Chapter 8

Greg pushed the door to Doug's office open and peeked inside. Mike and Doug were playing chess while they chatted about what to do with Gluey, but there weren't many options for someone that far gone. Doug was up a pawn and a knight. He had a satisfied little smirk on his face. Mike had the look a babysitter gets waiting for her ride home to show up.

The management team at Punanai were not so much a pair as they were an adversarial pairing. Button-down, no-nonsense Doug and never-have-your-tie-on-straight Mike. The irresistible force and the immovable object. The indomitable will and the unfettered imagination. And yet, they were in perfect agreement about the fundamentals of addiction.

All of which put them at odds with the heartfelt views of the provincial funders whose heads had been turned by Life Skills. It was no longer a case of *if* but rather of *when* someone would have to say *après moi, le déluge.*

Mike looked up, happy for the interruption. "Can't you see we're working?"

Greg had a look at the board. "You think that's complicated? Wait until you hear about Mr. Canon's crocodile."

Doug had a final look at the board, reluctant to leave the game. Mike loosened his tie as the three men took their seats around the conference table. It earned him a frown.

Greg pushed the newly completed file across the table. "Mr. Canon claims to be a clairvoyant."

Doug opened the file. *If he is, we're in it up to our elbows.* He dialled the thought back into a more professional statement: "Is he credible?"

Greg smiled at the galloping ambiguity dripping from the question. "*He claims to be clairvoyant, I don't.*"

He turned to check out Mike's reaction, but Mike was lost in thought. Greg soldiered on. "I'm not even sure what clairvoyant means. When he plays the tune, I could swear drug-induced psychosis laid down the chords and schizophrenia wrote the lyrics." He smiled brightly. "It's got a lively beat. You can dance to it."

Mike shook his head. "Second sight is a new wrinkle. Cocaine psychosis lands on paranoia. Crystal meth makes everything fascinating until the formication starts."

Greg playfully anticipated the punchline. "You mean *fornication.*"

Mike leaned back in his chair and put his arms behind his head. "You often get some of that too, but formication is imagined infestation from burrowing insects. Hellish torment. First an itch they can't scratch and then one that leaves them bloody."

Doug baited Greg. "Have we moved on from reptiles to insects?"

Greg was playfully indignant. "His name is Croc, and he has impressive chops in the financial community."

Doug restored order with a frown. *Croc tells me everything I need to know.* "Bob told me he thinks we're going to let him cart the damn thing around with him while he's in treatment."

Greg pointed to the window. "Look outside, there on the patio — he's doing it now."

Doug slid over to the window to sneak a glance. Lou was talking with the other guests, holding Croc in his left hand the way that you'd hold a wine glass at a cocktail party.

The scene suddenly struck Doug as being desperately funny. "Oh dear lord, no." He started to laugh. He pulled out his handkerchief to wipe the tears from his eyes and flopped back down in his chair. *I should be out there swinging him by the ears.*

Greg was giving way too. He could feel himself losing control. "It's hard to get serious when a rubber crocodile is holding court."

Mike was feeling the same vague inappropriate urge to laugh. He blurted out. "Does it speak?"

Greg gave way to a fresh wave of giggles. "No, it's a strong introvert."

Doug stuffed his handkerchief into his side pocket and put his glasses back on. "I looked up *clairvoyant* on the internet. Lou listed it as a medical condition on his intake. Crazy prick." He glanced out the window again, keeping an eye on the young man. *He's worse than that drug dealer last year who came in for an interview so he could hand out his business cards.* He put that thought out of his mind. "Most of what was there struck me as bullshit. This is the part that sounded reasonable," he said, holding a paper at a comfortable focal length. "It's from *The Theosophical Glossary* by Helena Petrovna Blavatsky. It says, 'It's a faculty of seeing with the inner eye or spiritual sight. As now used, it is a loose and flippant term, embracing under its meaning both a happy guess due to natural shrewdness or intuition, but sometimes it is, and can be, genuine if it is linked to deep spiritual insight.'" He put the paper down on the table and slid it across toward Mike. "No mention of crocodiles."

Mike piped up. "The kind of thing you would expect from Gandhi or a Bishop Tutu?'"

"Or you when the moon is full and you're on one of your hot streaks," said Greg, starting to settle down a bit. He was slowly getting his game face back on after the giggles. "This guy is smart. The nonsense is there to confuse. It's his first line of defence." He looked over at Mike, who was drumming his fingers on the table as he gave the definition of clairvoyance a closer reading.

"Let's start with the bits we can be certain of," said Greg, returning to his notes. "Lou doesn't smoke or drink very much. We're looking at a psychological addiction if we're looking at anything at all. Then there are the distractions. I asked him if Croc was coming with him to treatment. He insists they're inseparable." A look of satisfaction stole across his face. "He was counting on that being the end of the discussion."

A scowl formed on Mike's face. "I'm not having the crocodile for a month…"

Greg shrugged. "It's not against the rules."

While Doug worked on his next objection, Greg finished making his point. "Croc is a smokescreen. I think the clairvoyance plays well with his friends. But it isn't real." Greg held up the index finger of his right hand. "The most incriminating thing I could get him to admit was that he uses the alcohol and pot to stop the clairvoyance, which rhymes with annoyance and avoidance and tells you everything you need to know about his relationship to the adult world."

Doug got a sour look on his face that said, *Oh that old thing.*

Mike came out of his trance. He'd been busy behind those vacant eyes. "We can't treat what we don't understand. This kid is playing us. The game is five-card stud, and we've only seen three cards. If he can't or won't tell us the truth, there's nothing we can do for him and no point in bringing him in."

Greg spoke softly. "I think there is something seriously wrong with this kid's plumbing. Maybe something that can kill him. The nonsense is entertaining but nothing adds up."

Mike smiled. *Who's playing at clairvoyant now?*

Doug shook his head. "When did rich families give up on name-dropping and threatening to get everyone fired?" He pushed his glasses back. "The boy has us thinking about whether to bring him in or not in terms of swamis and swamp creatures. I'm not having it! Greg, I want you to grill his girlfriend. Find out her impressions of his drinking and his mental state. Mike, you sit down with the kid and explain how this is going to work in the absence of magical friends. Greg went in soft; try medium. And while you're all busy doing that, I'll strangle Bob Bourns for bringing this lunatic to us in the first place."

***

Greg picked up the telephone on the third ring as he bustled through the office.

A man with a very pronounced German accent spoke into the receiver. "This is the crazy place?"

"It can be — this is a treatment centre for people with substance abuse problems."

"Ya, the crazy place. You must speak to my son, Klaus. Yell if you must. He is very drunk, but also he is very stubborn."

"I don't want to talk to him if he's drunk, Mister…"

Klaus came on the line. "Don't believe my father's lies. He is very bitter. It comes with being a failure your whole life."

The voice sounded as if the man had been drinking but was not impossibly impaired. Good manners demanded that Greg give him a chance to speak. "So how can I help you today, Klaus?"

"My father says I am a drunk-hard, a disgrace. I want to come over and see you, prove there is nothing wrong with me."

Greg shook his head and smiled. He didn't have time for this. He had to speak with Lori. "Klaus, we're not doing any interviews today, but what I can do is take some information over the phone and make an appointment to see you early next week. That's the first slot we have open."

Klaus was yelling at the other end of the line. Greg took the receiver away from his ear and punched the speakerphone button.

"You hear that, old man? They say there is nothing wrong with me!"

Greg started to laugh. Both these bastards were bombed. "Klaus, is there anything else we can help you with?"

"No, you are a miracle worker, you have been a godsend. There now, old man. I proved I am not a drunk-hard, what you have to say about that?"

With that the line went dead.

Greg hung up and went over to the window. The sunshine streaming through the pane warmed his face. He wanted to stand there for an hour and just be. But there was no chance of that. He had a lot to do before 4:00 p.m. He had to smile at his two new friends. *It's only two in the afternoon. Where are those two going to be at midnight?*

Chapter 9

Fred burst through the fire door into an alley. The wind whistled off Lake Ontario and covered the streets of Toronto with lake-effect snow. The broad Danforth was buried under three inches of the impossibly light flakes. Gravity brought them down to earth only to have the wind take them aloft again. At a glance, they could've been mistaken for fog, except they were fluid and fast.

The arctic air that animated the flakes took Fred's breath away. He turned his back to the wind and felt his neck muscles cramp and spasm — a shout-out from the car accident that ended his career. Fred didn't know which way he needed to go, but if he could put a couple of blocks between him and the detox, the cops would have a devil of a time finding him.

As the sound of the door alarm faded, he became aware of a new sound, a jangling, the sound that a fat ring of keys on a chain makes. It was coming from deep inside his body. He patted himself as he ran, then stopped to listen. He wondered if he was dragging some of the tubes from the detox behind him. It was too cold for that kind of introspection. He'd come out wearing only jeans, a T-shirt, and a pair of rubber flip-flops that looked and felt ridiculous in the snow. He wondered if the cold was why he was hearing things. His gut still felt empty, bloated, and full of fire.

At least I'm outta there.

He hoped running would keep him warm, but his legs felt thick, the way they had the night of the car crash. *Don't go there.* The large, square flakes of snow were clinging to him like moths to a streetlight.

He looked up in time to see the subway entrance and pushed his way through the heavy door. He tried to brush the snow off his hair, face, and clothes with his fingers. The big flakes melted easily in the warmer air, leaving him shivering. His T-shirt was soaked through and clinging to his skin. People took one look at him and hurried on their way. He could hear the splash from their feet as they retreated through the half inch of water that covered the station floor.

His hands were so cold that his skin burned when he tried to reach into his pocket. His fingers refused to move, and it took a long time for him to realize that he had no money. He'd left his shoes and his wallet behind. He didn't even have a pocket comb. An older woman came through the door and stopped beside him while she searched for something in her purse. He thought about asking her for a subway token, but when she looked up and saw him, fear and distrust formed in her eyes. It filled him with self-loathing. No one had ever looked at him that way before. Well, at least not for a very long time.

Don't go there.

The subway rumbled below. If he timed things right, he could leap the barrier and be on a train and gone in less than a minute. The thought pleased him. When he felt the movement of warm air against his face, he made his move. He ran at the turnstile. He was astonished when he failed to clear the barrier with ease. His wobbly legs couldn't deliver the thrust he needed. He landed badly, ending up face down on the wet, filthy cardboard that had been put down on the floor to sop up the melting snow.

The surprised ticket taker stuck his head out of the booth to see if Fred was injured, but when he saw the size and condition of the offender, he closed and locked the door to the booth. Fred got to his now bare feet, numb with cold and rage. He gathered up his flip-flops and limped down the escalator as quickly as he could.

He got the sandals back on his feet, but as he neared the bottom, his way was blocked by an elderly homeless man with a bundle buggy. He was going to spoil everything. Fred wanted to push him aside but contented himself with dancing from foot to foot. As he slipped past him, he heard the warning chimes. The doors to the subway cars were closing. With his last reserve of strength, he made good the distance between himself and the train. The doors pressed on him like big, mechanical jaws, but they could neither bite him in two nor spit him out. After two chomps they relented and allowed him to enter. The voice of an angry conductor came over the loudspeaker. "Don't rush the doors. You could put a whole subway out of commission doing that." Everyone was staring at him. They wanted him to go away as much as he wanted them to vanish.

Fred lurched through the subway car, trying to get as far away from the people who saw him jump the barrier as possible. A well-dressed young woman was letting her little dog nose its way around the car while she read a magazine. Fred was still looking back over his shoulder for pursuers. His flip-flops found the leash and gave the dog an awful yank. The frightened animal began barking and running in circles around Fred, winding the shortening cord around his legs. When the dog ran out of rope, he bit Fred.

Fred picked his assailant up by the collar and held him at arm's length while he untangled his feet from the leash. The owner was furious. She began to strike Fred with a rolled-up magazine and curse him in a language he didn't understand. What he did comprehend was that he was once again the centre of unwanted attention. He put the dog down and moved to the far end of the subway car. There were no pursuers. Everyone was glad to see him go. He felt a moment of supreme satisfaction — he was going to get away with this.

He glanced around a final time, then took a seat and shut his eyes — now was the time to hide — and hope this would put the other riders at their ease. It worked, everyone settled down.

Fred could've been home in ten minutes if he'd chosen the right train. But choosing was becoming difficult. He was operating from somewhere outside the rational.

He became aware that he'd gone the wrong way when the train came to the end of the line at Kennedy Station. He looked out the window for a long time, trying to remember the order of the train stations. He decided to stay put. Sooner or later it had to make its way back west. The heat from the vent felt good against his skin. He was having a hard time keeping his eyes open.

The odour of fresh-brewed coffee seeped into the subway car. He thought about coffee and mornings and feeling good after a workout and arriving at the station. He thought about pushing and shoving in the hallways, sitting in Captain Clark's office with Sergeant King, smoking cigarettes and telling stories about what happened on the night shift.

Where did it all go?

Fred opened one eye when the car lurched forward, and he forgot about the past and belonging and feeling good. He picked up a discarded newspaper from the floor and pretended to read it. From time to time, he lowered it from eye level to his lap while he took a bearing, making a show of turning the page while he eyed up the other occupants of the car. People were still looking at him but not with hostility. No one cared about a bum on the subway trying to stay warm unless they had to sit next him.

Sneak a peek and turn away. When I look at you, all I see is ferrets and parrots. You spend half your time rooting through a dumpster and the rest of it showing everyone what you found. You're never around when the shit goes down.

His wet clothing and unkempt hair were the problem. His best bet was to play the homeless card. That's what he'd done when he was undercover. Try as he might, he couldn't shake the feeling that his former colleagues were in hot pursuit.

A drunk taking off from the hospital was always a call you took your own sweet time responding to. The last thing you wanted to do was find the poor bastard. When Fred was a rookie, Sergeant King had shown him how it was done. They'd collared a homeless wino trying to finish off the quart of wine he'd stolen from the LCBO while he was still dressed in his hospital gown. Sergeant King punched the old bastard in the gut until the he vomited in the parking lot. "It's easier than having to clean up the back of the unit," he'd explained.

Fred let out a deep sigh. Now he was the one wearing the hospital bracelet.

He felt very empty. Thinking was impossible. Everything was wrong, rotten, and upside down.

Why is this train moving so slowly? It's rush hour.

As the subway got closer to downtown, the car started to fill up with commuters. The tight press of bodies held fresh horrors for Fred. The crowd made him feel dizzy and out of breath. He tried to shut them out by closing his eyes, but every little sound or jolt from the carriage made his eyes pop open. The buzz of their conversations filled him with a kind of rage that grasped his windpipe with an iron fist. He tasted copper.

It was impossible to see beyond the people standing in front of him. Without reference points, the car became phantasmagorical. A painting where the artist was deliberately fooling around with perspective. It gave him vertigo. There were coats, backpacks, briefcases, and hints of perfume and aftershave all swaying in front of his darkening eyes while a babble invested the scene with dark menace.

And he couldn't shake the feeling of being watched.

Everything looked grey and out of focus. A pane of dirty glass stood between him and the rest of the world. There were no people here. Only disarticulated parts of humanity crowding him, stealing his air. These people were not monsters, but he could feel their hatred and sense their desire to turn on him. There was no place to hide. Cold and fatigue had undone him. His mind landed on the day his dad had come home drunk and beaten him and then cried and said he loved him.

Don't go there.

He dropped his head into his hands.

A woman tapped his shoulder and he startled. For a moment, he couldn't make sense of what she wanted. Slowly it came to him. He was hogging two seats. She was carrying a heavy bag of books. He shoved himself against the side of the subway car, pulling his feet close to the hot air registers, and closed his eyes. As the train left the station, he found himself trapped in a 4G, ever-tightening spiral. He tried to open his eyes, but the pressure had turned his eyelids into paving stones.

Chapter 10

Greg found Lori sitting alone by the patio door in the living room, enjoying a book in the afternoon sunshine. The guys were still in class and the staff busy with assessments. She was a beautiful young woman, poised and graceful and blessed with an inner calm and dignity that was out of place in a treatment centre more accustomed to seeing significant others give way to angry tears and threats.

Greg stood a respectful distance away until she looked up from her book. "My name is Greg. I'm Lou's counsellor. Can you spare me a few minutes?"

Lori looked surprised to see a rock star in a pinstriped suit. "Lou asked me to wait here. Is he going to be a while?"

Greg smiled and nodded as if he and Lori were old friends about to catch up. "He'll be an hour or so. What are you reading?"

"*A Connecticut Yankee in King Arthur's Court.* I love Mark Twain."

Greg walked into the coffee corner and picked up the teapot. He gave it a rinse under the tap and then filled it with warm water. "Can I make one for you?"

"Yes, thank you."

Greg set the kettle to boil and selected the tea bags. He looked up from his task to ask. "Does he talk to you about clairvoyance?"

Lori looked mildly irked. "*Merde*, did he tell you that?"

Greg's eyes began to sparkle. "You seem to have some strong feelings about it…"

Lori made a face. "It makes everything harder. People think there's something wrong. Maybe not *wrong* … maybe *fishy* is the right word."

The kettle continued its slow drift up to the boiling point. Greg didn't want to push. He hoped Lori might come to him. "We're all a little mystified. Is it true? Can he do special things?"

Lori opened her purse and took out a lip balm. "I don't know. I mean, I take him at his word. I was afraid he was going to get all mystical on you, and you were going to say he was crazy. Refer him. That's how we ended up here."

The kettle rolled to a boil. Greg poured out the warm tap water he'd used to heat the pot and placed three tea bags into the vessel. Lori knew at that moment that he could be trusted. The kettle sound changed from exasperated to relieved as he poured the scalding water.

Lori sighed. "My brother was an alcoholic. He hid bottles, lied about everything, made trouble wherever he went. Used to set fire to the furniture with his cigarettes. Sometimes he stole things and didn't remember. This place would have made sense for him. But those things never happen with Lou. He'll go for months without taking a drink. Other times we'll go out to the pub and have a few."

Greg didn't look up from his ministrations when he asked, "So you drink?"

"I'm a one beer kind of girl." She smiled when Greg's inference became clear to her. "You want to check my purse for a mickey?"

"I can tell you play fair." Greg examined the coffee mugs, looking for two clean ones. "What's the most you ever saw him drink?"

Lori leaned back against the counter and searched her memory. She pouted while she thought. "Hmm, two bottles of wine. He was bombed. Sick for two days."

"How often does he get drunk?"

"Once a year."

"What about pot?"

Her face was suddenly alive with passion and subtext. She was channelling Norma Desmond in *Sunset Boulevard*, with those never-to-be-forgotten expressive eyes. "He grows his own in the garden. Not much, two or three acres."

"Do you know what denial is?" Greg had missed the film and, thus, the joke.

He lifted the teapot lid and gave the batch a swirl with a spoon while she tried to hide her pleasure at blowing a dramatic utterance right over the centre of the plate. "I'm not the one pushing him in here. You need to talk to mommy and the premier." Lori smiled sardonically. "That's the stink you smell."

"You think the family is the problem?"

Lori's face grew quizzical as she sized Greg up again. She admired the rock star looks and the pinstripes, but most of all she was impressed with his flat-footed honesty. "I love Lou, but I wish he were an orphan. I actually heard Thomas tell Kay that Lou turned out the way he did because she had a glass of Chardonnay while she was pregnant. It's all *her* fault." Lori looked down at the floor in mock solemnity. "Kay let them all down very badly with her *selfishness*."

Greg mirrored her tone. "And now it might cost the family the premier's office?"

"It's biblical — the sins of the mother."

Greg gave her a wink. "Now, never say I have no guts. What about the crocodile?"

Lori looked into his eyes. "He's an IQ test. If you get your feet tangled up in that, you really are an idiot."

***

Mike had formed an impression of Lou and of what needed to be done. But none of his information was firsthand. Bob and Greg were reliable, if slightly astigmatic, lenses through which to view the world. Mike lived at the intersection where their perceptions stopped overlapping and began to diverge. The similarities and differences they uncovered invited comparisons.

For the middle managers, the clients became creatures of the imagination. They felt as real as characters in a stage play. A conversation with a client was a rare treat, an opportunity for Mike to check his own perceptions. Was the wiring diagram of Lou that Mike had formed in his mind congruent with the living person?

Mike, as always, played the nicotine card. "Lou, do you smoke?"

"Not cigarettes."

Mike tried again to make him feel comfortable. "You're crazy, they're good for you. Full of Vitamin N. Let's go and have a talk."

"What about Greg?"

"It's his nap time."

Lou was disappointed when Mike took him out the front door and onto the patio. He badly wanted to see the second floor. That was where heat was building up. He could hear waves lapping and smell sea air. If he wanted a closer look, he was going to have to enlist, and in order to do that, he was going to have to tell a few lies about a subject he didn't know very much about.

Lou took a bearing. Mike was different in the flesh. He had an animal vitality that wasn't apparent in the visions. He wore the same kind of clothes that the other counsellors did, but he somehow managed to make them look informal. His movements were as fluid and graceful as an athlete's. This was the man who went with the face Lou had been seeing for weeks now. Quebecois, tough as nails — the kind of guy who would take a bullet for a friend. Mike wouldn't be easy to fool. But his compassion might make him vulnerable.

"You're the heavy, here to restore order?"

Mike took a smoke out from behind his ear. "Yup, my job is to make a few things clear to you."

He pretended to notice Croc in Lou's hand for the first time. "Is this Croc? Hello, Croc." He gave a little wave of his hand then looked back at Lou. "Why do you want to come in here? Your file says you're not an alcoholic."

Lou tried to look embarrassed, as if he had something big to hide. "I have my reasons…" It sounded as lame as he hoped it might.

Mike edged into Lou's personal space. He didn't want to intimidate him, but he did want him to feel crowded. "Not good enough. You have to be an alcoholic or a drug addict." Mike lit his cigarette and blew a plume of smoke toward the heavens. "Lou, straight up, do you have a problem?"

Lou looked down and shuffled his feet. "Not with alcohol."

"What about pot?"

"What about it?"

Mike was sweating the body language, waiting for the words to catch up. "If you don't have a problem, why come here? This is a very rigorous place. We get people up early in the morning and keep 'em busy, all day, every day. This isn't a rest spot."

Lou sized up Mike and decided to give reality a tweak. He wasn't lying. He had a legitimate reason for being here. He was curious to see what all these premonitions were going to give rise to. This was the downside to reading the last chapter of the mystery novel first. He was always out ahead of the curve, and it was boring waiting for everyone else to catch up.

How can you not smell the sea air? We might as well be standing on a wharf.

Lou placed Croc on the railing and turned to address Mike eye to eye. "My parents have ambitions. Political ones. I'm a liability. My parents want you to change me into what they think they need."

Mike looked at him blankly. This was the answer to a question not asked, but it was well worth listening to. He gave Lou a nod that said, *Tell me more.*

"Lori and I can't stand that world, politics, their snooty friends…" His voice softened. "We have each other." Lou put his foot on the bottom rung of the railing and lifted himself off the ground. "I've tried to tell them for years that there's nothing wrong with me. But I'm not the son they ordered from the catalogue."

About the pot. About coming in here. Any thoughts on that? Mike wondered.

Lou was warming to his topic. "My old man talks about the past, about hard work, commitment. That's the crap he'll be spewing on the election trail this summer."

He's not going to answer my question, which answers my question.

"Did you know the last three generations of men in my family all worked in retail? We aren't the blue bloods my dad would have you think we are. He made a lot of money on some shady deals, and because no charges were ever laid, well, I guess that does make him upper class."

You still haven't told me why coming in here is the right move. But what the hell, we're checking boxes. He gave Lou another up and down. *You're embarrassed about something, and you don't want to tell me. We might still get there.*

Lou spoke into the silence. "The reason I'm here is because my parents have an image problem." He attempted to look hurt without being obvious about it.

He reached over and took Croc down from the railing. "You get it? What the press could do with my name? Croc worked out the headline: 'Louis Canon Sinks the Premier.' The whole family is getting dry cleaned for the official photograph. That's what this is about. They're embarrassed by me. My dad's going to be very disappointed when he's elected. Being in the limelight isn't going to make him happy. He has no people skills. The media are going to tear him apart."

"And you know this *how*?"

"The fact that my parents even want to run for office tells you all you need to know. If they opened their eyes and had a look at their marriage, they'd — well, I'm not even going to go there. Fortunately, they have me to work on. I need to be fixed. And coming here is one more item to tick off the to-do list."

This guy never answers a question. If he got that from his old man, maybe the family is *destined for political greatness.*

Mike ground out his cigarette on the railing. He looked at Lou's youthful face and tried to put his old brain back into that much younger body. He couldn't. What passed for young these days was very different from his experience of rebellion.

Why should this kid trust us? I don't even know if he believes this stuff. It doesn't matter. We gotta shake hands and part as friends.

Mike felt a rush of compassion. It was hard to dislike Lou. "This is what I think should happen — and try to understand, I'm only talking to you here about the drinking and the pot. Try staying sober on your own. See how it works. If you can stop, then do it. But if you find you can't stop, or you can't stay stopped, well then, come on back and we can have another talk. I still have to run this by my boss, but I don't think it's a good idea to bring you in here. How do you feel about that?"

Lou pretended to be irritated again, but secretly he was enjoying baiting Mike. "When I say I don't need to come in, I'm told I have to. When I say that I'm willing to come in, I'm told I don't need to. Tell me, Professor Wagstaff, do you guys ever decide based on something solid, or do you automatically take the opposite tack of whatever the client wants to do?"

Mike bit his tongue and willed his face to remain blank. *I should have locked Lou in the broom closet and taken my chances with the crocodile.*

Chapter II

Fred found himself back in the bubble, propped up in bed by four pillows. His hands again restrained with cloth ligatures. *For Christ's sake.* He pulled at them, and the effort made the room begin to turn — the familiar spiral used in film noir when a detective takes a solid thump behind the ear.

He tried to go to a quiet place, thinking about the deck at the boathouse. On a summer afternoon he'd sit there with a cold drink, watching the gathering darkness that always precedes a powerful summer thunderstorm. But he wasn't tasting rum. There was another taste on his tongue. Copper — bitter and sharp. The same taste as when he'd put a penny in his mouth as a kid. His gut was burning with emptiness and gastritis, with a little room left over for fear and loneliness.

He tried to free his hands again, a little more calmly this time. They never tied these things tight enough, especially when someone was asleep or unconscious. How many times had he been called to the hospital to grab some crazy bastard and hold him down while new restraints were applied.

Something caught his eye and he ducked. A swooping grackle was loose in the room, taking runs at his head. Panic overtook him and he redoubled his efforts to get free.

"Damn these things. Why do they keep putting them on!"

His right hand came free and he used it to swat at the invader. A black light was swirling around the room, getting into the corners and underneath things. It took him a minute to make sense of it. The black light was emanating from a source above his head — maybe even from within his skull. It reminded him of a police siren, but instead of throwing a red beam into the shadows, it threw a black light into the well-lit hospital room. The darkness overpowered the light, leaving deep blue shadow where none should be. It made no sense. It had no cause. It couldn't be.

He heard a rotor blade. A whooshing sound from some kind of mechanical arm swirling around a fixed point above his head. He turned to the right and was astonished to find that he had X-ray vision. He could see his mother and father standing in the hallway outside his room, talking to a doctor. They were speaking softly, but he could hear every word.

The young doctor was hedging, trying to make up his mind about how much to say. Preferring to say nothing politely if he could. He clutched a clipboard to his chest. "We've run some tests. Until they're back, I'd only be guessing." The doctor put his arms down by his side, assuming his listening pose.

Fred felt his father's displeasure deep in his own chest. "We've tried everything with him, nothing works." Fred gasped. Every cell from his sinus to his Adam's apple burned as if he'd inhaled ice-cold sea water.

His old police captain was there. But that couldn't be right. He lived in Vancouver. Why would he be here and in uniform? He tried to sit up in bed, but his restrained left hand held him fast. He ripped at it in fury.

He tried to swallow, but his esophagus wouldn't open. The back of his throat burned the way it did that time he'd had tonsillitis. He choked as his eyes flooded with salt, the way they had that time when the tear gas blew back in their faces.

His mother was hanging on to her husband's arm. "Doctor, this isn't the first time." She looked at his father as the old man's head went down. Lois stood up straight. "He's fine until the darkness starts creeping in. He bathes himself in light, but his mood deteriorates. That's when you smell vodka coming off him even while he's in uniform."

How did she know?

The doctor looked down at his clipboard. "Is there a girlfriend?"

Lois looked sad. "They all leave. The OCD makes them crazy."

Captain Clark looked surprised. "He has OCD?" Then he shrugged. "He was a good cop. He did everything I asked him to." He took off his peaked hat and ran his fingers through his hair. "What's he going to do without the job?"

Without the job. That cut the jungle vine and he plummeted down through the foliage, expecting death at the end of it, only to wake drenched in perspiration and gasping for breath.

Chapter 12

Bob and Doug had worked together for fifteen years. They'd been a potent team. Sitting in the office, sipping coffee, they could easily have been mistaken for two luxury automobile salesmen — well-fed and sure of themselves. They were both impeccably dressed and wouldn't dream of loosening their ties for anything less than a gunfight.

"I miss this place. It's nice to get back, if only for an afternoon."

Doug smiled at his former mentor. "How long have you been gone now? Almost ten years?"

"That's about right. Which means you've been here for twenty-five. You getting tired yet, rookie?"

"I don't do tired. I figure when you retire, that's it, you're dead in six months." He gave Bob a playful jab with his finger.

Bob smiled. Everyone knew that Doug would die with a harness on his back. "I'm living on borrowed time, how cool is that? What do you make of my friend, Mr. Canon?"

Doug sighed. "How did you come across him?"

"His father, Thomas, was our family lawyer before he got into politics. He asked me to have a look."

"And…"

"His parents are nuts. Must be from reading all that legal fine print — that would drive anyone to drink." Bob went over to the wall and took down one of the staff photographs he was in. He looked wistful.

"I don't know, the kid seems harmless to me. The numbers are all wrong. If he's an alcoholic, then so is my dear old Aunt Tillie." He put the photo back on the wall and lowered his voice to a conspiratorial whisper. "She drinks more than he does *and* plays bingo with married men."

Bob looked at his nails and shook his head before he resumed his former tone. "Nope, something else is going on here. That's why I brought him in for a cup of tea." He selected another photograph and took it over to the window, where the light was better. "And," he said with considerably emphasis, "I thought I was doing you a favour. It occurred to me that sorting out the child of the next minister of health, or maybe even the next premier of Ontario, might not go unnoticed."

Doug crossed the room and righted the picture Bob had moved. "Messing him up might cause a few swirls too. This is risky business. This kid isn't a fit. It's not fair to the other guys to bring in colourful characters just for yuks."

Bob made a pained face. "Well, it's a dilemma. The doctors can't diagnose him. The family says, 'Talk to the experts.' The client says he's not psychotic, nor is he reliant on substances. What to do? What harm can it do to bring him in for a round of treatment? He may benefit in a way we can't anticipate."

Doug had heard a lot of these "oh shucks" preambles from his former chess master — he knew the best was always saved for last. "Who's playing at clairvoyant now?"

Bob had thought this through. "There are lots of people in twelve-step programs who have dodgy credentials as alcoholics and addicts. They're lonely, broken. I don't think Lou is one of those, but I wouldn't be surprised to find out he has a problem he's too embarrassed to talk about, especially when he is being prodded by a bunch of doctors. He might confide in us if we behave ourselves."

"This would be much easier if he had the ass torn out of his pants."

The volte-face delighted Bob and made his laugh. "What would you do then?"

"I'd show him a picture of the queen and send him back out to do some more drinking. There's no point in trying to pick the fruit before it's ripe."

"We cannot allow being rich and well connected to become a barrier to treatment."

Doug sighed. "We both know we're going to bring this guy in. We're going to put up with his nonsense because of his age and maybe because of his family connection. If we don't, well, the large brains are going to feed us to his crocodile…"

Bob couldn't help himself. "That picture is still crooked."

Doug wheeled to have a look. A look of merriment stole across Bob's face. "You're right about that. It's the politics and empire building that ramp up the old blood pressure. But, and this is the part that doesn't wash, why is the kid sitting still for this? He's young and financially independent, he's about to get married. Why are we even talking about his parents?"

A smile crossed Doug's face as he regarded his old comrade. Bob did have a way of putting things into perspective. He was right. The kid was up to something. Arthur Wilberforce Cardel had already treated them to a documentary, perhaps this was the setup for a companion tell-all book.

We are going to have to be so careful with this guy.

***

Greg was sitting at his desk in the back office where he stored his guitar. He had his headphones on and was adding notes to Lou Canon's file after his conversation with Lori. He looked up and saw the light flashing on his private line. *I could use a break.*

"You answer your own phone. Does that make you a winner or a loser? I can't remember."

Riana Peligroso. Greg took a sharp breath. *Where the hell has she come from?* If his wife, Zinna, got wind of this — especially after the last go-round — home would resemble the gulag for the rest of the winter. He hated the note of fear he heard in his own voice. "Riana, it's been a while. Where are you calling from?"

She sounded triumphant. "I'm back in Toronto. I've got a new job."

Greg felt his gut tighten. He wanted to sound disinterested, but a million years of life-and-death pursuits across the African Savannah had fine-tuned his predilection for outfooting predators. The energy to do just that was coursing through his body while he remained frozen in place. Small wonder that he felt a tremor in his leg as he spoke. "Well, that's wonderful. How's your family?" That question usually started a long-winded harangue that would give him time to think.

She didn't rise to the bait. "We're not close, but you know that. I'm coming to see you this afternoon."

Greg tried to master his feelings by sounding professional. His angel voice shouted down the choir chanting for him to run. "Today isn't a good day."

Riana was nerved up too and sounded every inch the aggrieved party. "Greg, we're going to talk about the *relationship*."

That word put the fear of God into him. He was done with trying not to offend. "We don't have a relationship. You drink. I don't. Stay away from me."

She was undeterred. "I'm sober now. Why can't you be a little bit kind? We used to get along. Don't you remember?" She started to cry.

Two minutes into the conversation and she has the tears flowing. Not again. Not ever again.

The foot race was over. "If you show up, I'll get a restraining order."

She shot back with some venom of her own. "And while you're busy filing the paperwork, I'll be having a quiet word in Zinna's ear. You can count on that, lover boy."

Greg's voice was failed calm. "I'm hanging up now."

Her delivery of the line was magnificent. "Very well, since you insist, I'll see you promptly at three."

Greg picked up his guitar and tried to strum a few familiar chords. It didn't work. He put the instrument back on its stand and then punched the wall.

***

Greg finished the report and took it into the counsellors' office. "Mike, I need to tug on your sleeve about something."

Mike handed him a tissue. "Your hand is bleeding. What'd you do?" Before Greg could make something up, Mike looked at his watch. The big meeting was looming. "We have time for a smoke."

The day was becoming overcast and cold, the front porch grey and bleak. The pots and urns that were awash with oranges and reds in summer now stood empty and forlorn. Overhead, four desiccated maple leaves curled against the fury of the north wind and clung desperately to the branch that once gave them life. The sky was full of dark scudding clouds being pushed furiously across the rooftops toward the beckoning lake.

"I had a call from Riana..."

"One of your groupies?"

"She's the one I got into trouble with when Zinna and I were separated."

"I remember her. The Life Skills lady. She got a teaching job."

"No, she got that big job in Calgary, handling addictions for the oil company."

Mike looked concerned. "Oh, *her*. You had to change your phone number a couple of times."

Greg nodded. "She's coming by this afternoon to talk about our *relationship*."

"Personal or professional?"

"Thank god only personal."

"Could have been professional. She was in the hunt for Erin's job. Got a second interview. If she wasn't so high-handed, she might have gotten it."

"Are you telling me that lunatic could have been Doug's boss? Oh shit, that would have been horrible."

"*Oh shit* is not the half of it. Your ex has a poor opinion of us and what we do. She thinks abstinence scares off the customers. She is all about the pharmaceuticals."

Greg scoffed. "Putting that one over with the board would require some life skills." But then his smile slipped, and the two shared a frown before Greg continued. "I told her not to come. I don't want anything to do with her. But she's going to show up one of these days. I want you to know what's going on. I don't want you to make this worse by being polite and inviting her to the Christmas party."

Mike got serious. "Being polite is your way of dealing with this, and clearly it doesn't work. You can rely on me."

"Thanks."

Mike stubbed out his cigarette on the railing before heading back inside.

"Greg, you're not blameless in this. It takes two to tango." He stopped at the door and turned back for a moment. "You have a wife and kids."

Greg couldn't look him in the eye. His voice lost its power. "That's the part that hurts most..."

***

Greg tucked his report under his arm and his forebodings about Miss Peligroso into an even deeper recess. He took a deep breath before walking into Doug's office. The mood was playful, which surprised and delighted him. He could feel the tension around his windpipe departing. Having Bob back, even for one afternoon, was a gift. Parliament was in session on April Fool's morning. Mike, Doug, and Bob were already sitting around the conference table with big grins on their faces.

Greg took the lead. "Canon's girlfriend was helpful. Says the family are wacked. She loves Lou but wishes he was an orphan."

Mike shook his head. He wasn't finished playing. "The guy is nuts, and no one will tell him. You'd think the crocodile would wait for a quiet moment to take him aside. If I had a crocodile, I would expect at least that much."

Bob gently chided him. "Maybe they're not that close. Besides, there's no such thing as nuts anymore — he's differently visioned."

Doug got to his feet, striking a heroic pose. "Before my enlightened reign, there was a period of dark despair and double dealing."

Bob got to his feet and chimed in. "Scoundrels abounded."

"It does you credit to own it." Doug put a fatherly hand on his old boss's shoulder. "Bob can be forgiven for much of it because, after all, he inherited an unholy mess from his predecessor." There was a dramatic pause before they said in unison. "The Major of Sainted Memory."

Mike was grinning from ear to ear. *There is a name we haven't heard for a while.*

Bob carried on. "The major didn't mince words. I can still see him lighting one of his unfiltered Camels with that Zippo he carried with him from Sicily to Rome. Looking at the flame and then snapping it shut as he pronounced his diagnosis: foof."

Mike burst into laughter at the familiar acronym.

Greg never met the major and was unfamiliar with this pronouncement. "What's a foof?"

Bob beamed. "It's a majorism: Fine Old Ontario Family."

Greg pressed on, smiling, "But what does that mean?"

"What it means," said Doug, "is that the cheque will clear the bank, but that's all the help we can expect from the family. They're fine, don't you know — *he's* the sickie, the one letting them all down. Families of this ilk treat this place like the dry cleaners. They expect prompt, courteous service and discretion because this kind of mess is out of place in their circle."

Greg joined in the fun. "I kind of hope we do bring him in. I've never worked with a crocodile. This could be an interesting addition to my resume."

Doug smiled. "Is that what your grandfather said when the *Hindenburg* hit the ground? *Interesting?*"

Greg started tapping his pen on the table. "I forgot to tell you the best part — Lori says the reptile is an IQ test."

Doug nodded. "I'll bite."

"If you don't laugh, there's something wrong with you," said Greg.

Mike wasn't having any of that. "Then there's something wrong with me."

"Okay," said Doug. "Enough fooling around. Let's go around the room. Tell me what you really think."

Mike went first. "He's not an alcoholic or an addict. Send him home. If he can't stay stopped long enough for the doctors to run their tests, then bring him back in for a second look."

Greg got a sour look on his face. He wanted him in. "The addiction is at a very low level, but the problems are starting to pile up. I think pot may turn out to be the real culprit. The big thing for me is this: he's using the clairvoyance and the reptile as a way of hiding — he's worse than an astrologer. He has an explanation for everything, but it's all bullshit. There's something going on that he wants to keep private and that says addiction to me."

Bob butted in before Greg was finished, eager to make his point. "I'd forgotten how much fun these go-rounds are." He leaned forward. "Look, this kid is adrift. It won't do him any harm to bring him in. The thing I can't square is why Lou is sitting still for this. The nasty, suspicious part of me that I disowned when I retired thinks the kid is pranking us. Maybe he's here to write a book. His old man told me he thinks treatment is a waste of the taxpayers' money and that what these young guys need is a good boot in the ass or trip to prison."

Mike couldn't resist, "But apparently not for his son or, at least, not yet."

Doug noticed Greg twitching. "Greg, you have a funny look on your face."

"Sorry, I was thinking about an impending catastrophe in my personal life. As to Lou, bring him in. We need to eliminate drugs and alcohol from the suspect list. My gut says all this odd behaviour is coming from a physical cause, and the quicker someone finds the tumour, the better."

As always, Doug had made up his own mind. He struck another heroic pose. "Mike, take a note. After a considerable period of intense scrutiny…"

Mike translated as he wrote. "After wasting an entire afternoon…"

"Having considered an array of arguments and treatment options…"

"…and not coming up with any kind of realistic plan…"

"It was decided on a balance of probabilities…"

"The cover-your-ass flag was hauled up the flagpole and saluted with a resounding oink."

"That the matter be referred to the medical director."

"That we pass the buck in the most craven and disheartening manner."

Doug had his happy face on. He was warming to the problem. "We're going to bring the kid in, give him a chance to settle down, build some rapport, and *maybe* get to the bottom of this. Let's see if he shows up sober."

"What's the morning line on that happening?"

"It all depends on what kind of mood the crocodile is in."

"If we had a hot tub, I'd like our chances better."

Chapter 13

John sat on the cane chair and watched Walter rock back and forth. He could easily have been mistaken for an air puppet trying to call attention to a dying tire store. An hour passed with nothing to distract the thin ghost but a young woman enjoying a cigarette and stroking a cat before she left for her afternoon class.

"If nothing else, being a ghost teaches you patience," said John as he examined Walter's fingers on the banister for the umpteenth time. "Don't your hands get tired, you old bastard?"

Walter looked neither right nor left, neither distressed nor surprised. John's words held no more interest for him than the sound of the surf does for a seagull.

Assuming a bow-legged stance that felt right for what he had in mind, John tried and discarded several placements of his right hand on his hip. Finally settling for fist and bent arm, he settled into character. "Peter, now you remember Peter — of course you do, the fat fellah — anyway, Peter has taken the position, not that I agree with him, mind you, but Peter seems to feel that you lookin' at the naked girls here is obscene."

John nodded at Walter as if he was hearing a point made in rebuttal. He ached to spit some chewing tobacco on the floor but settled for miming the action and then wiping his lips on the back of his sleeve. It felt right.

"Yup, I agree, Walt, that's the private school education screwing up his thinking, for sure. Your weekend either centres on Saturday night or Sunday morning."

John moved a little closer to the banister and tried to pry Walter's pinky finger loose. It was as if Walter's hand had put down roots in the railing.

John struck the pose of a colourful sidekick speaking softly to a hero — a posture that suggested friendly warning. "Now, Walt, you and I both know you can't hang on to that banister forever. The next time that light comes nosing around, well, ain't no doubt about it, you're outta here. But is that what you really want, to be scooped up to heaven or hell without any idea of what it means? No, sir. To my way of thinking, that kind of death is dee-grading. It does not advance the frontiers of human knowledge one peg forward. No, sir, that kind of death is beneath you."

The spent ghost's catatonic visage betrayed no interest in his impending exit. A brave captain going down with his ship could not have looked more resolute.

John put his hands behind his back and began to rock back and forth on his heels, all the while keeping his face three inches from Walter's.

"Bad enough you have to go, but I say, why not go in the cause of science? Now here's what Peter and I have in mind. Three doors down from here, at Punanai House — do you find the name intriguing, you old lecher — yeah, Punanai, how bad can that be? Anyway, we're going to move you down there and park you near another old gentleman who has overstayed his welcome. Mr. Jacob Hutton. Both of you bastards had your first smoke when Satan was in short pants. We were thinking you could pal up and share a cab to the big airport. Sort of be company for each other. Do you see where I'm going with this, Walt? A far more dignified exit."

John tapped Walter on the chin. The old poltergeist was surprised by the sensation and looked down. When he did, John flicked his nose with his index finger. Walter looked offended.

You can still react, you old possum. Good.

While John was mulling over his next move, a young woman mounted the stairs, wearing only a bath towel. Walter began to rumble the way volcanoes do. He turned his head to follow her progress. She took a long, elegant-looking cigarette from a folding case and lit it using a gold Dunhill lighter. Walter quivered. When a voice from below informed her that the shower was once again free, she stubbed out her barely begun cigarette and ran down the stairs, clearly intending to return shortly. All of this set John to wondering. What was it that had caught Walter's interest? He went with a hunch.

"Peter said you used to be a smoker. I bet you'd give anything for one more pull. I know about addictions, Walt." He looked over to where Walter's gaze had come to rest. The young woman had left an unopened pack of Du Maurier and her high-end cigarette case and matching lighter behind.

A new plan landed with a thud. John looked Walter in the eye. "You won't let go of that damn rail for love nor money. But there's more to life than them two."

John knew he would have to push as many buttons as he could. With a smoker, it was about more than the cigarette — it was all the little rituals that went along with the habit that made it irresistible. Walter couldn't smoke, but maybe he'd forgotten that. The way he was looking at the fresh pack suggested that he wanted one.

The inspired improviser squeezed himself between Walter's outstretched arms and braced the small of his back against the rail. An improbable pair preparing to dance. An effort this complex was going to burn until it cramped. John held the purloined pack of cigarettes under Walter's nose. He made a show of slowly tearing the cellophane ribbon. He flung the thin strand aside as assiduously as an erotic dancer giving up a veil. He kept the cigarette package front and centre for Walter and, with patient fingers, he pulled the two halves of the cellophane apart and let them fall seductively to the floor.

Dandruff, the cat, sprang up onto the railing, filled with purpose, her tail twitching. Objects floating in the air excited her. She watched in fascination. John was too focused on what he was doing to worry about collateral damage.

John felt a punishing wave of cold run through his arms. He was redlining — this was a real calorie burn. He pushed the bottom of the pack with his thumb until it sprang open. He waved the fresh deck of smokes in front of Walter's uncomprehending eyes, held the silver paper between his thumb and index finger, and gave it a quick tug. A wonderful warm smell of fresh tobacco jetted from the package. Walter's nose twitched. Dandruff's eyes narrowed to pinpricks.

Something stirred from deep within the lifeless pod — a glimmering of something long sought after and now finally at hand after having been all but forgotten, a grail memory.

John heard Walter say, "...moke..."

With a considerable effort, the thin ghost took one of the cigarettes out of the pack and pushed it between the poltergeist's lips. He reached for the gold-coloured Dunhill lighter he had set to rest on the banister. The stylish instrument made the act of lighting the tobacco seem elegant and reverential. In that confined space he had to be careful not to allow either of them to get too close to the flame.

Walters's left eye displayed another flicker of interest.

"Oh yeah, Walt, we got what you want right here."

Walter let go of the railing with his left hand as he attempted to light the cigarette. This was more than Dandruff could bear. She slashed the floating cigarette with her claws and watched it fall two floors below. She took off with a bump in hot pursuit. The pack of cigarettes fell to the floor as a wild look stole across Walter's face. John retrieved the pack from the floor and extracted another cigarette.

"That's it, Walt. These are real ones. You gotta focus, and you do remember how to do this, don't you? Good boy!"

Walter took the cigarette in his left hand and held it up to his nose, trying to identify this oh-so-puzzling and tantalizing piece of archaeology. He placed the cigarette underneath his nose and held it there by rolling up his top lip. The damn thing resembled a pencil-thin moustache. It gave him a rather comical appearance — Charlie Chaplin fooling around for the newsreels.

"That's what you really want. Who knew? But Walt, that's not the way to do it."

John reached over, gently pried the cigarette out from under Walter's nose, and popped it into his mouth. The old poltergeist's eyes, previously weak and rheumy, flashed excitement.

With his arms trembling from fatigue, John held out the glittering lighter for Walter, who desperately tried to grab it with his left hand, but John kept it outside his grasp. He wasn't fool enough to give a poltergeist an open flame to work with; that could make short work of them both. A fresh look of consternation crossed Walter's face. He was a soul in torment. Without thinking about what he was doing, he let go of the banister with his right hand as he strained to reach the lighter. To John's great amazement, Walter began to bounce slowly up and down on the spot. John ducked to get out of his way and watched as Walter floated past him toward the stairs. He bounced down the staircase to the landing below.

John followed him and marvelled at the way he moved; a helium-filled balloon caught in a gentle breeze. "Holy cow, Walt! Was that why you were hanging on?"

Whatever was moving Walter was powerful. The old ghost tried and failed several times to grip the banister. He floated and bounced, with his cigarette unlit in his mouth and a look beyond desperation in his eye.

John found that he could control the bouncing by holding Walter firmly by the scruff of the neck, but Walter's forward motion almost lifted John off his feet. By trial and error, he worked out that he could control the direction Walter moved by digging in his heels and leaning left or right.

"I don't know what's got into you, Walt, but let's not waste it. Let's get you tucked into your new room at Punanai. We can figure this out later."

As they crossed the street at Madison and Lowther, a car blew the stop sign and whizzed through the intersection. John dropped the expensive gold Dunhill in the crosswalk as he instinctively brought his hand up to protect his face. Walter closed his eyes and held his breath as if he was about to dive into a pool, losing his cigarette in the process.

The unseen force compelled them. Two doors down, they reached the front steps of Punanai. As they ascended, Walter started to pick up speed. John tightened his grip on the back of his collar, and to his astonishment, Walter's feet rose in the air. Something was drawing him into the house, into its orbit.

For one frantic moment, John was afraid the light was near. Was this what happened when it showed up? He looked around for signs of an ambush, but he didn't see anything. The heavy oak door opened as two thin youths departed. He dug in his heels and leaned left to direct Walter toward the elevator, but the force acting on him was getting stronger. It was harder to control him. His feet began to slip on the tile floor, and he was dragged right into the open elevator. He had to rest.

When he let go, Walter rose to the roof of the elevator car. They passed ten minutes in silence before the elevator sprang to life. The door of the car opened on the second floor. John had come to the end of his strength. Walter's collar was ripped out of his hand, and the old darling bounced and skipped his way down the long corridor, accelerating around the corner into Lou Canon's room. He came to rest on the ceiling above Lou's bed, beside another old ghost whom John had never seen before. They were stuck to the wall the way balloons are after they have been rubbed on someone's hair. As he stood there gasping and wondering what to do next, another poltergeist, an old woman this time, came skipping quickly down the hall. Where the hell were they coming from?

John knew better than to get too close. But he couldn't resist sneaking a peek into that room. A rubber crocodile was the only other occupant. He was resting comfortably on top of a novel by Ernest Hemingway, which was underneath a beautifully framed numbered copy of a Group of Seven masterwork.

John heard the sound of surf and smelled sea air. He should have felt a moment of pure triumph, but he was exhausted from his efforts. He couldn't wait to tell Peter what he'd accomplished. "Walt, I do believe you're getting the hang of this thing, yes sir. Why don't you old timers have a chin wag and catch up. I'll be back later."

It was hard to make his way down the corridor. He was not immune to the force acting on Walter. Whatever had pulled the old poltergeist in was making it hard for him to leave. It felt as if he was wading upstream. But as he rounded the corner, the force on his legs diminished.

Best not to get too close, *he thought.* Next time it will have me too.

Chapter 14

There was a lot of foot traffic between the Eddington Detox, St. Joe's Hospital, and Punanai House. Older clients always had a hard time getting detoxed. It often delayed treatment, sometimes for weeks. The question this morning was how much gas did Fred Grant have left in the tank? He'd lost a lot of weight by eating hospital food. His clothes hung off him. The new heart meds had left him pale with an undertone of grey. He needed a haircut and a decent meal, but most of all, he needed a reason to get out of bed in the morning. He wanted nothing to do with Punanai.

Mike wisely chose Greg to do the assessment. "What brings you in to see us today, Fred?"

Fred was taken aback. "Do I know you?"

Greg smiled. "You were here two months ago. We had a chat. Do you remember that?"

Fred was searching for something, something way back somewhere. "Yeah, something about this place is familiar."

It hurt Greg to watch him struggle. "How long have you been in hospital?"

Fred thought about it for a full minute. "Don't know, every day is the same day in that bloody place. But too long. They wouldn't let me out."

Greg made a note and looked down at the file. "Last year you made three appointments to come see us and you never showed, and then two months ago we had a chat and you told me you were drinking forty ounces of hard liquor a day. That's a lot. Is there something wrong at home?"

"I don't drink forty ounces every day."

"Okay. How much do you drink?"

"Nothing, I haven't had a drink in years."

"Do you remember what the Doc said?"

Fred shook his head. "Which one? They run around in packs. I can't keep 'em straight."

"Fred, who's the captain of the Toronto Maple Leafs?"

"The defence man, Ron Rampage."

"Close enough." He closed the file and put his pen down on top of it. Fred was still too spun to answer questions or decide. "We're going to bring you in for treatment today. Your mom has packed up everything you need and arranged to have someone take care of your place. As far as I can tell, you're still a little under the weather. I want you to relax and try and get into the rhythm of the place, and let's see if we can't get you well and home again soon."

Fred looked him in the eye. "I want to go home now."

"The only way you're ever going to make it home is to come through here. Give us a chance. We can help you."

The sour look on Fred's face told Greg he didn't think so.

***

Greg picked up the phone on the third ring. It was the man he'd spoken to the day before, the one with the German accent. Before Greg finished saying hello, Klaus bulldozed him.

"We spoke last night. I have changed my mind. I must come in."

Greg was surprised to hear this, but he didn't let on.

"I will set up an interview—"

"Tell me when and where and I will pick up some beers."

"That's not the way we do things." Greg smiled, knowing where this was going. Most clients would have gladly accepted an invitation to discuss their issues over drinks at the Madison Pub. "I need to take a little information."

"Go ahead."

"What's your last name, Klaus?"

"Why do you need that?"

"To start the paperwork. We need some contact information. We don't share it—"

"So it is secret?"

"Uh, yes, it's secret."

"But not more secret than if I do not tell you anything. *Ja?*"

"I can't give you an appointment if you won't tell me your name."

Klaus was playing to a larger audience. "See now, how he interrogates me in the manner of the Stasi. Such people can never be trusted."

The phone was slammed down.

I am going to take that as a maybe.

***

Lori put down her book and went to make herself a sandwich. She'd read on the plaque at Punanai that the institution's odd name came from a book by Christopher Ondaatje — about his father and the island of Sri Lanka. *The Man-eater of Punanai* had taken her by surprise. She had expected a novel not a coffee-table book. The wildlife photography and the moving stories of village life and connection to the land were compelling. The book possessed a beautiful metaphysical unity. How could three things as different as a distant parent, a wounded panther, and a beautiful nation on the verge of civil war be connected? In the eyes of a child, they were. Lori understood why Punanai was such a wonderful name for the house. The book was a profound meditation on the nature and consequences of brokenness.

As she buttered the toast and waited for the teakettle to come to a boil her thoughts turned to Lou. He'd only been gone for three days and already she wanted him home. His visions and mystical experiences were different from the ones in Ondaatje's book. But they had one thing in common: they both looked at the world from the point of view of a vulnerable child confronted with the unfathomable choices made by adults. *That first moment when our trust in the world fails us.*

When Lou hinted there was a part of him he was afraid to share with her, she'd felt a compulsion to know. What secret burdened him? Lou was patient. He began by telling her about the mysterious things that happened to him when he was eleven. He told the stories without embellishment and without sharing his personal thoughts about what the events meant.

He let Lori share his experience, as if she, too, were having visions. In time, the ragged edges of the images coalesced into a pattern for her. In the collage of impression, she sensed a loving presence gathering up the loose ends of the lost. She learned to love Lou all the more because he told her the truth as he understood it and gave her the space and time she needed to make up her own mind about what these images and sensations suggested.

But at the end of the day, what did she have to go on? This was ultimately something you could only know and be sure about if it happened to you. She couldn't authenticate the story, but she could love and respect the storyteller — his integrity made it all seem possible. Belief is a risky business.

She set her sandwich down on the kitchen table and turned on the radio, hoping to hear the news. Her eye caught a sparrow pecking at the dried stalks in her garden. *What would happen if we all took the time to listen? To let everyone work out exactly what they needed to say. To trust that maybe the stuff that wasn't quick and slick had value.*

Chapter 15

Larry Lorne had gone to his room to look for his toothbrush after a pastry that didn't sit well and instead found his bed taken apart and pushed into the hallway. A large man was on his hands and knees, scrubbing the wood floor in the closet. Larry hoped it was housekeeping dealing with the plumbing and not something worse.

Please don't be bedbugs.

He announced his presence with a friendly question. "Who turned the room upside down?"

Fred looked up from his work with a scowl. "I did. It's filthy."

Larry shrugged. It looked clean to him. "Are you maintenance?"

Fred straightened his back and turned to see who he was talking to. "This is my room. I can't sleep when it's filthy. They said I was on day zero and that I could do whatever I want today. I'm squaring this place away."

"Well, if this is your room, I'm your new roommate." He made his way into the bathroom and got to work on his teeth. "I'm Larry," he said agreeably as he foamed at the mouth.

"Fred," said the big man, returning to his task. "Do you snore?"

"No recent complaints. What about you?"

"Don't know. I've been sleeping solo. Besides it's only a problem if you snore."

Larry had a chipped front tooth that showed when he smiled. His nose had been broken and it marred his otherwise handsome face. He spat into the sink and gave himself a rinse. Satisfied with the result, he turned his attention to the ongoing renovation. *How long is this shit going to go on?* He glanced at his watch and said brightly, "I'd love to stay and give you a hand, but I have to be back in class."

After a moment of reflection, Fred grunted. He could tell Larry had never been to jail. He was too open a book. "I don't need your help. The cleaning makes me feel better. And you'd only make it worse."

Larry saw no reason to argue that point. "All right. I'll be back in an hour or so. You wanna take a little walk around the neighbourhood? I can show you the sights and buy you a cup of real coffee."

Fred had to lay his hands on the door frame to leverage himself to his feet. It hurt. He was still eyeing Larry up as he crossed the room to shake his hand. "I could go for that."

Glad to be on his way, Larry continued down the carpeted corridor toward the seminar room. As he rounded the corner, he caught the scent of a sick room. *Freddy should be down here.* The door to the common washroom was open and inside a very tired-looking woman wearing pink scrubs was rinsing out a white hand towel in the sink.

I've never seen a woman here before. "Do you work here?"

"I'm working with Mr. Hutton, down the hall."

Larry could see she how unhappy she was. "I'm going for a coffee later. Can I bring one back for you?"

She gave him a resigned smile. "Thank you, that's very kind, but coffee won't help me when I'm this tired. And besides, in three hours I plan to be asleep."

Larry nodded his head and left her to get on with the washing. The smell was coming from the room opposite the washroom. He slowed his pace as he passed to have a look. A huge man with a pockmarked red face was propped up in bed under thick covers. He wasn't awake but he didn't look as if he was asleep either. And the room smelled as if a careless foot had kicked over a can of cleaning solution containing ammonia. Larry shuddered as his feet did what every part of him wanted them to do.

***

Fred kept cleaning until dinner time. A guy with two canes came by and insisted that he put the furniture back into the room. Being rushed angered him, but he'd made a good start. Warm water and soap soothed him. The smell got up his nose and inside his head and did a little cleaning there too. And memories weren't as sharp-edged when he was doing something productive.

Another hour was all he needed. The room still didn't feel done to him; it didn't feel right.

A drink would've cut the ribbon on this.

Larry was sitting at their table in the dining room, waiting for him, when he arrived and that helped — seeing a familiar face. While the last of the stragglers drifted in, Fred took stock of the room. Half of these guys had their fingerprints on file. The tats and shifty eyes confirmed that. But he didn't see anyone here he needed to be concerned about. These were not hard men.

He might have busted one or two of them. There'd been too many of them down through the years. After a while, they'd all started to look the same until the day came when their features faded into a blurred jumble of unhappy creatures. They'd remember him far better than he'd remember them. Getting arrested is always much more memorable for the one in handcuffs.

It bothered him that he could be in the presence of someone with a grudge and not know. How humiliating would it be to die because of that kind of carelessness? He eyed up the scratched and dented fork, pulled a tiny bottle of disinfectant from his jacket and gave it a little squirt and a wipe with his napkin while his dinner companions made a point of not noticing.

Dinner was good, chicken pot pie and four scoops of real mashed potatoes and gravy. There was something green, but he didn't eat nonessentials. His dinner companions were good company. The Leafs had given them plenty to complain about. It was fun to hear the talk. It'd been ages since he'd eaten with anyone.

His stomach was tender, but it felt good to have food moving around inside him again. He always had an appetite for the first day or two of a binge, but then he'd begin to feel bloated and distressed, and as the days passed, he felt the need to eat less and less until, finally, the very thought of food was enough to gag him. At the end of one of his binges, he'd as soon stuff a well-used mechanic's rag down his throat as try to eat. Food was poison and poison was food. Even he grasped the insanity of that and yet some of that ethos lingered over this meal.

For too long his consciousness had existed between two fixed points — the blessed release of the first drink and the *coup de grâce* of the passing out ceremony. The usual measures of progress — days, weeks, and even hours — ceased to matter. Small passages of time were recorded in the ebbing level of a bottle of spirits, the larger passages in the thinning ranks of vodka bottles standing in parade formation on the bar.

Alcohol was a benevolent dictator. The thing that was causing his gastric pain was the only thing that soothed it. The first two or three drinks would kill the pain and give him an appetite. If he got distracted, the moment would pass and the drinking would take over. But if he timed his move right, he'd be able to get something bland down, something he could grab out of the fridge while he was recharging his glass. More often than not, it turned out to be a chunk of cheddar wrapped in a piece of stale brown bread.

He went for days without eating, feeling a horrible bloated empty sensation in his core punctuated by bursts of violent vomiting as his body fought to rid itself of the poison he kept swallowing. His dentist had noticed the acid wear marks on the back of his teeth getting worse and kept asking him if he was anorexic. After two such painful interrogations, he stopped going.

Despite all the pain, Fred couldn't imagine life without the sedative properties of alcohol. Booze castrated him, and for that he was grateful. Alcohol numbed his forebodings and stilled his mind while he was conscious, but it was only when he was passing out that he felt something akin to peace and connection. He could simply cease to be for a few hours.

The high-pitched chirp of a chair moving across the linoleum brought him back into the room. His gaze fell on a young thug sitting at the other table. The youth looked back at him, puzzled by his expression. A shudder of revulsion coursed through Fred. The young man reminded him of Stephen. He would be a grown man now, well into his middle years. Fred looked again, the face was the wrong shape, it couldn't be him. But this was the kind of place he'd been headed for.

The disaster with Stephen was the second time he'd felt exposed. The first was when he was just thirteen. He and his friend Marvin had been rolling around on the bed, but something about this wrestling match was different from the hundreds that had gone before, and it had surprised both boys. They hadn't gotten very far, but they'd gotten somewhere, and that was bad enough. He remembered the look on his mother's face as she opened the door a crack and then withdrew.

His mother had avoided talking to him for an hour after Marvin went home. She sat in her armchair, looking out the window while she sipped ever so carefully on a cup of tea that had long grown cold. Her face a study in turmoil as hope and fear took turns colouring her visage. When she finally questioned him gently about what she'd seen, he knew what nakedness had meant in the garden. She'd seen through to the heart of the matter. "Do you know what homosexuality is, Fred?"

His wits had been with him that day. He scoffed at her insight and said of course he did.

"Do you have … feelings for Marvin?"

"Mom," he'd said in a pained voice, "we were trying to throw each other off the bed." That statement settled the issue in the short term, but the world had changed. Nothing he'd done had felt wrong, but the look on his mother's face told him it was.

He spent twenty years working long hours in vice and wondering if what he was doing was futile. An endless line of broken, tortured people. And then he picked up a young runaway on a charge of possession. Stephen was lost and bewildered when they cuffed him and put him in the back seat of the cruiser. Instead of arresting him, instead of feeding him into the belly of the beast, Fred took him to his mother's for a meal. In all his years of trying, Fred had not been able to save one of them. There was something about Stephen's eyes that made it all seem possible, if only for an hour. But it was a mistake.

Stephen was terrified. The kids he was running with killed snitches. It never occurred to him that what Fred had in mind for him was a home-cooked meal and a bus ticket back to Sudbury. They might as well have been wearing figure skates in the apartment. Everything was wrong. They didn't speak the same language. Fred ended the awkwardness by putting the boy on the bus early. It never occurred to him that young Stephen would betray this act of kindness.

But betray he did, the very next time he was picked up.

Fred heard the outline of the story over the top of the lockers as he was going off shift. He didn't know it was Stephen they were talking about. He went along with the verdict of the other cops without knowing that he was the one on trial. One of his buddies gave him the heads-up the next morning. Fred was sick in the sink.

Fortunately, Captain Clark sorted through what happened and concluded nothing inappropriate had transpired, but it had shaken Fred to his very core to have to answer his questions. It didn't matter that he'd done nothing wrong or even that he'd tried to help the boy. There was a new, low note of dread in every quiet conversation he half-heard. A scent of sickening fear now clung to the uniforms of his colleagues. It was part of the air now.

Everyone noticed the change in him. The switch from beer to vodka. Red eyes in the morning and new holes in his leather belt. Complaints from the public and suspects alike. They made him see the psychologist. She told him he could trust her. He thought and felt otherwise as he looked deeply into her piggy eyes. She radiated a hostility and judgment appropriate for a rogue angel. He said as little as he could — enough to get him out of that chair and back to work — and turned down her offer of pills, knowing damn well that they'd be nothing but trouble.

Then the spiral, the repression of who he was mixed with the fear of what they thought of him bred more severe restriction. How he hated simple polite enquiries, their amused contemptuous looks. Misgivings made social connection a living hell. Even polite conversation had an edge of terror. He hated the feeling that evil thoughts were whirling around like dervishes inside his skull and that anyone looking into his eyes could see the deceit and chaos.

Until the car crash. The horror of realizing that his body was never going to be right again. Then back to the apartment, working security jobs, but on the night shift now, working alone, changing jobs every six months until none of the people he used to know remembered him anymore. Until his new bosses got wise, smelled booze on his breath and death coming out of his pores. Then all that was left was the cleaning, the drinking, the regretting — and doing it all again. He had to clean until it felt right, then he could stop, when it was done and done properly.

***

The phone rang as Doug was packing up for the day. He'd stayed well past his time, and he was tired and ready to go. Against his better judgment, he took the call.

"I just got off the phone with Kay Canon," a furious voice said. "Why didn't you tell me her son was in the house?"

Time slowed. Doug let the barrage of sacred words land where they wanted to as he slowly drew the phone away from his ear. Erin was a force of nature, a starry-eyed believer filled with the energy of certainty. She was up to the task of dragging him, and the entire profession, if necessary, to higher, firmer ground.

"There are twenty-eight other guys in treatment, Erin…"

"The Canons are front page news, and they have big dollars to donate."

"I'll be sure to ask Lou for a cheque."

"The tone that we've talked about is back in your voice."

Doug clenched his teeth and drew a short, sharp breath. He took a five count to remodulate his voice. He didn't say, *You mean the tone that never leaves yours?* and instead settled on a more defensible statement. "Mr. Canon is going to take a delicate touch. We've got it under control."

"Which room did you put him in? Tell me you put him in the one we decorated last week."

"He went into the first room that had an empty bed."

"Who is his roommate? There are no psychos in his room, are there?" Even over the phone, he could hear the air crackling.

"We're going to do our best for Mr. Canon by treating him the way we treat every other client."

"We'll see about that."

Chapter 16

The Pine Rock Discussion Group of Alcoholics Anonymous didn't suit Kaiser's palate — far too tame. He preferred the cut and thrust of the Bad Boys Meeting and would rather have gone there, even though it meant a drive to Brampton in rush hour traffic. This was Reg's kind of group — he'd been coming here for five years, listening to the same people week after week.

Kaiser grudgingly fired up the old Toyota and drove his colleague to meetings from time to time as a penance and peace offering. He half-heartedly went along with the suggestion that doing something together would help them wallpaper over their differences. Mike had come up with the idea after one of their more memorable brawls. But Kaiser did this only on nights when there was nothing worth watching on television.

The room itself was nice. It was in a community centre, one with ample parking and lovely plants and artwork in the halls. The space smelled of topsoil this evening, as the plants had recently had a good watering. A huge slab of transparent plastic served as the roof for the foyer. Young and old alike delighted in sitting on the benches to watch the progress of either rain or snow. But was what they experienced while sitting there watching the storm universal or particular?

Tonight's topic was an open discussion about how the big changes that happen in the middle of your life — things such as buying houses, raising children, getting divorced, and working in a corporate culture — affect your sobriety.

The group had a firm no-crosstalk rule — no one could comment directly on what another person had said. This rule was a godsend for people who grew up in abusive families. Open 12-step meetings were unfailingly polite. Reg believed this arrangement should always be tried first. Respect for the other was sacred to him. And that was the reason he clashed with Kaiser and struggled in the treatment business. Reg expected people to do the right thing once their dilemma was properly explained to them.

Kaiser, on the other hand, believed that not everyone responded to the respectful approach, that some people need that extra zing. He saw it as a logical next step for those who were forever trying to get sober but always coming up short. Allowing people to perish when the solution was at hand enraged him. Listening to them lie to themselves uninterrupted made him shake his head in dismay.

Small wonder, then, that the crosstalk rule was a bone of contention between the two counsellors. From Kaiser's perspective, it allowed people to talk about their addiction endlessly without ever resolving it. While from Reg's vantage point, it gave people the time and space they needed to make up their own minds and be convinced rather than browbeaten.

Kaiser let his looks convey his disapproval as the meeting came order. His pet name for this bunch was The Stuck and Stuck Up.

The first speaker, a young woman named Sonia, stood up and shifted her feet a bit, not making eye contact with anyone as she introduced herself and then said, "I wanted to go first tonight, to get the talking out of the way so that I can listen a bit more … which is what my sponsor suggested I do…"

Kaiser looked heavenward and shook his head. *Hip deep in the mud and praying for rain.*

There was a pause and then tears flowed. "I've been feeling … so wrong. The pain is … loneliness, too, I suppose. It's hard to bear… Other people get into trouble, I know that," she shook her head and continued in a steadier voice, "but they get out of it because they have friends and people to help them. But stuck in this alone, you're beaten already." Her head went down. She sucked in a huge, painful breath and looked up. "I'm sorry about the tears… There's hope for us. There's help if we want it." Sonia put her head down again, unable to look at anyone.

Kaiser was off the clock but that didn't matter, he was intrigued. *When she talks about herself, she falls to pieces, but when she's talking about other people, she's fine. I betcha there's a fancy name for that.*

Kaiser was still racking his brain, looking for the elusive word, when he heard Reg's voice. He'd lost track of him in the crowd. There had to be fifty people sitting around the big oval table. Everyone leaned in to hear Reg. He was a crowd favourite.

"Reg. Alcoholic." He sighed and smiled around the room. "I really am at a crossroads. I've been working on a novel. It's my dark lady. It's what I go home to in the evening after a hard day at work. Sometimes my lady is warm and supportive, while other times she's so damned demanding that she reduces me to self-loathing. This thing has been a killer to write." He put his hands on the table in front of him as if he was about to play the piano, his fingers open wide. "But now I'm finding out that the writing is the easy part. To get this thing published, I have to get an agent. But in order to get an agent, I have to have something published."

A few heads nodded gentle encouragement.

"And if an established writer doesn't vouch for you, or if you can't win an award, well then, you might as well be writing a diary. Who knows? If I will my manuscript to a university history department, someone might use it in a couple of centuries as the basis for studying neurotic behaviour in middle-aged men."

That earned him a chuckle from his fans. He paused for moment, waiting for quiet.

You're letting the side down with this humble shit. You're supposed to be a power of example. Kaiser turned to give him a look, but a woman who was new to the group stood up and broke the silence.

"I hate whining. It disgusts me. How can you sit there feeling sorry for yourself?" She looked around the table. "Imagine having to persist at something for a long period of time."

Reg and Sonia exchanged a look that said *I hope she's talking about you.* This month's chairman raised his finger to admonish the firebrand. "You need to qualify—"

She crushed him with a belligerent look and then turned and smiled sweetly at the group. "My name is Riana, and I'm an alcoholic." She smiled at the chairman and said, "Better now?" She had the floor. She was way out of line, and everyone was dying to hear what she was going to say next.

Riana's tone became even more aggressive as she swept the broken conventions of the past before her.

"My old Dad asked me to take care of him for the last six months of his life. He told me he'd leave me all his dough when he was gone. The old bastard put one over on me. He lasted five long years." She jabbed her index finger into the table. "Five years of bedsores, pill bottles, and nights without end. By the time he finally did cash out, he'd spent all the money he'd promised me on online gambling. I even got to pay for his funeral," she said brightly as she looked left and right up and down the table.

"Well, I got through that, and the addiction piece, too, because it was the right thing to do." She zeroed in. "Reg, stop trying to be charming about being a failure. Grow up. Take someone by the throat if you have to, but get the damned thing published."

There was a profound silence. The air was heavy with expectation. People were not allowed to talk that way. It was crosstalk! The chairman knew he should be on his feet restoring order, but he was dumbfounded. He sat there at the head of the table with all eyes on him, frozen in a moment of indecision, his face painted with the dreadful hue of shame and defeat.

The group likewise wavered in its resolve. In the lengthening silence, the regulars exchanged frantic looks. Someone had to answer this challenge. They couldn't let her get away with this. Finally, it was Reg's plaintive voice that pierced the void.

"Are you by any chance a literary agent?" The room roared with laughter.

Kaiser felt a surge of feel-good chemicals coursing through his veins. Reg knocked off his perch and the rest of the group looking outraged and helpless, all because they were afraid to say boo to this woman. He was glad now that he'd come. There was another meeting here on Thursday. He'd come back then for a closer look at this Riana. She was worth the drive.

Chapter 17

Fred was a bigger problem for Larry Lorne than Czombo had been. The old prick was same age as his dad — with all the same endearing quirks and a few additional irksome ones to boot. He talked over people, enforced rules that made no sense, and got mad when you questioned him.

It's like I never left home.

Guilt was a problem bigger than Fred and his father combined. Larry was certain that Paul had figured out that he was the one who had provided Czombo with clean urine. Czombo hadn't given him up when he got kicked out, but the fact remained that it was his urine they'd tested. Ending up with Fred as a roommate had to be cosmic payback for helping Czombo.

Thank God knowing isn't proving. Maybe that's why they put a cop in my room.

Fred didn't need to tell Larry he was a cop. It was etched in acid on his forehead. He was big and self-satisfied — always in the right. His eyes were video cameras continually sweeping the room for danger. He had that smartass, burning out patina of crumbling invulnerability that clung to all the members of his profession. Running around town with guns gives you the twinned sensations of peril and privilege. But the final tell was his use of questions. He'd listen to an answer but then pretend to need clarification when, really, he was trying to undermine the previous statement.

Fred's first edict was that shoes must be removed before entering his room. Larry did it to keep the peace, and afterwards was delighted to find that Fred had shined his shoes, applied some foot powder, and replaced his worn laces.

Larry took Fred to his first AA meeting, as was the custom. It put him in mind of watching a hen walk across the top of a tiger's cage. He sensed a coming disaster and decided he better talk with someone. Kaiser frightened him, but he felt safe with Paul.

Paul was sitting alone in the office, repotting a spider plant that had been tipped over and its container broken, a look of contentment on his handsome face. His fingers were thick and powerful, but they moved delicately as they restored order.

Kaiser could be pushy and intrusive. A conversation with him might end up someplace you didn't want to be. But then he went looking for trouble. Paul wasn't like that. He listened and tried to understand.

I still have to be careful what I say.

Paul was happy for some company. He tried to find the perfect spot for the plant as he listened to Larry. "I took Fred down to the corner to get a coffee before the meeting and we found a table at the Second Cup, and you know how rarely that happens, but he wouldn't sit there because someone spilled something. We had to go to the park. And it was freezing outside — but I couldn't let him go on his own." Larry shrugged at the memory. "I hate when people bully me. I wanted to give him shit but he looked like someone pulled a knife on him. I got him to sit down on a park bench and light up a smoke, but he wouldn't settle." Larry was still feeling the agitation.

A look of concern crept across Paul's face. Larry wondered, *Is that frown for me or the spider plant?* He soldiered on. "I said we could try the Tim's around the corner, but he said he couldn't. Not there. Not in a room full of strangers. He said he gets nuts in tight spaces."

The phone rang and Larry lost his confidence, but Paul only thumbed his nose at the instrument, which made Larry laugh.

"I didn't know what to say. But then it hit me. If he couldn't handle a coffee shop full of college kids, what was he going to do at a rowdy AA meeting with over a hundred people? I asked him straight up, 'Is a church basement going to be a problem for you?' He said he had to sit in the back and have a clear path to the door. And then something about him being the sun, and me being a planet. He said, 'You orbit around me.' And I just said, 'Okay, but we have to stick together. All the way to the meeting and all the way back. You'll get me in trouble if you leave.'"

The phone rang again, and this time Paul put his fingers in his ears and stamped both his feet on the floor like a child. Larry's mood brightened.

"Then he got mad." Larry got to his feet and took on Fred's imposing body language. "Said, 'Look kid' — as if he were my dad or something — said, 'You don't understand. I've traded hammer blows with monsters.' He actually said that." Larry's face was one part snarl and one part grimace. "He said, 'I've seen things that can't be *unseen*, the worst shit this city has to offer. I lived in it. But I don't wanna do it anymore.' And then he said something about the stink of it getting up his nose or in his bones or something." Larry flung himself into his chair with a look on his face that suggested confusion rather than exhaustion.

"And the whole time, his eyes were crazy, like, desperate. He started on about panicking, about his throat tightening... Said he was drowning. I don't even know if he was still talking to me."

"Did you ask him if he drinks when this happens?" Paul asked with a smile.

"He said it's the only thing that helps. Asked him if he'd talked to any of you guys, but he just said, 'None of their freaking business.' Then he started poking me in the shoulder, hard — I mean, it actually hurt — and he said, 'We have to take care of each other, have each other's backs.'"

Larry rooted around in his pocket. He pulled out an elegant object. "Then he gave me this." He handed it to Paul. A gold lighter with the Dunhill logo embossed on the side.

It fit comfortably in Paul's hand. When he depressed the plunger, a battery generated spark ignited a perfectly symmetrical tear drop of flame.

"He said he found it in the middle of the crosswalk."

Paul shook his head admiringly. "Someone is going to be sad when they find this is gone. Is it real gold?"

"Maybe fool's gold. I don't think so. Anyway, we got through the meeting, but this can't go on."

Paul's face was untroubled, his eyes soft and at peace. Larry felt an impulse to tell him about the urine, simply to be done with it. He wanted to. But he caught himself.

Paul handed the lighter back. "What's your gut telling you to do?"

"Run!" he said with some enthusiasm. "I'm not getting thrown out because of some crazy thing he does. He's gonna go off sooner or later."

"You did the right thing telling me. I'll have a talk with him."

"Are you going to rat me out?"

"Nope. If this is as serious as you say, I won't have any trouble getting him to talk about it."

***

Paul leaned back in his chair and gave Fred a moment to settle, but Fred stayed sitting up straight, digging his fingers into the armrests. The phrase *friendly chat* obviously didn't exist in his world. Fred looked desperate.

"I didn't realize last night was your first AA meeting."

Fred sat up straighter. Even this much intel was cause for concern. "How do you know that?"

Paul softened his voice, trying not to offer offence. He fibbed a little. "I heard the guys on the deck talking."

"Which guys?"

Paul tried getting him to do the work. "Why are you making an issue out of this?"

"I'm not." The look on his face was indecipherable.

Paul decided to chance it. "Do people talk about you, Fred?"

"Sometimes."

"How does that make you feel?"

"I don't care for it." Fred crossed his arms and looked away. No more psychologists. Especially not this nosy guy. *What's he up to? What does he want to know?*

Paul smiled at Fred. *Let's start with an easier question, maybe the one I should have asked in the first place.* "How did you enjoy the meeting last night?"

Fred had to change gears. He couldn't ask the question he wanted to ask without tipping his hand. No. The thing to do here was to play along and get as much information as he could while giving nothing of value away.

"It was okay. I didn't understand a lot of it."

"If you weren't in treatment, would you go back?"

"Not to that one, it's way too big."

"There are smaller ones you could go to. Would that help?"

"Yeah, maybe."

"I'll make you a list. But remember you still have to get someone to go with you."

As he got to his feet to go, Fred resembled every losing candidate who had ever come to the podium to concede defeat. Paul felt a stab of connection. "Do you feel any better about being here, Fred?"

"I want to go home."

Chapter 18

Reg cornered Riana when the meeting was over. She was standing at the centre of a small circle of her admirers, facing down a larger orbit of people waiting to give her a good talking to. She stood untroubled, calm, and magnificent. Reg looked at her, but she ignored him for a full two minutes. He upped the ante by stepping into her space. "May I talk to you for a moment?"

There was a collective holding of breath in both camps. Was this a showdown?

Riana fired the first shot. "Are you stalking me?"

"Not after what the judge said last time." Reg smiled at her sweetly and lowered his voice. "He got right personal in some of his observations."

She was not in the mood for charm. She looked at her watch with a frown. Reg stared at her with hope and then shook his head and dropped his gaze.

"Speak up," she said finally.

He couldn't help himself. "I was kind of wondering…"

Riana appeared very angry now. "I said speak up!"

Reg did his trademark shuffle with his canes. He frequently looked as if he might tumble over, but he never did. "Well, as I was about to say, I was wondering…" Words failed him again as he glanced from side to side.

Her toe began to tap. "Wondering what, you annoying man?"

Reg looked around her circle. They all had the disapproving eyes of conquerors. "Wondering about what's going to happen when I complain to you about what you said. Are you going to storm out of the meeting hall and make me limp after you on my canes?"

She was deeply offended. "That would be rude!"

Reg smiled at her. "See, they were all wrong, you do know what rude is."

Riana hated pranks. She wanted to smack Reg. Her look belonged in the witness box — an outraged woman in pearls asked by the prosecutor if her assailant was in the courtroom. She smirked. "You're a friend of Greg's, aren't you?"

The question surprised him, dripping as it did with venom. "You know Greg?"

She sneered in the certain knowledge that she'd fired one right over his pointy head. "Evidently better than you do."

The circle of admirers closed rank, aching for the serpent or the mongoose to strike a fatal blow. This was turning into a tug of war with historical overtones. Reg decided to make his point and call it a day.

"Riana, do you know what crosstalk is?"

"Counter transference is a very big word for a short-dicked cretin such as yourself." Mouths opened with the sharp shout of embarrassed laughter.

Reg shook his head. He still wanted to know what this lady had to do with Greg and why she'd crosstalked him but, having reached his fortieth year with all his parts still attached, he decided, after consulting the actuarial tables, that it would be easier to take the matter up with Greg.

His face beamed satisfaction. "Have a safe trip home."

Kaiser was waiting in the Toyota, amusing himself by trying to remember what all the warning symbols on the dashboard meant. "Did you talk to your sweetie?"

"I tried. She can be difficult. A woman of rare insight though. She can estimate penis size from behavioural clues alone."

"She was right, you know."

"About the size of my johnson?"

"Getting your novel published."

Reg felt the horror a fat kid experiences when cornered by the skinny bitches. "Can you elaborate?"

"Get it done." Kaiser turned in his seat to face Reg. "You know, now that I think about it, that new kid that came in last week — Seymour — his mother's a big wheel in publishing. I bet you we can get him to give her the novel."

Reg cringed. "That would take unethical to new heights."

"What are you talking about? If one of the clients had a dry-cleaning store, would you feel bad about dropping your suits off there?"

"It would be wrong if I was looking for a freebie."

"Don't you believe in your own novel? When you talk about it, you always make it sound stupid. Why is that? If you don't believe in this thing, no one else will either."

There was a prolonged silence. Reg coloured and his words, for once, failed him. "Well…"

"Well what? Give me the damn thing and I'll get it published."

Anger was finding its footing but had not yet prevailed. "I don't think that's a very good idea. You're not a literary agent."

Kaiser looked heavenward, "That's why it'll get published. I don't know the rules of the game. I'm not trying to build an empire of make-believe friendships and Facebook connections. I want to get the damn thing published so you can win or lose and move on with your life. You're stuck on the fly paper and you're making everyone crazy with this longhair shit."

Reg was undone. A look of horror in his eyes told the story. He felt like a child pushed onto the stage with his half-remembered first line drowned in terror. He needed privacy and some loving support to bring this off. There was no point in saying that to a man who was certain this could be accomplished with bravado and intimidation. He drew a breath and a line halfway between what he was thinking and feeling. "Kaiser, this is important to me."

"It doesn't show. Jesus, crazy women are picking up on this stuff at meetings. When you get mad at people you always want to fight a duel — very formal, very civilized. Where I come from, if someone calls you outside, you kick 'em down a flight of stairs. No fuss, no bother. If I leave it up to you, we'll still be talking about this twenty years from now. That's why you come to this group. The swamp group is what I'm going to call it from now on, for people bogged down in their own crap."

Reg had to smile. He loved Kaiser's rants. "You're talking in parables."

"You go to that group because no one there is going to hold you accountable and make you change. You've given up wine for whining. What would happen if we ran Punanai that way? I'll tell you what, a big fat nothing! We have a reputation in this town. People look up to us. We don't let anyone get away with making us look like idiots."

Next week I'll come alone — on the bus, Reg thought.

Chapter 19

At 7:00 p.m. Paul unlocked the big oaken front door and sent the guys on their way. They were eager to get out of the house and into as much mischief as they could handle. Most of them favoured the AA meeting at the corner of Spadina and Bloor, because the short commute gave them more time to chase the girls and drink coffee. Lou was enjoying the energy of the group. He hadn't been out with a large group of single males since high school, and he suddenly realized how much he missed the energy of the herd.

Lou didn't have a roommate — a concession to head-office views of how he was to be treated. He was accompanied to his first meeting, as was the custom, by an older gentleman named Dale. A high school principal by trade, it naturally fell to him to take the nutcase with the crocodile under his wing.

The meeting was a bust, as sometimes happens. Unfortunately, the speaker was not up to the task. It left Lou in the lurch. He listened for several minutes before realizing that the speaker had no idea what he was talking about, and neither did anyone else.

The speaker was aware that he was dying the death. He was unable to focus on what he needed to say, but he didn't have the good grace to sit down and shut up. He kept rambling, hoping inspiration would strike, looking more desperate by the minute. Lou looked over at Dale for a reaction and saw that he was dozing peacefully.

When in Rome, grab a toga off the rack.

Lou closed his eyes and listened to the slow rhythmic breathing of one hundred bored and restless smokers. He pretended that a choir of whales was the source of the asthmatic wheezing that filled the air.

With his eyes shut, and a big dinner being digested, the fragmentary images in his mind's eye were coming a little more sharply into focus. Psychic energy mimicked static electricity. It built up slowly as bodies collided and then discharged when it found a place to go. Lou was aware that a hot spot was forming in his room on the second floor. A strange energy was drawing everything that was no longer in a stable orbit into its magnetic field. That was scientific nonsense, but it was the perceptual model he used to make sense of what was happening.

He was also thinking about what Lori was doing tonight — probably a hot bath and a masterpiece of Victorian fiction. He patted Croc on the head and hoped that he could drift off down river too. He inhaled soft sea air — fresh, the way the shore smells after a rain.

***

Maurice, the night man, was dozing in his chair when the phone rang. It was 4:00 a.m. — a deadly time of night. With nothing to do but watch other people sleep, the hours moved slowly and amused themselves by filling unhappy eyes with sand. A ringing phone was a treat, it meant another miserable insomniac to converse with.

"Good evening, Punanai House, this is Maurice."

"I'm P.C. Ringer from 43 Division."

"Oh boy, what's up?"

"Relax. It's not that kind of call. When we have bad news, we show up in person."

"Oh, good. My old mom is getting on and she's senile. A call this time of night from you guys could be the start of a very busy day."

"We're at the scene of a domestic. I'm faxing over a letter of permission now. The father and son have both been drinking, but they're telling us about trying to get help from you guys earlier today."

"Let me check the book. What's the name?"

"Klaus Schaller."

"Uh… I don't see them here."

"The father said a counsellor named Greg was looking after them. Here's the thing. I don't want to arrest anyone if they're telling me the truth and trying to get some help."

Maurice pushed the call log button. "There's one more thing I can try. What's their phone number?" Maurice scrolled down the list. "Oh, here they are," he said after a minute. "They called us five times this afternoon."

"Could we drop one of them off there?"

"Sorry. You have to be sober to be in the building."

**

The following morning, Reg stuck his nose into the interview room to find Greg frowning over a file.

"You write the most interesting reports," Greg said, his tone setting a new bar for cheerful. "You need the room?"

Reg tried to look serious. "No, but I need to talk to someone sane, and until I find that person, I'm going to make do by talking to you."

Greg pushed his papers to the side and picked up his guitar, a small smile on his face as he started to soundlessly work out a chord progression that had thus far eluded him.

"You know that those guitary things plug in, right?" Reg settled into a nearby chair and got straight to the point. "I ran into a woman who knows you at my meeting."

Greg stopped picking and looked up. "Uh-oh."

Reg was intrigued. Was this guilty knowledge? "Why uh-oh?"

"Paranoid pattern recognition. I sense the approach of an evil presence."

Reg laughed. "Has somebody's alligator bitten you on the ass?"

Greg put the guitar away. "Not to my knowledge…"

Reg was enjoying matching witticisms with Greg. His voice changed to adolescent pique. "I met this girl, and she has feelings for me, you know, disgust, contempt and ridicule…"

"I know where this is going."

"See, you're clairvoyant!"

Greg frowned. "You've met Peligroso."

"Describe her."

"Dark hair, well dressed, good figure, and articulate as hell. Altogether quite a woman."

"Well if her first name's Riana, then we're talking about the same lady." The look on Greg's face said they were. "She and I got into a bit of an imbroglio." Reg hooked a chair with his cane and set his aching leg to rest on it. "I was sharing at a discussion meeting in my own even-handed, culturally sensitive, and altogether wonderful way when suddenly..."

A broad smile crossed Greg's face. "You got torpedoed."

Reg gave his sore limb some rough loving with the palm of his hand. "Well, I wouldn't have put a nautical spin on the imagery, but yes, that's essentially what happened. This strange woman lit into me as if she'd known me since high school, lent me money, slept with me, and been disappointed."

Greg sighed. She was as good as her word. There was a major note of resignation in his voice and a minor one of embarrassment. "That would be Riana."

Reg realized how tender this subject was. "Don't mistake my tone, but what I found rather distressing was that she knew who I was and what I was all about, which is odd because we've never met."

"She does her homework, that's for damn sure."

Reg couldn't resist teasing. "I got the sense she thinks you're the antichrist, and I popped in to discuss the matter of how the end times are going to proceed under your watch."

Greg got to his feet and looked out the window. He wanted to come clean, but was the office the right place for this? He managed his discomfort by speaking to Reg with his back turned. "She's going to take another run at me."

Intrigued barely covered what Reg was feeling. "Another run?"

Greg turned to face him. "She and I were an item a while back."

Reg looked nothing less than shocked.

"Zinna and I were separated. You remember when we had all that trouble with my son."

"Did my look give me away?"

"Only a professional would've noticed."

"I've always thought of you as a very married man."

Greg sat down and picked up his guitar once more. Moving his fingers soothed his soul. "It was one of those Saturday nights. Pataphysics was playing at the Silver Dollar, and I was feeling like a rock star, not the guy who had to take the kids to Sunday school the next morning. Zinna and I were split for six months. We were barely even talking. And Riana was just … there. She was so damned comfortable. And when the band took their break, she bought me an iced tea."

Greg's head bent as he observed his technique on the fret board more closely. "It always feels like I'm high when I play. The music acts on me the same way the drugs used to — well, the way they used to before they stopped working. When the music starts and the crowd gets into it, I feel immortal. I get the whole cocktail — dopamine, endorphins, serotonin, with a little side of GABA to keep it all from becoming too zesty."

Reg was intrigued. "So what happened?"

"We talked. I was actually feeling pretty flustered. I hadn't dated in twenty years."

Who knew?

"Say what you will about her, she knows how to dress. Tight in all the right places. Six wifeless months takes a toll on a guy."

"She stayed the night?"

"And we made good use of the time."

"She wasn't drinking…"

"No, she'd been off it for a couple of years. It made all the difference."

"Was she doing meetings?"

"Back then, yeah. Now she's into Life Skills."

"Are you still an item?"

"She started drinking again and we had a huge fight. She headed west and then Zinna and the kids came back, and I prayed that would be the end of it."

Reg sat quietly for two minutes. When he finally spoke, his voice was soft and comforting. "I need to put you on your guard. She told me last night that she knows you better than I do. Which, I think, suggests a certain hostile intent on her part."

Greg had recovered. "That doesn't surprise me. A week after we met, I found out she'd copied all the numbers on my cellphone. Inside a week, my friends were her friends. Then one day I was working back here alone. Doug came in and said he'd spent a very pleasant half hour talking to my wife. I went out into the living room expecting to see Zinna, and—"

"Riana."

"Yup." Greg put down his guitar and tucked his pick into the watch pocket of his pinstripes. "You know, she was okay when she was sober. But she'd go on benders and lie about it."

"Oh, that."

Greg picked up the manila folder he had been working on with both hands and hit himself over the head with the file three times. "She had a funny way of keeping track of sobriety. If she was sober for five months and then drank, she wouldn't choose a new dry date. She said sobriety wasn't destroyed by drink any more than love was undone by death."

Kaiser's face appeared in the window for a second. When he saw Reg, he shook his head and left. Greg saw him but Reg didn't.

A look of *I wonder what he wants* crossed Greg's face, which Reg misinterpreted as discomfort. "You know how people who have been sober a long time lose the markers of addiction? She never did. I could tell if she'd been drinking the night before when we spoke the next day on the phone. There was a darkness in her soul. For her, the world is a cheap rip-off and everyone in it despicable. Nothing's worth the effort. To make herself feel better, she claws her way to the top of the heap then tears it all down again. She's convinced herself that the agonies of early sobriety are as good as being sober ever gets and that anyone who says any different or who claims to be recovered is a fake."

Reg picked up his cane and gave it a vigorous shake as he thundered. "But are her views on publishing to be relied upon?"

***

Kaiser was enjoying his unhealthy preoccupation with the life and work of Riana Peligroso. She figured in his thoughts more as a grail quest than a destination. Reg was doing the Thursday overnight shift at Punanai, which would keep him out from underfoot. Kaiser slipped into the Pine Rock meeting embarrassingly early and found a seat at the back with the other old stagers, where he knew that he could observe his quarry and the group dynamic without being noticed.

Riana's sharing at Pine Rock was becoming the talk of the town. She had a unique way of looking at things. People who hadn't been to this meeting in years were dropping in to see what all the fuss was about. Her recent pronouncements had polarized the group. Some people came to scoff, and others to wonder. The treasurer pointed out that they were all dropping a toonie or two into the collection plate and, as a result, for the first time in the group's history, they had enough money in the bank to pay the rent for the next three months. There was even some wild talk about buying a new coffee pot — these were heady times.

Riana had taken to dressing up for the meetings. She encouraged others to follow her example and the members of her circle obliged. She was fit and attractive, with glowing skin and a smile that broke down doors. She wasn't encouraging unwanted advances. But there were, here and there about her person, little frills of lace, perfume, and jewellery that hinted at sensual pleasures lurking below the surface. She did not smell of sea air. Neither could one hear the sound of combers coming ashore. Even so, some kind of enchantment was afoot.

The way she engaged the stares of her admirers was telling. One time the look said, *possibly*, the next time it said, *but not just yet*.

The chairman had recently had his teeth fixed, at considerable expense, and he was wearing his new sports coat. Riana knew that she had carte blanche to say whatever she wanted with him running the meeting. This place needed to be dragged, kicking and screaming if necessary, into the new century and a new way of doing business.

As the meeting came to order, there was a tacit recognition among the faithful that they were speaking either before or after Riana. The casually dressed camp eyed up the well-dressed in the measure of suspicion they received in return. This was no longer one group. It was two camps on the eve of civil war.

When her turn to share came, Riana got to her feet and surveyed the expectant room. She was wearing a colourful print dress underneath a high-end white sweater. The floral pattern spoke of the spring everyone in the room was aching for. She kept her thick brown hair shoulder length, and it reflected the light and bounced when she moved. A smile was her opening gambit.

"I work in the addiction business. I want to be upfront about that. There are people who do well simply by attending these meetings. They don't need any more help than the twelve steps. Thank God for that. But a lot of people need more. When I attempt to talk about them — about what they need — the rank and file become very annoyed with me. Why is that?"

She stopped to look for trouble, but no champion wearing the colours of the status quo appeared.

"Lots of people who attend these meetings earn a living working in the treatment business," she continued as she let out of a puff of air. Kaiser pointed at his chest and, looking around at his neighbours, mouthed the word *Me?*

She looked toward the back of the room and smiled. "To hear them talk, they're above petty concerns like money. Even if some of them do prowl the meetings looking for the rich and gullible to seduce with their glossy brochures."

That was too much for the traditionalists. Chair legs scraped tile. Their discomfort encouraged Riana. Tradition required all present to listen with an open mind and give a fair hearing to whatever was being said. She exploited that courtesy to goad them. Her voice dropped an octave as it rose ten decibels.

"There's nothing wrong with charging a living wage for a service rendered. If people can't get what they need here, what's wrong with them trying something different?"

Oliver, the longest-sober member of the group, got to his feet and started to walk toward the door, looking neither left nor right. After a moment, two other old timers joined the exodus.

Riana smiled and raised her voice half an octave. "That's right, walk out. The Flat Earth Society is serving tea in the solarium."

Oliver made a dismissive flip with his hand by way of a reply.

Her voiced changed again, from firebrand to intimate. The troubled eyes of the group shifted from the departing elders and refocused on her. Some of the faces looked frightened. She was different — vulnerable and showing it.

"I know a couple of these so-called professionals."

"Louder," called a disembodied voice.

She took a breath and overshot the mark. "One of them sent me his son as a client. His own son. Now why do you suppose he'd do that? What with him having all the answers and knowing everything there is to know about this problem. Then he cried poor. Said he couldn't pay." She checked out her supporters for a reaction. "The nerve of the guy."

There was a flash of embarrassed laughter as everyone hazarded a guess as to who it was. Several people wanted to speak and were making their wishes known to the chairman the way bidders signal the auctioneer. But none of them dared to butt in and talk over Riana. She had the floor, and she was uncharacteristically working out what she thought by talking about it.

"You'd think someone with that kind of juice would take care of his own kid. But no! First he tries to boink me, then he expects me to pick up the pieces of his failed marriage, and then, just for yuks, he wants me to sober up his kid. It was like my first job at the call centre when I was in high school asking, 'Is there anything else I can do for you today?'"

The mask slipped a little more, and sorrow flashed across her face like a single bolt of lightning across a clouded summer sky after sunset — there and then soundlessly gone again. Only those near her heard what she said next. "Now he won't return my calls. Now I'm a troublemaker."

There was a sharp intake of breath on both sides of the growing divide and a look of pure desperation on the face of the wretched chairman.

She smiled triumphantly as her voice rallied. "His son is sober today, thanks to me. Life Skills is shortly going to be the talk of this town. Lots of people around here are unhappy about that. But does that mean you shouldn't check it out?"

The chairman had the exhausted smile that dancers in a chorus line boast, but to no avail. Everyone was blaming him. Angry hornets on both sides of the divide swarmed him, demanding a return to order and reason.

Kaiser smiled as he connected the dots. Looking at the distressed and anxious faces confirmed his opinion of this group. *What kind of lunatic tries to start a revolution at the stuck-in-the-mud group?*

The rest of the meeting was a burden of platitudes. The chairman's face radiated sorrow. This was not the baptism of fire he had hoped for. His new suit and teeth had come to nothing.

Kaiser couldn't take his eyes off Riana. He regarded her the way he admired himself in the mirror. She sat at the table with a look that suggested she hadn't caused the fuss. He couldn't leave it there. He needed to know. *Did you pull the fire alarm at school when you got bored? Yeah you did. You like firetrucks, don't you? Firemen too. What in the world do you want with Greg? Is it the rock star thing?*

The group predictably broke into two sullen camps when the meeting adjourned. Those who believed the 12-step program was the way to go rallied the faithful in the hall, while the usurpers — those who favoured Riana's harm-reduction approach — gathered around their leader and the coffee pot.

Posing as a suitor, Kaiser insinuated himself into her circle as she was adding cream to her coffee and shaking her head at the gooey sticky rolls.

"Did you mean that?" he asked as he helped himself to a cup and saucer.

She looked at him with a studied disinterest. "Did I say something?"

"I knew you'd be fun to talk to."

Riana was trying to place him. She hadn't yet connected him to Reg or Greg.

Kaiser was enjoying the advantage of a secret identity and her discomfort with him. "It's the Shirley Temple in you that compels me."

She took it up a notch and stepped into his space. "Well, Kermit, let me lay down the law for you. This is my AA group now. This meeting is going to be safe going forward. Mind your manners and you and I will get along fine."

Kaiser managed to look hurt without going over-the-top. "That's where you're wrong. I'm a man among men."

There it was again, that more-than-Mona Lisa smile. "I'll admit, if I were twenty and starry-eyed, I might go for that mane of curly blond hair and that bad-boy presentation. It hints at some kind of animal strength," she patted his paunch, "which, sadly, has long since vanished."

"So you do care."

There was some heat in her voice this time — enough to put a lesser man to flight. "Every twenty-year-old girl who ever ended up in family court, chasing a bum for her half of an entry-level paycheque to support her kids, has come to the same conclusion. Bad boys are prickly weeds. If you let them, they'll choke your garden. This room is full of them."

"You and I both know you don't mean half the things you say."

She smiled. "Even so, you wouldn't know which half is which, now would you?" She turned on her heel and moved back toward her circle of admirers.

Kaiser sighed. The rocks in his head would fit perfectly into the holes in her skull.

Chapter 20

Kaiser walked into the office and landed with a thump in the chair recently vacated by Reg. A spray of aftershave and words mingled in the air. "I want to talk to you about your pal Riana."

Greg made the sign of the cross with his two index fingers, which coaxed a smile out of his guest. As Greg settled back in his chair, he picked up a subtle hint of discomfort around Kaiser's eyes, a highly unusual event that set him wondering. *That's two of you now.*

Kaiser didn't wait for an answer. "You were an item."

Greg was still trying to work out how his colleagues had succumbed to enchantment. This was upsetting bordering on frightening. His voice was quiet, suggesting wariness. "She taught me a few things about personal and professional boundaries, lessons that I'm sure she would be delighted to teach you."

"She knocked the hell out of Reg's AA group last night."

"They'll survive."

Kaiser tried another approach, looking around the office as if he was worried about being overheard. "A friend of mine is smitten with her, and I don't want him getting suckered. What's the scoop?"

A friend? Greg tried to look offended as he worked out what he wanted to say. "I would rather not say. It's un-gentlemanly."

Kaiser smiled as his toe began to tap. "Don't give me that crap. The woman is a wrecking ball. What I want to know is how she does it."

Greg relented. He was proud of himself for working it all out. The index and middle fingers of his right hand found a comfortable purchase on his upper lip. "She's patient. She does her homework. Finds out what you're interested in and bones up on it. The real fun starts when she introduces herself to all your friends, flirts with them, flatters them, pays them all kinds of attention — and before you know it, she's part of the gang. I don't even think she's aware that what she's doing is wrong. It's instinctive." He looked over to the corner for his guitar but thought better of it. He needed to concentrate on Kaiser's face. The real purpose of this conversation would be visible there first. "But once she has her man in the trap, the tune changes from disco to polka. She starts to chip away at your sanity. Infiltrates every area of your life and tells you that if you don't put yourself into her capable hands, you'll remain a mutt for whatever's left of your miserable life."

The bachelor in Kaiser feigned a studied indifference not supported by the hot trickle of sweat running down the small of his back. His consciousness didn't formulate the thought, *Then why doesn't she want me?* Instead, he landed on a rougher plank that let him pretend a little longer that her hook had not found purchase in his flesh. "So how is this different from marriage?"

Greg reached for his guitar after all. They were going to be here for a while. "I never stopped to consider that, but there are two points. The first sign of trouble is that she has no female friends. She despises other women. The second sign is that nothing satisfies her. As soon as she gets the tower built, she sets fire to it and then moves on to her next project. That is what passes for dating in the borderline crowd."

Kaiser was trying to square the circle of what he'd experienced with Greg's mystifying insights. He landed on psychology: *Is she narcissistic?* But he might as easily have landed on astrology: *Is she a Taurus?* The real question still eluded him. *Why you and not me, rock star?*

Greg wasn't going there. Slapping around feeling with thinking is what the clients did. He was beyond that now with this woman. He had an asset that meant everything to him, and it was in peril because of the whole cocktail of human frailty.

"I'm not allowed to diagnose conditions I can't spell," Greg said. "But I do know this. If you're out for dinner and a chandelier falls on your head, she'll laugh, finish her dinner, and put the cheque on your credit card. No feeling for other people. And the reverse side of that coin is even worse. Criticisms cannot — will not — be tolerated."

Kaiser's face showed the deep hue of disappointment. "Thanks, that's been helpful. Is there anything you want to know from me?"

"No, but I need to put you in the picture. Reg was in to see me about her too. She phoned me and told me we were going to talk about *the relationship*. She's gearing up for another run at me. I don't know how to stop her and I'm terrified Zinna is going to throw me out again. If she does try to co-opt you, could you give me the heads-up?"

I'll do better than that, buddy. I'm going to break her heart.

Chapter 21

Tartu College was Reg's favourite dinner spot. It was an independently owned student residence built by the same people who erected the infamous Rochdale College in 1968. Despite its stark appearance, owing to its brutalist architectural principles, it boasted a fine restaurant, albeit one done along cafeteria lines with steam tables and covered aluminum trays.

The steep stairs at the front of the building were a formidable obstacle that made Reg think twice about dining somewhere else, but the memory of the cooking always lent fire to his ascent. The staff knew him well enough to say hello, but never to inquire further. They always assumed, or so Reg fancied, that he was an academic given dinner money on those occasions when his wife entertained. His bow tie propped up that erroneous assumption better than any handkerchief embossed with the U of T staff logo.

Reg glanced into the main dining area where several academics were each enjoying dinner and a book in silence. Reg had brought his elevated bookstand along with him as a dinner companion. Here was a special place for an introvert to unwind after a day of noise and interruption.

The choice tonight was no choice at all. There was a breaded and therefore, in his view, a to-be-dreaded fish dish and a homemade meat lasagna with a side of Caesar salad and garlic toast. Reg eyed up the steam table. His timing was good. They were putting out a fresh tray, and judging from the tables he could see, the pasta was outselling the fish five to one.

Leaning against the rail and rising to his full height, Reg tapped on the thick plastic partition and pointed to the lasagna below with a predatory look in his eye. He felt a whisper of pleasure as the pleasant woman behind the counter cut a square from the tray with a spatula and moved it to the waiting plate. Long ropes of cheese protested the move. A plume of steam rose in tandem with Reg's expectations. Tongs flashed from below as the lasagna was crowded on three sides by the salad. The garlic toast, encased in a cocoon of silver paper, was served on a separate plate. His mouth began to water.

He thought about adding a piece of lemon meringue pie but slid his dinner tray along the rails toward the cashier instead. He stopped to pour himself a coffee, but as he was adding the cream, his resolution failed. He shuffled back for the pie with his head down. The lady who had served him took the cash and he gave her a good tip as she pressed an abundance of paper napkins onto his tray.

As he was tucking in to the crucial first bite, an interloper hovered in his periphery. He glanced up from *Barney's Version* to see the silhouette of a well-dressed woman backlit by the setting sun streaming through the window. Reg squinted for a second, waiting for the bright gold brushstroke on his retina to clear. His hope was that the woman was only invading his space long enough to put away her change purse. He heard the scrape of a table leg and felt a bump that rippled his coffee.

"Oh shit, it's you," she said.

Reg opened one eye. "There are lots of *other* places to sit."

"I'm here on business." Riana draped her overcoat over the back of the chair to her right. She was wearing a pumpkin-coloured silk blouse set off by a pale-green soapstone carving of a seal suspended on a leather cord.

Riana had ordered the fish. He was looking forward to the pang of disappointment that was sure to cross her face. Dinner, though ruined, might yet be turned to some advantage.

"What kind of business brings you here?"

"Mommies and daddies get very worried about what little Buffy and Billy get up to on their own when they're away at college. I slap them around."

"Is this addiction stuff?"

"Not your kind." She placed a real cloth napkin over her lap. "Life Skills is the wonderfully ambiguous term we employ. That way, no one gets embarrassed later in life, when files get hacked. The families I deal with aren't bottom-feeders." She gave him a look that said, *That would be your bunch.*

She took a bite of the fish. Her top lip curled as she put down her fork. "Needs salt."

It wants freshness.

As she assiduously gave the saltshaker a workout, his entrée took on a new meaning. His was a banquet and hers a bust. He smiled a little Buddha smile imbued with garlic and butter.

Riana tore the paper lid off her juice container while she surveyed the room. "Is this where you write?"

"No, wrong vibe."

"Where then?"

"At home. I have a special spot that overlooks the park."

She squinted at him as she tucked in to a perfectly browned home fry. "Are you really a writer?"

Reg was delighted by the barbed-wire ribbon this package came wrapped in. *Why are you here? And why am I putting up with this?* These obvious questions were no match for the feeling of being the sole focus of her attention. The lasagna cried, *Reg, over here,* but to no avail. Was it her guile or her gall that fascinated him?

While his instincts and intellect took turns whispering warnings, he gathered himself enough to ask, "What else do you think I'm pretending to do?"

She pressed her napkin to her lips. "That tribal stuff you do at Punanai … total abstinence, total honesty, total bore. It's not what people want these days."

He never missed a beat. "Don't I know it! It shames the face right off me sometimes…" Reg knew enough about lying to look her right in the eye when he said it. He wanted more than anything else to get into this woman's head, and a lie he could later confess or attempt to pass off as a prank seemed a small price to pay to find out what this woman — who, when last they met, had called him a short-dicked cretin — was up to.

She looked at him warily. "Addiction is no longer the preserve of down-and-out do-gooders. It's a science now. You guys need to change with the times."

Reg smiled and pointed to the drink cooler. "What say we order a glass of wine while we talk?"

She put her palms face down on the table. "Don't tell me you drink."

He beamed with sincerity. "You misunderstand. Uncorking a bottle with you would be the same as pulling the pin on a hand grenade in the presence of my enemies. God might forgive me a final drink if it put an end to you too."

"Very funny." Riana set her fork down and leaned back in her chair. "Tell me about your writing."

He stayed in the charming lane. "I only discuss that with naked people."

"The people at the meeting weren't naked."

"Are you more beautiful or annoying? I can't decide."

There was some colour in her cheeks and her left eye closed halfway. "Are you putting the moves on me?"

"Rumour has it you're against that sort of thing."

"What?"

"My friends say you run off all the men from your AA meeting."

"The last thing a woman in early recovery needs is an alcoholic boyfriend."

"You're right. Those kinds of romances never make it past the first fight. My question to you is this: Why make that your issue?"

She leaned even deeper into his personal space. "I love to watch them crawl."

Reg couldn't stop himself. The lie leapt from his lips. "Me too."

She was wary and scented deception but only had enough evidence to obtain a warrant, not lay charges. Her faced radiated a faint hope, as if she was puzzling something out before she ventured further. "I knew we had that in common."

Another forkful of the rich, moist lasagna made this a perfect moment. Reg gave her a look that said, *How cool are we?*

Her con light came on immediately, and she went from defence to offence. "Why all those *ah shucks* moments at the meetings. You embarrass yourself."

"Strictly for the suckers, my dear, strictly for the suckers."

To his amazement, a look of familiarity and ease stole across her face. "Well, now that we're finally talking, what do you think about my friend Greg?"

Reg wasn't prepared to take the game that far. He'd had his fun. It was time to fess up. "Greg is a prince. The finished product. What you look like when God finishes putting you back together."

"He stuck me with his son, you know."

"God or Greg?"

She turned her head and smiled. "What a clever thing to say … but your poster child has secrets. He's not the darling you imagine. His son was making the cocaine disappear by the kilo last year, and Greg sent him to *me* for some Life Skills training."

"What—"

"He conned me. Said his wife's plan would cover it. He promised to pay, and he didn't."

"Greg would never do that. He thinks Life Skills is crap."

"Everybody does until it's their kid."

"He wouldn't—"

"The old bullshit wasn't working so…" Riana shrugged.

"He knows better."

She smiled demurely. "His wife thought otherwise."

"And what did you promise his wife? A cure?"

"He owes me four grand," Riana snapped.

"Did you sort Gordon out?"

She looked toward heaven and rolled her eyes. "No, the little stager's a worse con artist than his old man. He never even slowed down."

Reg did the math in his head. "For a Punanai guy, four thousand dollars is a wallop."

"I don't care about the money. What I want is the satisfaction of hearing him admit that when the going got tough, he sent his son to *me*."

"Gordon didn't stop using."

"Well, duh, neither do your guys."

Reg felt a nascent war cry forming in his craw, but a mouthful of the beautiful lasagna and the wet, buttery garlic toast combined to restore his perspective. He kept his blade in the scabbard. After all, here he was, talking very dishonestly to a woman who obviously had some deficits. He was where he shouldn't be, doing exactly what he shouldn't be doing, having fun torturing a torturer.

Riana took a sip of water and set her glass down. "Am I in your book?"

"Keep talking and you will be."

"It might be worth reading if I was."

"The topic wouldn't suit you. The book is about finding authenticity."

"There's no such thing!"

"You and I both know that, but the suckers don't." Another lie out of his mouth before he could stop it.

Her face changed from anger to insight. "Are you planning to ride this book for the rest of your life?"

"You obviously know more about this than I do. Be my teacher."

She picked at her fish with a disdainful look. "Writing fiction is a waste of time. You make something up. Who cares? What you want to be writing is nonfiction. Go find yourself a grad student. One who prefers smoking dope in the early afternoon to doing real research. Get 'em to do a study, and the next thing you know you have science to support any claim you want to make." She leaned into his space. "But you always keep the sample size small. That way you can claim it was an anomaly if someone ever checks it for accuracy. You say it's promising, not conclusive." She tapped the side of her nose.

"Is that how it's done?"

She laughed with delight. "You can prove that your morning cup of coffee causes cancer and that your afternoon cup cures it if you know how to manage expectation. Real science is about the age of rocks and how atoms behave. Soft science is for manipulating people by telling them what they want to hear." She reached into her purse and pulled out a high-gloss brochure that she slapped down beside his tray. "Life is about wanting to be satisfied. Life Skills!"

Reg was willing to trade lies for a good cause, but not if it involved his friends and certainly not if it involved his book. His thoughts raced. *What a mess. I lied to get inside her head and now look where I am. Do I come clean here or brazen it out?*

He took a forkful of salad while he contemplated his peril. *No wonder she thinks I'm a whiner. It's all a game for her. Ah damn it, I still need to know what goes on behind those crazy eyes.*

Reg changed gears. "You're going to laugh at me for saying this, but writing is sacred for me."

She gave her seal pendant a tug. "You're not one of those."

"Fiction is the ultimate addiction."

Her face flushed with displeasure as she pushed her dinner away. "There's something wrong with that fish."

He picked up a paper napkin and wiped the layer of garlic butter from his fingers. "Maybe you're right about psychology and science, I don't know about those things. I could never bring myself to read social science. The way they footnote in the body of the text drives me mad."

She glanced at her phone before returning it to her purse. "Which explains why you work for chump change at Punanai and eat dinner here alone."

"Making money has nothing to do with this. When I write, it drowns out the noise. I get to dive into the water. I prefer that world to this one."

"Which explains the rest." Her eyes flashed insight and then sympathy, which unnerved Reg and put him on the defensive.

"I want to look at my book when I'm old and be proud of it," he said. "I want enough time to pass so that I can see it with fresh eyes, maybe pretend for a moment that somebody else wrote it. When I read it again in twenty years, I hope it makes me cry. I want it to tell the truth. About how we helped people. Who we were and how we all fit together. In a hundred years, that's all that will be left of us."

She saw the opening and didn't miss a beat. "You'll never get published by daydreaming. Put yourself in my hands. I know people, media people, who are in the business of making connections and getting things done."

Reg was stunned. She hadn't heard a word he said.

She threw her linen table napkin on top of her dinner. "You know how the world works. There's never enough to go around. You need an in. A fixer. No one gets there on their own."

"Which kidney would you want in return?"

She smirked. "I may need your help on a project I'm working on. We can talk about that later. Let's get you sorted out first." She took out her phone and started to scroll. A look of peace crossed her brow.

Reg let the offer hang in the air as soft and beckoning as the autumn harvest moon. Riana was a good closer. She knew that whoever spoke next was the loser. A new, fantastic way of engaging the world was on offer. She made it sound as if getting his book published would be no more difficult than picking up the dry cleaning. He wouldn't have to go knocking on doors and being ignored. This was beyond tempting. His palms dampened and he felt a hollow feeling in his gut. He looked into her face for clues. *What is she after? What could be worth all this effort?*

He pulled the pie closer and took a sip of coffee. After the lasagna, the lemon filling was powerfully present on his palate as he took the time he needed to sort this thing out. *She's a flame and you're a moth.*

This is what she'd done at Pine Hills: told them what they wanted to hear, rounded up the suckers and taught them how to dance. She probably told them they could drink again if they worked with her for a year or two on their core issues.

What she was saying wasn't true — it couldn't be. *Why then does my heart want to do this when my head knows it's nonsense? Why would I want to turn the most precious thing in my life over to anyone, let alone Riana? Oh, the power of words! There's something to be said for Life Skills.*

Reg finished his pie and sipped on his coffee, trying not to let Riana know how deeply her offer had disturbed him. She was prepared to give him all the time he needed to think this through. Riana understood introverts.

He thought about the famous line attributed to Martin Luther: "The Word of God cannot be bound." However, in light of his conversation with Riana, he now understood how, in the right hands, the immutable could be tweaked, fluffed, and repurposed to suit another outcome, but as with her fish entrée and her offer of friendship, this new creation was flawed. The thing that gave it away was not the presentation on the plate, nor the aroma, but rather the faint taste of decay it left on the tongue. This woman was salt.

He waited in silence until she looked over at him. "A handsome offer from a handsome woman, but I can't accept. Thank you for taking the time to speak to me. I hope we can still be friends."

Riana left the offer and her unfinished dinner for someone else to clean up. "Try and separate a loser from his misery — it cannot be done."

Chapter 22

Kaiser got the Toyota fired up and was watching the light show on the dashboard to pass the time while he waited for Reg to cross the parking lot. It was an icy morning, and a fall was a real possibility. A look of relief crossed Reg's face as he pulled his legs into the vehicle one at a time and shut the creaking door behind him.

A ride to work in the Toyota was a mixed blessing. It shortened the commute by an hour each way. But you had to listen to whatever Kaiser was obsessing about all the way there and all the way back. Whatever was top of mind for him was naturally top of mind for you too. Kaiser showed up at your front door with a U-Haul of issues.

Reg was struggling with his seatbelt when Kaiser announced, "Give me your manuscript. I'm going to get it published."

Reg turned as best he could to face Kaiser. "First Riana and now you!"

Kaiser kept his eyes facing forward but the rest of him was fully attuned to his companion. "What has she got to do with this?"

"She made the same offer over dinner last night." Reg took off his gloves and held his hand over the air vent. It was blowing cold air. "Why do you have the air conditioning on?"

"Riana had dinner with you?" Kaiser's voice papered over his displeasure at this latest turn of events. This complicated matters.

Reg smiled without seeming to. "She insisted."

Kaiser stayed on point. "Is she a publisher?"

Reg put his gloves back on and pulled his scarf tighter around his neck. "She has Life Skills and that is all one ever needs."

"You said she was a psycho."

Reg secured the high ground. "She thinks you're nice — dreamy is the word she used. Got all misty eyed when she said it too. Thinks about you constantly. She wanted me to make an introduction. Can't get you out of her head."

Kaiser stayed on the glide path. "What's the title of your book?"

"*Folie à deux.*"

***

Paul, Reg, and Mike were sitting in the office. Mike was at his desk, trying to get his cellphone to accept a new battery. For him, Friday afternoon had already been supplanted by the weekend. He was focused on his Sunday pickup hockey game with the well-past-it gang. He looked up from his labours to see Greg enter the office shaking his head.

Paul gave him a quizzical look as he came in. "Why the long face? You get to go home in two hours. I'm the guy stuck here alone all weekend."

"I just broke up a debate between Millie and Fred Grant. He had some particular insights to share with her about the dishwasher and about disinfecting in general."

All eyes landed on Greg. "What did our Millie have to say about that?"

"With her mouth? To her credit, not a word, but with her eyes … volumes. I got Fred by the ear and reminded him that he had no business being in her kitchen."

Reg piped up. "How did he take the news?"

"Badly."

Reg smiled. "Hard to believe this guy used to play cops and robbers in the bigs."

Paul who had gone back to attending to some paperwork looked up. "Did this guy ever have a life?"

Mike sighed. "He's damaged. Kaiser and I found him dead drunk on the floor of a surgically clean apartment."

Reg's face registered mild irritation. "Has anyone asked him about that?"

Greg shook his head. "In our first interview we got stuck on what year this is. He's better today but not much. His brain is too full of ammonia."

Reg got to his feet to stretch his aching back. "He puked bile on the subway when he had the seizure."

Greg playfully straightened Reg's bow tie. "Liver and gallbladder is a bad combination."

Reg started rotating his shoulders. "We should take him back to where we found him and leave him in a basket."

Mike finally got the battery to fit. "I'm going to keep this guy for as long as I can. If he drinks again, he's dead. He's defenceless and doesn't realize it."

Reg sat down again. "So now we have three of them heading for the last roundup."

This was news to Paul. "The others being?"

Reg brightened. "That's right, you weren't here yesterday. They brought Jacob Hutton back from the hospital."

"But he just left."

Mike got to his feet. "Well, he's back, sicker, fatter and stinkier than ever."

"And the third?"

Mike took a cigarette out from behind his ear. "My old roommate, Mr. Charles Dorn."

Reg placed his open palm on his face. "The same Charles Dorn who scared the shit out of Arthur Wilberforce Cardel simply by bumming a cigarette?"

"The very same." Mike headed toward the smoke deck.

"I got an idea," Paul said as Reg and Mike departed. "Why don't the rest of you dilettantes take the weekend off and leave me here all alone to deal with this whole sorry mess."

Reg and Mike exchanged a look. "Well, we could do that, but you'd definitely owe us one."

***

Seymour Dunn was a pleasant young man, well regarded at Punanai by both the staff and the guys. He had thick, dark hair that he kept short and was tall and sturdily built, though he had an odd way of moving his right leg. His gait suggested a charley horse, but he actually had a congenital problem with his hip. Paul noticed he also didn't match his parents, who were both short, round, pasty-skinned Scots. They arrived forty-five minutes early for visiting hours on Saturday afternoon. Seymour and the guys were still down at the corner, getting themselves a brew from Tim Hortons.

Paul saw an opportunity to get some insight into his young charge. "You're Seymour's mom," he said brightly as she ascended the stairs. He held the door open for her.

"Yes, and you're…"

"I'm Seymour's counsellor today, Paul Bethune. I met you on Wednesday when you dropped him off."

"That's right," she said. "I'm Verna, and the lovely fellow sitting out in the car is my husband, Kingsly."

Her playful tone provoked his next question. "Why is he sitting out in the car?"

"He's listening to the end of the symphony."

Paul understood that. He gestured toward the office door.

Verna looked at all the chairs available before she selected one. "How is Seymour coming along?"

Paul took a seat opposite her and tried to look relaxed. Somehow this woman had put him on his back foot.

"I haven't made up my mind about him yet. The guys won't be back until one o'clock. What say you and I have a chat?"

Verna was approaching retirement age. Her hair was silver grey and came to a curl just at her collar. She wore a dark skirt and white blouse that boasted a rather ornate pendant made from a red gemstone.

Paul pulled his chair a little closer. "There are a couple of things about Seymour that don't add up."

Her face softened. "You suspect that he's a changeling?"

"Well, that's a new one." He smiled. "What's that exactly?"

"A fairy child that secretly replaces a human." She smiled. Her love for her son was clear. "Did you ever see *A Midsummer Night's Dream*?"

"I saw it a couple of years ago in High Park."

"What did you think of it?"

Before he could answer she held up her right hand. "Think carefully before you answer. I produced it, you know." Her smile was wonderful.

"Well, Mrs. Shakespeare, I thought you did a good job. But your bunch sure talk funny English."

She ignored his witticism. "Seymour was a godsend. We couldn't have children. Seymour's family were Vietnamese boat people. He was left in a hospital in one of the processing camps. It is hard to get your brain around that level of love and desperation."

"No problems as a kid?"

"The usual stuff. He was a serious child. Bright as they come but reserved and kind of private. When he got his driver's licence, we let him take his friends to the cottage for the Labour Day long weekend. We worried about his friends but not about him. He could be trusted around motorboats and gas stoves."

"When did he start drinking?"

"The first time we saw trouble on the horizon was when he came of age. We had a party at the house. That was the first time I saw him drink. Everything changed. The way he walked. The way he talked. The way he held his body…"

"How was it different?"

"He was angry. Almost hateful…" She started to cry and rooted around in her purse for a handkerchief. "Until it happens to someone you love right in front of your eyes, you cannot believe it's even possible. He started gulping drinks and insulting people, and the next thing we knew, he was passed out in the bathroom. We put him to bed and when he woke up the next morning, he didn't remember."

Paul felt her sorrow. He needed a way forward. "Do you ever watch *Trailer Park Boys*?"

"The television show? The one they shoot in Nova Scotia?"

"That's the one."

"Seymour and Kingsly would watch it. They loved it. But the humour was always lost on me."

"One of the gags that I loved in that show was that one of the characters, Julian, always had a drink in his hand. If he was in court, if he was in jail, if he was in a shootout with someone, the glass was still there. Once they were being chased by the police, and the car they were driving rolled over three times and ended up in the ditch. When Julian crawled out of the wreck, he had a drink in his hand."

Her face suggested that his ploy was not working. "I'm failing to take your point."

Paul sat up straight. "Julian is what we call an inveterate alcoholic. The guy who's always drinking, but very seldom gets totally drunk."

A look of distress crept across Verna's face. "I could've put up with Seymour's drinking if that had been the case."

Paul got to his feet and looked out the front window, hoping to see the guys returning. He turned and found a perch on the edge of Mike's desk.

"Then perhaps your son is a better match for the other main character, Ricky. The people who wrote that show really understood addiction. Episodes would often start with Ricky waking up after sleeping all night in his car. He'd talk about his relationships or the problems he might have that day. He was rational. Then he'd roll a joint or have a drink, and he'd turn into a lunatic. Popular culture is full of examples of decent young men who get into trouble almost as soon as they start drinking."

Verna found herself warming to both the conversation and to Paul. It was easier for her to talk about addiction in the abstract. "That's the great thing about movies and books. They allow strangers to have friends in common. I've read several books about addiction since Seymour hit the skids. The character who intrigued me the most was a dark figure. Have you read *Under the Volcano*?"

"Yes. Does Geoffrey Firmin remind you of Seymour?"

"No, except that Firmin is always circling the hospital. He knows he needs to go there, but he resists. I've seen the same process at work in Seymour. He knows what he needs to do, but he can't bring himself to do it. It's a blind spot. Before he drank, I would've trusted Seymour with my life. Now…" She looked at her lap.

"When did it become intolerable?"

"At the cottage. Oh, it must have been about a year ago now. Seymour is a good painter … well, at least, he was."

"Oh?"

"He did splendid watercolours of the lake. In the warm weather, there's a mist at the water's edge in the morning. Seymour breathed life into that shoreline. His images remind me of the Impressionists' but with more human feeling. We planned to rent a gallery on his twenty-first birthday, have a show to celebrate, but then one weekend he brought a bottle of something vile with him to the cottage, and in a rage, he broke all his canvases into pieces and flung them into the fire."

Paul was horrified. "All of them?"

"Yes, and the paintbrushes too — the whole lot gone. All that beauty and promise destroyed. Seymour doesn't remember doing it. He only remembers feeling angry. Something about what some fellow had said to him at school, how he couldn't get a date with a girl." Her words were heavy with sorrow. "I still have photographs of his paintings, but it makes me sad to look at them. I can show them to you." She reached into her shoulder bag.

"Yes, please."

She fumbled with a high-end iPad for a few moments as she searched for the right folder.

"Here they are." She held the screen up for Paul to see.

Kingsly came through the front door and stood in the vestibule, waiting for his eyes to grow accustomed to the low light. As his eyes found their focus, he smiled. How typical of Verna to have the snaps out. He spied a newspaper sitting on the coffee table and sat down to read it. In an instant, he was gone, as comfortable as he would have been in his easy chair at home.

Paul was awestruck. There was something about the way Seymour had captured the mist on the lake that was at once comforting and mysterious, maybe even erotic or narcotic. The land lay half hidden, arising from slumber, a translucent veil crowning her glory. The nervous lake waited for her, eager for their dance to begin. His tapping foot sent gentle waves breaking onto the shore. The portals in the mist revealed his waistcoat of deepest blue. But his secret heart could only be inferred through the opaque lens of the mist. The photographer in Paul was amazed.

A wave of excitement coursed through his body. "These are wonderful. I would love to spend a morning on that shore. I have exactly the right lens to capture the spirit of that painting."

"I wouldn't want you stealing Seymour's thunder."

Paul felt a little hurt by that. "Verna, this is exactly the kind of thing I was hoping to find. Seymour needs to connect to something that's going to lift him out of himself. Art, music, and literature can all make the difference between life and death for an addict. It's possible to stay sober working in a factory, gluing labels on cans of baked beans, but it's so much easier to recover when you find something you're good at, something that fills you with energy and allows you to connect with other people. Seymour could spend his life doing paintings like these, never making a dime at it, and still die a happy man."

Paul kept flipping. "The world needs to see these. This is what Seymour was born to do, anyone can see that. Not doing this will kill him."

Verna paused for a moment. "Then why did he destroy them?"

Paul wasn't ready for that question, and he let it slip by. "I'd bet five bucks against the value of my house that he can't paint the bathroom when he's drinking."

"He tries, but they're awful. He can't make them work." She blew out some sad, stale air. "He's not seeing the world in the same way."

Paul was smiling. "For the first time, I have some real hope for your son. *I can use these to get him out of his funk and interested in life again.*

"Speaking of which, here he comes."

The conga line from the coffee shop returned. Seymour had recognized the ancient Volvo in the driveway and was scanning for two familiar faces. He smiled when he saw his father absorbed in the newspaper. He shook his head and felt a warm sense of being at home. Pop would've gone to his cabin on the *Titanic* for a nap on that fateful night if he'd felt sleepy.

When she saw Seymour come in, Verna closed the lid of the tablet and put it back in her purse. Paul would've appreciated more time. The images were still moving around inside his head.

"Hello, Mom." They hugged each other. "I thought you were off to the cottage this weekend."

"We are, dear. This is the new Friday of my work week. It's the only way to miss the traffic, don't you know, to be out of sync, as your father puts it."

The words ran out and the silence embarrassed them both.

Paul's eyes narrowed. *What happened there?*

Verna took the initiative desperate to fill the space. "I was talking to your friend Paul. I showed him your paintings. He thought they were nice."

Seymour cringed. It was the word *nice.*

"God, Mom. Those are personal. The guys — well, you know what guys are like!"

Paul would've loved to watch more interaction between Verna and Seymour, but they wandered off, and the other visitors were starting to arrive. Paul had to let it go.

Chapter 23

Seeing Walter — bright, funny, full-of-life Walter — manhandled by John had been too much for Peter. The jingoistic impulse that had moved him to cast his old friend into the flames — if that is what it took to master the light — dissipated when he'd seen Walter's face, so deeply steeped in distress.

Once he'd careened down the stairs away from them, he found himself exhausted by his efforts and overcome with sorrow. Now his thoughts turned to his love, Terri. What if her situation was as difficult as Walter's? Was she at risk? Could the deep freeze canister keep the light at bay? He needed to be sure that she was still safe, slumbering in the deep snows of winter.

Peter made his way past the reception desk at Granite Glen and waited until someone finally took the elevator to the basement to catch a ride. The viewing room was open until eleven p.m. If you didn't know what you were looking at, you might well mistake The Chamber of New Life for a meditation room. There were comfortable benches and wonderful art and rich fabrics draping the wall. From time to time, a wandering oldster from the facility upstairs would find their way down, but there was nothing they could meddle with that would inconvenience the slumbering guests. The entire process had been automated and the controls hidden in a room that used to be a broom closet.

Peter found the waiting room for eternity soothing after the debacle in the sorority house. The lights were low. Terri's name still shone on the burnished surface of the masthead. He used his finger to feel the letters of her name. But he'd come at a bad time if he was looking for peace. The sound of approaching voices resonated in the hallway with the rattling of a cart.

Two men entered the room with a stepladder. The older man, Barstow Higgins, was the one Peter had dealt with when he arranged his passage. Pritpal Virk, who was wearing an aluminum suit, followed him. Barstow watched the younger man climb up the ladder and then handed him a pair of long-handled tongs. Pritpal unlatched the top of the tank and dipped the tongs inside.

Peter was aghast. These grave robbers were disturbing the order of things.

Barstow turned and left Pritpal poking around in the tank. He returned a moment later, pushing a cart carrying several frozen heads wrapped in heavy plastic. Peter looked on in horror as Barstow wheeled past him looking matter of fact about his sacrilege.

"We should have room for ten more in this one," Barstow said, checking the schematic on his clipboard.

Pritpal's aluminum suit made an odd noise as he lifted one of the heads and slid it into the mist inside the tank. "Some of these deadbeats haven't paid in years. We should toss them."

Anger flashed across Barstow's face. "It doesn't cost any more to keep them. If we get to the point where we need the room, we'll decide then, but I won't break faith if I don't have to."

"Fine. But I'm not storing them at the bottom," Pritpal said as he rearranged the frozen heads to his liking. "The delinquents stay on the top row so we can fish them out when we need the room."

Peter was furious. He had his tongs on Terri. "Leave her alone! Oh, I'll get you bastards!"

Peter had paid extra to have Terri's head in the spot next to his. When Pritpal moved Peter's head to the top row, it all came clear. But how could it be? He'd left a million dollars in trust for this very purpose!

Pritpal lowered the lid of the canister and resealed it. There was a satisfying hiss of air.

"We'll need to monitor the temperature for a day or two. This should stop them from icing up."

The older man took off his lab coat and had a seat on the couch. "I haven't cleaned house this thoroughly in twenty years."

The silver man climbed down the ladder. "The tanks work better when they're full. Besides, that old clunker you had them in was leaking. We had to move them."

"This tank is even older — I don't feel right about using it."

Pritpal carefully took off and folded his protective gear.

"Don't worry, I fixed this one myself." Pritpal did a final once-over, looking for leaks. "You know what we should do with these NSF guys?"

"Not again..."

"I'm telling you, we don't need to save the whole head, just a little bit of tissue. In a tank this size, we could do thousands."

"Your thinking is too narrow, Pritpal. Yes, a tissue sample on a slide is all we need to clone them, but what if they develop a new technology that allows them to recover their memories? These people want to come back as they were, not as clueless clones."

Peter stood more frozen than his head in the tank just a few feet away. Then he ran at the men, without effect.

"They're also expecting to wake up in their old bodies, wrapped in a warm flannel sheet, as if they'd emerged from a nice little day surgery. That's what they're paying for," said Barstow.

"They also expected to come back while their grandchildren were still alive."

The two men gathered up their tools and left.

Peter flung himself on the bench and considered his options. Murder was foremost on his mind. He was up against a frightful deadline. An eternal eviction notice had been tacked to his door. But it wasn't only him, it was his beloved Terri too.

He had no idea how to get to his lawyer's office in Don Mills from here. Even if he did, what could he do when he got there — hire another lawyer to look into the matter? Oh, why hadn't he hired two lawyers? That would've solved this problem. One lawyer could be corrupted, but surely not two.

Peter sat in silence until calm returned once again. His anger and his fear wore themselves out. He couldn't, he wouldn't, talk to John.

If he makes light of this, I will have to strike a match.

Behind his back, out of his field of vision, a flashing green light turned to steady red.

Chapter 24

Lori was the next visitor through the door. Lou and Croc were waiting for her in the living room. Lou helped her hang up her coat before giving her a big hug.

"Croc said you weren't coming."

"Why?"

"Well, it's winter, and when it gets this cold, he buries himself in the mud."

"That certainly explains why he has such pretty skin. Have you explained down-filled parkas to him?"

Lou leaned into her personal space and whispered. "He misses feathers. He wishes crocs still had them."

Lori gave him a kiss.

Lou ushered her down the hallway into the sitting room where they found privacy in the afternoon sun. The room offered a glorious view of the brownstone mansions on Madison Avenue and boasted three comfortable, red-striped barrel chairs — one for each of them. There was a faint scent of baking bread in the air that suggested wonderful things were developing in the kitchen. It put Lori in mind of something she'd brought.

"I smuggled in some real food for you."

She reached into her bag and produced a thermos. "Real coffee, prepared not thirty minutes ago in your very own kitchen."

He opened the lid and took a sniff. "I love you."

"And..." she added rather grandly. "Looky, looky."

Lou watched Lori produce a slender package of scones.

"With honey?"

"And walnuts."

"I think I'm going to cry."

"I thought the food here was good."

"It is. But how many people thank God for coffee and scones the way we do?" Lou was beaming. "What can I do for you in return?"

Lori leaned back and thought about it. *Is this the time? More to the point, is this the place?*

"Well, I want to know more about the things you experience. I've been thinking about it a lot since you got here."

He looked at her with love in his eyes. His face grew serious, but his eyes remained untroubled. There was a long pause that neither found distressing. "You've been very patient with me. I'll tell the whole story now, if that's what you want."

Lori settled her hands on her lap. "I'd feel better if you did. Simply to know."

"Do you remember high school physics?"

"I was good at that. I had a gorgeous teacher, Mr. Wilson."

"Well, he lied to you."

"With *his* eyes, I wouldn't care."

"Do you remember the atom? Protons and neutrons huddled together in the centre, while electrons whizzed around them the way planets circle the sun?"

"Yes."

"That's a simple way of making sense of the universe. You can do chemistry with that model and even build an atomic bomb and blow up the world if that's what you want to do, but it's not the whole story. At the subatomic level, amazing things are happening. The particles that hold our universe together are complicated. We have to infer and deduce the things we don't know from the things that we can measure."

"Hit the dumb button, please."

He picked up one of the scones, took a bite, and chewed while he considered how to say what needed to be said. "I see people who are dead, and sometimes other creatures I'm not sure about. Some of them are good but some aren't." His voice dropped. "Croc is mobbed up with them."

"Do you see them the way you see me?"

"Not with my eyes open. But I see them in my thoughts, the way people appear in dreams, the way you can shut your eyes and see the face of someone you love."

They shared a smile.

Lori poured him a cup of coffee from the thermos.

"And, I hear them too."

"Actual voices?"

"More people can hear them than see them."

That didn't answer my question.

Lou took a breath and tried again. "When I try to explain this, people frown. Most of the time they're being paid big bucks to talk to me, and they don't believe a word I say. They want to direct my thinking to an acceptable conclusion. They're so certain that they're right, they always miss the point. The fact is, what we see and can measure isn't all there is." He reached out and took her hands in his. He looked her straight in the eye with a face brimming with love. "We don't die."

Lori returned his gaze. "Well, actually, we do."

"But it doesn't happen the way we think it will. We're all stuck on protons, neutrons, and electrons. That's all we see because we think that's all that there is. There's way more going on."

Lori was struggling with content but otherwise enjoying herself. "Okay. So what happens when we die?"

"Most people simply go. One minute they're here and the next, they're gone."

Lou paused and looked into Lori's eyes before giving her hand a gentle squeeze. "But some stay here. They're the ones I see. There are three of them upstairs."

That was a dramatic utterance if there ever was one, but neither of them went there. Lori raised an eyebrow and he nodded, both of them glancing at the ceiling.

"They're like babies," Lou continued. "They're alive, they're in the world, but they can't do anything but cry."

"How is that a good thing? It sounds terrible!"

Lou ran his fingers through his hair, leaving a tuft standing straight up. "Something is coming to take them home."

"Home? Like to heaven?"

"No. Home to the future."

Lori reached over and smoothed his hair. "But why the future?"

Lou took a sip of coffee as he considered his answer. "I could never solve a Rubik's cube. It was one of those problems that got worse the more I tried."

Lori smiled asymmetrically. "Lots of those in life, cupcake."

He put his mug down. "But then one day I picked it up and looked at it and the mush turned into the Rosetta stone."

Lori leaned back in her chair, looking as if she was attempting to whistle. "I love that moment."

"Well, that's what happens. Somehow you get taken to a place in the future where everything suddenly makes sense. You have all the answers. You come back different."

"But Lou, what about you? Do you get the answers?"

"Not so far."

"Why not?"

"I don't know! If I get a chance, I'll ask."

They talk to you?

Lori sat in silence, searching for something that would validate what she'd heard. What was this really about? She went for the easiest piece. "So the only reason you came here was for this?"

Lou's face said, *You got me.* "I can sense when these things are about to happen. I start to smell sea air and hear waves on a beach. I get this feeling of excitement deep down in my gut."

"So there's no booze problem?"

"Nope."

"No drug problem?"

"Nope."

"The rumours about the tumour?"

"Sadly, no."

Her face lightened as she saw the humour for the first time. "So all that go-round with your parents and the counsellors…"

"It was a necessary preamble, *and,*" he added rather grandly, "it served a noble purpose."

Her eyes narrowed. "What purpose?"

He popped a chunk of scone into his mouth and answered as he chewed.

"Don't know the answer to that one as yet. But I do know that I need to be here. This week. In this physical location. I can't say no to this. Lori, there are only two times in my life when I'm happy: when I'm with you and when I'm doing this. I don't know why, but when I do this, when I make myself available in this way, there's a ton of feel-good energy. I feel alive in a way that never happens otherwise."

Lori turned from Lou and stared out the window.

What are you thinking?

Chapter 25

Peter was frantic. He had to find John. He hurried to Punanai because he didn't know what else to do. The closer he got to the house, the quicker and easier his path became. He was skating downhill with the wind at his back. This had never happened before.

He made his way to the second floor, where another surprise awaited him. Walter and four other poltergeists were huddled together where the wall met the ceiling. They were all talking. Not one of them was listening to anything the others said or making any sense themselves, but even so, it was good to see even this much life in Walter.

Lou was fast asleep on the bunk below with a novel perfectly balanced on his nose, while his beloved Croc rested on his abdomen, trying to find a comfortable spot for his tail.

Peter tried to talk with Walter, but the old poltergeist looked through him as if he wasn't there. The old boy was pretending to smoke a cigarette. Peter lost interest and decided to keep looking for John. They needed to talk about this. As he left the room and began wading upstream against whatever unseen force was roaring through the halls of Punanai, he heard a child's voice.

"Hey, mister, you look sad."

Peter turned on his heel. It was the young girl they had seen through the Holt Renfrew window. But now she was dressed in a school uniform and had shrunk to the size of squirrel. He wondered if she was old enough to understand what had happened to her.

She read his thoughts. "Peter, I'm not dead. I'm not a ghost."

He towered over her. "How is it then, that you can see me?"

"Isn't it enough that I can?"

Peter felt his back go up. He sniffed the air for danger. The light was nearby! Closing in on him. He froze in a moment of indecision as his body ached for the release of fight or flight.

The little girl crossed her arms. "Why are you afraid of me?"

"I'm not," Peter said, full of bluster but taking a half-step backwards. "I'm simply trying to get my mind around this sacrilege. I've been betrayed by my attorney. When I find that four-eyed thief, I'm going to push him into the path of an oncoming bus, even if it leaves me a poltergeist and heads me in the direction of hellfire. It will be worth it."

The little girl was nonplussed. Her head tilted to the right. "You miss her, don't you?"

Peter's face darkened.

The young girl pixilated. For a moment, Peter couldn't make out more than faint red and purple sparkles in the air. Then she came back into focus, now a teenager and five feet tall. Peter stared at her dumbly as she took him by the hand. He was overcome with vertigo underpinned by pillars of nausea and alarm. His senses oppressed him for an agonizing interval until he felt himself zipping backwards. It didn't feel like a free fall, but a journey on a waterslide.

He came to rest at last, blinking frantically until the horizon righted itself and his stomach settled. The world was once again as he relied upon it to be. He was standing near the cryotank with the now sporty-looking girl dressed in a track suit. She was tracing his name on the masthead with her perfect, tiny fingers as if nothing had happened. Peter was terrified. He tried to speak but could only manage a guttural cough. He reflexively covered his mouth with his hand. A sensation of moisture on his lip alarmed him. His hand came away from his mouth slick with perspiration. Ghosts are dry and they never cry and they sure as hell don't sweat. But here he was oozing worse than a fat drunk in a sauna.

His question was directed inward. "What's happening to me?"

The bouncy teen pointed at the cryotank as she chewed on a wad of pink gum. "Do you see that light flashing?"

He looked around, his eyes still quailed by the experience of vertigo. "Yes, I do. Oh no, it's supposed to be a steady green!"

Peter felt the same outrage he had experienced when those two monsters laid tongs on Terri. His agitation made short work of his better angels. He began to pound the side of the tank with his fists. "We have to do something."

The young lady blew a perfect pink sphere until it burst. "What do you want to happen?"

The question froze him. "You make it sound as if you could fix it!"

"I can and I will, if that's what you want me to do."

Peter hated that juxtaposition more than the tongs. If that's what you want me to do indeed. How many times have I been in this very spot? Quid pro quo is not a game. Is this child a demon here to devour me, heart and soul?

"Peter, your thoughts are taking an alarming turn."

He looked at her in terror. You're inside my head!

He heard her unspoken response. I'm as near as your next breath of air.

Peter flung himself against the cryotank with his arms spread as wide as they would stretch.

"Oh Terri … dear God … sweet Terri."

The young girl drew her arms back above her head, growing in stature as she did, until she towered over Peter. She wanted to pick him up and set him down on her knee but thought better of it. While Peter hugged the tank and sobbed, she placed her index and middle fingers on his temples. It had an immediate narcotic effect. Peter's knees gave way, and he started to fall to the left in slow motion. His eyes rolled back in his head until only the whites showed. His feet left the ground and he began to float in the air, looking like a man in an isolation tank buoyed by Epsom salt and tepid water. But Peter wasn't warm and safe. He was cold. A dead astronaut in space, perfectly preserved but capable of nothing.

She whispered in his ear, "A glacier is the cold blue harbinger of the unseen forces that shape our world. One year, oh so very long ago, all the snow in an alpine meadow did not melt in the spring. What of it? The wildflowers still blossomed to the very edge of the frozen patch."

She gathered a handful of topsoil from one of the potted plants and sprinkled it gently over his eyelids. She smoothed it with her thumb until it resembled a cosmetic mask. Satisfied, she placed her open palm on this forehead.

"What invisible hand can turn such an unseen screw and to what unfathomable purpose? Was the downward slope shaded for the first time by the shadow of a rising mountain peak? Continents are forever adrift, and lands rise and fall as tectonic plates jostle beneath them. Did this doom the Brome and the Buttercup?"

Peter lay floating on his back, enveloped in a mix of fog and snowflakes. His formidable eyebrows caked with snow. His expression beatific. He was a Greenland mummy floating in an ice river, his body forgotten in a crevasse, his sorrows locked away in deep, icy sleep.

"The accumulation of snow and rain went on for eons, and as is the case with all self-perpetuating injuries, it gained in depth and breadth until its ministrations ran miles deep. Ice rolls imperceptibly down the side of a mountain, the way that stained glass flows downward in a church window frame. Nothing can resist its steady progress. It tills everything in its path, right down to the bedrock. The very stuff of life turned and reduced and crushed by its indominable will."

She gently scraped fresh snow from Peter's wild eyebrows and let it melt in her hand. She let runoff drip into the soil that covered his eyes like pennies on a corpse, turning it into a paste. Satisfied with her work, she blew on his eyes until the mud turned silver and then vanished. The old ghost looked at peace. She stroked his cheek with her hand.

"And that is where the matter lies with you, Ötzi."

He groaned a sleeper's groan and mumbled his true love's name.

She smiled and mussed his hair.

"Peter, the love of God should flow unhindered down from on high like a mountain stream. But this brooding ice cave you've devised for yourself frustrates that purpose and holds your life captive. There are two oceans, one of salt water, comprising the freeing sea, and one of frozen fresh water, denuding the land. In your winter slumber, you cannot hear the sea birds cry or smell the healing waters. Until the sea floats you up and breaks your spine, you'll remain trapped in sight of the ocean but powerless to rejoin it."

She looked at the device in her right hand and frowned. "You and John are quite a challenge."

Chapter 26

Jacob Hutton was living the life of a foster kid. He moved between three institutions in a way that was eerily similar to an unwanted child caught in a power struggle between deficient parents. The detox didn't want him taking up a bed he didn't need, the hospital couldn't put up with his drinking on their premises, and the treatment centre regretted ever taking his money. He was back at Punanai for the third time this month.

Kaiser looked in on Jacob a few minutes before lights out. Jacob's evening nurse was looking badly used. She was sitting on a plastic chair beside the bed. Kaiser smiled at her. "Can you give us a few minutes?"

She couldn't believe her luck. She'd been praying the old bastard would fall asleep for over an hour. Her ass hurt from the hard-backed chair and the sick-room smell was harder to take this evening, particularly after Jacob called her a bitch.

Jacob was sitting up in bed, staring at the wall and muttering imprecations, lost in glorious thought. He was imagining the scene where his upstart board of directors got their comeuppance. What had he ever seen in any of those place seekers? Kaiser dragged the chair closer to the bed and waited for a greeting. There was none. The mischievous part of Kaiser gained the upper hand. He cleared his throat and gave Jacob every chance to finish what he was doing and acknowledge his presence.

Jacob's heart was pounding. He looked Kaiser in the eye and took his measure. His displeasure was obvious. Kaiser was well built, solid through the chest and the arms. The look in his eye announced to the world that he was fearless. He was here to lay down the law, no doubt. Not a good time for a battle. No, the thing to do here would be to let Kaiser stand in the rain for a day or two until his resolve vanished into self doubt.

Jacob turned his head away and continued to ignore Kaiser. Kaiser couldn't help but smile. After ten minutes of silence, he put his head down as if he were a beaten man about to skulk out of the room. As he turned and got to his feet, he suddenly leaped up onto the chair and pointed frantically into the corner. "How did that get in here?"

Jacob launched himself out of bed and got his feet tangled in the blankets. He would've fallen if Kaiser hadn't caught him by the scruff of the neck and returned him to a sitting position on the bed.

"What, where?"

"What, where, what?"

"Why did you scream?"

"I didn't, you did."

"What's in the corner?"

Kaiser looked into the corner as if for the first time. "Dust bunnies."

"What the hell do you think you're playing at? You scared me to death."

"I heard you scream, and I came running in from the hall."

"Liar, you were sitting right there in the chair!"

"Oh, so you did see me."

***

After lunch on Sunday, Paul invited Seymour into the counsellor's office to have a cup of tea with him before the Straight Up meeting. The two men moved the office chairs closer to the window to better enjoy the afternoon sun on their faces.

"I have to keep an eye on the phones. Hope you don't mind."

Seymour looked around the office: he was one part kid finally seeing where his dad worked and one part artist feeling the gentle caress of his muse. "You sure made an impression on my mom."

"A good one or a bad one?"

"She asked me if you were a drunk or a do-gooder."

Paul smiled. "You didn't tell her, did you?"

The young man smiled broadly. "I gave you up."

Paul took off his glasses for a moment and rubbed his eyes with the broad palms of his hands. "I brought you in here to talk to you about something near and dear to my heart, but before we get to that, I want to know how your family feels about addiction."

Seymour struck the ironic tone that people over forty can only remember and marvel at, the way they remember flat stomachs and joints that purr when they're stretched. "They hate it! Sometimes I worry that they hate me too."

Was that what the silence between you and your mom was about?

The young man sighed. "They think *it's* the real me."

Paul gave him a little nod. It was enough.

"My parents think that they love me to death, but I'm damaged goods." A sorrow stole into his eyes. "They tried their best to save me from myself and failed."

Paul fanned the flame. "So you're a bad seed?"

"My real parents left me in a doctor's waiting room. What does that tell you?"

Paul rubbed his eyes with his index fingers without taking off his glasses. "You mean your birth parents? Aren't the people who raised you your real parents?"

Seymour looked pained. "It took me years to work this out. My parents didn't know what they were getting when they got me. I'm the kid who's never going to grow up. The one who will never find love or have a life."

Paul gave him a nod and a look that said he understood.

"God didn't give them children. That's a judgment on them," Seymour said.

Paul smiled as he gently shook his head. "Yes, He did. He gave them you."

Seymour leaned into the space between them, brimming with the energy of disbelief. "Yeah, and they've spent their lives trying to save me from my evil self. That would be a kind of proof, wouldn't it, that they were all right and that not having children — that would be on God. They'd be showing him that he was wrong about them all along. It wouldn't matter that my dad never spoke or that my mom was the ultimate control freak. All the bad stuff would be somewhere else."

Paul's eyes looked wise and sad. "When I was a kid, I didn't see myself as different. That happened in high school, when everyone started to date."

Seymour was wary but intrigued. "Me too. I was popular in public school, but … high school, well, that was a different story. It's why I started doing art."

Now it fit. "Was that your passport?"

"My passport?"

Paul got to his feet and removed his suit coat, draping it over the back of his chair. The move was intentional. "Yeah, how you prove to everyone that you're not only as good as them but — hell, let's just come right out and say it — better. Way above their petty prejudices and game playing."

Paul settled back in his chair, transformed from interrogator to friend by the absence of his coat. "You found that something in your painting, didn't you?"

"I don't know. I just know that hiding in my room got me a slap on the head and a trip to the guidance counsellor." There was a long pause as Seymour traversed the emotional distance from his past to the present. "For a while, painting was enough, but then it got so messed up. I started to hate it too."

Paul opened a tin of shortbreads and offered one to Seymour. "That's the experience of being different. You put your heart and soul into doing something wonderful with your life, and after a long struggle, you succeed, you build yourself up to the point where you start to see some results, and you begin to hope that, somehow, all this effort is going to come to something, that it's possible to earn the respect of the world. You pretend that they'll stop hating you when you show them what you can do."

Seymour started to fidget in his chair. Shells were falling all around him.

Paul flattened his voice. "Then one day, some halfwit racist at school called me redbone and everybody laughed. And do you know what I hated the most? Not the loudmouth, not even the people who laughed. I hated myself. Because of the fear I felt in my gut."

Paul did a slow turn in his chair and swung for the fence. "It seeped into me. It was dissolved in my baby formula. Fed to me like medicine on a spoon. It's in my bones and teeth and hair."

Seymour was shaken. "So you do know."

Paul nodded. "You don't need to prove anything to them, because they can't give you what they don't have."

Seymour was on the edge of his chair. He'd made it this far countless times, only to fall short. Could Paul provide the math that would finally balance the equation?

Paul took his time. His voice calm and linear. "But that's only the half of it. This all plays out when you drink. Imagine laying your hands on the bastard who was talking about you behind your back. How would it feel to finally have him by the throat? To see the look of surprise in his eyes give way to fear?"

"That would be awesome."

"Take a deep breath and dream large with me. Those two images belong together. There's an order to them. Reacting and acting. Two sides of the same coin. Reaching for a drink satisfies in the way choking that bastard would, but it's only a soap bubble in your head, the self-hatred comes when the bubble bursts and all you have in your hands is an empty glass."

Seymour's face reddened and his eyes looked plumper, as if they were suddenly ripe.

"Your mom showed me your paintings."

"She shouldn't have done that."

"She told me what you did with them."

"They were mine. I did what I wanted with them."

"I want you to talk about the paintings in the Straight Up group — Seymour? Where are you going? We're not done."

Chapter 27

Paul loved the Straight Up meeting. What could be simpler than a group of strangers, sitting in a circle in the lunchroom, asked to comment on two straightforward questions: When did you realize that you were in trouble? What has given you hope that you can change?

Marriages and careers could end for some of the participants in the next thirty days, but not because of what they said here. Time and again, decades-long addictions had perished in this circle that looked out onto the terraced winter garden. The wonder of the thing was its simplicity. Here, the most artfully crafted lies lost their cohesion and dissipated into air. The manipulations and self-deception that prospered everywhere else fell flat.

Not surprisingly, the guys who still wanted to drink couldn't get away fast enough. The guys who wanted to change struggled to find words.

Lou sat with his back to the patio door. The great imposter. He was here on an undercover mission, certain he was about to give himself away with a slip of the tongue. He had flashed over this meeting a week ago while enjoying a Sunday afternoon snooze with Lori. He remembered seeing Daniel and Larry, their faces serious and involved, but the subject under discussion had eluded him. He experienced a second splashdown a few seconds later: a callous young man near the heavy oak doors, speaking rudely to a thin shivering woman. Always a glimpse, but never a look.

The talk on the smoking deck before the meeting provided him with the unofficial list of dos and don'ts. But, as Croc had pointed out, you have to know the truth before you can tell a credible lie, and with no experience of addiction to draw on, Lou was in a tight spot. His best option was to listen hard and learn what he could.

Every counsellor had their way of doing this meeting. Last week, Greg Bass invited the participants to centre themselves by listening to classical music. Paul liked to have the guys sit in a circle and pay attention to their breathing with their eyes closed. It gave him a chance to say a little prayer — Father Phil's prayer: Lord, put these guys in harm's way and keep them safe.

While they were breathing, in the heavy, wet way that smokers breathe, Paul gave them the once-over, his voice deliberately warm and comforting. "I want you guys to remember that this is hallowed ground. It's not only the speaking that makes this sacred, it's the listening. Hearing voice after voice talking about the thing that's shamed and defeated you ... a secret you vowed to take with you to the grave..."

A smoker's cough said, in effect, *Do tell us more.* Paul's voice was compelling. "Recognizing that you belong here is the first step. Understanding that people recover comes next. Deciding to give this thing a fair chance and the time it needs ... well, enough said."

Sensing the natural entry point, several of the eyes popped open.

Paul smiled and looked around the room. "If this is your first time, I won't call on you until you've had a chance to hear a couple of the other guys. Remember, you can talk about the moment you realized you were out of options ... that you had to do something ... that addiction had ruined your life. But what I hope to hear about is an experience or insight that's given you a new perspective. Something that happened this week. An event that's changed the way you understand the problem ... maybe given you some hope."

Chair legs scrapped the floor, a book fell over and furtive glances were exchanged. Tension revealed itself in balled fists and clenched jaws.

"What you're not going to hear this afternoon are lectures, shaming, or friendly advice. You've had enough of that."

Paul rose to his feet and placed his broad hands on the back of his chair.

"Now I want you to nod to the men on either side of you, let them know you're down with this. And, even more importantly, I want you to notice that empty chair in the middle of our circle. It is there for a purpose. An empty chair is an invitation. That chair is there to remind you that there's a distance between where you are and where you need to be." Paul's eyes carried the weight of his final remark. "We're swimming in the deep end of the pool. If you can't or won't tell the truth, you're done. Don't waste this chance. Who wants to start?"

A cane slammed down, and all eyes followed the sound to its source. The old man who ate in his room and had a nurse was struggling to get to his feet. His pant legs came up just below his knees to reveal a red mass of sores and bruises. Jacob Hutton looked around haughtily. "I'm not going to sit through an hour of this crap."

Paul felt his gut go sour. Sure, Jacob was ill. His physical condition was altering his perceptions. But it was obvious to everyone in the room that, drunk or sober, Jacob was a son of a bitch. The conversation to come was a rare opportunity. One Jacob could ruin. Paul asked himself the two centring questions: *What's best for the house? What's best for the client?* Polite needed to give way to pointed. "It won't be an hour of crap, Jacob." He didn't say, *You'll only be talking for a few minutes.*

The old bastard had game. "How much do they pay you to run this shabby piece of navel-gazing?" He glared into the room. A wicked smile turned up the corner of his lip.

Lou couldn't take his eyes off Jacob Hutton. Sea water was pooling around his feet. How could he not feel it? Croc started to twitch so violently that Lou was forced to put him in his coat pocket before he yowled.

Paul confirmed his suspicions by looking around the room. The guys were embarrassed. They were ready to have this conversation. But they weren't going to do it with Jacob yapping.

Paul rose to the occasion. "Jacob, you have two choices: listen or go back to your room." It cost Paul something not to add, *The adults are talking.*

The old man surveyed the room, looking for allies. But he found none. That moment of hesitation invited aggression.

Fred hated Jacob. He didn't know or need a reason why. This meeting, like all the others he had attended in this nightmare of captivity, was pointless. A way to pass the time. Even so, he wasn't going to let a cheap crook hijack the agenda. He hadn't planned to speak, but now he felt impelled to.

"My name is Fred. I'm an alcoholic." That word reverberated painfully in his ear. He looked at Paul. "Do I have to say that every time I speak?"

Paul smiled, flushed with relief at so improbable a rescue. "No, not this afternoon."

"Good, because I hate saying it." He saw the faces around him begin to cloud over. Fred's eyes narrowed and his voice dropped. "The first time I had to say it out loud, I almost died."

The men roared their approval. The only one who didn't get it was Lou, who was otherwise occupied sorting out what was happening in Fred's periphery. Dust devils kept coming into focus and then departing. Lou could hear two women talking, but he couldn't make sense of what they were saying. Something about poking someone with a broom. Jacob and Fred were corner pieces, and this house was rocking with energy.

Fred had a wary look about him, a defensive posture, as if he expected something to jump out from the shadows. Paul had seen this many times. The effects of delirium tremens make a person hypersensitive to changes in the light for months afterwards and they cannot abide things scurrying around.

Fred's initial impulse had been to shut Jacob up, but now he found himself speaking without understanding what it was that he was supposed to be commenting on. He let loose.

"Being a drunk is much simpler than being an alcoholic." His face brightened as if he was seeing the humour in the thing for the first time. "There's a schedule. You get up in the morning. You have a little drink. Then maybe a nibble of breakfast, and you square your place away. Then it's off to your den to check on the vodka supply and the fridge to check on mix and food, then out the door you go with your list. There's only one rule: don't run out of booze."

The guys were not expecting to hear that in a treatment centre, and they roared their approval a second time. Fred blushed slightly, but he was enjoying himself.

"Don't laugh. With blackouts, it happens all the time and then you're really screwed." It cost him something to add. "They ruin everything."

Paul was taking stock. Fred was off topic, but so what. He was talking and Jacob was fuming. Not a bad start. *But how are the guys taking it?*

He noticed that Larry and Daniel Philips were sitting together. The way they were leaning forward with their elbows on their knees suggested that they'd formed a bond. They occupied the two chairs to Fred's left.

Sitting next to them was the rather subdued Charles "Chuck" Dorn — he was back after a prolonged stay in detox. Doug had given him a lift in his car after Mike had lost his temper and thrown him out. It was hard to believe that Chuck and Mike Sage had been friends and roommates when Mike went through treatment. There wasn't much of that version of Chuck on display this afternoon. His dreams about a career in aerospace had vanished. Twenty years was a long time in active addiction for anyone, let alone a crack addict, and it showed on Chuck's worn face.

Seymour and Jacob were opposite Fred, their faces lit by the natural light from the garden. Lou was sitting with the other new guys. Paul had yet to attach a name to most of those faces. He'd had a few days off, and the house had turned over in his absence. He would know the newcomers soon enough.

Fred was warming to his subject and basking in the attention. He left his chair and walked to the centre of the room, something participants seldom did. "I go to the movies in the afternoon. I take a mickey with me. He's good company. Mick and I sit there and take in the show."

Fred was profoundly off message, and Paul considered trying to give him some direction but then thought better of it. This was the most anyone had gotten out of him. Fred alternated between looking sad and a little defensive, the way a man does when he's not certain how his words are going to be received, and then almost joyful when the men nodded their approval. The guys were attentive, so Paul let go of his agenda and decided to let this river find its own way to the sea.

"Movies make more sense than life. There's a point to them. You go after something hard, something you want. You succeed and have a happy ending, or you die trying. Either way, it gets settled." His shoulders slumped and his head lowered.

"Life is different. It leaves you hanging. Stuck in the middle. Aching for an ending. That's where I've been. I don't know how much longer I have to live..." His eyes seemed to be fixated on some faraway point, but his focus was inward. The way we talk to our ghosts while we look at ourselves in the mirror. Opportunity was staring him in the face. Staring him down. "I hope it's not long. My accident took everything I ever loved."

Paul noticed that Daniel had an odd look on his face. That vacant look that comes most often when you're lost in a book.

Fred paused and looked around the room, suddenly aware of how exposed he was. He plopped himself down in the empty chair.

"I see my life on that screen. All of it up there, the way it was. I can hear it. I feel it in my gut. I want it. The way it was when I still mattered." A nascent truth escaped his lips. "Booze makes that feel possible."

Paul eyed the nugget in the fast-flowing stream. "Possible?"

Fred didn't respond to the prompt. But Chuck did. His lips disappeared inside his mouth as his eyes closed in anguish.

The battle raged on inside Fred. It cost him to continue. "Everyone thinks I'm nuts. They're always asking questions. 'I don't know' is how you say 'drop dead' around here without getting shown the door. But I do know. That relief I feel when I finally get a drink to stay down in the morning." He stopped for what seemed like an eternity. His mind as empty as an overturned drum. "It comes at a price. More expensive than that little bag of nuts in the hotel fridge — the one that costs eleven dollars. When you open the door, it's the first thing you see."

The guys started to laugh. They knew about fridges in hotel rooms.

Fred brightened as his audience pumped their arms and clapped.

"Those cashews are a bad deal. Having one bag won't put out the fire. The greasy punk in the lobby smiles when he adds them to your bill. He knows you're going to eat two of them. That bag of nuts is too small. Someone with the soul of a hyena did the math."

Fred stretched his back by bending at the waist then stood up again. "But even at eleven dollars, the nuts are a way better deal than that pipsqueak bottle of brandy." The men were enjoying themselves.

Lou's eyes were riveted on Fred's feet. A pool of water, salt water by the smell of it, was forming around him. "I got to say this out loud right here and right now or I'm never going to get it said. Am I the only guy in the world who gets too sick to drink water? Am I the only guy in this room who drinks and pukes until he finally gets one to stay down? My nose runs, my throat burns, my stomach heaves, my eyes blur. But I keep forcing it down." His eyes clouded over.

The room was full of silent *amens* and an unspoken *hallelujah* from Paul.

"Why can't this shit give me what I want or kill me?" There was a long pause. It sounded as if sorrow had finally gotten the upper hand. He spoke in a choked whisper. "I can't do it the other way."

There it was. The marrow — visible through the compound fracture — no longer protected by the bone. The anathema we attempt to cut from our still-living flesh. Without realizing that they were doing it, the men leaned in to the circle. Fred's gaze strayed to the garden. "But then a little bit of the poison stays down — and I don't give a damn about anything. But that sweet spot, it never lasts."

Jacob was talking to himself and shaking his head the way wrestlers do when their rival has the microphone. Everyone else was hearing a damning diary entry read into the court record — everyone but Lou, who was struggling with content instead of meaning. *People do that?*

Fred sighed. "I can't stand what I'm doing, and I can't stop myself from doing it." He clenched his teeth and rolled a sore shoulder, the pain radiating into his chest and causing him to bark out his words. "Do people stop? Or are we a bunch of jailbirds memorizing scripture? Guys do that in the can because there's nothing else to do. It passes the time. Is that what this is — more pretending?"

There was a silence full of dark shadows. This was the thought they'd all been keeping at bay. Was one type of self-deception being replaced by a new one?

Lou felt a tear roll down his cheek as Croc squirmed in his pocket.

The pain kicked Fred again. Harder this time. Burning everything within a foot of its epicentre. His voice dropped as he struggled to take a breath. "I can't say anymore. If I offended anybody, I'm sorry. But I've been talking to myself about this for years and today is the first day it ever got said with someone else in the room." Fred returned to his seat in the circle and sat down heavily. The jet of escaping air blew the onus of speaking next one chair to the left, where it landed on Larry Lorne.

Larry's crooked nose and chipped front tooth reminded Lou of an all-star centre-ice man giving an interview on *Hockey Night in Canada*. Larry was stuck on last week. *Do I have the guts to tell them?* Czombo running wild in the house, leaving him exposed, about to get caught for fiddling the urine tests.

He'd had an awful moment when Paul and Mike ushered Czombo into the back room to confront him. He expected to be next. He needed to talk about that. How that felt. To be betrayed, lied to, and then nothing.

Paul was wrong about truth. Truth can't exist when someone is in charge. If he piped up, Paul would send him home. He wouldn't have any choice. Larry's jaw tightened, the tension most noticeable in his forehead. *Damn the truth anyway. What use is it? Or this stupid Boy Scout circle. Or talking about shit. None of it matters because truth is shit.*

He blew out a long slow breath of air as he wiped his damp palms on his blue jeans and closed his eyes for a moment. *There's no way I'm the only guy to ever get caught in the rat trap. It would do these guys good to hear what happened to me — from me, straight up. Crap, if this was Fred's movie, I'd look them in the eye and tell them. Paul would be so proud, but sad. I'd be the son he couldn't save, and out the front door I'd go — straight into the arms of my adoring girlfriend. That's what the story needs.*

He opened his eyes and they landed on the empty chair. He dried his moist palms on his shirt this time before instinctively feeling around in his pocket for the lighter Fred had given him. It felt good in his hand. He wanted to light it but dared not. *There's nothing. That empty chair really is empty.*

Jacob could stand it no longer. "You. Bellhop." He shook his cane with his right hand. "Yeah, you, jackass, with the stupid, pious look on your yap. Get over here. I'm going home. I've heard enough shit for a lifetime."

A flush of anger pulsed through Fred, who had to will himself to stay in the chair. The anger felt good. Cleansing.

Paul considered the possibilities. Put up, double down, or walk away. Jacob was about to make or break this meeting. The good shepherd leaves the many unguarded when he abandons the flock to try and save the one who strayed. But would he risk everything to return this blackleg to the fold? He looked around the room. The guys were not embarrassed this time. They were frustrated. Fred had taken them where they needed to be.

Inspiration struck. "On one condition. Tell us the truth and I'll take you back to your room. What do you think about what Fred just said, Mr. Hutton?"

The old man's eyes grew wide. "You make me sick. Listening to you blather is as bad as watching one of those religious films they show at Easter." He waved his cane. "You all have that same true believer look on your faces. You ought to be ashamed. A real man goes into the world and takes what he wants." He banged his cane on the floor. "Doesn't even matter if it's legal. That's what lawyers are for."

Fred's eyes narrowed on Jacob. His suspicions were confirmed, he was a cheap crook.

The red-faced oldster looked pleased as he used his cane to draw his walker closer. It was well used, with off-putting stains best not thought of. "People respect power. That's right. That's how I made my money. I took.

When people complained, I sued. If they went to the press, I slandered them. Nobody stands in my way."

Fred would've thrown him into the unit and driven him down to Cherry Beach for a tune up in the old days. He drew some satisfaction by picturing himself dragging the old bastard by the scruff of his neck back to his room. *Miserable old prick...*

Jacob glared at the pack of them, enjoying their outrage. "I don't care what you think of me. But are you scared of me? If not, I have work to do."

Paul got to his feet and started to move across the room. There was a puzzled silence as he did so. Larry Lorne felt as if they'd been scolded by an angry child. He couldn't help himself. "Who wipes your ass, old man?"

"Who said that?" Jacob searched in vain for the culprit as disembodied voices called out from every part of the room.

"It doesn't matter, we're all thinking it."

"Get out of here."

"We have no time for bullshit."

Jacob beamed. "Well, boys, no hard feelings. Tell you what. I'll send a case of stale tobacco and rolling papers down to the mission. It'll help you with your mid-winter blues. It's the least I can do." He patted down his jacket pocket. "Sorry, I don't have any change on me."

Then a curious thing happened. A ballpoint pen fell out of the old man's shirt pocket and landed on the linoleum, just outside his reach. When Jacob bent to retrieve it, he flushed a deep hue of red that left him dizzy. Frustration flashed across his face. He used his cane to try and move the offending pen closer, but it was to no avail. Fury replaced concentration. Paul let him struggle for a few more seconds before scooping up the pen and placing it back in the old man's pocket. He got Jacob to his feet by supporting him under the arms. As he turned to grasp the walker, a leg cramp caused the poor man to hop in pain. His legs were as thick as tree trunks and moved slowly, in painful increments.

As Paul edged the old man carefully toward the door, the mood in the room changed. "Carry on, fellas. I'll be back."

Lou squirmed in his seat, trying to restrain Croc, who was trying to wriggle out of his coat pocket.

Seymour saw opportunity. He jumped out of his chair when the door closed behind Paul. "I'll start and then Daniel can go next."

The men were intrigued by Seymour's energy. Most of them responded with a nod.

Chuck piped up. "I need to go for a smoke."

Seymour held his ground. "Do what you want. I need to get something said without Paul in the room and I would appreciate it if you stayed."

Fred got to his feet and took up a station by the patio door. His body language said it all. No one was going for a smoke. Chuck looked annoyed but came around when the nervous young speaker found his voice.

"My name is Seymour. I'm a drunk." *Why do I have to say this.* "I hate myself…" His larynx betrayed him. The young orator tried to restore order with an unnecessary cough. It, too, rang hollow. His brain raced as sweat frothed beneath his arms. He could smell sneakers and wet towels. He looked around the circle for encouragement and he found it. Breath returned and words with it. "But that's not it. I think I love the real me." He let a moment pass. "I hate what the drink does to me as much as I love to drink."

Only Larry still looked concerned. The rest of the men were mulling over this new paradox.

Seymour was outing himself. Saying aloud for the first time his silent prayer of self-loathing. Working the hateful beads of recrimination through his fingers. The prosody that moved with difficulty through dense thought and tangles of emotion exploded when it encountered the porous air. "People only want one thing from me. 'Be an artist,' they say. 'Make us all proud.'"

There was a very long pause.

Croc kicked Lou in the ribs in a way that said, *pay attention.*

"I can't be an artist feeling the way that I feel. Having talent only makes it worse. My parents try to soothe me with psychology. They tell me what I'm feeling is normal for someone my age. Why can't they say they don't know. Why can't they be honest the way Jacob was?" Taking his cue from Fred, he made his way to the empty chair, placing one knee on the seat.

"My birth parents abandoned me. I don't know if the union that produced me was a moment of love and hope, or of brutality and despair. It makes a difference to know if you are a child of light or darkness."

He turned the chair around with the back support now facing his audience. "Think about what that poor old bastard just said. Is that what he did when he looked out at the world and found nothing? Figured if he got rich that the rest of it would fall into place. Sad old tub of guts. I hate the look of him because he reminds me of me."

Larry looked up at Seymour and then over at Daniel, acutely aware of the passing of time and the closing portal of opportunity. *Get on with it. He'll be back in a minute.*

Seymour mistook his look of concern for support. "Maybe this is where I belong. I want to paint. But to do that, I have to belong. I have no sacred truth. No stories. The world confuses me. I don't even understand the little bit of it that I live in. That's why I paint plants." His hand came up covered his mouth. "I don't know if my parents love me. They say they do. But they're hooked on the same bullshit as Hutton. I'm the monument that's going to make sense of their lives. Oh crap, it hurts to say that."

The sound of the elevator door opening and closing sent Larry into a panic. But Paul did not appear. The young man tapped his foot frantically.

Seymour was still talking. "Can I make my dreams come true? Can I turn this thing around? That old man is haunting me. He's what my self portrait is going to end up looking like." He paused as if a canvas stood on an easel before him.

"I don't want to stop drinking only to find out that I'm nothing. Oblivion doesn't cut your guts to ribbons the way being nothing does. I can control oblivion with a shot glass. There isn't a damn thing I can do about feeling empty."

The group sat in silence for a few seconds. The sound of the phone ringing in the cook's office brought them all back into the room.

Larry couldn't move. Couldn't get a breath. Couldn't make a start.

Daniel Philips couldn't contain himself. His voice was agitated. "Last week, I lied to you guys. I said there was something wrong with me, and I didn't know what. But I knew. I was … ashamed… But I've always known. The drinking is all about forgetting, the drugs are all about killing the pain, and the lies, well, they tidy up the loose ends."

He looked around the room until his eyes came to rest on Fred. "I can't tell by looking at your faces if it's safe to say what I need to say." *Why can't one of you give me what I need?* Fred looked past Daniel from his station near the patio door, but it was clear from his eyes that he was not comprehending.

Daniel reacted. "I just felt … fear. It happens every time. Why can't I look at you and say what I need to say? It's the looking that kills me. I feel stupid. In the past, when I've tried to tell the truth, it always ends bad." *Don't say it. You'll be the only one left in the room.*

He looked around, starting with the feet. Willing himself to look at the faces. Faces have no manners. They tell the truth straight up long before the lips can deploy foam and fire suppressant. An iron fist seized his throat from the inside, stopping his breath.

"I have to stop now because I want to drink. For the first time since I got here, I want to do a line. Of all the friggin' places to have this happen. My secrets are killing me." The room was silent. The most respectful hearing he'd ever gotten. "Be patient with me. I'm trying. But it's so hard." His head went down.

That should have occasioned a silence. A *what* to puzzle out and pair with a *why*. But the clock was thundering for Larry Lorne, who imagined he could hear the sound of Paul's returning footfalls. He practically jumped out of his chair and spoke the way a younger child does when they know they're about to be shushed. "I'm the guy that Czombo was getting his urine from. You guys deserve to know that. Daniel, what you said about how you feel when you can't tell the truth … that's right."

The point was well taken. The gazes were inward around the circle. Each man looking at his cargo as if for the first time. There was the part of the story that could safely be told. The part that made you a lovable villain. But the rest of it — what to do with the rest of it?

Larry was trying to convince himself that he'd done the right thing in spite of his rising terror. "What do I care about Paul? How bad would it be to get thrown out of here? Why do I care about what people think of me? I do stuff all the time that hurts me thinking, somehow, it'll make other people love me. I don't care about them. I'm kind of getting the idea that maybe they don't care anything about me either."

The threads of the narrative were becoming interwoven. Larry's words, Seymour's thoughts, and Daniel's evasions swirled like meltwater in a fast-moving stream. Pushing dead plants, silt, and even boulders toward the ocean. They weren't talking about the same event, but they were talking about the same thing. The barbed wire that so neatly separated one private hell from the other snapped, coiling back on itself with a hiss, leaving a useful passageway. What is secret about a shame universally shared?

Larry considered occupying the empty chair, but his legs thought better of it. "Booze is porn. A fake. It can't happen and maybe you wouldn't even want it to. But is sobriety going to be any better? Or is it going to be a flop too? Am I going to go to meetings in church basements every night until that becomes my whole life? I've seen guys that live that way. They talk tough in the meeting and then hit you up for loose change on the way out."

Why can't I tell when people are lying? I wish people glowed a faint shade of blue when they told the truth. How can I be real when every instinct in my body is telling me not to? Where do you find that kind of courage?

Chapter 28

Getting Jacob back to his room was taking forever. The wheels of his walker left tracks in the carpet that were uncannily similar to the imprints his socks left in the hot, red flesh around his ankles. Jacob knew that Paul wanted to be rid of him and back in the meeting and so he made a point of dragging his feet. He paused to catch his breath every ten steps and took a bathroom break. Paul didn't say anything, but irritation was showing around his eyes. Kim Ji-woo had gone for walk. Two hours away from her troublesome patient and that hot, smelly room was as appealing to her as a two-week vacation by the sea.

As they made their slow progress together, Paul realized that he was going to have to keep Jacob until Monday morning. There was no place to send him on a Sunday afternoon. He got some satisfaction knowing that Jacob was going to hate wherever he landed. Detox couches, gurneys in hospital hallways, and unwanted treatment beds share one thing in common: no one loves them. Paul decided to use that as his theme.

Jacob was a doomed airliner, but Paul decided he was going to try and fly this baby until he only saw turf through the front window. When the old man emerged from the washroom with a satisfied smirk on his face, Paul knew what he needed to say. "Jacob, have you been a difficult son of a bitch your whole life?"

"How dare you." The old man could have held his own in an amateur theatre production.

Paul took up a position beside the walker. "I get paid to dare. What if I talk to you the way you talk to everybody else? You're a fat, stinky, horrible old drunk. When people see you, even when you're hiding in one of your two-thousand-dollar suits, they want to run the other way. You're a living corpse."

"I'm still more of a man than you are."

"No. You're a parasite. You don't produce anything. You abuse people. You break the law. You steal from your investors." That one landed. The old man picked up the pace, unconsciously trying to outfoot his tormentor.

"I must do it well. I'm not in jail."

"Really? Not in jail. Is that what you think? Look around, smart guy. All that's missing are the bars and jumpsuits. How is this different from jail?"

Jacob's lip turned up in a sneer. "Jail is free. This song and dance costs money."

Paul got in behind him. "Jacob, you're stupid into the bargain. This is only a jail because you're making it one. You're a drunk, and this is a place of healing. Healing that cannot take place as long as you're being an asshole."

"Where did you learn your clinical language?"

"From talking to guys like you."

"I'm nothing like those guys." His voice dripped perfect condescension.

"None of them are as far gone as you are."

"I'll make a note in my journal."

Paul sensed the small crack in the old man's armour for the first time and smiled wickedly. "Let me tell you what I do know about you, Jacob. You live to cause trouble. You figure out what makes people crazy and then you feed them a steady diet of it. But that's not enough. One thing could never be enough."

Paul gave him a gentle poke in the shoulder with his forefinger. "Shady stock deals and muscling the planning committee and finding loopholes in municipal codes are the meat and potatoes of who you are. A dirty game. One that you rigged."

Paul got a funny smile on his face as he warmed to his argument. "And then there are the women, of course. Lots of stylish escorts who'll do whatever you want for a stack of green."

The old man rounded the corner, picking up speed as he went, but Paul was right behind him.

"And you have a wife too. Someone to stand beside you and look elegant."

Paul thought he heard Jacob swear. He got in front of Jacob and put his hands on the walker, bringing the old man to a full stop. "But that's still not enough. The booze. When you can't cheat and hustle and control the world, you get it straight out of the bottle."

The old man tried to move past him, but he was trapped.

"You can lose it all, your business, your health, your office with all the bullshit awards, your mobility — and let's be honest about it, Jacob, you lost your edge — but the bottle, it's always right there, razor sharp and ready to make you feel immortal any time you want." Paul's voice slowed and lowered half an octave. "But you only get to *feel* it. To imagine it. You never get to be it."

Jacob screwed up his face. "Do you smell a faint stink from the sewers?"

Paul looked at him fondly as he began to walk backwards. "My question to you is this, Jacob. Was there ever a real you? Did the cheating and pretending start so early that you never knew anything else?"

Jacob rounded on him. "I like this game. Making up lies and serving them up hot off the grill. Let's play some more."

"Nope, here's your room. Ji-woo will be back shortly. You can tell her how you made all of us look stupid."

Jacob was furious. "You said you were sending me home."

"I have. You're here."

***

Paul opened the door to find the lunchroom silent and the men subdued. Fred was standing with his arms crossed by the patio door. Paul wondered what he had interrupted. Larry's anguish was still hanging in the air. The expressions were troubled. This was not the group he'd left. Whatever had transpired had also transformed. *What have you been talking about? I'm not going to ask.* He looked at his watch. The first hour was almost gone.

"So, how did you guys manage without me?"

Seymour smiled at him. "I chaired. It was a great success."

"Did everyone get a chance to speak?"

"No, still half a room to go."

Paul did the math in his head. Something had happened that the guys wanted to keep to themselves. "All right. Go get a smoke. I'll see you back here in fifteen minutes."

***

The guys formed a semicircle on the smoke deck. They were shivering, but it was too much trouble to run up two flights of stairs to get their coats. Nicotine and cold air were what they wanted. Powerful external agents to numb their sense of unease.

The pecking order had changed. Fred was the new tribal chief, replacing the recently departed Sean Miller, who was sleeping on an air mattress at Channing Hart's apartment until the end of the month. Jacob had replaced and, frankly, outdone Czombo as evil outcast, while Charles Dorn had taken up new duties as the head of her majesty's loyal opposition. That left the rest of them jockeying for cabinet posts.

Larry had spoken his truth in the presence of the empty chair, but now what? Looking people straight in the eye and coming clean was supposed to change everything. That was the big promise. What everyone had been telling him since he got here. For a moment in the middle of it, he had been free. But cooling passions were eroding that certainty.

This was Czombo and the urine fiasco all over again. A moment of profound regret gave way to a vague feeling of fear. What had he been thinking? *Had to play the hero again.* Why did he think that telling them about piss of all things was going to change anything?

Daniel thrust his pack of cigarettes under Larry's crooked nose. "I'm impressed."

Larry shook his head. "Am I going to get burned for what I said?"

"That's fifty-fifty. No one who heard what you said would dare." He put his hand on his friend's shoulder. "What you said in there mattered."

"It did?"

Daniel extracted a cigarette. "Got a light?"

Larry produced his beautiful gold-plated Dunhill. It sparked a perfect tear-shaped flame.

Daniel took a puff before continuing. "No one in this world is going to look after us except us. What you said in there … if we don't tell the truth … we're done…"

"You haven't told me the truth yet."

"I know…"

"When?"

"I need you too much right now to take that chance."

Daniel blew a plume of smoke skyward. The cold, dry air made short work of it. The hint of trouble in Larry's eyes got his lips moving again.

"Half the guys in that room think that some kind of shit show caused their addiction. They figure if they can fix that, the addiction will stop. That's the crazy hope. That we can fix ourselves and get control again."

Larry gave him a quizzical look but didn't interrupt. Daniel was shouldering his way through a crowd, trying to get somewhere he didn't want to go.

"I spoke the truth — the whole truth — once… Most of the time, I say as little as I can get away with. My guidance counsellor went nuts when I told her. Secrets are dangerous. When you tell, you lose control. I was months convincing them that I didn't mean what I said. They didn't believe me."

Larry did the math. "Is that why you use?"

"I made my first connection in the group they put me in. At least then I knew what I was, what I wanted."

"What happens when you stop the drugs?"

"This…" he said, pointing at the circle.

Larry was struggling to understand, but most of his focus remained on his own remorse. "This…"

Daniel took a frantic pull from his cigarette. The coal burned bright red as he turned his attention back to Larry. "Wanting is what gets me going. I feel bad about myself. What I … when I…" He sighed and looked over at Fred, who was standing outside the circle, smoking alone. The pair watched the older man move past them as he headed back toward the warmth of the lunchroom. Daniel's eyes followed him the whole distance. His voice rose in anger. "My old man tells the same stories over and over. He thinks he's helping by telling me the way things used to be. He and his buddies would go looking for a summer job by knocking on doors. He could pay for college doing that." He snorted. "I'm a barista working twenty-two hours a week. I can't even afford a one-bedroom."

He threw his cigarette butt into a nearly full coffee can. "I'm stuck in my parents' basement. No privacy. I'll be stuck there forever. Then I'll be the nurse. I'll get to make stupid rules for them." He gave the smouldering can a kick to put himself upwind. "Seymour's right. We all end up looking like

Hutton. I want to live before that happens — smoking a joint and doing lines and drinking." He took a breath and ran the middle three fingers of both hands against his brow like a washcloth.

Larry took up the thought. "Your parents never charge you enough. You have enough money to get high, but you can't stay high. There's always big talk about next year and how everything is going to be different."

They made their way back toward the lunchroom. "I can't get from where I am to where I want to be," Daniel said. "What they're saying in here is as useless as the stories my old man tells. Don't they know that what used to work doesn't matter anymore?"

He stopped just short of the patio door. *Why can't someone show me how to be me.*

***

Charles Dorn kicked off the second half of the meeting. He had to raise his voice to overcome the restless shuffling of feet and chairs. The meeting felt awkward with Paul back in the room. The frantic truth-blurting of the previous hour was finished. It set Chuck to wondering, *What is the connection between the empty chair, the counsellor, and the truth?* Chucky had seen a lot of different treatment centres, all with competing beliefs and totems.

Chuck had arrived from the Eddington with mismatched socks and donated clothes ten years out of style. A volunteer had cut his pants down to size but neglected to remove half of the now unnecessary belt loops. They gave him a comical appearance. In spite of that, he felt himself the senior spokesman in this group.

"I want to talk about hope. Something good is about to happen. I want the addicted part of my life over. Some days I don't even care how it happens." He looked over at Fred, but the big man was looking out the window. "I've spent everything I ever had on dope. I stole from people I love. I boosted big box stores. I took chances at the border that no sane man would — and for what? To feel horrible and make my parents cry."

Chuck caught the first scent of a roast from the oven. His mouth watered as he remembered his mother's kitchen and coming in cold and hungry from the rink.

"I've been back and forth between the street and treatment forever. Christ, I could teach this stuff." He got to his feet but stayed near his chair. With Paul in the room in seemed presumptuous to occupy the empty seat.

"When you look at me, what do you see?" He extended his arms and did a slow twirl. "Crackhead. Thin as a rail."

That got a laugh. He pulled back his bottom lip with his thumb and index finger. "My bottom teeth are all gone from the pipe. The heat melted all the enamel right off 'em." He pulled his T-shirt away from his shoulder. "I have ink on my neck I don't remember getting."

One of the new guys laughed and rolled up his sleeve. "I got a few of those too."

Chuck felt the room warming to him. "Weird shit happens to me all the time now. I feel like a kid being dragged along by an older brother. When I'm wasted on a run, I see myself standing there. I watch what I'm doing." The natural pause lengthened into a noticeable silence. "I want the drugs so bad. So bad. I want that feeling. I'm not alive without it." He wanted to cry but couldn't. The wound was too old to bleed. His voice faded out. "Am I ever gonna feel something again?"

Paul was taken aback. This wasn't the Chuckster who had called him "Mister man doing a woman's job," the one who terrified Arthur Wilberforce Cardel simply by bumming a smoke and then butting it out on the carpet. That version of Chuck — the emblem of cocaine psychosis — was the more familiar twin. The one that Doug had taken pity on and driven to the detox for the umpteenth time. The Eddington staff had worked another miracle.

Torment was written on his strong features. "I taught Sunday school. I have my grade eight piano. I got scouted by the Cleveland Indians when I was in high school. I won a trip to Spain for writing an essay about aeronautics. Do you believe any of that shit looking at me now? I was there when it happened, and I don't believe it."

That got a sad sigh of recognition. Chuck felt encouraged. "I'm not the only one suffering. My parents moved heaven and earth to make a life. They don't talk to me. I see them sitting in the court or talking to a doctor in the hallway. They loved me, but none of that mattered."

A few heads went down.

"What makes me do what I do? Everyone has a different answer. I go one place and they tell me I can drink and smoke pot as long as I stay off the crack." He smiled like a vaudevillian and threw up his hands. "Good luck with that. I'll go right home now and write that on the fridge."

The men laughed.

"Another place tells me I have letters dancing around my head — PTSD, ADHD, OCD. But what does any of that shit mean when you've been on the phone with your dealer and help is on the way?"

That crossed a line. That feeling was sacred, a precious soap bubble that could float you back over the wall and out of hell.

"Don't get me wrong. When the doctors gave me contradictory answers, I was delighted. I didn't want there to be an answer. I wanted this to be fatal. A mind-blowing rush followed by an aneurism. Is that too much to ask the universe for? Is that too hard a deal to put together? To finally find a way to separate the pleasure from the pain?"

Chuck dropped out of warp and took in his surroundings. "Paul's looking at me. That means I better come to the point. I want to talk about hope. I've found some. When my dealer shows up, I'm filled with a kind of overwhelming excitement. It feels as if everything is going to be all right. But that's not hope. Hope can't be the wrong thing to do. Hope is looking over at that empty chair. When I'm high, sometimes I have out of body experiences. It scared me the first time it happened. I thought I died."

Even Paul had to laugh at that. Chuck felt the velvet touch of inspiration.

"Most of what you hear about in detoxes is bullshit. Harm reduction — that's the worst fraud ever. Those bright, shiny faces who tell you about it look so professional — they're frauds and don't even know it. Took me ten years to see through them. They bill insurance companies a hundred and fifty dollars an hour. Think about that. Why do they need to charge that much? To give you, the consumer, some confidence in the crap they're peddling. They're not addicts. They read about shit in a textbook, and they get everything wrong."

The guys were all looking at Paul, trying to understand why he wasn't interrupting and wondering if he was allowing Chuck to talk this way because he was nuts.

"Don't believe me? Try this on for size. Cocaine, morphine, and amphetamines are illegal. Know why? Because they're as addictive as hell. But what do they tell us when we get our feet tangled up in the barbed wire? They tell us that our choices matter."

Larry gave Daniel a dig in the ribs that said this was going to be good. But his friend's attention was elsewhere.

"Think of the three best people in the twentieth century." He started to wave his arms in a way that said, *but don't take all day.* "I'd go with Gandhi, Mother Teresa, and Einstein. Get those three going on speed, oxy, or coke and look out. Gandhi would jack the tires right off your Cadillac while you attended your daughter's christening at St. Paul's. Einstein would have the radio and airbag out of your ride lickety-split. And Mother Teresa, why she'd have the girls down at the convent chop what was left up into parts before the sun went down."

The room roared with approval. A wave of satisfaction transported Chuck to a nobler space, even if he did stay in character.

"All of 'em would do the same shit we do. What they did before wouldn't matter once they got going on the downhill. The talent they used to make the world a better place would simply find a new direction. That's what happened to me. I used to be one of them." The tear he swallowed this time was about gratitude, not sorrow.

"That psychobabble stuff doesn't work. They're trying to make the water run uphill. I need the truth and I need it straight up." He looked directly at Paul. "And I need someone to slap me around and make me do what I need to do. I'm hoping not forever. But for as long as it takes."

Another taboo was held up to the light: that sobriety was simply the natural resting point between prior and future excess. Anyone can stay sober in treatment — the problem is that eventually everyone has to leave.

"When I look around the meetings, I see lots of sober faces. They tell me this works. That's the basis of my hope. I'm trusting the old timers to tell me the truth. I'm waiting for God to show up the way my dealer used to." He sat down for a second before adding. "That sounds nuts, but it's not."

Paul had the good sense not to say a word. He looked around the room at the pondering faces. The new guys didn't understand any of what Chuck had said, even though they enjoyed it, but the more experienced guys did. A couple of them were giving Charles a thumbs up.

Paul sat in wonder. *That man contains multitudes.*

Lou was up next. He'd been mulling over his options while Chuck spoke. He smiled at Croc, who was once again sitting quietly on his lap, enjoying his friend's discomfort. *Here's an odd spot for a clairvoyant to find himself, answering the question, "When did you know you had to be here?"*

Larry wondered why Lou always wore a sports coat. *Does he think he's a counsellor?*

Daniel was fascinated with Croc. *Why can't I do that? Get away with being outrageous.*

Seymour was sketching the pair in his head. *I'm going to make Croc twice as big as Lou and have Lou sit on his lap.*

Croc poked him with his tail. Lou looked over at the empty chair and saw a thin ghost with grey hair. The apparition was agitated: he sat down for a few seconds and then leapt once again to his feet, running the length of the room before vaulting onto the side table and vanishing into a dust vortex. The third corner piece. Who was he and how would he fit in?

How can they not know that something big is happening all around them? This place is a thunderstorm building up over water. The rain clouds are rising faster than birds riding the thermals. Paul is giving me the heads-up. It's my turn. I have to say something.

He put Croc back in his pocket to keep him out of trouble.

These guys remind me of a variegated leaf — all different shades and shapes and textures on a single leaf. No two stories exactly the same, and sometimes they even contradict each other. Not that that matters. They're connected. No single story is as important on its own as when they're heard together — that changes the meaning of all of them. That's what I want to tell them.

Lou looked around the room. "I think we can all agree that I'm the oddest duck floating around in this pond. But I've noticed, after the initial shock of ending up here, most people lighten up and start to enjoy themselves. I see guys who are lonely starting to make friends. I see angry guys thinking about what they should do before they explode. I see guys who are afraid starting to take chances. This place is full of energy."

He checked the faces around him for a reaction. They were listening.

"I'm a poor excuse for an alcoholic. My credentials aren't nearly as impressive as yours." That earned him a laugh.

"But I do know about hiding who I really am and being afraid of what the world thinks of me. That's the bond I feel. I know about keeping two sets of books. I understand that loneliness."

Larry gave him a funny look — his attempt to say nothing was speaking volumes. But what were the other guys making of what he was trying very hard not to say? Lou had a bad moment as he weighed his options. They needed something real. Something about addiction. Nobody else had chickened out.

He wanted to go deeper still. He wanted to tell them everything. But he knew — deep down inside he knew, and he'd always known — what he saw they were blind to, what he heard was white noise to their ears, and what he'd come to understand about heaven and earth was his privilege.

The words were out of his mouth before he could weigh them. "The future isn't fixed. There is nothing inevitable about our lives. Seasons come and go, mountains get worn down by wind and rain. They're things and things get changed by other things. They can't change themselves."

There was a respectful silence. A few of the men nodded as if they'd glimpsed some deeper meaning. Most figured he'd chickened out and politely looked away. The energy in the room dropped to zero. He had succeeded in disappointing them. It was his best option.

Croc squirmed his delight at Lou's discomfort.

Chapter 29

By chance, Kaiser stopped into the office a few minutes before dinner was served. The subway had lost power and shuttle buses had been summoned but had not yet arrived. Paul, feeling awkward, invited him to stay.

The roast beef was lean and pink and flowing with juice. The cook slipped an extra piece onto Kaiser's plate, even though it was against the rules. He was losing weight, and she was worried about him. After the feast, the house was full of lazy yawns and happy, digesting creatures.

After dinner, Kaiser set to work on Mike's computer. The piggy bank at home couldn't pay for the internet and it was too embarrassing to use the office computer when everyone else was around. He had a stack of emails to catch up on. His plan was to stick around until it was time for the guys to head out to their meeting. He was the speaker that night. He didn't tell anyone. He wanted it to be a surprise.

He didn't look up when Seymour pushed the office door open without knocking and flung himself into the chair opposite Paul, who was busy transcribing his notes into the daybook.

Seymour had a sad and serious look, one that was out of place on his youthful face.

Paul looked up at him and smiled, relieved to be back on speaking terms. "I thought you hated me."

Seymour looked him in the eye before relenting. "I do."

"Tell my boss — he sees that as a plus."

Seymour didn't want to chit-chat. He got right to the point. "You're right about the drinking. When I reach for it, I'm angry at the world and I think it will solve everything. Then, before I know it, I'm throwing my paintings into the fire."

Paul tread cautiously. "Is that why you hate me? For saying that?"

Seymour put his head down. "I had the million-dollar lottery ticket, and I tore it up."

"You could buy another one. There's a draw every week."

"No, it's once in a lifetime."

"We'll go halfsies."

Seymour leaned back in his chair, trying to find some comfort. "I'm too beat up to try again. The guy who painted those pictures died in the fire."

"I need to blur a line here from professional to personal. I want to photograph your lake."

"Why?"

"As a photographer, I'm dumbstruck with what you did in your paintings. I need to get up there myself and have a look at that shoreline through a lens."

"Not happening."

"How do you mean?"

"Mom would have a fit."

"Over photographs?"

"Over anything. You wouldn't know it the first time you met her. She's very good at hiding what's going on with her, but she has issues. She's terrified of the world."

"She seems reasonable."

"Well, she's a control freak, and when things are the way she wants them to be, it all looks pretty good on the outside. But there are things that give her away. When I was a kid, going to the cottage was sacred. We'd all pile into the Volvo and off we'd go. Every weekend was a perfect duplicate of the one before: same food, same route, suitcases always packed exactly the same way. The only thing that changed from week to week were the manuscripts."

"Manuscripts?"

"Mom is batshit crazy about a lot of stuff, but she's deadly with young authors. She can pick a good one out of the herd. But for her to do her stuff, she needs everything to be just so. If things aren't the way she wants them, she gets distracted.

"When we got to the cottage, we would give her some peace and quiet. Dad would go down to the boathouse and listen to his records. Hell, he could stay there the whole weekend if you slid sandwiches under the door. I would go to my studio and paint. Mom sat on the front porch in her special chair and read."

They wanted to be alone, but what about you?

"When she reads a book, she reads it from cover to cover. If someone interrupts her, she has to start all over again, right from the beginning. That's why the phones are turned off. There can't be any running in and out of the cabin for water or to use the washroom. Dad and I get it. We give her space. When she's done, she gets all otherworldly and cooks and bakes for the rest of the day."

"Where is this place?"

"It's on a point of land on Georgian Bay — a piece so tiny it doesn't even have a name. We're surrounded on three sides by water and half a mile from our nearest neighbour."

"Sounds ideal."

"It is, for Mom. She grew up there and had to take out three mortgages to pay off her sisters. It's her favourite place on earth, and she says it's where she does her best work. All the books she loves and all the manuscripts she's ever published are all there for her. When I was a kid, sometimes I would tease her by moving a couple of books around or pulling them a quarter inch out of the bookcase. At first she wouldn't notice, but then she'd get this frantic look in her eye, and the next thing you know, she'd pounce on the imperfection."

Paul had to ask, "What would happen if the place burned down?"

"Dad and I carry cyanide capsules."

"I want to take photographs of the places you painted, and next weekend I'm going to stand over you and make you paint them again."

"It's a waste of time. I told you. I've lost my talent."

"No, worst-case scenario you've lost your confidence. It happens all the time with drunks. You can't do anything creative when you're potted. Even if you do manage to produce something, it's junk. It's how people ruin their reputations. You've hypnotized yourself. Because you can't paint drunk or hungover, you've convinced yourself that you're through."

Kaiser looked up from the computer and shook his head. *So that's how novels get published. No wonder pointy head is getting nowhere.*

Chapter 30

The young girl, still dressed for the gym and sitting on the edge of the bench, waited for Peter to wake. He rubbed his eyes vigorously, thinking the hard grains tormenting his vision were the work of the sandman.

"Did I sleep?" Peter sat up and gave himself a shake.

The girl's hand touched his forearm gently. "You're moist."

"That can't be. Ghosts are as dry as gunpowder."

"Not supposed to sleep either." She ran her forefinger over the back of his wrist. "How do you explain this?"

Peter got to his feet and examined himself in wonder. His arm was covered with thin patches of frost that melted when he touched them, leaving tiny beads of water.

The girl watched as his terror sought safe harbour in make believe. Her face remained serious and her focus unwavering as the stout ghost's eyes darted from side to side, from conjecture to possibly landing on futility and despair. There was no explanation. His body sagged as the fight went out of him.

"What's happening to me?"

A look of satisfaction crossed her face. She stood up and ran her fingers along the seal that separated the lid from the body of the cryotank.

"The chamber is leaking. It's letting in moist air that freezes when it touches your head. It's going to be much worse now that you're on the top row."

"But I'm not in the chamber — I'm here!"

"You're in both places, Peter. This is a sympathetic reaction. Bodies are funny things."

"*This can't be!*"

"*Well, if it's any consolation, this is the first time it has happened.*"

He threw his arms in the air. "*You're making me crazy. You sound as if you understand this!*"

The young girl flickered for a second the way a fluorescent tube does when it's warming up. "*How many ghosts do you think there are in the world at this very moment, watching their heads frost up in a cryogenic vault?*"

Dark fury returned to his brow. "*Naff. How could I possibly know that?*"

"*You're it — the whole population.*"

Peter was horrified. "*There are hundreds of us in there.*"

"*They've all moved on.*" She watched his head fall to his chest. "*Why haven't you?*"

He turned, expecting to see the menacing adolescent giant but finding only a child colouring in a book. The five-year-old in him exploded, unable to contain his disappointment. "*You promised to fix this.*"

The little girl didn't look up from her page, but she did select a different crayon before continuing. "*I can, but you have to want me to, and before I can do that, I need to know that you understand what you're asking me to do.*"

Peter knocked the book off her lap and onto the floor, towering over her in his rage. "*You're a liar. I hate you.*"

She calmly retrieved her book and took up her pencil once again. They sat in silence. She drew until his head lowered a second time, listening to his snorts give way to deep regular breaths before turning to look at him.

"*What is it going to take to make you change your mind?*" she asked.

"*I don't want to talk about that.*"

"*That's not true. I can feel what's in your heart.*"

"*No, you can't. No one can!*"

She selected another colour before resuming her drawing. "*Terri did. At least she could once. Long ago. You're staying for Terri, aren't you? It's always been Terri.*" She turned in her seat and held up her drawing for him to see.

It was of a young girl at the river's edge holding up a crayfish with a broad smile on her face.

"*Stay away from me.*"

Chapter 31

Sunday afternoon rolled into Monday morning without anyone leaving on a gurney. Jacob Hutton tugged on the blankets, desperate to find a more comfortable position. He felt a shiver run down his spine that threatened to send his neck into another spasm. He ached to see the amber glow of whisky on the bedside table but found only tap water that had been sitting long enough for gas bubbles to attach themselves to the inside of the glass. *Is that worthless idiot never going to get the heat going? I'm freezing.*

He lifted his head warily and looked around. No art on the wall, no flowers in a vase, no fruit baskets from flunkies, and, of course, an absent self-serving caregiver. *This place has all the charm of a storage shed.*

He gave way to despair. *I don't belong here.*

He tried to sit up fully and found that he'd been tucked tightly into the sheets, like an infant. His fury mounted and he kicked at the corners until his legs burned.

He lay back on his pillow and groaned and swore at the same time, producing a sound not unlike that of a floorboard giving way to a pry bar. *I have to sit up. My guts hurt. It's the food they serve here. Oh shit, that hurts!* He banged his fists on the mattress, but it brought him no relief.

Of course, the minimum-wage hag is off somewhere. Probably scaring up a Canadian husband. Fat lot she cares. Her and her goddam Buddha smile. If I wanted ibuprofen, I'd send a boy out to pick up a bottle. I need real painkillers, not laxatives.

A baser urge asserted itself. He had to piss. He looked over at the wall where there was a call chain. It was the last vestige of the nursing home that had occupied this space prior to Punanai. But it no longer worked. *Too much trouble to get off your ass and help someone. Lousy bastards. They left that there to annoy me. I can tug on it until I piss the bed. Shit, I gotta go.*

He sat up more cautiously. *No wonder I'm cold — I'm covered in sweat.* He swung his pale, swollen feet down to the floor. His legs were red and angry. A cramp was gathering strength in his calf. Hopping around on one foot with a full bladder wasn't going to fly. He looked around for something to help him lever his bulk out of the bed. The dresser offered him half a hope.

He rocked himself on the edge of the bed, the mattress groaning beneath him. When he felt some momentum, he tried to lurch to his feet but found, to his horror, that he couldn't achieve the perpendicular. He threw out his arms as he lost his balance and sat back down hard on the bed. A hot squirt of urine was all he had to show for his trouble. "Shit!" His war cry worked. Rage propelled him into a standing position. He wobbled uncertainly on his feet for several seconds until he found his balance and started to shuffle stiffly toward the bathroom. His feet refused to flatten on the floor.

The first building he ever owned had these same off-white sinks. Broken pieces of them could still be found washing up on the Leslie Street Spit. They were all cast in the depression, for Christ's sake. Still, it was a solid and reliable chunk of porcelain, and he knew he was going to be able to lower himself onto the john if he hung on to it. His boxers were missing. In their place was a diaper. He tore it off with disgust and flung it into the corner.

"Who the hell put that on me?"

He soon felt a blessed relief. He hefted his bulk more easily this time and regained his feet. He turned and examined the bowl. The sharp odour of the B vitamins they forced him to swallow made him gag. It smelled the same in the toilet bowl as it did in the bottle.

He flushed and turned his attention to washing his hands. He still had a hospital band on his wrist. He tore at it with his teeth but couldn't get it off. *Leave it on then. I'll go back. At least I'll have television in my room.* He put both hands on the sturdy wash basin and attempted a hurdler's stretch. His legs were weak, and they burned with the effort.

How do they expect me to get the condo deal done? Idiots! Those ingrates on the board are in for a firestorm. They'll pay for putting me in here again!

He looked up and caught sight of himself in the mirror. His salt-and-pepper hair was thinning and looked oily and unkempt. His once handsome face was red, angry, and swollen. His eyes had a veined, tortured look. They showed yellow. He pulled the loose flesh away from the eye socket to reveal red, inflamed tissue.

"Look at what they've done to me with all their meddling."

He heard a faint knock at the door and turned to see who was intruding. Reg was standing in the doorway, leaning on his two canes.

Oh crap, the cripple. "What do you want?"

"I came to see how you're doing." Reg looked uncomfortable. He took off his suit coat and hung it on the doorknob. "It's hot in here, how do you stand it?"

"What are you talking about? I'm freezing."

Reg limped over to where Jacob was towelling himself and touched his pyjamas. "These are soaked. Do you have another pair?"

"Send for my nurse. Where is she? That lazy woman is never around when I need her."

Reg took a step back from Jacob and steadied himself on his canes. "She's a person, Mr. Hutton. She has a name. Ji-woo has gone out of her way to make you comfortable. You should be thanking her. She volunteered to go to the pharmacy to pick up your new meds."

"A proper painkiller, I hope."

"No, not with your liver. Another diuretic."

"I won't take them — they make me pee the bed."

"Well, while she's gone, I'm your nanny. What say we get to know each other better?"

Jacob did a slow and magnificent turn that left the small of his back leaning on the sink. "What makes you think I have any interest in getting to know you?"

Reg smiled. "Does keeping this preachy and hostile suit your mood? We can pretend to be on Larry King."

"Do you realize how much it's costing me to be here every day?"

Reg made a face that said, *Really?* "Are you squawking about the per diem?"

"No, you piker." A look of merriment stole across his face. "I'm going to buy this building right out from underneath your feet. That will be my revenge on all you halfwits."

Reg looked into the red, swollen face of his adversary and felt his instinctive revulsion and anger give way to something better. He softened his voice.

"Mr. Hutton, let's take a step back from anger here. We're going to try and help you with your drinking, but before that happens, we need to get you physically stronger."

"I'm not a drunk. I don't belong with those pathetic whiners downstairs." He felt exposed standing in the bathroom with wet pyjamas that smelled of urine. Not knowing what else to do, he pushed himself away from the sink and traversed the twenty steps from the washroom to his bed with flat-footed care. His attempt to land gracefully on the edge of the bed failed. Reg reached out to steady him.

"Get off…"

Reg steadied him anyway. "Do you know why you're here?"

"Someone's idea of revenge."

"It's your wife's doing."

"I might have known."

"When your assistant called about you, we told him we wouldn't take you back for all the money in the world."

That pleased the old man.

"The only reason you're here is because your wife soaked the manager's shirt with her tears. She asked us to take you back as an act of charity."

The way that Reg punched the word *charity* got Jacob's back up. "If I'm sick, I should be in a hospital, not some faith healer's tent. I swear sometimes that Filipino woman is going to do some of that slight-of-hand healing I saw on television. Palm a hunk of bacon and pretend it's a demon that she's pulled out of my guts. Does that kind of show come with the room, or is it extra?"

Reg kept his voice level. "Your wife thinks you're dying."

A look of disgust amplified his response. "She thinks she looks good in a pencil skirt. She doesn't. Her legs are skinny and her ass is too fat."

Reg's voice stayed in the strike zone. "I think you're dying too, Jacob. That's what I came up here to talk to you about."

Jacob considered trying to dress himself as further proof that he was still his own man. But he knew he couldn't manage it just this moment. He lay back down on the bed and struck a thoughtful pose.

"Well, I'm glad all you pea brains are voting on this. Let me tell you something, boy. I'm in the middle of the biggest condo project anyone in this country ever put together. My deal is going to be the centre of Toronto for the next two hundred years. It's going to be my monument, and it's going to have my name on it."

Reg hit the mark again. "Your name…"

"That's right. All the biggies in the business have come to kowtow and try and get their mitts on this one, but no dice — it's all mine."

Reg took a seat on Ji-woo's chair. "Is that why the lot has been standing empty on the corner for five years? Your wife says you're drunk all the time. You couldn't even manage to get a permit to pave it and turn it into a parking lot."

Jacob's face turned sick with rage. "Where's my nurse? I need to get out of here." The old man started to thrash around, trying once again to regain his feet. But with Reg there he thought better of it. A failed lift off or a fall would be disastrous.

"As I told you, Mr. Hutton, she popped out to get you some medication and some more Pampers."

Charity bruised, but *Pampers* cut his flesh. "How dare you!"

Reg was delighted to see his bolt find its mark. "How dare I what?"

"I don't need Pampers."

"You do. You're pissing our bed."

"It's those damn pills. I won't take them."

"If you don't, you'll be right back in the hospital. You're full of fluid because of all your drinking."

"Do I look like a drinker to you?"

"What does a drinker look like?"

"You, and all the other mutts around here!"

Reg smiled and pointed his cane at his adversary. "I guess you don't breathe the same air as the rest of us."

Jacob drew in a breath and sat up straight in the bed, assuming a heroic aspect. "I make things happen."

"Then why don't you make yourself well?"

Jacob held his two hands in front of his face and then, frowning, dropped them in a dismissive gesture. "I'm tired of talking to you."

Reg brightened. "Then why don't you get up and walk out of the room? Here, use my canes. Call a cab or have someone from the office come by and take you to the club. Order a couple of drinks and put together a deal that's going to make you millions."

Jacob's eyes narrowed. "Who the hell do you think you are, talking to me that way?"

"I'm the only guy still talking to you, Jacob, and they have to pay me to do it."

"That Kaiser fellow told me you worked your way up from teaching the bears to dance. I should offer you a job in my new building commensurate with your skills. Do you think you could run a floor polisher, boy? I mean with your gammy legs and all?"

Reg leaned forward in his chair and rested his chin on his cane. He couldn't have looked more certain of himself if he'd been wearing a top hat and white gloves. "Jacob, I can smell death clinging to you. Are you going to try and do something about this or continue to pretend?"

"You have a lovely way with people. Did you ever consider parish work?"

"Nice doesn't work with you, Jacob. You're an asshole."

"You can't talk to me that way."

"The booze has addled your brain. You're so far gone you can't even remember what you said yesterday."

"Windbag!"

Reg smiled at him a little sadly. "Nothing you say is going to stop the disease from eating you alive from the inside out. You might as well have cancer and spend your days pretending you're curing it with fruit juice."

Jacob was out of threats and too tired to argue. He dismissed Reg with a wave of his hand and turned his back on him. To his great relief, he heard the counsellor's canes contacting the floor.

I'm going to put a pink slip in that moron's pay envelope if it is the last thing I ever do.

Chapter 32

Badly shaken, Peter started his search for John. He wasn't in any of his usual haunts. It took most of the afternoon for the fat ghost to methodically work his way down the street to Punanai. He abhorred the place, though he couldn't think why. But he knew that John used it as a rehearsal space. An inkling directed him to the second floor. He felt himself quicken as if he had the wind at his back. Sure enough, there was John, an impresario standing with his arms folded, staring into one of the rooms from the hallway.

Peter vented his anger. "I've wasted the day looking for you."

John held out his arms with his palms up, obviously delighted with himself and confused by Peter's combative tone.

"No doubt to congratulate me for this prodigious piece of stagecraft."

"What are you talking about?"

"Come and see for yourself. I got Walter sorted out, and now he has a whole room full of poltergeists to keep him company. Don't ask me how they got here, because I don't know, but every time I turn around there's another one. Can't you feel the energy all around us?"

Peter shook his head. He felt invigorated but he had no time to talk about anything inconsequential. Terri was in danger.

"Allow me to demonstrate," cried John, full of himself and enjoying the moment. He ran down the hall away from Lou's room and then slid on his heels. As his momentum spent itself, his slide slowed. But then, as if he were made of metal fillings caught in a powerful magnetic field, he did a slow U-turn and began to slide back down the hall toward Lou's room, picking up

speed as he went. He playfully tackled Peter to come to a stop and the two ghosts fell in a heap.

John rolled on his back, laughing with delight.

"Oh, Peter," he said, as he helped his startled friend to his feet. "Can't you see? The light is here. We've forced its hand."

Peter sputtered in the throes of despair. "I spoke with it. The light is a demon. It's after Terri."

John had a horrible moment. He looked at his one confidant and sighed. How could Peter not see what was right in front of him. You're going to end up in Lou's room if you don't smarten up. *He shook the image off, it was too terrible to contemplate.*

"Hah! You can't talk to a light."

Peter ran his fingers through his hair, trying to master his anger and his tone. "This thing moves around. It takes any form that strikes its fancy. But no matter what form it takes, it smells of cigars."

John grew serious, a look of concern crossed his brow and he spoke in a slow, precise cadence.

"Peter, we have a plan. Remember, we agreed. Put Walter in a room — the process of elimination."

"You're thick enough to make a mother weep."

The word ingrate *was on the tip of John's tongue. He was about to fling it across the room when he took a step back. The venom got loose in spite of his best efforts.*

"Where were you when it was time to stop talking about moving Walter and start the actual hard work? I'll tell you where, you were off mooning over your frozen head."

Peter gave way to the panic that had been steadily eroding his confidence all morning. "You're dancing on fly paper, you idiot. The light is here, and it's hunting us. It knows our names and our secrets and it's seductive, oh so very seductive! It knows what we want and it's ruthless."

"Peter, focus. What are you talking about?"

The fat ghost turned on his heel and fled down the hall, shouting as he went. "Anything that sounds too good to be true is always a lie. Look to your defences." And with that he was gone, leaving John alone in a ruined magical moment.

Chapter 33

Kaiser was still mulling over what to do about Riana. He had this image stuck in his head of the two of them cutting a rug. Their eyes locked in mutual wonder and admiration. But if he wanted to continue that vision, he had to put another quarter in the machine.

He'd seen the logjam of suitors hanging around her at the meetings. And he knew that flowers and invitations to dinner and a show always met with a put down, at least for the guys who didn't drive high-end vehicles. Kaiser reckoned you had to own a Porsche to enter the derby. Uncle Oren's Toyota, with it's impressive display of lights and symbols, closed off that whole realm of possibilities to him. Just as well. He needed the quarters for laundry.

He had given up on romancing Riana to pursue an achievable end when, very much to his surprise, he heard her sultry voice on his answering machine. He smiled. Had she finally put a name to his face? Was the pursuer to become the pursued? The idea of her chasing him was titillating. He landed on a more realistic probability: she wanted something.

Her voice was abrupt and rather clipped, sounding outraged that she had to leave a message, fully expecting that he'd be sitting beside the phone, waiting for her call.

Greg had opined correctly. Riana was putting down roots in his extended family. Kaiser returned her call and left a message on her voice mail, suggesting that they meet for a coffee at an upscale specialty shop across the street from the community centre. It was expensive and thus safe to assume she knew the place intimately, even if she couldn't have told you where the cash register was.

He arranged for the table by the window. The sun was warm on his face as he waited. Riana strode into the restaurant with the authority one would expect of a Hollywood vixen from the golden age. She was no cheap knockoff — she was a knockout. As Kaiser rose to his feet to greet her, he tried to reconcile what he was seeing with what he was feeling.

Not only does she own the restaurant, but the staff and customers as well. If she thinks she can turn my head with this juvenile bravado, she's right. If Greg hadn't told me what she was up to, I'd be stuttering. What am I seeing in those Jessica Rabbit curves — seduction or relapse?

Riana observed him for moment. "So you do own one good suit."

Kaiser smiled broadly and shook his mane of curly blond hair. "For an occasion such as this, nothing but the best."

He helped her take her seat. This was fun. It was reminiscent of nightclub manners in old movies. *Oh, wouldn't it be grand to light up a smoke and order a glass of wine?* Too bad. The world had moved on. No more elegant carcinogens in public places.

"You look wonderful! Is this all for me?"

Her body language was closed. "Don't flatter yourself, I dress this way for work."

Kaiser bit his tongue. He was on a mission. "Well, I'm glad we can finally sit down together and have a chat."

The waiter took their order. When he left, Riana made a point of looking at her expensive wristwatch, which matched both her purse and her smart-looking business suit.

"Are we pressed for time?"

"Always," she said sweetly. "I'm here to talk to you about your ridiculous friend Reg. Does he have Asperger's?"

"Sounds as if you two had quite a conversation!"

"He's infuriating. Don't give me that look, you've heard him at the meetings. Whining about his precious book. No one wants to hear that. I told him to give the damn thing to me. I would as soon throw it in the trash as get it published, but I had to do something — whining grates on my nerves."

"He told me he turned you down."

Her smile lit up the room. "Not a brain in his head."

"But let's get back to you. I didn't know you had a publishing connection. Does your family own a house?"

She looked equal parts perplexed and annoyed. "They own a lot of stuff, what are you talking about?"

Kaiser smiled. "I meant a publishing house."

"Specify, darling. Specificity is the key to clear communication."

He felt a wave of pleasure move through him. *What a woman! She lies about having a publishing connection and then when I ask her about it, she ducks the question and tells me it's my fault because I haven't specified. Is it any wonder I'm in lust?*

She noticed his look of admiration and chose that moment to nudge the conversation back in the desired direction. "You strike me as being too bright to work at Punanai. What keeps you there? Does being allowed to power trip make up for the small paycheque?"

The waiter arrived with the coffee, and they paused their conversation while he poured. Kaiser took the time to bask in the symmetry of her face.

"It's a job, a place to go on Monday mornings." He prepared a path for her. "I get a little bit bored with it sometimes, but the thing that fills me with terror is the thought of losing it and having to find something worse."

Riana looked at him with the smile she reserved for all high-IQ idiots. "Don't you want a better job?"

Fully in character, he responded. "I'm not convinced that such a thing exists anymore."

Her displeasure was becoming palpable. "Why *anymore*?"

"People used to get better jobs as they got older and then retire with a pension. These days, employers want young people with university degrees and massive debts to pay off — you can get them to do anything. But you only get to stay as long as you don't make a fuss or get too wrinkled."

She was enjoying the gentle provocation almost as much as his charm. "I suppose if you can't measure up, you have to say derogatory things about the people who can."

His body language was an invitation to tell secrets. "The rest of us have to work three part-time jobs to make ends meet, and then we have to hope we die before our strength gives out, because we're never going to be able to retire on what we make."

"You need Life Skills."

"It's always something. The last time I had this conversation, it was hot rocks and acupuncture."

"You Punanai guys all read from the same songbook. You know the one, *Stuck on Stupid*. Kaiser, there are a million ways of doing things. Why are you and your pals so afraid to try something new?"

Reg's literary prospects were glowing dimmer by the moment. Kaiser found it impossible to concentrate on anything other than *he* and *she* combining to become *we*. "I might as well be a high school teacher. I get a good salary and lots of vacation time, but the thing is I have to spend my whole life in high school, and every year the kids get younger and stranger. It leaves a bitter taste. Helping people is cool, but the job is routine. I do what I do because the guys in treatment need it."

She produced a smile that changed the intake of Kaiser's breath.

"A girl could go for you if you had a decent paycheque."

He swallowed hard. "The power of love."

She leaned across the table. "Love doesn't mean shit when the rent is due." She patted the back of his hand. "If you can't afford the vacation, don't get on the plane. It's all well and good to help the other guy out from time to time, but you've wasted the best earning years of your life working for a not-for-profit. Now you're bored and restless and blaming everyone but yourself." She tried a sip from her coffee, but it was still too hot. "Why did you choose that life? Have you got a criminal record?"

A quizzical smile crossed his lips. "Is this the Life Skills talk? Are you going to put some fire in my belly. Help me screw up my courage and go get what I really want?" His look was pure Valentino minus the Vaseline.

Riana leaned back in her chair with a dexterity that suggested she had cat genes.

"That's not half of what I could teach you," she said seductively. "But it would be a start, and better than what you have going for you now. You're a bottom feeder. Full of resentment toward the people who do the real work. You've become toxic. Has anyone ever turned the Punanai tables on you and given it to you straight?"

"Yeah, the addicts in treatment tell me why I'm a loser about once a week."

"Well sit back and let Mamma tell you the real story."

Kaiser picked up his coffee, which was perfect and well worth the five dollars, and took a long satisfying sniff followed by a more fulfilling sip. *Why do I want to seize her by the collar, wipe that red lipstick from her lips with my thumb, and kiss her like I've never kissed anyone before? Did she get all dressed up just to come down here and spin my head? Is her heart racing as fast as mine?*

"Sorry, not interested."

Her smile trumped his denial. "In what? Success, being real, giving up the bedbugs and the droopy suits? What is it that you're not interested in, cowboy?"

Kaiser felt himself blush and decided not to waste it. He managed to look a little uncomfortable — burdened somehow. "If I tell you the truth, straight up, the first time, and don't hold anything back, will you answer one question in return?"

Her face lit up.

Kaiser reached across the table and gently laid his hand on top of hers. He made eye contact but then turned away, as if he couldn't bring himself to do it again. Then, after a moment of indecision, he took his hand back, as if he was genuinely afraid of a reproach. "I came here tonight because I need help."

His silence prompted her to respond. "Go on."

"My friend Reg has written a book…"

She released a pulse of air. "Yeah, I know all about this."

Kaiser put his head down as if he was having a hard time reaching into his pocket to get this bet up onto the table. He held out his hand, palm out. "Please don't interrupt, it makes this harder. I'm having trouble finding the words I need."

Riana felt sorry for him. He was all hot air and melted butter after all. She ran up the score by looking at her watch again.

"I want to help him, but I don't know how." He glanced up at her with the look of a little boy asking for something he knew he wasn't going to get. "We were talking about it in the office and then someone, I don't know, maybe it was Reg, said you had a publishing connection." He looked up at her again — a soul in torment. "Like, you know, someone maybe could have a look at the thing and fluff it up a bit. It's not Tolstoy, but if it got published and he made a few bucks, it would make him so happy."

"You want me to turn on the tap and change water into wine?"

"Well, you sure give the impression that's what you do for a living."

"Is that it? The thing I had to pull your toenails out with pliers to hear?"

Kaiser's head went down again. "No, I left the hardest part to the end." A profound silence intrigued her. Had she really hooked this guy?

"Well?"

"I was going to seduce you and then ask you to publish the book. But here's the thing. You don't have a publishing connection, do you?"

Riana's eyes grew wide.

"That's what I thought." He smiled wickedly at her and pointed at the coffees. "Are you going to pick these up?"

"Yes indeed," she said as she emptied the contents of her cup on his head.

Chapter 34

Peter looked at the long and lean adolescent apparition that confronted him — an amalgam of angelic face and impossible stature, smelling not unpleasantly of peppermint gum this time. The universe's final hateful attempt to blot out his dreams. Her eyes were kind but that didn't fool him.

"Why, Terri? Why only her, why not another?" she asked him.

Peter lowered his massive head. Silence was his friend. He experienced a moment of peace instead of the rage of wanting and coming away with nothing, that horrible emptiness. He was left with only his heartfelt belief that speaking the truth aloud would destroy any remaining chance of success. One dare not ask. Tell them what you want and they will take it away. That tandem had scored his soul, leaving deep furrows on his face and micro fractures in his teeth while he was alive.

"I want to be with Terri. I always have. When we were kids, she'd show up at my place on a Saturday morning and off we would go down to the creek to look for crayfish. You couldn't eat them, and we never found very many, but it felt as if we were picking nuggets of gold out of that stream. We'd keep them alive in a jar until they started to fight. Then Terri would insist we put them back — and not just anywhere. We had to put them back where they belonged, exactly where we found them."

Peter's eyes were locked on a point far away. He had a child's eyes, despite the massive grey tangle of brow that shielded them, and for the moment they were incapable of either deceit or insight.

"I loved my parents and I guess I even loved my wretched brothers and sisters, but Terri is special."

The girl's voice was one decibel above a whisper. "Did you talk to her about this?"

Peter's brow furrowed as his eyes shifted from the past to the present saying, Back off or die.

"I ... that's not a ... you should really ... young lady, you're being impertinent!"

The little girl placed her fingers on her brow. "You're ashamed of something, something that happened later. I can feel it."

A small circle of illumination, about the size of a silver dollar, attached itself to Peter's boot heel. He didn't notice.

"I fell in love with Terri the first day of school. Our mothers walked us there together. Holy cow, that schoolyard was big and full of kids running around, screaming. I wanted to be a part of that. I don't remember much about the classroom, only that first recess. Jeff Arnold. I don't know why they let that little pyro into the school. He spent recess trying to trip me, calling out to the other kids that I was a crybaby. Then I heard Terri's voice. 'Jeff Arnold, you're telling wicked lies! Peter is my friend.'

"Arnold tried to think of something clever to say, but that was never going to happen. He said she had smelly underpants while he held his nose. There's no comparable insult in the adult world. All the children who heard those words froze. It was in that moment that I found my courage. I walked the five paces and planted a beauty right on Arnold's bugle. As he fell over backwards, I turned toward the other boys who had joined in the fun. I grabbed the biggest one and gave him a good shake and then watched him turtle, turn tail, and run. The king was dead. Long live the king."

Peter looked up from his reverie. "That was the outside of things. Inside it was only Terri and me. When she smiled at me, the world changed."

The little girl's voice was suddenly indistinguishable from his own thoughts. "So why didn't you tell her?"

"I did as a child, but I ... missed my chance as an adult."

"Peter, you can't ever be with her, or anyone else, carrying on this way."

The anger was back. "You said you could fix this."

"I can. I'm here because a lot of people have been praying for you."

"I want to talk to Terri."

"Who do you think sent me?"

A slap in the face couldn't convey the anger and shock released by that last remark.

"Wait. That can't be. She's not with you! She's with me ... in ... in the..."

"Peter, find your courage."

He looked at her in wonder as she got to her feet and took his hand in hers.

"I am the angel of death. Look, you're standing in the pool of light."

Peter's mouth opened wide with horror. A klieg light was illuminating his feet.

The little girl shook her head and smiled. "Go ahead, step out of the light."

He did as she asked and immediately felt old and weak. The light blinked out.

"Think about what I said. Let go of whatever is holding you here. Do whatever you need to get yourself free. I'll bring Terri along with me tomorrow."

"Back here?"

"No. In Lou's room."

"Where is that?"

The little girl smiled wickedly. "Ask John."

Chapter 35

While Kaiser soaked in the implications of being doused with hot coffee, Riana took a final bite of her cherry cheesecake and wiped her smiling lips, leaving a vivid red imprint on the linen napkin. When Kaiser reached for a clean napkin to dry himself with, she adroitly snatched it up and put it in her purse before she departed, looking neither left nor right.

Kaiser knew from countless old films that the thing to do was to sit quietly at the table with as much dignity as he could muster until a fawning server came to his aid. But the kids these days don't watch black-and-white movies. As he mopped his brow with what was left of his used napkin, he thought about finishing the cheesecake, which looked rather good and still had to be paid for, but the stares of the onlookers put him off.

When the server finally arrived, Kaiser slid his credit card into the reader and saw word *Declined* appear on the screen. He kept his final stash of cash in his invisible pocket and used a few of the bills to settle the account.

With all eyes still on him, he headed for the restroom, where he rinsed the coffee out of his hair as best he could. It hadn't left a burn. His best suit was a little worse for wear.

He sent a one-handed text to Greg while he was waiting for the hand dryer to work its magic on his clothes: *Wounded panther on the prowl. Look to your defences.*

He glanced in the mirror. He was looking the part of a damp and disheartened feline. His mood grew introspective. *That went surprisingly well for a first date. What is she playing at? Greg's married, and he's nuts about his wife and kids. If I'm a bottom feeder, he's a carp. Well, maybe the rock band moves him ahead a square or two. But how is having me or Reg on her payroll going to help her with Greg?* He gave his damp hair a twist, hoping to restore the curl.

The engines of imagination began to whir. *Wouldn't it be great if she could deliver the goods. Imagine it being that easy — deciding to fix ourselves. Sit down with a coffee and a brochure in a brightly lit office and watch a presentation. Rod Serling introducing an episode of* The Twilight Zone. Kaiser leaned forward, his hands on either side of the sink as he replicated the famous voice and invented a few lines. "Learn to operate the hidden springs and levers of your mind. Pass through the swinging bookcase down the dank, dark, stone staircase until you arrive at the chamber of hidden desire."

That was the note to strike. Kaiser was sure of it.

If we understood the "why" that powers the crazy things we do, we could regain control of our addiction without anyone else ever having to know. Go back to the moment where you first put a foot wrong and change it. That's the active ingredient in a bottle of Life Skills.

He remembered being ten years old and falling ill the night before the family was supposed to go to the zoo. Terrified that his parents would cancel the trip when they found out, he climbed into bed and willed himself to get better. He imagined white blood cells kicking the hell out of the invading horde of germs and drifted off to sleep, convinced that he was going to see an elephant after all. We never entirely get over believing in magic.

That's her edge — that belief that we can fix ourselves. There's no harm in believing in magic if all you want to do is see a tiger. She tells the suckers something is possible and then stands back and lets them run wild with the idea. Her looks help the con. Lots of happy tears and fuss, and then when the bottom falls out of the paper bag, well, who's to blame, you or the miracle worker?

Even if she could deliver on her shit, she'd still just be what she is: a poor, sick little girl screwing the world over because that's all she knows how to do. It must be awful in the quiet moments when the wardrobe and jewellery fail and that empty feeling gets around her defences. I wonder if she cuts herself.

With that, he genuflected to his image in the mirror and departed.

Chapter 36

Paul enjoyed the drive north from Toronto. It gave him an opportunity to simply be. His snow tires hummed and thumped along the highway with the confidence and familiarity of back-up singers on a concert tour. The Bruce Peninsula had been enjoying a week of spring thaw. The roads were dry and the skies blue and sunny. His wife, Lilly, accompanied him as far as Owen Sound, where he dropped her off at her sister's. He made his way the final forty miles to the cottage on the unfinished county road. The ping of gravel hitting the undercarriage was all the company he needed.

He arrived precisely at noon and parked his Civic on the side of the road as instructed. The blood flowed back into his cramped legs and arms as he stretched and inhaled the intoxicating mix of thawing pine and fresh air. As he made his way up the deserted driveway, he pondered Seymour's warning to leave no evidence of his having been there. It was easy enough to do, not unlike removing your sandals on sacred ground. The long driveway that led to the cabin was a little overgrown and smelled wonderfully of rotting leaves and autumnal damp. It bent sharply to the left at the halfway point, and from there he could see the outline of a cabin hidden among the thick growth of pine trees.

A rusted oak leaf had fallen into a puddle, where it was suspended in a thin shell of transparent ice. Only the bubbles in the ice betrayed its presence. Paul changed the lens on his Minolta for one better suited to close-up work and photographed the leaf from several angles, then did the same again with his digital camera. When he was satisfied, he stood silently in the half light and looked about for other possibilities. A thousand people could walk down this driveway and not see the treasures he took in. Paul had a mystic eye. He saw eternity in the curling tendrils of a climbing plant and the possibility of love in the pattern that decorated a snapping turtle's shell.

He could smell the ashes from the fireplace as he got closer to the cottage. Humans had been here and departed.

He approached the cabin and snapped a few reference shots. The place was not much to look it — handmade in the late forties, if he was any judge of materials and craftsmanship — but he could tell the place was deeply loved. It had a fairy tale look. There was no peeling paint or cracked windowpanes.

Paul tried to imagine how this place had evolved for Seymour as he grew. What special memories of longing and belonging were caught up in the ordinary objects that populated this landscape? Was the woodpile the German front line at Vimy Ridge? Did dragons lurk in the soggy undergrowth of the swamp? Rotten rope hung from a pine branch high above his head. The scuff marks left from the tire swing had not healed. Was this the first place that Seymour had dragged his feet?

What was in your heart when you last stood here, Seymour?

He walked down the steep, wooden steps to the lakeshore. The stairs were slippery with frozen lake spray. He paused halfway down and took out his phone. Seymour had provided him with a couple of the images he'd painted to orient himself. He didn't need them. Any fool could see the natural beauty that graced this space. No interior decorator working with the finest furs and fabrics could ever engineer anything as perfect as this stretch of shoreline.

In summer, the water from the stream was cooler than the rest of the sundrenched lake, but in winter it was warmer and had gently eroded the layer of ice that formed a necklace around the shoreline. Paul saw the pulse from the stream, as it moved an aquatic plant the way a dancer twirls a ribbon.

The saplings that Seymour had painted in the summer now stood bare and resigned to winter. What had been soft and full of life on the canvas was flint edged and spare on the frozen shore. The life that had vitalized the leaves had retreated down to safety in the roots of the plant, stored along with the promise of new love for the first days of spring. In the noonday sun, a layer of white hoarfrost was beginning to melt off the long, graceful stems and thick, desiccated leaves. Even in their dotage, they possessed an elegance.

Paul snapped pictures from every angle. His hands shook with excitement. He sensed the presence eternal. Each spiky pattern of frost on each rock, leaf, and stem was unique. Paul recorded the light while his heart leapt for joy.

He felt grateful to be alive. If Seymour couldn't paint from these images, then he was finished both as an artist and as a man. Paul found an agreeable rock to sit on and watched as the water birds wheeled high overhead. He offered up a prayer of thanksgiving and with that he was gone.

Chapter 37

Kaiser was putting on his overcoat, intent on taking an afternoon walk when Seymour crossed his path. The young man locked eyes with him for a split second and, in that moment, Kaiser saw an opportunity he didn't want to miss. *Why is he afraid?* He gave his young charge a fearsome look as a possibility took shape in his mind. "Put on your coat. We're going for a walk."

Seymour was astounded. Here was the counsellor the guys had nicknamed the Terminator, and he was demanding that Seymour drop everything and go with him. Seymour wanted to make an excuse, but the look on Kaiser's face made it clear this was not an offer that could be negotiated. He clamoured up the stairs and came running back down with his coat in his arms. He was more curious now than afraid. What would this most intriguing of the suits have to say?

Kaiser possessed a certain élan when he walked. Seymour was still shoving his arms into his coat as he struggled to keep pace. The Terminator was not someone you could ask to slow down and so he pushed himself and felt a rising soreness in his hip. Kaiser had the young man where he wanted him.

"What's wrong with your hip?" Kaiser asked, knowing the answer full well.

"Birth defect."

"Can anything be done?"

"I can suffer."

Kaiser smiled and took out a cigarette. "That'll be good for your art."

Seymour stuffed his bare hands in his coat pockets. "It hasn't helped so far."

"Is art important to you? Paul makes it sound as if that's the reason you're here."

Seymour's look said, *Not this again.* "It's the only part of my life anyone around here seems to be interested in."

"What happened when Paul let you sketch on the weekend?"

"It was amazing."

Kaiser stopped where Bernard crossed Madison as a van full of excited students barrelled through the four-way stop, honking the horn and jeering as they went. Kaiser smiled at them fondly. "How do you feel about those paintings you burned?"

The north wind was blowing. Seymour extracted the hood of his sweatshirt from under his coat collar. "Have you ever destroyed something you loved?"

"In my life, it's been a regular occurrence."

Seymour didn't offer more, so Kaiser prodded him. "If you sold them, you could have bought a lot of hooch."

Seymour's eyes narrowed. "There's a guy down on the corner who does that. I can tell he drinks. His hands shake when he's drawing, but worse than that, they sweat. All his work sticks to him and gets smudged. He has talent, but he's working with such cheap materials, and in the street. Everything's dirty by the time he's finished. It's pointless. He hates those drawings."

"Are we talking about you now, Dr. Freud?"

Seymour sighed. "I'm cursed. I use my talent to poison myself."

The intended edge to Kaiser's voice failed him. "That sounds heartfelt, but you're still overlooking something obvious."

"What's that?"

"The bum leg isn't the only thing you inherited."

"You mean the booze?"

"Yup. It's a package. You can't change the hand you were dealt."

They arrived at the playground east of Spadina. The benches were deserted except for a few pigeons working the afternoon shift and an old man sipping out of a pint bottle wrapped in a brown paper bag. The sun felt warm on their faces when they found a place out of the wind.

"Kaiser, answer me one question — and I won't rat you out. But I need to know."

"I don't dye it. I'm a natural blond."

It took a moment for Seymour to compose himself and remember his question. "Does this work?"

Kaiser had to smile. "Go ask the guy over there."

"I'm a good judge of people. You're rough but you're real. I can't make sense of all the stuff you guys are teaching. It's too abstract, too overwhelming. It makes me dizzy. My gut tells me I can trust you. If you were me, would you go down this path?"

"I did."

"You don't need to be special or lucky?"

"Just willing and stubborn."

"I get the willing part, but why stubborn?"

"Alcohol changed you into a rat bastard. But here's your problem — you couldn't stand your life before you drank, and you're scared to death that the sober you is going to be an even bigger loser. You figure that you're going to spend the rest of your life sitting around feeling miserable and bored, wishing the whole time that you could have a drink. That's why you keep relapsing."

"I hate that you know this shit." He gave his hoodie a good tug and a jet of warm air escaped.

"You have to be tough to recover. Bad things happen. People get scared, or greedy, or bored, and they go back to what they know — and that's often the end of them."

That's what the guys on the smoke deck say.

"If you get drunk before you're fully healed, it'll all start to spin on you. You'll look back on what happened to you in treatment and write the whole thing off. Lots of people fail, thinking that what we do is bullshit. A way of keeping our spirits up while we wait to relapse and die."

"That's pretty stark."

"It has to be."

"Why?"

"The bullshit we believe is durable."

"What changes it?"

"Experience. It eventually hurts more to stay the same than change."

They both fixed their eyes on the old man drinking from the brown paper bag just out of earshot. He was in love with his companion. His take on this would be interesting.

Seymour's rejoinder slipped out. "What am I going to do about my mom and dad?"

Kaiser depressed the soft pedal. "Why do you have to do anything?"

Seymour looked the part of a diner taking a hard, round object out of his mouth and wondering if it was a pebble or part of a tooth. "I can't go back. If I go home, I'll die." His head went down and his voice changed. "They swamp the boat faster than I can bail it out. That's why the paintings went into the fire. That was the part of me they wanted, the only part of me they loved. Without my paintings what am I?"

The look on his face said, *Nothing.*

"You can't bear to hurt them, but you need to get away?"

"I don't want to be anyone's kid."

Kaiser brightened. "I'll see what I can do."

What the hell does he mean by that?

"Now, you answer a hard one for me," said Kaiser. "I got to tell you, straight up, I have no business asking, but I'm going to, because I'm desperate."

What in the world…

Kaiser rested his elbows on his knees and allowed his gloved hands full access to the sides of his head. "Reg has written a novel, but he has no idea how to get it published. It's got him all jammed up inside. He reminds me of you and your paintings. The reason I brought you out here is to find out how to get the damn thing published before he flings it into the fire. I hoped you might have some sympathy for him. Paul says your mom is the one who decides these things."

The hoodie came off. "Is the book any good?"

"I don't know. I haven't read it."

Seymour started stroking his face, marvelling at the feel of deeply chilled flesh. "There's a process that books go through before they get published."

Kaiser's energy flickered. The divine right of kings left him for a count of three. In that moment Seymour, saw the truth. The painter's fingers reached for his brushes, but nothing came to hand. He sat motionless, allowing the expression on Kaiser's face to imprint in his memory.

"Reg said please and got nowhere."

Seymour did a quarter turn on the bench to face the older man, his keen vision taking in the hue of his subject's skin around the eyes. "Kaiser, my mom loves books. She sees her job as sacred." He paused as he examined the pattern of the Kaiser's curls where they met and bent at his collar. They would be difficult to capture. "Everything has to be the way she wants it before she can look at a manuscript. The last thing in the world that you want to do is shotgun her in her office."

"What should I do?"

"Do what everyone else does — get an agent."

"Nothing is that simple."

Seymour liked being treated as a confidant, but he wasn't sure if he wanted to be in Kaiser's gang. What he needed to do was get started on the portrait. The simplest path forward was obvious. He spoke in a distracted way. "Well then, let me read it. If it's any good, I'll show it my mother."

Kaiser couldn't look at him. He knew that what he was doing was wrong. "I don't have a copy."

The old man on the bench opposite held his now-empty bottle fully upright over his lips. When the last drop fell on his grateful tongue, he gave the bottle a shake and attempted to suck any remaining goodness out of it. When he was certain it was empty, he removed it from the brown paper bag and examined it in the sunlight while the pigeons hopped around wondering what they could gain from this shining object. The expression on their faces matched what was happening with Kaiser: something beautiful had shown promise and then disappointed.

Seymour pulled back his hoodie and felt the cool air wick the moisture out of his hair. *This dude is a madman. That's how I'm going to paint his face. He's waiting for me to say something. The novel has to be crap. Is this willing and stubborn in action?* Inspiration struck him. Seymour started to laugh. "Do you like dogs?"

"I'm crazy about them."

"My mom too. Why don't you give her a dog, then kidnap it and make her publish the book?"

"What kind of dog does she go for?"

***

Lou was reading *The Sun Also Rises* in his room. He was tired of endlessly rereading the "Big Book" of Alcoholics Anonymous. When he took a novel downstairs to the living room, some over-the-top young counsellor would invariably take exception and chastise him and then insist that he once again take up the sacred text until he'd wrung every last drop of juice out of it.

Unlike the other guests, Lou's brain had not been fogged by alcohol and drugs. He was a careful and meticulous reader who never turned a page until he understood everything that was on it. The other guests were having terrible problems with retention and comprehension, a situation that would persist for months. Half an hour before the start of class, the living room was full of scholars reading the required text. But somewhere in the process of ducking out for a smoke, gathering up their books, and helping themselves to a coffee on the way to class, what they'd studied would mysteriously vanish. When asked by the counsellor leading the seminar what they had read, eyes would turn down or escape out the window. Was it any wonder they were all terrified they'd fried their brains?

It was 6:15 p.m. An hour after dinner and forty-five minutes before he had to put his book down and join the other pilgrims on their nightly journey. Lou enjoyed the AA meetings. The ones held in the downtown core were an anarchist's dream. If the dominant discourse of the human race was a smoothly polished jazz symposium, then recovery was where the intricate varices of the countermelody were stamped, scored, and etched onto the sides of abandoned railroad cars. Ah, the world of human experience, endlessly caught between the rough and the smooth.

Lou could feel the spirit world impinging on the human. Tonight would be high tide and the full of the moon — no place for darkness to hide. He'd been smelling ocean air nonstop since the Straight Up meeting on Sunday, and half an hour ago he began to hear the sound of surf advancing and retreating on some uncharted shore.

When he rested his eyes on a faraway point and then looked away, he had the impression of an otherworldly image fading from his vision, the blue dot you see after someone takes a photograph with a flashbulb. He looked at the beautiful, numbered print of Tom Thomson's *The West Wind* hanging on the wall across the room from his bed. Sometime tonight it would come crashing down onto the floor without breaking. That would be the harbinger of coming events. The moment he'd find himself immersed in the surf. Until that happened, there was nothing for him to do but wait. He patted Croc on the head.

"Put on your alligator shoes. We're going downtown tonight." The reptile's painted eyes showed no sign of life yet.

The increasing clarity of the insights was the other confirming sign. The little teasers he'd been seeing and feeling for months were coming fast and fierce as he lay on the bed. Brush strokes enriching a canvas. The seemingly trivial and haphazard elements combined to evoke a larger cogent image.

Lou felt the part of a broken gambler looking at the football scores on Monday morning. How could he have been so mistaken about what was now painfully clear? His earliest insights were seldom more than pixelated glimmers into the future, like images on the screen when the cable TV froze. These coming attractions jolted his senses the way an approaching migraine did. But when a tidal surge this powerful occurred, the mood was different. He felt at peace.

Lou closed his eyes to offer a prayer for the tortured poltergeists hovering above his bed. He tried to see them as they must have been when they were still young and untainted by the horrors that had landed them here, the way they had been before they gave way to anger, despair, and self-seeking. They were here to scratch the itch from a wound long gone septic — one that they could drain but never heal.

When the tide came rolling ashore as powerfully as it did this evening, it wasn't only ghosts and familiars who quickened. Like leaven working in bread, Croc changed not only the mood but also the behaviour of the people around him. Straightlaced people came out of their stays. Freudian slips abounded. Things locked and forgotten in magicians' trunks gathered themselves for a journey. He was Aaron's staff, the first breath of spring, and that song from the old days you've been longing to sing to a dying friend. Things that should never have been joined, but which convention and convenience had epoxied together, started to come unglued and unravel. There was going to be a lively scrap outside the barn dance tonight.

**

The wind started to pick up as the sun went down and it poured rain. The slush and ice blocking the storm drains caused Madison Avenue to flood.

The power flickered on and off three times before it finally went out for good. The emergency lights came on and Greg sent Charles Dorn down to the corner to see if the church still had power. It did and that meant the meeting was a go.

Greg was trapped in the office. The damned phone wouldn't stop ringing. Everyone knew they were not supposed to call and ask about their loved ones, but they all did anyway. There were lots of special people, all with particular needs, requiring an exception to be made to the silly old rules. Greg ran upstairs to check on the guys at 6:45 p.m.

There was always someone asleep or fouling up somehow at this time of day. The guests had to leave for and come back from the meetings in pairs, and the last thing he wanted was for some dough-head to get left behind. Greg checked the rooms, but for once everyone was doing what they were supposed to be doing.

The last two rooms were on the second floor. Lou's door was closed. Greg knocked politely but didn't receive a reply. He knocked a little louder, sometimes people listened to their iPods. He tried the handle and got an electric shock. He took a step back and tried to figure out how that could've happened. He tapped the door handle with one finger and this time it was cool and compliant. The handle turned but the door did not open. This had Greg thinking it was a prank. Someone was bored. He gave the handle a real heft, but the door wouldn't budge. It wasn't the lock. That was moving the way it should. He examined the door in the frame. It was wedged in tight. *Holy cow,* he thought. *It's swollen shut.*

He banged louder. "Lou, are you in there?"

There was no reply and that didn't sit well with Greg. He went looking for Lou. When he asked the guys, they all said they'd not seen him since supper. This wasn't good. He was AWOL and that meant discharge.

That's a shame, thought Greg as he made his entry in the treatment record. *I had some hope for him. It's hard to figure him going for a cocktail. Well, at least he's settled the burning question — he's an alkie after all.*

Greg finished his log entry, and when the hands of the clock reached 7 p.m. exactly, he shooed the guys out the door. He told them that if they ran into Lou acting the fool on the corner, they were to send him back to the house PDQ.

It was nice to have the place to himself for a few minutes. He still had four hours to go before he could take off his shoes. A sinister thought struck him as he was pouring a coffee. What if Lou had fainted or had a stroke? This was the guy who he thought had a brain tumour. What if Lou was lying dead or disabled, blocking the door? He got another rush of foreboding. Something felt very wrong about this. He got on the phone to Doug and told him what he was thinking.

"Go try again. Put your shoulder into it this time. If it's his body blocking it, you should be able to at least move the door."

Greg knocked a lot harder and tried the handle again. He got another shock. Not as strong as the first one but still a jolt that left his hand numb — and it still wouldn't open. What could possibly account for this? The hallway wasn't damp and there were no wires running beneath the carpet.

Inspiration struck. Greg went back down to the office and grabbed a wooden yardstick that had been lying around since the days when Punanai had been a nursing home, and he grabbed the night man's flashlight. He went back to the hallway and shone the light under the door. There was a good-sized gap of an inch and a half, but he couldn't see anything. The lights in the room were out. That was a good sign. He took the yardstick and swept the floor on the other side of the door. The metre-long ruler met no resistance. This allayed Greg's fear a bit. If Lou's body was blocking the door, he'd have either seen it or felt it when he probed. Of course, he could be unconscious in his bed…

"It's a good thing I'm more than just another pretty face," he said as he rushed the door with about half his weight. He bounced back. He remembered himself being stronger than he actually was. He hit the door again. This time at three-quarter speed. A crash came from inside. *The West Wind* hit the floor but didn't break.

Greg was about to hit the door again when he heard something never heard in a men's treatment centre — a woman's scream.

Chapter 38

The rain pounding against the window in Lou's room was the soft treble clef, the deep sonorous echoing roar of the inrushing tide, the hard bass note. The resultant harmony had a narcotic effect. Lou heard the music of the spheres and felt the warmth of the summer sun on his chest. He returned to partial consciousness only for the second it took to feel the jolt of Greg's shoulder hitting the door and to hear *The West Wind* crash to the floor. The sounds, both real and fancied, mixed and echoed as if the collisions had happened inside a church bell. Lou felt himself lifted out of the chaos by powerful hands and propelled backwards down a long waterslide that eventually deposited him in a comfortable restaurant booth.

He freaked the first time it happened. Too afraid of where he was going to enjoy the trip, certain he could not trust his senses. Not anymore. He was glad to be here once again and anxious to see what would transpire.

Croc was waiting in the plush oval booth for him to arrive. He was happily perusing the dinner menu as his tail swished along in time with the lively dance music.

***

Jacob took his leave. He went quietly. Ji-woo was in the hallway getting some air at the time. Jacob's room was stifling hot and smelled of disinfectant and ruin. She'd worked forty-five hours and faced the prospect of two more unhappy days of his abuse.

Jacob was hard to take. She'd stopped caring about his opinions and tempers. When he went, the world would be a better place. It saddened her that any human life could be so vile and self-absorbed. She was still thinking foul thoughts about her patient when she discovered his body and let out the scream that drew Greg from down the hall.

***

Jacob sat up in bed, feeling very much better. His stomach didn't hurt and his back wasn't throbbing. And then he looked around and panicked — he was seeing double. There he was lying in the bed, and here he was sitting up. He could move his arm, but the arm of the man in the bed did not move. That took a moment to sink in.

He got to his feet easily this time.

"Holy crap! I'm dead."

A funky dance tune was playing somewhere down the hall. It sounded inviting, as if it was something put on only for him. It put him in mind of his favourite bar from way back in the age of disco. He put the music out of his mind, leaned over the bed, and poked himself in the chest. His fingers passed through the body.

I can get back in. I know I can.

Jacob lay back down on the bed and allowed his new form to accommodate itself to the wreck lying there. The remains felt cold, and for the first time in weeks, he noticed the sick-room smell and gagged. He sat up and moved away from the deathbed. He would as soon have picked up a rat as touch himself again.

"I'll get these bastards if it's the last thing I ever do."

He passed his nurse in the hall, drawn toward the familiar beat of Disco Inferno. He stopped at the door to Lou's room. Greg was lying on the floor, trying to fish something out with a yardstick. Stupid man, what's he doing?

Jacob was drawn to the door and when he reached for it, his hand passed through, as did the rest of him. He found himself in a grand ballroom full of elegant people drinking and dancing to the disco beat. His heart leapt. He headed over to the bar and pushed his way through the crowd of milling people, looking wildly out of place in his pyjamas and bathrobe.

"Scotch!" he bellowed. "As big as you can make it." He smiled and looked around the room.

A well-dressed man in a tuxedo was sitting at the bar, tapping his finger to the lively beat. He'd just finished one cigarette and lit another off the smouldering remains. He looked up at Jacob. "I needed that, it's been a very long time."

"Jacob Hutton," cried the man in pyjamas above the din, and then he downed the scotch as if he were drinking pink lemonade at a fair.

"Walter Glannon," said the man in the tuxedo as he took a long pull from his cigarette.

"What's the party all about?"

"No idea, old boy, but look at all the pretty ladies. I was down the hall when I heard the music."

"This must be about something." Jacob spotted a large and ornate banner on the wall. "Look, it says Man of the Year."

Both men smiled wickedly. "Have we crashed this thing?"

"I know I have — look how I'm dressed, and I don't know a soul."

They laughed like evil children.

"We'd better load up on the goodies before someone takes note and boots us out."

Lou and Croc were sitting in their booth in the anteroom, just out of earshot. They were watching the well-dressed partygoers move in and out of the rooms. Lou ordered a glass of wine for Croc and a small beer for himself.

"I'm in treatment after all," he explained. "I think it would be wrong to have a whisky."

Croc loved to party whenever he got the chance. The wine glass looked silly with a straw sticking out of it, but it was necessary.

"It's been a while since we've had an evening out." Croc examined the tip of his tail, delighted to find that it had grown back.

"I wish Lori could join us."

"Not in the cards. Different gifts."

Lou nodded as his attention landed on a passing party girl.

"Look over there."

"Where?"

Croc nodded to the far corner of the room. "There's a pile of newspapers."

"So what?"

"Go get one, dummy!"

Lou walked over to the rack and helped himself to a paper. He returned to the booth and put it down in front of Croc.

"I suppose you want the financial page. You told me you didn't need to cheat to make money."

"I don't. Turn to the sports page. I want to buy us a Pro-line ticket."

Lou looked at the box scores. "I've never heard of two of these teams. What's the date?"

"Let's simply say that you're now last year's man."

"Wow, that's a jump!"

"Do we know anyone here?"

"Well, there's a yardstick poking back and forth under that door, which I imagine is attached to one of the suits. And Jacob and Walter are over at the bar, disgracing themselves. It seems that vascular disease and liver failure aren't the deterrents they were once imagined to be. Other than that, it's the usual gang."

"What a pair. You'd think they'd learn."

Croc rather improbably pursed his lips and took a long satisfying sip from the straw. The contents of his glass disappeared.

"You're a fine one to talk. You're drinking beer."

"I never claimed to be anything but what I am. I drink, but I'm not a drunk."

The impact of a palm on a microphone brought the room to attention.

"Good evening, ladies and gentlemen. I would like to welcome you all to the annual awards dinner for Neville, Burns and DeWitt, the world's foremost think tank. I'm Brian Burns, and I'll be making all the off-colour remarks this evening." There was a roar of approval.

"But before I start embarrassing my wife, my family, and my colleagues I have a few household announcements to make. In a few minutes, we're going to hear from our keynote speaker, and it's important that we all hear this without interruption."

He leaned into the microphone and tried to sound conspiratorial. "They have worked very hard to get this right and it would be a shame to spoil it."

The younger people knew what he was talking about, and what with the wine and the merriment, one of them let out a war whoop that was out of place among the tuxedos. Brian laughed at the response. "Well, someone is having a good time. So, if you need to run an errand or top up on some of this splendid food or drink, do it now."

Jacob looked at Walter. "This is going to get serious in a moment."

"Serious?"

"Seriously boring. I'm leaving. You coming?"

"No, I'm perfectly happy here for the moment," Walter said as he blew a smoke ring that hovered in the air for five seconds before it dissipated. "I think that I'll linger until security comes to take me back to my room."

Jacob polished off his third double Scotch and, feeling very much the better for it, he made his way to the entrance. His board of directors needed a combing and he was now in the mood to do it.

The security guard assessed Jacob's pyjamas as he approached the exit. He was obviously an interloper.

"I'm sorry, sir, you can't go in there. They're preparing the entertainment. You will have to use the main door."

The Scotch had done its work.

"Buzz off, asshole! Do you have any idea who you're talking to?"

The security guard smiled. He enjoyed the cut and thrust of conversation. He put Jacob in a cobra hold and moved him into the hallway.

Jacob's arm and his shoulder hurt like fury. He wanted to strike the man, but he couldn't get his arms free. He was in agony when he heard the voice saying, "Stop struggling." When he did, the pain subsided. After a moment, he dared to take a breath and opened his eyes. He was on the floor wrestling with Greg and Ji-woo.

"Jacob, stop hitting me!"

***

Greg got Doug on the phone as the firemen and ambulance crews trooped wet boots through the living room. He couldn't spell defibrillation but Ji-woo could. You don't often need an AED, but when you do, you do. The paramedics were doing their workup on Jacob before transporting him.

The boss said, "I'm on my way," and hung up before the subject of what to do about Lou came up. When Doug arrived, Greg outlined the Lou problem.

Doug was distracted and gave hurried directions. "Have a look in the basement and around the outside of the building. There's a stream deep underneath the building and, who knows, maybe something has shifted and caused the door to stick. But if you ask me, that mad bastard crazy-glued it shut."

Chapter 39

When Kaiser got home, he gathered up his towel and bathrobe and made his way to the shared bathroom, where he waited for the enormous clawfoot tub to fill. Steam whispered of ease and comfort to come as it fogged the mirror over the sink.

Steam...

Kaiser's weakness was boredom. His father had once inquired of him, "Are you one those guys who simply can't stand prosperity?"

Kaiser got his kicks provoking people. Riana was an adrenalin junkie as well. She got him and he got her. Their views on addiction were bookends. Both had a nose for trouble and a fear of quiet, rainy Sunday afternoons with nothing to do but watch the cat lick his paw as he looked out the window.

The other counsellors took a half-step back when a biker or a career criminal came into the house with an air that cried, *Watch out, I'm trouble!* Kaiser always beat the advance toward the sound of the cannon. Everyone who disagreed with him paid a toll. Bravado made the underlying boredom bearable, but now it, too, was beginning to spall.

I wish I were steam.

His home life was drab. His housekeeper, Hy Campbell, did her best. She bullied and threatened him, frequently quoting scripture in her attempts to turn his sterile rooms into a home. He craved stimulation, not comfort. He needed to push in order to feel alive. Action was meaning and risk the most precious reward. His *kaiserschlacht* could be an epic success or a tragic failure. The outcome wasn't the issue.

I wish I could change…

He had his legacy to consider. Getting Reg's novel published was a capstone project. A Hollywood producer adopting a street kid. In his mind's eye, he saw Reg advancing with cane in hand and murder in his eyes. *Yeah, that image doesn't work.*

Outwitting Riana and whistle-blowing the geniuses at head office were also possible notes on which he could put out to sea. Oh, there was a layer of wanting to help Reg, but damn it, this final time had to be about him. He was cock of the walk and what he said mattered, and it always would, as long as strength remained in his body.

It didn't matter that a van was coming Friday to take his furniture to the auction house. Who cared if he got his spending money by feeding credit cards into bank machines. If they didn't want him to have the money, they shouldn't have sent him the cards.

He tested the bath water with his toe. He hadn't lost the contest with Riana, but he hadn't distinguished himself. He'd enjoyed the skirmish, but when it was over, he felt let down, his spirits dampened — as if the quarrel hadn't really been about them.

Two adrenalin junkies should have ended up between the sheets, striving to achieve mastery to the end. That would've parted the waves that led to a generous exile. A chariot ride through the triumphal arch with Riana whispering in his ear, *Life is all about wanting and being satisfied.* Surely those words had the power to drown out Reg's dreary eyes. In such a sunset he could've let the novel slip into the accumulation of decaying possibilities that we all tread over every day of our lives.

Promises made are leaves in the fall, wet and decaying underfoot, an accumulation of lies, boasts, and wishful thinking that we waft into the air. We watch them rise and fall and get trodden underfoot until their newness and their promise fail. When the tangle of our intentions gets deep enough, it becomes a trip hazard to even the nimblest foot.

Kaiser badly needed to hear the jazz band playing up close, blaring and only for him. He wanted to dance his way out of the racket. The satisfaction denied him by a blundered seduction must now be made good by other means. The Riana angle had showed promise, but it hadn't panned out. That meant his last best hope of a legacy was telling off the louts at head office and getting the book published.

Kaiser mulled Armageddon over as he soaked in the tub. The hot water and the soothing bubbles put an optimistic spin on things. This final week was about more than publishing a book or dodging creditors or trying to look nonchalant while he skipped town. The Kaiser show was going off the air after twenty seasons. The brown spot that started where the spade had nicked his skin now ran right through to the heart of this potato. Had any of it been real? He turned on the hot water faucet with his left foot, adjusting the temperature by shimmying his legs. Water sloshed out of the tub and onto the floor.

Crap I remember when there was nothing I couldn't do. I was always two steps ahead of the bad guys. When I got jammed up, inspiration would just come. I'd still be laughing at what I was pulling when I made my first move. I was immortal.

"Where the hell did that go?" he asked himself.

He took up a handful of bubbles and examined them before bearding himself. He wiped the steam off the oval shaving mirror that hung from a hook on the tile and examined the effect.

Years and warts are hateful things. They turn brilliant boys full of mischief into oily pockmarked old men who sit in hot bathtubs and plot revenge.

He recalled Riana's dismissive touch and looked down at himself. "Poor abdomen." He gave it a pat. "Mocked by a mad woman."

He sat up and turned on the hot water again. *When did I become creepy? Suddenly my jokes are inappropriate and my attitude unacceptable. I can't remember the names of all the new gods at head office. They get that offended look when I say something. Riana would fit right in with that bunch. The crap they're spewing is going to kill a lot of people. They don't know that yet. But they are starting to worry. They'll have their own tub of hot soapy sorrows soon enough.* He gave the waters a swirl.

Kaiser ran his wet fingers through his hair. It was thinning on top. The sides and the back still cut it.

His voice rang out loud and clear. "Simony — that's what Hy calls what we do. Hijacking the work of the Holy Spirit. Taking credit for something that is not ours to give."

He held the mirror up to his face.

"Is it any wonder she's convinced I'm hell bound? When I was the rookie, everyone was terrified of getting recovery tangled up with religion. Didn't want to offend anyone." He looked around for his face cloth.

Didn't want recovery to end up looking like Belfast. That was a mistake. We should have stood our ground and bellowed our truth to the heavens. Now we're on the verge of becoming a dull footnote in a brilliantly reasoned and researched fraud. Funders have preferences that make short work of modesty. I'm not the only bankrupt tycoon on this stretch of Wall Street whose been handed a copy of Life Skills and a bowl of soup.

He grasped the soap in his right hand with sufficient force to send it skyward. It landed with a satisfying splash…

"Annoying."

Ah, but annoying to whom? Offensive to what? God's loving purpose for the world is now the prevue of administrators and bean counters. So serious. Seriously flawed and seriously full of shit.

The face of Erin Fogbriar, the managing director for Punanai, came to mind. She needed a talking to — or three. *She and Riana were probably washed in the same tub.*

"Seymour is right. There's a long line of good little boys and girls waiting to hand teacher their homework. But not one of them is going to get the smile they want. Geez, if Puddin' Head wants to be a writer, why can't he do westerns."

There was a polite knock on the door. Reg asked. "Almost done, prune boy?"

"Five minutes."

Seven days from now, I'm gonna have both feet firmly planted in a pair of sturdy Wellingtons. Me and old Chester, nose to nose, living in a tool shed and fighting over bees. But before that happens, I'm gonna give them all something to remember me by. Then a little mystery about my whereabouts to tug at their heartstrings. He smiled ruefully.

"They'll be sorry I'm gone."

He laughed. *I'm gonna have to do something seriously goofy to get this book published, something outrageous, something that makes up for its lack of literary talent — and there needs to be a reckoning at the end of it. It'd be something if the story of how the novel got published was better than the book. That could be the note for me to go out on.*

"I can do this. One-stop shopping."

He lay on his back, allowing the soupy water to cover him while he let the individual frames of film pass in front of his imagination.

I can't play the hero. I need to fail with the whole world watching. Let my disappearance fan those serious doubts they have about my character. Then let a year pass in silence. Let my absence drip poison into their perspective.

He pulled the plug and eased himself out of the tub and into the gentle embrace of his bath towel. The tub gurgled its approval of the man and the plan.

He gave the mirror over the sink a smudge with his palm. *Now to the details. What do I know about this? Seymour needs to get away from his mom for sure, and maybe his old man too. Reg has gone as far as he's ever going to go as a counsellor. That smile he gets on his face when he wants to scream, I see that once a week. Doug has been fighting a rearguard action. Holding back management. They're afraid of him because they have no idea what he does or how he does it. But that won't last. Life Skills is on the horizon.*

Kaiser wanted Doug to wake up in six months and see right through to the bottom of this charade for the first time, to know, in that instant, that Kaiser had done him a favour.

Calling these weasels on their shit is invariably fatal. He can't. But I can. In fact, I don't see how I can't.

He set to work drying his hair with the towel, trying to frame his argument into something more noble than revenge.

I could leave Reg to rot on the vine, and I could stand by and let Seymour go home to his perfect mom and silent dad. What's it to me if a book gets published or a kid gets a shot at a real life?

Kaiser thought about Lakefield. There were going to be long nights at the bee farm, times he'd want to give up and come home.

Well, this'll make sure that I can't. At least not until I have a piss pot full of honey money. Nope, when I'm watching Chester bolting down sandwiches, I want to be able to say to myself that I'm taking my shot, my way and the world be damned. Why not go out in a blaze of manic glory? Set fire to the whole glorious mess and watch it burn.

Kaiser set to work cleaning the tub. That was one of Hy's rules. It gave him time to consider ways and means. Reg was knocking at the door with his cane, but he ignored him. He started with something easy.

How do I get my hands on the novel? Reg carries that damn laptop around like a Stradivarius. I don't know his password. I'll fiddle that part tomorrow when he's in class. I bet he uses his cat's name. I'll try Upset first.

Another knock at the door. "Kaiser, I need to go."

How do I get Mrs. Dunn to read it?

He recalled the famous story about Kris Kristofferson hiring a helicopter to deliver the sheet music for "Sunday Mornin' Comin' Down" to a reluctant Johnny Cash. No money in the budget for that.

Would this be a variation on setting a bag of dog poo on fire and ringing the doorbell or ordering twenty party-sized pizzas?

He poured a dab of cleaner on the orange scrubber and set to work on the ring.

The first principles need to be adapted to fit the character defects of the mark. Mrs. Dunn is an order freak. She's gonna jump on the bag of burning poo. It's in her nature to restore order and bellow for the cops. She'll get this in one take. But how do I get her mad enough to do it? What does the end of the world look like for her?

And there it was. He leaned back, resting on his elbows while the tub filled with rinse water. She kept her manuscripts at the cottage.

Don't send her twenty pizzas. Empty out her fridge. Hire a truck to take the manuscripts and leave Reg's book on the table with a note:

iF you EVER want to zee YOUR books aGAin PUBLiSH ThiS One!

Kaiser started to laugh and caught himself.

I need to do something to keep Puddin' Head out of jail. Nah, on second thought, a night in the slammer would be the perfect punchline. I can be the one to bail him out and give him a lecture on the way home.

Kaiser opened the door to find Reg squirming.

"You took your time."

Some day you'll thank me.

Chapter 40

Peter fussed over his appearance in the looking glass at the entrance to the Granite Glen Nursing Home, but it was in vain. He was, if anything, in worse shape in death than he'd been at the end of his life. The supple flesh and pliable muscle that had once made him a fine figure of a man had taken on the appearance of a helium-filled balloon left too long in cold air.

He looked out the window at Madison Avenue. The street was awash with a mixture of slush, ice cakes, and dirty, brackish runoff. The storm drains were clogged and the backed-up water was now deep enough to stall vehicles foolish enough to drive through it.

"What will Terri look like? Will she have aged? Has she been someplace nearby watching? Could we have been together?"

Without thinking, he pushed open the front door and made his way down the ramp that led to the sidewalk. His cresting anger could no longer be contained in thoughts.

"Why are churches so ignorant about what happens to us after we die? If I had known this was going to happen, I could've managed things." His hands flailed the lapels of his suitcoat as if he were trying to remove something offensive. I had a whole closet full of better suits than this one. Why did they bury me in this rag?

Peter looked down into dark freezing waters.

Will she still be able to see some facet of the me that she once loved? The boy she befriended. The adolescent she kissed. Oh, if she's indifferent, I'll die.

Peter laid hands savagely on a passerby. As luck would have it, the fellow was heading up the street toward Punanai. He stayed with the man until his feet found dry pavement once again. He had gone half a block further before he came out of his trance and realized he was walking — and there was a spring in his step. He felt the way he had the first day after he'd died. The closer he got to Punanai, the stronger the force acting on him became. It was intoxicating.

He bounced up the stairs that led to the great oak door and let himself be carried by the unseen force through the house and up to the second floor. A muscular man was down on his knees in the hall, pushing a yardstick under a door. Peter, to his enormous surprise, hopscotched over him, floated straight through the door, and into a darkened room.

It took a minute for his eyes to accustom to the gloom and a further moment for him to make sense of what had happened. He'd never passed through a solid barrier before.

He saw a pinpoint of light a fair distance off and heard the voices of a hundred happy conversations. He floated forward and found well-dressed people, chatting and enjoying snacks and drinks. Off in the corner, he spied the little girl sitting by herself in a booth.

What an odd choice of presentation for the angel of death to take — a beautiful, curly-haired child. Well, I'm not fooled. Children are innocent and loving, hardly the case with this wizened old life-taker. But if I want to see Terri, I'm going to have to get past her.

The little girl was staring at the screen of a device she was holding in her hand. As if death weren't annoying enough, now she had a cellphone.

Peter sat down on the opposite side of the booth and waited for the child to look up. She showed him the screen she was watching.

Peter was flummoxed. "What is that?"

"*It's my flowmeter. Do you see these red and yellow lines on the screen? Those are human timelines.*"

"*I don't understand.*"

"*The yellow lines represent the living and the red lines, the dead. Each line should be heading across my screen in a predictable pattern. A yellow line starts to slow and then turns red and flashes three times as it comes to a halt. A short time later, it flickers to blue. That's how this works ninety-nine-point-nine-nine percent of the time.*"

Peter felt a surge of hope. "But not always?"

"*That's right, Peter, not always. From time to time someone like you or your friend Mr. Canon over there mess up a perfectly lovely design for the universe.*

"*Who's Canon?*"

"*He's the one sitting in the booth reading the newspaper with the crocodile. He's responsible for this logjam. He's what we call a psychic catalyst — one in a trillion. That little piece of stone that clogs the gears. Things back up and overflow their natural boundaries. Things that shouldn't mix begin to blend. Look at this metre. The yellow lines go crazy when he's around. He spikes the living with the energy that was set aside for the transmutation of the dead. Some of them lose their inhibitions. They become as free in life as we are in death. It's a bad bit of business.*"

"*What's with the crocodile? Is he one of your crew?*"

The little girl rolled her eyes. "He's a Chromidon. Another nightmare for a person in my line of work. They follow psychic catalysts around the way remora follow sharks. They keep them from collecting unwanted bits of the future and bringing them back to the present."

"*What?*"

The pained look on her face left no doubt that she found this subject objectionable. But it didn't reveal why.

"*They're believed to be dark angels who inhabit long-lived lower life forms and act as the eyes and ears of certain other beings who, shall we say, prefer to keep a low profile.*"

Peter was frozen in a moment of longing, a distress that was overriding every possible concern and focusing his being on a single point of unquenchable desire. Yesterday he'd prayed for this very explanation, fantasized about slapping the truth out of this little body that confronted him. The mystery underpinned the methods and goals of the light — and now she was laying it all out for him and he couldn't care less.

"*I'm here to talk about Terri. Terri, my Terri — nothing else matters.*"

The little girl came around to his side of the booth and sat next to him. She placed her delicate hand on his massive paw and felt the churning of his soul as it came to a boil. She tried again.

"*Look at what's happens to the dead. Each red line should be straight, but they're not. You're all stuck. Something is stopping you from going where you need to go.*"

Peter had to get her off this nonsensical subject. "Why are we sitting in a bar? Heaven can't be this way!"

The little girl's eyes sparkled. "People see what they expect to see, Peter. It takes a ton of energy to move you from a yellow line to a red and finally a blue line. That energy makes people feel giddy — at least until they get used to it. That's why a lot of them see this place as a bar. They confuse spiritual energy with intoxication."

She pointed to the revellers from Neville, Burns and DeWitt. "That's also why the other crowd are here. Those parasites live on this energy. Without that, they have nothing." She tried to take Peter's hand, but he pulled it away.

He was through listening. He was tired of theories and wishful science. This explanation sounded as pathetic as one of John's hare-brained schemes. "You said Terri would be here."

The little girl smiled. "That's her on the dance floor."

Chapter 4l

Doug pushed against the door to Lou's room several times without result before having a moment of inspiration. He went to the tool room and selected a pry bar from its place on the wall. He placed the claw under the door and lifted it a quarter inch by stepping on the chisel end with his foot. The door sprung open to reveal Lou lying on his back, fully dressed, with a copy of *The Sun Also Rises* perfectly balanced on his nose, while Croc enjoyed an exquisite repose on his abdomen.

Doug stood in the doorway for a full minute trying to master his feelings as triumph gave way to naked fear. The figure on the bed was still. Lou looked as one departed. All of Doug's senses abandoned him with the exception of sight. A pane of dusty glass stood between him and the scene, clouding his perception. He stared at the prone figure with a foreboding not consistent with experience or reason. Youth and high spirits had no business ending up this way.

His mind raced to fentanyl but his lips refused to produce the word.

In that horrible moment it occurred to him that he should have instructed Greg to get the firemen to break down the door. They had been down the hall giving oxygen to Jacob. Blame and censure for that oversight were going to rain down on his head the way hailstones do in a microburst. Breath could neither enter nor escape. His skin ran to water while his knees implored him to take a seat.

He fought an urge to cry out as he moved toward the bed. He removed the book and placed both it and Croc on the night table. He touched Lou's shoulder but got no response. He sniffed the lifeless figure. No smell of alcohol. Lou's flesh was still warm to the touch, and he was breathing. Doug experienced a thunderous roar of blood moving through his eardrums. His hands began to shake, and he took a moment to calm himself.

Inexplicably he began to giggle. It offended him, the way that crying in public did, but he couldn't stop. *You little bastard.* He reached for his handkerchief and wiped his eyes. A good blow went a long way toward restoring his resolve. Any fool could see what was going on. *You're high and you're going to lie about it.* He tapped the sleeping figure firmly on the temple. The young man's eyes opened.

"I dozed off. What time is it?"

Doug struggled to keep both the dread and the relief he was feeling off his face and out of his voice. This was the next premier's kid. He gave way to a short, sharp burst of unwanted laughter once again. With difficulty, he mastered himself. "It's eight o'clock."

Lou sat up. "Crap, did they leave without me?"

There was a flash of anger in Doug's eye. *Who do you think you're kidding?* he thought, but he said, "Greg has been banging on your door!"

"Oh shit."

"Stand up and walk around. Show me you're all right."

Lou moved around the room easily. "See for yourself, I'm fine."

Doug moved into his personal space and peered into his eyes. "You're not fine. You took something."

Lou's pupils protested his innocence. "I didn't take anything," he said, hoping that the beer Croc had bought him in the ballroom no longer scented his breath. "I lay down on the bed to read before the meeting and the next thing I know I'm talking to you."

Doug shook his head, still fighting the urge to laugh. "Go downstairs and tell Greg you're all right. I will be down shortly."

Lou noticed a fireman walking the length of the hall. With a quirky smile on his face, he went to see what the fuss was about.

Doug shook his head a second time as he looked around the room for signs of villainy. There were no empty bottles or drug paraphernalia. He gave the room a good sniff. Everything was in order. He examined the door lock, but as far as he could tell no one had tampered with it. He opened and closed the door several times without it sticking. He took a breath. This wasn't adding up.

Does he have a tumour? Was its deadly fruit coming into season? Was this the beginning of something that had to end so very badly?

"Thank God he's not dead."

He took another deep breath, wondering for a second if carbon monoxide might be the problem and not other things equally deadly and invisible. He sat on the bed and took a bearing.

We're right back where we started. Tumour or drugs. The higher-ups are going to cover their asses by making a gift of my head to the board.

He looked over at Croc, who was now standing guard on the night table. He picked him up and felt a silly impulse come over him. "Spill your guts, prune face, or I'll throw you to the shoemakers."

***

While the rest of the house straggled back from the AA meeting, Doug and Mike talked over what to do next. Doug wasn't himself. Mike wondered if he was in shock. Finding bodies can do that.

"How are the guys taking this?"

"Tongues are wagging, especially after Czombo using. Everyone knows that Lou was AWOL."

"Since the door wasn't locked and there wasn't evidence of intoxication, it's possible that this was innocent."

"Not with this guy and never in a treatment centre."

"What time did Hutton help himself to a coronary?"

"Ji-woo said when Greg threw his weight against Lou's door, there was a crash that should have woken the dead. When Jacob didn't react, she checked him for a pulse. That's when she realized he was in trouble. She and Greg used the defibrillator on him. Apparently, Hutton came out of it swinging and Greg had to restrain him." Doug paused and shook his head as he pictured the scene. "No one could sleep through all that racket. He had to be using."

"So how do you want to handle this?"

"I'm going to give him a chance to come clean. Then I'm going to piss-test the little bastard."

Chapter 42

Peter couldn't believe his eyes. It was Terri, exactly as she had been on her wedding day — eighteen years old and in love.

He checked his appearance in the mirror behind the bar, hoping to see a similarly youthful version of himself. That glass handed out a lot of bad news. What he saw was the familiar silhouette of his enormous girth. His appearance hadn't changed. He was wearing the same sad old suit that he'd been buried in. But surely none of that mattered. He was still the man he always had been.

He walked onto the dance floor with as much dignity as he could muster. Not even a man leaving prison could feel more spring in his step.

Terri was dancing alone, swaying to the music in the spotlight, and when she saw him, she smiled. Peter reached out and Terri took his hand in hers, and in an instant, they were dancing.

He looked into Terri's eyes, and for him, the years fell away. They were back in the schoolyard, holding hands for the first time, locked in the wonder of their first innocent embrace.

"Is it really you, Terri?"

"Can't you tell?"

"I've missed you so."

"Has it been long for you?"

"I don't understand."

"Time ceases to matter."

"*I still don't understand.*"

"*Don't even try.*" She touched the end of his nose playfully with her index finger. "*Eternity takes practice.*"

She twirled expertly and then leapt into the air with a big goofy smile on her face. Peter missed the invitation to do a lift and instead caught her in his arms, looking the part of a groom crossing the threshold. She wriggled enough to secure her release.

Peter stood flat-footed before her, sensing a turn. "*Are you happy?*"

She began to move once again with the music. "*I always have been.*"

That didn't sit well. "*You looked so sad when you were dying.*"

She danced into his space again, hoping to resume. "*I was! That was my low point. I lost heart for a while. Did they really freeze my head?*"

"*Yes, your husband had it done.*"

She stopped and looked up at him. "*What a silly thing to do. And you kept it safe all these years?*"

Peter was hurt. "*It wasn't silly!*"

"*Peter, look around you, look at me, now look back at yourself.*"

Her words fell with the force of a hammer blow on his ears. It was a startling noise. The futility of it all started to come clear to him. Sitting in funeral parlours for days at a time, hoping to garner a clue about what was waiting for them. Watching friends deteriorate into poltergeists and endlessly theorizing about the best way to cheat and get ahead of the game, when, in fact, no such thing was possible. The weight of it was suddenly too much.

Dry as gunpowder no longer, Peter began to weep. He held Terri in his arms as he sobbed.

But her attention was somewhere else. There was a commotion in the hallway. A belligerent man in pyjamas was being escorted out by security.

"*Poor man,*" said Terri, making Peter look up and then over at the man. "*They have tried and tried and tried with him.*"

"*Where are they taking him?*"

"*Back to the world, Peter. Back to his old life — what's left of it.*"

"*So you and I could go back too?*" There it was.

Terri put her hand on Peter's shoulder. It was a touch that suggested both a renewed invitation to dance and a moment of intimacy. "*You could, but I was hoping that you would want to come with me.*"

Long overdue second thoughts left Peter trembling on the dance floor. His heart's desire was at hand, and yet a profound reluctance incapacitated him. It took forever to distill into words. "I'm afraid."

She placed her fingers gently on his temples. "Yes."

"I want—"

"That's the problem, Peter. You think you want something, and that wanting is stopping you from having anything."

"But—"

"Do you remember that day in the schoolyard? When you punched poor addlebrained Jeff Arnold in the nose?"

Peter went rigid. "He had it coming."

"Indeed, he did. It was a good prep for all the horrors life had in store for him."

Peter was suddenly wary. That last remark was savvy. It had a strange perspective. The thing a buyer says before they ask to see another property. Was this his Terri, the girl of his dreams, or a counterfeit?

"How do you know that?"

"Peter, when you struck him, you weren't afraid, and I know that you did it more to protect me than to either hurt him or defend yourself. That was always your best quality. Peter, that's why I'm here. I remember how it was."

"But I—"

"Peter, our time here is short. This window is about to close. Look me in the eye and tell me what you want to do."

"I want to go with you."

"It won't be the way you think."

"I need you, Terri. Life has taken everything. One more loss will be the end of me. I would rather put my trust in you than take my chances."

"Well, if that's the case, let's finish this dance. We have exactly enough time to do that."

The little girl tugged on Terri's sleeve.

The couple stopped and looked at her.

"He's lying."

Terri was surprised. "About…"

"Most things."

Peter started to sputter. "What are you saying?"

"He's thinking about throwing you over his shoulder and following Jacob Hutton out the side door."

The little girl looked wickedly into the trembling man's face. "You can't lie to an angel, Peter. What about your buddy John? Are you going to leave him in the lurch? And what about your old kick Walter? Is he on his own now? Don't you care what happens to them?"

Peter was gobsmacked. Since when had he become responsible for them?

He grabbed Terri far more roughly than he intended. "Terri, tell me one thing — when we go together, are we going to be all right? It's going to be you and me..."

"Oh," said Terri with a look of distress.

"The way it was always meant to be."

"I told you so," said the little girl.

The old ghost buckled inside. "What? Why are you looking at each other that way?"

The little girl calmly closed her flowmeter and put it back in her purse.

"Peter, we can't take you, not this way. Go back and do whatever you need to do to let go of your old life. Something is holding you there."

"I want to be with Terri."

"I'll leave you two to talk," said Terri. "It would be a shame to miss this dance."

Peter was horrified. The love of his life was dancing alone on the floor while he stood dying inside.

The little girl took him by the hand and returned with him to the booth. "The Terri you want to be with doesn't exist anymore, Peter. If you love her, accept that. If you care about her, be glad. She's truly herself now."

"You don't understand."

"Alas, in this job, I do."

"Everything in my life, everything I ever did, I did for her!"

"No, Peter, you did it all for yourself, for something you thought you wanted, and that's why you're sitting here talking to me."

Chapter 43

Doug reread all the reports on Lou Canon twice before he called him into the office. Every counsellor had good things to say. Lou wasn't doing anything objectionable. However, he wasn't doing what the staff hoped he would either. Lou's public utterances were cryptic when they weren't out-and-out bizarre. But so what?

The consensus was that he was suffering from something other than alcoholism. The staff had all tried to pigeonhole him without success. Paul's entry was the most compelling. He observed that the staffers were caught in a loop of logic. Since Lou was here, it followed that he was an alcoholic, and since the defining characteristic of the disease was denial, that had to be what was going on. Unless it wasn't. What if his denials were justified?

Paul and Greg agreed Lou needed further medical examination. Something was happening to be sure, but it wasn't booze. His behaviour didn't fit the profile.

That, thought Doug, *is the only reason for having him here — to rule out addiction. If he'd behaved himself, I could let him slide through. What he heard here will do him no harm and maybe wise him up a bit about the ways of the world. But now what? No one makes us look foolish. I have to think about what's best for everyone. Which leaves me right back where I started. What's best thing I can do for Lou?*

The door to his office received a sharp rap. Lou walked in with a triumphant grin on his face, which did not sit well with Doug, and settled himself in the big chair opposite Doug's desk.

"Where's Croc?" Doug asked.

"He's packing. We're going home."

Doug was taken aback by his confidence. "I wanted to talk to you about that very thing."

Doug reached into his pocket and took out a urine sample jar as he perfectly replicated Lou's triumphant grin.

Lou wasn't fussed. "You're going to want to watch me fill this one up, aren't you?"

"I'm afraid so."

Lou took the jar and tossed in grandly in the air. "It won't answer your question, but I guess it will rule out a possibility or two. You guys do a lot of that around here."

Doug sighed. "Still playing the mystic?"

"Nope, I have cards to play."

Talking to someone you feared dead not an hour ago caused a disorienting mixture of relief and anger. Was there a worthwhile insight waiting for him at end of this tunnel? Despite his misgivings, Doug had to admit that he wanted to hear this whole large and lugubrious lie without interruption. "Do tell."

"Doug, when my folks get back into town, they're going to kick you around like a piñata."

"Is that a threat or simply more juice from the beyond?"

"Giving people shit is their cardio."

Doug tried to edge Lou back onto firmer ground. "Since it's only the two of us talking, let me give it to you straight. You broke the house rules by not going to the meeting. I could cop out and use that as an excuse to send you home." He paused and let a look of concern form around his eyes. "I could as easily find a way not to if I knew the truth."

"I was locked in my room."

"It's the unconscious part that interests me more."

"What happened is hard to understand … but not impossible."

There it was at last. The distant hope of reconciliation. "Did I just hear the faintest glimmer of some interest in what we do here? Is there a scintilla of hope that you want to stay?"

Lou was surprised by that question. "No, I'm going home. My work here is done. But I'm leaving without ill feeling. I enjoyed my stay. I admire you and the work you do."

Doug gave him a lipless smile. "My gut is deeply troubled by that remark. Are you playing with me, or trying to get your nerve up to tell me something embarrassing? I'm up for both."

Lou sat in silence for five minutes. His face resembled a windmill as he calmly and efficiently sifted through the possibilities. From time to time, a hard bit would narrow one of his eyes or curl up a lip. Doug keenly felt the absence of Mike, whose observational superpower was badly needed.

Lou produced a serious face. "I have to be careful about what I say. There are consequences to knowing. Sometimes they're obvious, but other times they sandbag me." He felt around in his coat pocket, hoping to find Croc. "I travel to the future. That's what happened last night. That's why there are all kinds of loose ends to deal with that have no rational explanation."

Doug had his stone face on.

"And, Doug, you're a man who does not care for mysteries."

Lou reached into his sports coat pocket and passed an envelope to Doug. "Croc gave me this for you. These are the box scores for a Pro-line ticket. We got this from a newspaper last night. Two of the teams won't start playing until next season."

Doug looked at it and smiled. "Oh really? How thoughtful."

"Let me finish. I want you to hang on to this — treat it the way you would a post-dated cheque. The closer you get to the actual date on the ticket, the more you're going to begin to doubt your senses. The names of the teams will be consistent. The dates of the games will be right. The venue they're playing in will also check out. But that won't convince you. You'll still be suspicious, because that kind of information could be known by a few organizers long before an event. But when the score turns out to be right, not only in one contest but across the whole ticket... Well, that's when things are going to start to change for you. You're going to abandon the idea that *this can't be* and get to work on *how is this possible.*"

Doug flashed back to the image of Lou lying motionless on the bed. He wanted to say something, but years of training and experience told him to nod and give the young man a quarter smile.

"There's an energy in this house that changes lives. It makes me giddy. But here you sit, Doug, a spider at the centre of this web, curiously immune to what's going on all around you. Don't close your mind to what's possible simply because it's unexpected. You tell your clients to do this every day. I wonder, can you swallow a dose of your own medicine?"

Doug smiled. "You're the mystic, you tell me."

Lou got to his feet and moved over to the window. "There's no way for you to know that what I'm saying is true. I'm asking you to take what I say on faith. Trust me for a little while. Have some hope that what I'm saying could be true. Use this ticket to orient yourself and to give you some confidence that what I'm saying is possible."

Doug got to his feet and handed Lou a urine jar. *Bob Bourns was right all along. He's been pranking us. But you have to admire his stagecraft. Sometimes you win and sometimes you lose, but the spoils always go to the victor. Well played, Mr. Canon.*

Doug took the ticket and pinned it to the bulletin board. A performance of this quality deserved a souvenir. He had to bite his lip. The giggles were back. Where the hell were they coming from? "Come and have lunch with me if your troubles ever get worse."

Lou saw right through him. "I'll be back when the two new teams start playing in the league. We can talk some more then."

"Let's go have a piss to celebrate."

***

The following day, Lou made a beeline to Lori's place. A leg of lamb sang its roasting praises to his nostrils as he entered the door.

"Baby face, you're sprung!"

"I had a big night."

"Everything's okay?"

"For now, for us, yes."

"What about everybody else?"

"Ever watch a juggler throw clubs in the air?"

"Whose head are they going to land on?"

"I didn't pick up any personal stuff this time, save one image."

"What was that?"

"I had a vision of us sitting together in a hot tub with Croc."

"As long as you take the spout end, I can see that happening. Now get in here and help me with the vegetables. I've missed you so much!" She had to ask. "Is *daddy* going to be premier?"

"Yeah, his name is all over the paper. 'Clouting Thomas: From Landslide to Landfill in Less Than Six Months.'"

"Too bad. I was hoping something would make him happy."

Lori took the roast out of the oven and placed it on the rack. She was suddenly overcome with a fit of giggles. She crossed the room and hugged Lou. "Why am I laughing?" she asked, wiping a tear from her eye.

"Aftershock," said Lou. "Croc says the stink of the future stays on my clothes for weeks after I come back. Talking about what we shouldn't know makes us giggle."

"The stink of the future," she said as she felt a roar of laughter exit her frame.

"The stink, the stink, the glorious stink."

Chapter 44

Peter came to his senses in the hallway outside of Lou's now-empty room. His heart was beating at a frantic pace while he bounced slowly up and down in place. A man with a wood plane was shaving a door that had been taken down from its hinges and laid on its side. Inside the room, one shabby and bewildered poltergeist stuck to the ceiling above the bed. The rest of them were gone.

Peter felt the way he did that time his doctor gave him diet pills — frantic with energy. Ordinarily he'd be delighted to be able to do things again. But what he wanted now was quiet. He needed to think, but he couldn't. Terri was eternal. What they had was forever. More durable than even the love of a parent. But Terri had changed. And what had the little girl meant when she said Terri was exactly the way she was supposed to be?

Who the hell does she think she is, lecturing me about John, of all people, and Walter? That wasn't right. What could I do for those guys? When did they become my problem?

This was quite a turnaround. He had spent years hiding from the light. But now that he'd stepped into it, he knew better. Terri came back for me. She knows we need to be together. Why is that horrible little girl causing trouble? What needs settling on this side anyway?

The forlorn ghost couldn't control the trembling in his limbs. He was a man stuck in a train station for days while a storm raged outside, desperate for a way home.

They need me to do something. Something they can't do themselves. Something off the books. An injustice. That has to be it. They have no power here. They need me to act because they can't. But what? Tell me what you want. I'll do it. Why do I have to guess?

The moon face of his bespectacled double-dealing lawyer came to mind. Peter's bounces became more energetic. Then there was that defiler with the tongs who had threatened Terri. Peter felt the breath come right out of him.

Chapter 45

Riana sensed the initiative slipping away. She couldn't let that happen. Men fawned on her, did foolish things to please her, and that was only right. Yet in her pursuit of Greg, she'd suffered two rejections in the space of a week — and by the likes of Reg and Kaiser, chaff destined for the flames.

She resolved to act before Greg slipped away too. She changed into a cool-blue pantsuit that suited her mood and purpose. She put her hair in a bun and tried to look the part she envisioned herself playing. She sent Greg a text: *We're going to Vegas.*

She called a cab and soon found herself in the Junction. She was greeted at the door by Greg's wife, Zinna, who looked her up and down coolly. Riana couldn't get a read on her. Her face was enigmatic, but her body language was fluid and relaxed.

She spoke first to establish control. "My name is Riana Peligroso. We spoke earlier on the phone."

Zinna invited her in with a hand gesture. "Let me get my husband."

Greg was upstairs listening to Bob Marley on the headphones while he tried to work out the fingering to "Redemption Song." The pattern of metrical accent, and the uniquely Jamaican rendering of the words, had thus far defeated him, but he was determined to master this most glorious of anthems.

Zinna entered the study and pantomimed taking off a pair of earmuffs. Greg reluctantly pulled one earphone away from his skull. He wanted to convey that he was very happy where he was, doing what he doing, and that he had no desire to move.

"An individual named Peligroso is downstairs," she announced with a slight upturning of her nose.

Greg felt a twist of fear and anger rip through his gut. His voice was loud and then broke as he sputtered. "What does she want?"

"Let's find out," said Zinna brightly.

As Zinna made her way back down the stairs, Greg picked up his phone and read Kaiser's perplexing email about a panther on the prowl. Riana's missive about Vegas gave him more to work with. *She can't be serious.*

He began to see the outline of his peril. What in God's name had passed between Riana and Kaiser? This could be the end of his marriage. His eyes were hard at work as he descended the stairs, trying to pan the stream for clues. He felt exactly the way he had when he was ten and forced to face the mother of the girl he'd played doctor with.

She's here about the money. No, some kind of insane accusation. It'll be about the sex. Oh God, why did I ever let this woman into my life?

Riana had taken the power position in the living room, sitting in the large armchair. She'd draped her coat over the back of the chair adjacent and positioned her Christian Dior handbag on her lap after placing a manila envelope in front of her on the coffee table. With her game face on, she looked the part of a woman whose patrician patience and forbearance had been sorely tried.

Greg folded his arms and remained standing in the doorway to the living room, making an unhappy face that he prayed would convey outrage. He hoped to turn the tables on Riana by refusing to sit down. The faint trace of sweat on his forehead said, *Lie in progress.*

"Riana, I asked you to leave me alone."

The clipped precision of her response undid him. "We have business. It's this or disgrace in the courts."

"The courts would suit me better."

"You owe me four thousand dollars."

Greg drew in a breath, but never got the chance to say, *In a pig's eye.*

"Let me insert a word here," said Zinna. "Greg, please sit down over there. I have something I need to say to both of you."

Riana's eyes betrayed her — there was a flash of excitement, one that she quickly got under control. It didn't matter that Greg was angry. All that was required was for Zinna to throw him out. The rest would follow.

Greg recognized that he had no choice but to comply. He sat down in a way that communicated he was spoiling for a fight. His head felt as if he was spinning at the end of a centrifuge waiting for his eyes to explode and relieve the pressure.

"Riana, would you care for something to drink? Some water or juice, a coffee perhaps?" Zinna's offer was as assured as it was gracious.

"No, thank you," Riana countered with equal poise.

"What's in the envelope?"

"A bill you haven't paid." The delivery of the line was worthy of an Oscar nomination.

"For a service you never rendered," said Zinna, putting the Oscar's final destination beyond doubt.

To her chagrin, Riana's voice went up fifty decibels. "I took good care…"

Zinna's blood was up. She seized upon Riana's words with a ferocity that would've silenced a ballroom filled with waltzing couples. "You took very good care of yourself."

Riana frowned. The anger was appropriate, but the recipient was wrong. Why wasn't this falling on Greg's head?

"Well, if you feel that way," she said, getting to her feet. "I'll see you both in court. I came this evening as a professional courtesy." She started toward the door, hoping to provoke a stronger response. She turned on her heel and looked at Greg. "But clearly I'm not dealing with a professional."

Zinna moved past her and barred her way. "You're going to stand there and listen to me. Greg and I agonized about Gordon's addiction. Greg said we had to let him take his lumps and find his own way in life. I didn't have the heart for that." Her voiced softened. "Gordon is everything to me."

Riana let herself down badly by taking a half-step back. Her eyes lost their fire and her composure, for once, failed to save her.

Zinna went wild. "You told me you'd fix him. Of course I agreed! And you'll no doubt be very satisfied to know that Greg and I fought about what to do and ended up separated for almost a year." Her eyes welled up.

Greg raised his finger to interject.

"I'm talking, dear. Please shut up." She turned back to face Riana, her focus undiminished by her tears. "When I found out that you did Gordon no good whatsoever, that you actually told him he could drink again if only he followed your every instruction to the letter, I couldn't believe it. Then, when the Employment Assistance Program people told me they don't even deal with your company…"

Riana was barely managing to maintain the façade of being the offended party. A gentlewoman scolded by a fish wife. Greg's face reflected the surprise and outrage occasioned by having a foot run over by a shopping cart.

The half-step that Zinna took in Riana's direction suggested impeding fisticuffs. Her voice crested. "Greg told me about a 'lapse with a bimbo.' I figured out it was you when our youngest told me the lady who helped Gordon was with Daddy in the car on the way to Sunday school."

Riana stood ramrod straight and, this time, delivered her line without raising her voice. "I don't have to stand here and listen to slander. No one would believe a word of this, coming as it does from two deadbeats."

Zinna took another half-step into Riana's personal space. "You're going to stay, because it's safer than trying to push past me before I'm finished."

Riana and Greg were frozen in place, trying to work out where Zinna was going next.

"I documented everything and sent it to your employer — with a note from my lawyer. If Greg still wants you when you're unemployed, disgraced, and likely drunk, he's welcome to go with you now." She looked at her husband for a long moment and then turned back to Riana. "You can leave now. Get out of my house and never come back."

Life Skills must have had a paragraph or two about tactical retreats after a failed intervention, because Riana managed hers adroitly. She looked at Greg on her way out. He didn't want her. Her face registered fright as she slid past Zinna.

The front door closed, and Greg was still looking at his wife in awe.

"Did you really get a lawyer to write a letter to her employers?"

"It was the most satisfying letter I ever read."

"Why didn't you tell me?"

"Why didn't *you* tell *me* about *her*?"

"Oh." He had to admire the propriety of the sentence.

"Are we finished with keeping secrets?"

Chapter 46

Peter fled to the safety of Flannerman's, where he took a pew and curled up into a ball. There were no services scheduled until noon. He had the place to himself. Two dignified-looking attendants entered the chapel and began to embrace, but Peter ignored them. He would have been hard-pressed to decide what frightened him more, the blinking red light on the cryotank or the damned flowmeter that horrible child carried with her everywhere she went.

"It has to be our heads. That's the connection. My one link to Terri. I have to take our heads with me when I go. It makes sense — frozen heads, frozen time. Can't be in two places at once… Oh I don't know."

He cradled his massive head in his hands. "Dead people leave body parts scattered all over the place. Some even get transplanted and they live on in a new body. That line of logic goes nowhere."

He looked up at the hardwood ceiling. "Why can't someone just come right out and tell me. Why all the shilly-shallying?" *His tone changed to ridicule.* "Maybe this and maybe that."

He picked up a hymn book and shied it at the two lovers in the alcove. "Naff!"

He lay on his back, using his entwined fingers as a pillow. Well one thing is for sure, I'm back at full power. I don't know how or why or for how long, but standing in that pool of light did me good. *He sat up and felt better for it.* I don't know what to do about Walter or John. It's not right that she put that on me. How am I supposed to make things right for them…

The look on Peter's face went from doubt to certainty. He nodded slowly in response to the jack boots beating the pavement behind his eyes. "There are two bastards I can set right before I go."

Chapter 47

Kaiser waited until he saw Paul sitting alone, obsessing over the images he'd downloaded onto his phone. He wasn't texting the way the kids did, but he'd adopted the same round-shouldered posture. No, he was weighing the photographic possibilities inherent in the images he'd produced. He had enough material after his road trip to keep him occupied for months.

Kaiser tried subtlety for this interrogation. "Does Doug know you're running an art school?"

"I haven't told him yet."

"Show me what all the fuss is about."

"No, you'll try to either flatter or bully me into revealing what I'm doing, and then use the information to sandbag me at the census meeting."

"Whatever gave you that idea?"

"Ten years of watching you work."

"Well if, as you say, the thing was a flop, then we're done with it."

"Subtle."

"Show me what you got, or I'll accept your wife's next invitation to dinner!"

Paul had to laugh. "Anything but that! Do you at least know the general story?"

Kaiser fanned his ten fingers. "It's all anyone talks about these days."

Paul got to his feet and moved into the centre of the room as he scrolled through his pictures, looking for the image he wanted to begin with.

"On my day off, I drove up to Georgian Bay and checked out Seymour's cottage. It ought to be a national park. It's the most gorgeous piece of shoreline

I've ever seen. Thinking about it gives me goosebumps. If Tom Thomson had seen that beach, the painting of it would be on a postage stamp."

"What did Picasso do with it?"

Paul shook his head. He couldn't find the image he wanted. "For that, you're going to have to come into the other room. I helped myself to a few of the sketches he tossed into the trash."

They made their journey. Paul unrolled a sheet of drawing papers from a roll and smoothed it out onto the desktop. "Did you ever take an art class?"

"I got to fingerpaint once."

"Not in the psych ward, in school. I mean an art appreciation class."

"I took auto shop."

"Art is something everyone can do, but something that very few people do well, and something that only gifted people can do at the highest level. In my photography, I'm competent and I take solid images, but nothing that breaks the image out of the frame. I'm only occasionally that good because I'm still a hobbyist. I started at this rather late in life. My point is that there's a line between competence and genius. It has everything to do with perspective. It's going to take me a long time and a lot of hard work to get to where this kid is starting out. He does stuff that's so fresh and alive, I can hardly believe it's possible."

Kaiser looked at the sketches, but he didn't see anything that looked even vaguely interesting. "I'm not seeing it."

"The talent's there. I saw the actual shoreline and I played with the images in a darkroom for a week, and nothing I came up with is as good as his initial sketches."

"What about Mummy? She's a mad genius too."

Paul's con light came on. "Kaiser, what are you up to?"

"I want her to read Reg's novel."

"Why?"

"Doesn't matter. I need the inside track."

"Why don't you send a copy?"

"You have to stand out in the crowd. I'm not sure Puddin' Head's book is any good."

"Have you read it?"

"No time. Far too busy on important matters. Lots of bees buzzing around inside my head."

"Why don't you ask Seymour about it," said Paul, dripping sarcasm. "Maybe pull him out of class and ask him how to outflank his mother. It would be good for the kid. Help him with his addiction, no doubt."

"I already have — he was quite helpful."

***

Kaiser waited until Reg went upstairs to teach the morning session. Reg, as always, left his laptop in the office. Paul was busy doing paperwork at one desk while Mike had his head down, frowning at a computer screen, at another. Kaiser got to his feet, put the laptop under his arm, and left the office. He set himself up in the back room. There was an icon labelled NOVEL. Kaiser slid his memory stick into the device and downloaded the book.

Mike looked up at him when he re-entered the office. Before anyone could think to ask what he was doing with Reg's computer, he announced, "He's going to lose this damn thing, leaving it out there."

Mike lost interest. Kaiser taped his breast pocket. Mischief was afoot and his chest was beginning to swell with manic magic.

After lunch, Kaiser walked down to Spadina and College and got a cheap pay-as-you-play cellphone. The clerk obligingly registered it in the company name provided.

Back at the office, he called Wiarton Movers after spotting their ad in the *Wiarton Echo*. He could hear the photocopier tirelessly printing Reg's novel in the background as he spoke.

"Can you guys get a truck up to Pike Bay?"

"Sure. What have you got in mind?"

"We're shooting a scene for a movie up there and I need a couple of guys to empty the living room and then very carefully put it all back exactly the way it was. The bookcases are sacred to the owner. She'll have my hide if her treasures are disturbed."

"We've done this before. We'll shrink wrap them."

Kaiser was becoming concerned with the amount of time it was taking to print. This was a big manuscript. Someone was going to come in. "I want you to take pictures before you move stuff, and then use them to put everything back exactly the way it was. Do you know what OCD is?"

The voice at the other end of the line laughed.

"Can you keep the stuff on the truck overnight?"

"That depends on how busy we are. When are you planning to do this?"

"This Friday. I'll courier a cheque and the key. We need the stuff out as early as you can manage and then we need it back as if it never left at precisely eleven a.m. on Saturday. That's the deal we made with the owners. They have something planned for the Saturday evening…"

"The name of your company?"

"Miracle Publications."

"And your name, sir?"

"Edgar Demain."

Chapter 48

Peter walked the length of Madison Avenue searching for John. He headed into Punanai and up to Lou's room. There were still poltergeists hanging around, but the tide was receding. Yesterday's energy was abating. The hallway no longer lent fire to his assent. Doors were once again impenetrable and whatever glue was holding the two spooks to the wall was giving way. They were slowly descending to the floor.

Peter went back downstairs and waited by the front door until a group of the guys formed up to go for coffee. He grabbed the biggest guy by the scruff of the neck. As the men lurched out the door, Peter calculated his options. He let go of the brute as he passed the Granite Glen Nursing Home and made his way inside the lobby, where he pressed the elevator button to take him downstairs to the Chamber of New Life. He sat quietly in the waiting area, waiting for inspiration. What needed doing began to take shape in his imagination.

He made his way to the small office behind the cryotanks, where he found Pritpal Virk working away at his desk. Peter couldn't stand the sight of the man. This was the prick who wanted to throw Terri into a dumpster.

We'll see about that. Peter sat down in the corner and plotted.

After an hour, Pritpal finally left.

Peter was still feeling chuffed after his invigorating baptism in the light. He used his extra energy to stand up and walk to Barstow's desk, where he used the phone to order an Uber.

Then he retrieved his file and Terri's from the cabinet and opened both of them on the desk.

There were three letters from his lawyer. The first explained that Peter's estate had a liquidity problem. The second acknowledged that Peter's investments had gone broke. The final letter had a cheque stub for two hundred dollars attached to it.

Peter was furious. For once he had something worth doing when the sun went down. It took him ten minutes to familiarize himself with Pritpal's computer. The last thing he installed on his computer before he died was a Y2K patch, which turned out to be a waste of money. This newer version had a few bells and whistles he'd never seen before.

He composed a letter to the Toronto Police and copied the Legal Society of Upper Canada and the three leading daily newspapers. His hands burned as he typed, but he didn't mind. This was for Terri. He would be a poltergeist in a week if he kept up this pace, but he was past caring.

"Wait until they see a dead guy's signature."

He printed out the letters and set them with the two files in a plastic bin liner that he had placed in the trash basket.

He sat in silence for an hour watching the screen saver — a shopping cart that rolled end over end in outer space. The cleaner startled him when she opened the door. She emptied the trash baskets into the big green bag hanging on her cleaning cart in the hall. Then she went to work giving the office a lick and a promise.

He followed her on her rounds, taking advantage of her access to locked rooms to obtain a stack of clean white towels from the linen supply. While her attention was elsewhere, he secreted them on her cart. Inspiration struck when he spotted a suitcase with wheels. Everything he needed would fit perfectly inside it.

Chapter 49

Paul worked in the darkroom, transfixed, aching to see an image equal to the one he'd obsessed about for years. He had come across it quite by chance, wandering alone in the woods. His burning bush that was not consumed. A waking dream that did not vanish in the first moment of consciousness.

He'd been camping near a lake, tucked away in the forest, carrying a pail of water back from the spring. A quarry stone a yard wide covered in moss. Out of the green, wet mass grew a wild rose, almost, but not yet fully, in bloom. He gasped and dropped the pail. His senses swam. An excitement from deep inside him set him to shaking.

It was a timeless incarnation of the eternal. The lens through which to view creation. The love behind both the giving and the taking of life. All of these inherent in the image but not contained by it.

The Romantic poets had it right — beauty is truth, truth beauty. Simpler forms evolve into increasingly complex ones. The natural world was full of the signs of God's passing. Every living thing bears the mark of the carpenter's pencil and the kerf chatter of the saw blade. Before and after visible both in the flesh and the DNA. The nascent human skeleton visible in the vein marks on leaves. The wonders of the human eye, in its vestigial form, at work in a field of sunflowers orienting themselves in tandem to changes in the light.

His senses swam. He stood transfixed, looking at the rose, the stone, and the dark-green moss, until he couldn't see his hand in front of his face.

It took hours in the darkness to find his tent. Once he did, he couldn't settle and sleep never came. He sat staring into the fire, watching the sparks and the stars become an unbroken field of fireflies.

At first light, he returned to the spot. This time he brought his camera. He found the pail where he'd left it, the trees all looked the same, he could see his own heel prints in the soft soil, but there was no trace of the moss, rock, or rose. He wept and wondered, had they only existed in his mind?

The image was indelible. He'd never seen its equal — until now. The shoreline at Seymour's cottage compelled him. It was a symphony building toward its next climax, the mystery at the centre of ongoing creation. He could almost see it in his photos, but he hadn't managed to coax it out of hiding. He sighed as he downloaded the images onto his tablet and headed off for his Friday shift at Punanai.

**

Kaiser was smoking on the front porch when Greg arrived for work. He planted a Padrón Series cigar into the breast pocket of Kaiser's suit and saluted him. "Thank you for the best night of my life, you conniving son of a bitch."

Kaiser's head tilted to the right. "What did I do?"

"You wound Riana up and my missus mounted her head above the fireplace."

"You speak in riddles."

"I speak in riddles."

Kaiser looked skyward and opened his arms wide. *No idea what he's talking about, but who cares? This is a nice cigar.*

He went back to thinking about the business he'd planned. There was no way to be sure that it would land where he hoped it would. He had a moment of doubt that touched the edge of sorrow. *I should think this thing through again.* But it was only a moment. He had to stifle a giggle as he headed inside. The image of outrage on Reg's face settled the issue.

Kaiser didn't hear a word of the census meeting. His gears were grinding fine particles into explosive dust. Mike, of course, picked up on his absence but could not make sense of it.

As the staff gathered up their papers, ready to depart, Paul hung back and took the seat opposite Doug's desk. "I want to talk to you about Seymour."

Doug looked up from his computer. "A quiet desperado by all accounts."

"There are depths to this one." Paul noticed that Doug was restless. Missives were flying back and forth between head office and Punanai about Lou Canon's abrupt departure. Doug had a full day of pointless interference and second-guessing to look forward to. Getting him interested in anything else was going to be difficult.

"About the paintings he burned…"

Doug was sitting on the knife's edge of *go away* and *tell me what you want and then go away*. "Your colleagues can't leave that alone. Every day they discuss it in great detail, as if they were breaking the Watergate story. I'm actually bored with it."

"I want to try something unorthodox this weekend."

Doug's reluctance was finding a focal point. "Are you going to come in early and work hard all day without complaining?"

Paul allowed a look of horror to pass across his face. "Hardly! I want to get Seymour painting."

Doug waved his arm grandly. "Wonderful — have him start in here and then do the living room."

"You know that's not what I mean."

"What's wrong with him doing the same thing that everyone else is going to do? Why does he have to paint on my time? We only have twenty-one days to explain to someone who would rather be anywhere else why they need to make changes to their life. Changes, I might add, that scare the hell out of them." He paused and pointed at his screen where ominous emails continued to arrive from every point of the compass. "A lot of people are annoyed with me. Doing the right thing is a career-limiting move. Don't you want me to have a nice weekend?"

"I know, and maybe I shouldn't ask, but I have to admit this has me hot under the collar." Paul could tell that he finally had Doug's interest when he turned away from the screen and faced him.

"Explain it to me. You're usually the most level-headed."

"This kid needs to paint or he's going to die."

"That's a bit dramatic. We used to say things of that nature about sobriety — and in almost that tone of voice."

Paul pleaded with his eyes. "His sense of self-worth is tied up with his painting."

"We can't play favourites. When the other guys see him painting, they'll want to give it a try. There'll be chaos and hard feelings if we don't — all of which will take their energy and focus off what we are teaching them. We need to stay in our lane. He has the rest of his life to find himself."

Paul sighed. He wanted to say, *One size doesn't always fit all*, but he settled for, "Let me show you something." He took out his tablet and scrolled until he got to the image he wanted. Then he looked up at Doug and pointed at the artwork on the wall across from him. "That print that you stare at all day while you work ... I gotta be honest ... it's pedestrian."

"It makes me happy."

"It does the same thing for the guy at the dollar store; he sells forty of them a week."

Doug looked hurt but said nothing.

"Now let me show you some real art." Paul turned his tablet toward Doug. "These are the paintings Seymour did before he went nuts. With his permission, I went back to the place where these plants grow and took pictures. It's winter now and the patch looks very different. I've photoshopped a couple of these and played with them in the darkroom. They're stunning."

Doug's face mirrored an interesting blend of disappointed and confused. "Looks like weeds."

Paul almost smiled. "They're much more than that. I don't expect you to share my passion, but I've been working on these since I took them. They're dynamite. I haven't felt this alive or happy in quite some time."

"Now we're getting somewhere. You're having a breakdown. But what has that got to do with Seymour?"

"He needs to feel what I'm feeling."

"He'll get drunk."

"He'll get drunk if he doesn't."

Doug looked over at the growing list of emails and despaired. "Go away for an hour."

***

Kaiser was helping himself to a cup of coffee in the kitchen when Paul emerged from Doug's office. "Who were you ratting out?" Kaiser asked playfully.

"You," said Paul, looking up from his tablet.

The big man shook his mane of golden hair. "I've led a blameless life of Christian example."

"There's where you made your mistake!" Paul went back to the images. Kaiser failed to pick up on the clues that pointed toward a desire for privacy.

"You've been looking at that since you got here. Whaddya got — pictures of the missus?"

"My new obsession. Wanna see?"

"A part of me wants to, but another part is afraid … very, very afraid."

"Kaiser, are you trying to hurt my feelings?"

"Hard not to, bonehead. Show me…"

Paul handed him his tablet. Kaiser squinted, trying to make sense of the images. "Is this your garden?"

"It's the shoreline at Seymour Dunn's cottage."

"This is gonna be a real sock in the eye to everyone around here who thinks you're nuts."

"Can't you see the beauty?"

Kaiser smiled. "It's a weed patch."

"On Judgment Day, that statement will be remembered against you. That's the most beautiful image the world has yet to see. And when Seymour paints this, it'll leap off the canvas and change the world."

"Like Reg's novel."

"I don't know. I haven't read it."

"Neither have I, but take my word for it, it's a peach. I've decided to have it published."

"You have opinions about books you haven't read?"

"Why not? You have opinions about paintings that aren't even painted yet."

***

Doug was drained and ready to call it a day even though it was only ten thirty when he put the phone down. A new idea had come to him. He tried to settle himself by putting on the stereo, but even that let him down. He felt too punched out to think — and yet more than a little manic. Something was coming to consciousness that required time and space to germinate. On went the coat as he went looking for Mike, whom he found in the counsellors' office, staring at his computer screen the way that aging actors fret over their appearance in a mirror.

"We're going for coffee."

Mike looked up with a smile. "A real one?"

Doug smoothed the brim of his hat. "Yes, and you get to choose where."

Mike looked over at Paul, who was reading a file, and said, sotto voce, "There has to be a catch."

Paul didn't look up. He nodded the way soon-to-be divorced husbands do.

Doug squared his shoulders. "I'm tempted to do something stupid and I'm counting on you to talk me out of it."

Mike headed for the coat rack. "You're right. That's worth a coffee and a pastry."

"No one said anything about a pastry!"

They made their way into the glorious morning sunshine.

"Paul's come up with an idea for Seymour Dunn."

"A job with the fire department?"

"Paul wants to let him paint while he's here."

"I'd rather see him do that than worry about our dumb old program."

Doug flicked his keychain and his car winked at him. "That is where this starts to blister. It's a good idea. Paul's instincts are sound. He wants to use what the boy loves to reset his compass."

Mike eased himself into the passenger seat. "There's something profoundly disturbing about him burning those paintings. It's medieval in its ferocity."

Doug closed his door and put on the belt. "The guy who runs the Trent canal has the same problem I do. How much water do you let in? Let it fall too low, and nothing works. Let in too much, and you burst the mechanical doors. I've read about painting and art working miracles in people's recoveries. I'd love to give it a try—"

"—but we're not set up for it," Mike finished the sentence for him. "Next weekend they'll be lined up five deep demanding interpretive dance and Reiki."

"Shoemaker, stick to your last," said Doug as he eased out into traffic.

"Meaning…"

"Stick to what you know."

Mike sighed. "Life Skills is shortly going to kick everything we know and love to the curb. I'm surprised you've been able to hold it off this long."

Doug adjusted the settings on the fan, allowing the warm air to heat the interior instead of the windshield. "Remember this when I'm gone. Punanai is a fish and chips shop. The kind of place that's been open for forty years and has moved from serving cod to halibut to haddock to pollock and, finally, to plaice. We can handle that much change."

Mike nodded. "Restaurants close when the owners get bored. They hire people to do the drudgery. Eventually the accountant gets loose in the kitchen and ruins the product. While the bosses dream about franchising the business, rats are loose in the storeroom. If you don't love food and don't love watching happy people eat, you've missed the point of owning a restaurant."

"What we do is repetitive. Make your batter, clean your oil, cut your chips, and count the cash. We don't need a maître d' or a sommelier," said Doug as he came to a stop at the light. He used the time to give his windshield a spray.

"The board were told flat out to get with the program or have their funding cut off. That's why they hired Erin — who didn't have a clue what we do here when she started, by the way. Two weeks later, she was talking about our program as if she'd invented it. Ten weeks later, she reads an article and decides to turn everything we do upside down."

Mike lit a cigarette. "The funders believe in numbers. And Life Skills has the numbers."

"Numbers are bullshit."

"Bullshit that keeps the lights on."

"Tinker, tailor, soldier, Doug."

"What…?"

"Some days I don't know if I'm an MI6 mole or a KGB plant."

"Meaning…"

"Life Skills is obliterating my sense of right and wrong."

Mike turned to look at his boss with a knowing smile. "Better and worse are the new right and wrong?"

"All the government cares about is keeping drunks out of the emergency."

Doug honked his horn at a cab driving the wrong way down the one-way street. "That fellow there has Life Skills."

Doug turned right when the traffic relented. The drive up Bathurst Street was torturously slow.

"You said I got to choose."

"Do you like Bagel World?"

"Yeah…"

"You've chosen."

"You really do get this choosing thing."

"I'm going to let the kid sketch. The painting can be a part of his aftercare. Paul can supervise it."

As they pulled into the always overcrowded parking lot at Bathurst and Wilson, Doug had to ply his way through several formidable-looking potholes. An elderly man in a car far too big for him was trying to back out of a space without looking by doing it in three-foot bursts, putting the onus on his fellow motorists to honk if they hated bodywork.

Doug had dibs on the space and gave the old boy some hand signals that, unfortunately, he couldn't see. As he cleared the space and made his way to the exit, another car loomed into sight, intent on cheating Doug of the prize. Doug lurched into the space and made a threatening appearance as he got out of the car. The intruder did the math before taking the point and driving on.

"Why don't they fix the parking lot?"

"They do bagels. That's enough."

Chapter 50

Moose Nevin and Bucky Brill drove the Wiarton Movers' five-ton truck to the diner early Friday morning, where they took advantage of the weekend getaway special. Four strips of bacon and four rounds of sausage with eggs and home fries for under ten dollars put them in the mood to work. A second envelope stuffed with twenty-dollar bills from Miracle Publications had arrived just before they left the yard. There was a note from Mr. L.E. Demain explaining that the cheque he'd written them was going to bounce because his secretary had mistakenly closed that account and couldn't reopen it. He apologized and hoped they wouldn't mind being paid in cash. They were delighted and decided to splurge.

They got the chef to wrap them up roast beef sandwiches for lunch, and off they went toward Pike Bay with a thermos of hot coffee sitting on the seat between them. It was a beautiful morning. Last week's snowfall had eroded, leaving only traces of white visible in the woods.

Bucky found the cottage without any trouble. It was a familiar landmark when the trees were bare, easily visible from the road. In summer, it hid behind a wall of foliage.

He and Moose were able to negotiate the narrow driveway, but the moving van was ten feet high, and it brought down a couple of dead branches as it squeezed under the canopy. The truck got stuck and they spun their wheels in the soft mud for a few minutes before they could free themselves.

The thing that stumped them was the key they'd gotten in the mail. It was labelled in neat handwriting: Dunn Cottage Side Door. But it didn't fit the lock. It wasn't even close. Bucky got on the phone while Moose poured the coffee.

Kaiser picked up the call in the hallway outside the meeting rooms. He had to teach in five minutes. "What's up?"

"We have a problem, Mr. Demain. The key doesn't work."

"Oh crap. Did you try all the doors? Never mind, of course you did. That's the key they gave me." He paused as if in thought. "I can't get anything up to you until tomorrow." His voice dropped. "Can you guys give the lock a gentle twist?"

Bucky didn't like where this was going, but he had come all this way. "Yeah, I suppose we could." That *suppose* told Kaiser he didn't want to.

"The whole crew is going to be on site tomorrow. The carpenter can fix any damage you do. Break a small window and put some cardboard in it, it will only be for the one night. I'll settle up with the owners."

Bucky was still unhappy but willing to be convinced. "Would you send us an email, so our tail feathers are covered?"

Kaiser's voice moving Edgar Demain's lips sounded reasonable and reassuring. "Gladly. I'll copy the Dunns on it too — that way everyone will be on the same page. Any other problems give me a call at this number."

Bucky put away the phone and motioned to Moose. "Bring the toolbox."

***

After work on Friday, Kaiser made the long drive up to Pike Bay. He stopped and had dinner at the Wiarton Diner. The waitress suggested the small steak. She was right — it was good.

Even at night, this was spectacular country. He used his GPS to locate the cottage and parked Oren's Toyota on the side of the road, unwilling to risk the perils of the driveway. He made his way up the dark path before he took out his penlight. He spied the broken window covered in cardboard by Moose and Bucky and had the side door open in a minute. He propped Reg's manuscript on the wooden windowsill and taped the ransom demand to the glass. In the empty room, it drew the eye.

iF you EVER want to zee YOUR books aGAin PUBLiSH ThiS One!

He started to giggle, partly out of anxiety and partly out of sheer giddiness. As an afterthought, he snapped a picture with his phone. A souvenir to show Reg. This one might be his masterpiece. He carefully surveyed the room one last time, fastened the door behind him, and carefully made his way back down the driveway. He could have sworn that the moon winked at him.

Chapter 51

The cleaner gave the cryotanks a few swipes with a wet cloth to discourage the dust. The floor didn't get enough traffic to warrant a nightly washing. She finished the room just before the end of her shift at 11:00 p.m. When she left, Peter had the place to himself.

Peter had watched Pritpal and Barstow work on the tank. He knew how to turn off the alarm on the old Lawrence Meteor and open it. The old tank belched vapour when he raised the lid. It took a moment for it to clear. There they were — two lovebirds frozen in a moment of time. Two desiccated astronauts that NASA couldn't bring back to Earth, floating forever in the dark and the cold. Peter ached to touch Terri's forehead with his loving hand but then thought better of it. Who knows what could happen with these very low temperatures? He might become paralyzed for fifty years.

He emulated the hated Pritpal, putting on the very gloves and using the same tongs he had employed. Peter had to work as hard as any mother to accomplish this rebirth.

He looked at his old head and sighed. Nothing left there. Terri, who'd been the wonder of the world in her youth, didn't look any better. Two bald heads in thick plastic bags, labelled Specimen 42 and Specimen 938. Peter didn't get much for his million.

He placed the two heads lovingly on the towels he'd brought along for insulation, then wrapped them and placed them in the suitcase he'd borrowed from upstairs. He had to fight an intense desire to kiss Terri. Caution only won out because of the intense cold.

He affixed a label to the suitcase with his lawyer's name and address, and the notation, in his own hand. "FOR PICK UP." He closed the cryotank and reset the alarm. He made his way to the elevator, where he sat down on the suitcase to rest.

That took a lot out of me. I have a long way to go. I don't want to run out of juice at the last minute. Every calorie counts. I won't get a second chance.

Peter waited with the suitcase out of sight in an alcove until the security guards changed shifts. They took the elevator to the basement and did their customary walk-through, making sure that no one had purloined a water heater. When they were out of earshot, Peter took the elevator to the main floor, where he positioned the suitcase out of sight on the floor behind the security desk. Exhausted but satisfied, he sat down to wait for his ride.

***

The Uber pulled up in front of the Granite Glen at 1:22 a.m. The driver came through the front door looking for the package he'd been sent to collect. The security guard was at a loss, but when he stirred himself from his fried chicken and looked around, he found the suitcase where Peter had left it. The label said "For pick up" and so he handed it over without looking inside. Peter grabbed the stout driver by the belt loop and let himself be towed to the car.

The ride to Don Mills took forty minutes. Even at night, the city was full of traffic snarls and backups. Peter had not been in a car for a while, and he enjoyed the ride. The city had changed since he'd last seen it. He noted with some satisfaction as he exited the vehicle that Pritpal's personal Mastercard was on the hook for the $38 fare. It served the little slumlord right.

Security at Fairview Mall signed for the package and left it on a shelf with dozens of others.

When the guard went on his rounds, Peter laid hands on the bag, which was starting to weigh a ton, and rolled it over to the escalator, which, thankfully, was still operating. The fat ghost needed to pick his spot very carefully. This cargo would be worthless if it was intercepted in the wrong place.

There were only cleaners and contractors working in the building at this time of night, but even so, it would be disastrous for someone to hear wheels growl on marble and look up to see a suitcase out for a stroll without its owner. But Peter had to take the risk. This cargo had to be detonated at an exact time and place in order to bring about the desired outcome. Normally ghosts didn't have the energy to move something so large, but Peter had stepped into the light. The energy he felt was more than anything he'd experienced as a ghost. He could move ten suitcases if he needed to.

Peter no longer recognized the hallway that led to his lawyer's office. The restaurant was gone, and the barber shop now sold telephones. He sat down on a stone bench to rest, and when he looked up, there was the office. He had almost walked past it.

He realized he'd come to end of the paved road. The rest of his mission had to be improvised in locations that he had never seen. There was an alcove to the right of the entrance that would serve to hide the suitcase. Then he reached into his pocket and produced a penknife that he used to jiggle the lock on the office door. A silent alarm went off at the security desk and the night watchman came running — well, running as fast as a sixty-five-year-old commissionaire ever cared to run to the scene of a false alarm. He shone his flashlight through the window and into the darkened office. He didn't see anything unusual, and nothing made a break for it. After fumbling with his keys, he opened the door and went exploring, calling out, "Security!" Peter moved quickly from the alcove, heaving the luggage in his arms. He dared not roll the suitcase. He hefted the heavy burden inside the door and then collapsed into a swivel chair, exhausted but with a look of triumph on his face. His short stay in the light had given him just enough energy to do what needed doing.

The guard found nothing amiss in the office. He logged the incident and locked the door behind him.

Peter hadn't been in this office in over twenty years. There was a picture of his man on the wall. He wasn't young anymore; he looked the part of a fat crook with perfect white teeth. Back in the day, when Peter knew him, he used to fight for lost causes and represent the wrongfully convicted. He was a man of integrity then. Or maybe that was just the beard.

The rest did Peter some good. He felt his strength returning, but he was glad that all the strenuous work was behind him. He now had to stage his crime scene. He took the thawing heads out of the suitcase and placed them reverently on a desk. There was a funny-looking plume of frost that resembled steam coming off them. He put the letters he'd written inside a plastic shipping envelope and hung them on a computer screen. The label simply said, "Evidence of fraud. Attention police."

Certain that all was now in order, he stood up on the desk and touched a match very carefully to the fire alarm. It took a minute, but the lights started to flash. Peter got under cover beneath a desk before the water began to spray.

The old commissionaire could run when his ass was on the line. This time, he made it back downstairs in less than a minute. When he saw two frozen heads where before he'd seen none, he got on the radio. There was no need. Peter had already thoughtfully dialled 9-1-1.

It wasn't hard to get a ride back to the nursing home. The cops went right over to see Barstow and Pritpal when they read the note.

Chapter 52

Kingsly and Verna didn't stop in Wiarton to pick up groceries. Kingsly had put together what they needed from the provisions in their apartment. It was only the two of them, after all, and they didn't eat much. If they'd stopped in town, the people at the farmers' market would've asked them about the movie. Moose had a lot to say last night at the legion. Everyone was excited and eager to hear all the details.

Kingsly allowed the Volvo to slow to a crawl before he turned off the side road and into the driveway to the cottage. As he began his turn, Verna grabbed his wrist.

"Tire tracks — big ones!"

Kingsly hadn't noticed them. "Someone turning around…"

"In here, never." Verna was shaking.

Kingsly stopped the car and turned to comfort his wife. "You stay here, I'm going to peek around the corner and make sure we're not walking into something. There will probably be a new water heater or some such foolishness on the front porch."

***

The OPP detachment in Wiarton took the initial call from Mrs. Verna Dunn at 10:00 a.m. on Saturday. The corporal who took the call noted that she was especially agitated.

"We've been robbed. They took my whole life. There's a ransom note making demands."

The investigating officers filed their initial report as Break and Enter and Mischief. Stunts of this sort were commonplace on the peninsula. When cottagers got too full of themselves and threw their weight around in town for long enough, they always made someone angry enough to reformat restorative justice.

Watching Mrs. Dunn lose her fur in clumps strongly supported this possibility in the minds of the investigating officers. No doubt she'd belittled someone, or maybe her kid hadn't taken someone else's kid to the prom the way he promised to. Maybe it was simply her turn. Who knew? These things were driven by petty impulses. This was probably nothing more than a bunch of high schoolers with a bottle of rum and nothing better to do on a Friday night than work out a little hostility on the adult world.

Still, it was a lot of work to pack up a whole cottage full of books. The complainants were adamant that there were ten bookshelves containing over five hundred hardcovers and twice as many manuscripts. There were obvious signs of a break-in and tire tracks in the driveway. It wasn't going to be hard to find whoever did this. In winter this road was practically deserted. The Ministry of Transportation traffic camera kept a steady eye on the comings and goings along this stretch of road. How many trucks could there be?

***

When Moose and Bucky arrived back at the cottage on Saturday morning, they were mildly surprised to find crime-scene tape blocking the driveway. They assumed it was something the film people had used. After their previous difficulties, they had the good sense to walk down the driveway before they tried backing the loaded truck down around the treacherous dog leg. They came upon an OPP forensic technician using plaster of paris to make casts of the tire tracks they'd left yesterday in the soft mud.

They looked at the policeman and then each other in wonder. Before either could utter a word, a wild woman came pelting out of the cottage.

"Do you have my books? Are you the ones?"

Bucky and Moose exchanged glances, wondering what the hell they'd let themselves in for.

***

Newly minted detective Clinton Culp was assigned to the case. It was a slow day for crime on the Bruce Peninsula and the duty officer was more than happy to have him out from under foot for the day. He listened to Verna's third telling of events as he examined the cottage. He put on surgical gloves before picking up the manuscript that Kaiser had left on the windowsill. Someone had thoughtfully left the author's business card taped to the back cover. The note made him smile.

He got on the computer and soon knew all there was to know about Reg Topping. The cheeky bastard had a picture of his cat holding the manuscript on his web page. *This guy's an idiot.*

Verna was fully engaged. The hook Kaiser had baited for her held fast. Self-referentially incoherent plots were her kryptonite. She never put down a manuscript until she had read it from stem to stern. This boondoggle was no different. Besides, this Reg Topping was staff at the treatment centre where Seymour was staying. Verna was furious that he had dared to touch her books, but part of her was curious too. She wanted to meet the man behind this. After conferring with Culp, she called the number on the business card and left a brief message. "My name is Verna Dunn. You know my son, Seymour. I have your manuscript. I want you to come to my office this afternoon to discuss things."

Reg was dumbfounded by the message. He'd planned to take in a film, but after the call, he lost all interest in the cinema. He went straight to his room and started to pull his marrying-and-burying suit out of the closet. His manuscript had been returned last month with a note that said what all the others had said. But none of that mattered now — she'd called. His heart sang for joy. This was the most wonderful thing that had ever happened.

Seymour has spoken to his mom.

***

Detective Culp had Verna's office wired for picture and sound. He'd never had a chance to use the recording equipment before, except in training exercises, and it was exciting to put it to use on a real criminal. Well, *a real idiot* might be the more apt description. His superiors had given him a hard time about the costs involved. Culp badly needed to uncover some serious charges to justify this expense.

In the end, his boss relented when Culp pointed out that they had nothing in the way of physical evidence that they could use and that it they didn't hear what happened from Topping himself, they might never know. If he was as crazy as he appeared to be, there might be no point in charging him. Video tape worked wonders with jurors. A drunk unable to walk a straight line is hard to misinterpret.

On the drive to Toronto, Culp had glanced through the manuscript, looking for something that might help him better understand who and what he was dealing with. The book was well written. Several times he actually forgot he was reading evidence left at the scene of the crime by a lunatic. How could anyone bright enough to write this be dumb enough to do that? He wondered if Topping was going to turn out to have a few gaps in his personality. Or, considering the material Topping was writing about, Culp wondered if the author had not gone over to the dark side.

Verna was still incapable of civil speech. Yes, Wiarton Movers and Moose and Bucky were obviously stooges. She'd held her tongue and her temper as they described how they'd taken a contract to rob her cottage without ever seeing the client. When they produced the cheque that was later replaced with the envelope full of cash, she noticed with interest that it was signed L. Edgar Demain. She saw a literary mind at work.

When Culp phoned the number used to communicate with the mysterious Mr. Demain — oh hell, why not just call him Topping and be done with it — they were told that Mr. Demain had been killed by a panther in a misadventure at the Toronto Zoo. Well wishers and those wishing to pay their last respects to the deceased were directed to attend a memorial dinner being held that afternoon at the Wiarton Diner. The cheeky bugger had even added that, in lieu of flowers, a gift to the WWF would be appreciated by the family.

Detective Culp called the diner, but they had no idea about any special functions planned for that afternoon. The cook had done a rather nice pot roast and some fresh pies and suggested that Culp bring some of his buddies over before the best ones were gone.

Verna's beloved books and manuscripts had been expertly handled by Moose and Bucky, who obviously took great pride in their work. They were able, with Verna's unnecessary assistance, to put everything back within a millimetre of its original position. They'd even given the books a good dusting. Though that did not sweeten her mood.

Ted McKing from town showed up in his pickup an hour after Moose and Bucky arrived. He told Detective Culp that a Mr. Demain slid a photograph of the damage through his mail slot. He'd also included $100 in cash and a note asking him to come to the cottage and fix the window.

Those were the facts that informed Verna's mood as she waited at her desk late Saturday afternoon. When Reg limped into the office, Verna was locked and loaded with a round in the chamber. This bow-tied vandal had wiped his boots on her holy of holies and he was going to pay for it.

Her tone was a marvel. While she thought, *You bastard*, she said, "Are you Mr. Topping?"

Reg was all smiles. "I am."

He tried to shake her hand, but she was having none of that. Reg put it down to Seymour's description of his mother's idiosyncrasies. Detective Culp had very carefully coached Verna about what to say. He wanted her to be gracious and get the man feeling relaxed and talkative. He needed Reg to incriminate himself, and the best chance for that to happen was simply to let the conversation flow.

But Verna's anger couldn't accommodate itself to Culp's patient strategy. This hoodlum had violated her privacy and here he was now, all smiles and insouciance, mocking her in her own office.

"How dare you!"

Reg looked behind him to see if he'd tracked dirt into her office.

Detective Culp wished he was a director able to shush Verna and put the scene back on the desired trajectory. But alas, this spacecraft was out of control and re-entering the atmosphere at a suicidal pitch and yaw.

Reg was struggling. "Mrs. Dunn, what's happening here? Why are you upset?"

She flew at him from across the room like a blitzing linebacker. Her extended arms made contact with his shoulders. Reg was too slow to get out of her way and was knocked onto the floor. He rolled on his side to collect himself before he regained his feet with great difficulty. There was murder in his eyes.

The primal part of his brain wanted to say, *If you were a man, I'd be clubbing you with my canes.* After a considerable personal struggle, he managed something less raw and memorable.

"Mrs. Dunn, unless you're a complete lunatic, I would advise you never to do that again. I'm partially disabled, but only partially. I can and will take care of myself."

Her blood was still boiling. "You stole my books and violated the sanctity of my home."

"I did ... what? I have no idea what you're talking about, but you look predisposed to some serious craziness. Good day, madam."

"You're not going anywhere, you little thief." She ran ahead of him to the door and barred his departure with her body.

Reg was genuinely at a loss. "Are you often this way, Verna? Is there someone I can call?"

She roared her defiance. "Don't you play the innocent with me. That room is my whole life. You stole my soul!"

Put me in harm's way and keep me safe indeed.

"I need you to tell me what it is you think I've done."

"So we're back to that game, eh?"

When Reg rose to his full height, looking the part of a prime minster about to restore order in the fractious lower chamber, something inside her broke and his demeanour served to further inflame her passion.

"Oh, you think you're being clever. But there are things going on here of which you're very much unaware."

"Oh shit, here we go," said Topping and Culp in unison.

"You used your position at Punanai to cultivate a relationship with my son. You then took what you learned and concocted a ridiculous charade to get me to read your book. Well, I won't have it."

Oh, Kaiser, what have you done...?

The familiar scent of mischief filled the air and acted on his voice like a tranquilizer. "I'll say you won't. You rejected the book last month."

"I've read your book?"

"You signed the letter."

"I sign all the letters. What's it about? Refresh my memory."

Reg suddenly felt seven years old. "It's about the treatment centre where I work. It's about addiction. I assumed that was why you sent us Seymour."

"I never read a book about that." *It must have been one of my juniors.*

Reg's legs were giving way. Without asking permission, he took a seat on the couch. "Then why did you call me here to discuss a book you have never read?"

"I called you here to discuss the burglary."

Reg held up his canes. "Do I strike you as the burglar type?"

Culp waved at his assistants as he put on his coat. "She's going to blab all the details. We have to separate them."

He burst through the adjoining office door with his badge displayed in front of him. "Reg Topping, I'm detaining you to help me in my investigation of a felony."

Reg looked over his shoulder at the camera and recording equipment in the other office. *Is that coming off my fifteen minutes of fame?*

Chapter 53

Culp took Reg to police headquarters on College Street. Reg was angry when Culp shoved him into the back seat of a police cruiser. It was not a comfortable ride for someone with spina bifida. He was angrier still when they took his canes and replaced them with a walker with one flat wheel. Dashed hopes and wounded pride gave way to a mounting sense of terror as he was herded down one hallway after another. His usual cool and control slipped away. Culp left him sitting in an interrogation room for two hours. When he asked to use the washroom, the officer assigned to see if he had hanged himself yet replied that there was no one available to escort him, which sounded uncannily like, *Go piss in your hat.*

Suspecting that he was on camera, he calmly relieved himself into a coffee cup he found in the waste basket. He proudly displayed his trophy on the interrogation table. It worked a treat on his mood. His anger crested and his fear passed. He focused himself and thought about the hour to come.

Why am I getting fussed? I haven't done anything.

Culp burst into the interrogation room and made a great show of turning on the tape recorder before pulling menacing paperwork out of an accordion file.

Culp looked over at the cup. "Is that what I think it is?"

"Yup."

"Did you learn that one drinking in the back seat of a Greyhound?"

"Your officer could've taken me to the washroom. How very odd that he wouldn't. Would it have been better for you if I had soiled myself?"

Culp didn't care for either his tone or that suggestion. "You're here on a very serious charge." He pushed the coffee cup with the end of his pen, moving it further down the table as Reg willed it to overturn. "Where were you last night?"

"I was at home," Reg replied.

"Good, we'll check into that. What do you know about Mrs. Dunn?"

"Her son is in our care at Punanai."

"Why did you break into her place?"

"I didn't do anything of the sort."

He removed a manuscript from the banker's box and leafed through it for several minutes before he spoke again. "We found your manuscript," he said, placing it on the table and sliding it toward its author, "and the note you left."

Reg's cheeks flamed red as his eyes popped and his mouth fell open.

His look hardened the detective's suspicions into facts. "You do know that mixing up fonts on a computer screen is not as effective as cutting letters out of a magazine." He placed his pen on top of the note with considerable satisfaction and slid it across the table. "You forgot to sign it."

Culp's look said, *Gotcha.* Toppings gut said, *Kaiser.* His DNA was all over this. Under the electron microscope of long acquaintance, he could pick out the familiar strands of metaphysical mayhem. It could only belong to the man with one name. This insight doubled the wager. *How do I get myself to safety without throwing shit-for-brains under the bus?*

"Apart from the fact that this is a copy of my book, why do you think I had any part in this?"

"You fit the profile. Psychologists have a name for guys like you. Answer the question, Dexter. Why did you do it? Was it a thrill? Did you get off on it? Our technicians are looking at your laptop. Who knows what kind of funny pictures we're going to find."

Reg knew from his long experience of interrogation at Punanai that Culp was attempting to provoke him in the hope that his feelings would overpower his thinking. That wasn't going to happen. Reg had seen through to the bottom, and getting there first mattered. Stick to the monogamous truth.

"I haven't done anything wrong. Ask me straight questions that I can answer."

"Shut up! You don't make the rules here."

Reg looked at his watch. "That's true but only for one more hour. That's how long I'm giving you. If you continue to play at intimidation, I'm going to call my lawyer."

Culp didn't care for the look of confidence on Reg's face. He barked at him. "Innocent people don't need lawyers."

"The hell they don't."

Culp kept the tone hostile. "We talked to the two guys you conned. They've both identified you as Edgar Demain. What do you have to say about that, smart mouth?"

"You made that up. Don't know them, don't know him, and if you have witnesses who say different, either they or you are lying."

Lying was a trump card. Reg braced himself for a slap.

Culp tried to ramp up the pressure by rising to his full height and leaning across the table. "You sicken me. We see a lot of your kind. Scammers. Well, you're neck deep in it now. We have you dead to rights. The only piece missing is the why. Were you drunk? Are you crazy? Give me some hope that you're not a monster. Because believe me, if you keep skating, we're going to have to take a much harder look at you. There's been lots of these break-ins and now that we have you in custody, we're going to see how many of them fit." He sat down and locked eyes with Reg. "Play your little games and, by all means, call your lawyer. That's all I need to satisfy myself that you did this."

There was a very long silence. Reg prayed with his eyes open but without moving his lips. *Help me keep my wits about me.*

Culp counterprayed, but Reg didn't need to read his lips. His thoughts were transparent. *Spill it, you bastard.*

Reg sorely missed his canes. They should have been resting beneath his chin, supporting his massive head. "From what I can gather, according to what you and Verna have said, this is a prank. My book is important to me. I would never involve it in anything shabby. Verna isn't the only one feeling violated."

For the first time, Culp doubted himself. His gut felt the way it did when acid reflux was about to get the upper hand on a good night's sleep. Reg saw it in his eye and made his move. "Charge me with something or let me go home. I'm done talking."

"You're done when I say you're done!"

Reg smiled as he theatrically checked his watch. "Whoa, that hour flew by. I'm going home. If you won't let me, I'm calling Harry. He can sort this out." He squirmed in his chair, trying to find a good position from which to launch himself. He put his arm flat on the table for additional lift and lurched to his feet.

Culp had a frantic moment. He wasn't sure what, if anything, he could charge Topping with as matters now stood. He needed a confession.

Anger got the better of him. He turned to the officer. "Put him in a cell."

The policeman handled Reg rather roughly. Reg overbalanced and almost took a tumble. "Let go of my arm. It's hard for me to use a walker. I need my canes. Are you afraid I'm going to outrun you?"

This time, "Regulations, sir," could not be mistaken for anything other than *Go piss in your hat*, a phrase that Reg was certain was going to be the preferred answer to every subsequent question.

Reg shook his head. *Some bastard fifty years ago put one over on them and now they treat everyone on crutches like a runner. I'm going to kill Kaiser for this!*

Reg was ushered into a lobby that looked out onto College Street, where a disinterested sergeant left him standing for a full five minutes while he worked away on some papers. Reg had done this a thousand times to clients, and he wasn't in the least surprised when the sergeant looked up at him with disgust.

"Reg Topping, I'm charging you with mischief and break and enter."

Reg felt the water rising over his nose. He took a deep breath, shut his eyes, and prayed. *Keep me safe.*

"I want to phone my lawyer."

"In due time. We have to process you first."

Reg thought about it. This was the haunted house of his youth. *The mean kids are going to stick my hand in cold spaghetti and tell me they're worms. Let them. I'll get a chapter out of this.*

They put Reg in a cell beside a man with a thick German accent and an angry disposition. He paced like a big cat in a cage, waving his arms and shouting that they had the wrong man as Reg tried to wipe the finger printing ink off his hands.

"It is my father you want. He is the monster!"

Reg nodded to him as if he was in complete agreement, but he was rebuffed. A few minutes later the man put his face up against the bars and beckoned to Reg, who could smell an abundance of whisky.

"My father was in the British internment camp at Bremervörde, him and everyone else lucky enough to survive the shooting and the looting. The big joke was Himmler coming into the camp. His papers said he was Heinrich Hitzinger— but that didn't fool anyone because everyone knew his face from the newsreels."

Reg was sorry he'd made an overture to conversation. Because the man was clearly impaired, he wisely kept his distance from the bars. But good manners required an encourager, which he provided with a nod.

"Before the very stupid English guards caught him out in his lie, he spoke to my father about how the war was for him. He was bitter and the camp schnapps made him weep. He blamed Göring for everything, always said that Fat Hermann didn't even know all the words to the 'Horst Wessel Song.'"

Reg nodded his head sagely as if in agreement. *This must be the unreliable jailhouse informant.*

Reg's lawyer arrived looking as if he too had been drinking since noon. "Why did you call me, Reg?"

"Look at me, Harry. And focus on the bars."

"I do copyright law."

"Well, someone stole my book. Have them arrested."

"They told me on the way in that you were here for mischief and break and enter."

"I've had the mischief. What I want now is the break and exit."

"That's very clever. You should write that down."

"Harry, I didn't do anything. One minute, I'm as happy as a clam because I'm finally going to get my book published. Next thing I know, this deranged harpy starts calling me names and runs me over like a raccoon on the Don Valley Parkway. Harry, I'm in the mood to sue."

"Good, because it costs $780,000 to sue someone these days, and I was wondering how to pay for my retirement villa."

"Is it really that much?"

"You wouldn't want to pay any less than that, would you?"

"What can we do?"

"I'm going to go talk to them and see if they're going to follow through on the charges. The case against you is thin. I think the only reason they put you in the cell was to scare the hell out of you. Button it."

"How much are you going to bill me for doing nothing?"

Drinking had muddled Harry's judgment. "We could cross complain."

"What's that?"

"Charge Mrs. Dunn with copyright infringement. Claim she stole your book."

"But that's bullshit."

Harry shrugged. "Yeah, you're right."

Reg shook his head and exhaled as Harry's soberer angels asserted themselves. "You may have to stay here tonight. The judge will see you in the morning. Sit tight and enjoy your tax dollars at work."

Reg gave his aching legs a vigorous rub. The rough handling he'd endured had a cumulative effect. A hot bath and a thick bathrobe might have restored him and made a good night's sleep a possibility.

"Yeah, I think in the bewildering array of happy options open to me this evening, I choose to do this thing, yes, this very thing and none other."

The sarcasm propelled Harry out of the cell corridor.

Chapter 54

Peter arrived back at the Granite Glen in the middle of the night, very much the worse for wear. He was beyond exhausted and too rundown to enjoy the spectacle of Pritpal and Barstow in handcuffs looking at each other for clues as they tried to come up with a plausible story. He curled up in a ball on the bench near the cryotank and watched the red light cry out its silent warning. A serious young police officer draped the room in yellow tape before locking the door behind her.

No Terri, no me, he thought. Just a big popsicle machine. But it was quiet and familiar, and that's what he needed.

If the light had shown up, he'd have gone with it. He ached to feel it's comforting warmth again. Maybe have someone to talk to. He had expended his newfound windfall of strength and tapped out his original reserves as well. He was running on fumes, not that it mattered. His was a good kind of tired.

The little girl's voice was niggling in his head. He was angry about what she'd said. What am I supposed to do about John and Walter?

It wasn't fair that she had hung that on him and turned Terri against him and ruined everything and then said, and this is the part that burned, that he had done it all for himself.

"I did it for Terri…" *he said to the empty room.*

John was a force of nature. A self-sufficient loudmouth with an opinion about everything.

He thinks nothing of standing on the coffin at a funeral and making fun of the mourners in the middle of a eulogy. *He sat up on the bench, feeling the quarrel's energy quickening him.*

There is no talking to him when he's holding court. He doesn't listen. I can't talk to John about the light without talking about Terri. If he laughs — no, *when* he sneers — well, that's when the matches are going to come out.

His thoughts turned to the expression on Walter's face as he clung to the banister in the sorority house.

"Naff."

When Peter came to himself, he wasn't sure if he had fainted or slept. Without Terri, the Chamber of New Life was of no interest. He made his way haltingly to the main floor, where he waited in the pleasant sunlight by the lobby window until the mailman bearing John on his back made his way through the doors.

"There you are. I've been all over town…"

Peter's voice was scarcely above a whisper. *"John, I need to talk to you."*

"Where did you go? You left me to deal with your pal Walter all by myself, which, incidentally, I managed extraordinarily well. In fact—"

"John, I'm all in and I need to talk with you about something very important."

John looked cross. "There is nothing more important than this! I got Walter into the room. He's not hanging on to that damn railing anymore. You remember… your master plan, throw the old prick into the light."

Peter sighed. That had been his whole life two days ago.

"I want to talk to you about the light, John."

"That's right, we'll throw him in and see what happens."

"John, I need you to listen. I've been in the light. Walter too. It's not what we thought."

John took a step back. But then curiosity got the better of caution and he approached Peter slowly, examining him for the first time in detail and not liking what he was seeing. "No one survives the light."

"John, the light is a good thing. We don't need to be afraid of it."

"It's damned near killed you."

Peter smiled. "No, that was a little job I did on the side. Now listen—"

"No, you listen. I told you this was going to happen — you're slipping over the edge."

"I'm fine, I have enough energy left to do what I need to do."

"You're not fine; you're getting that poltergeist look."

"John…"

"Shut up, look at me, and tell me straight, are you still playing with a full deck?"

Peter shook his head. "A full deck got me here."

"What the hell does that mean?"

"I'm thinking with my heart now."

"That's bullshit."

"Maybe it is."

"You promised…"

"Yeah, I did, and a fat lot of good it's going to do either one of us."

John shoved him. "You want the truth? Go look at yourself in the mirror, you old fool."

"John, not now, I don't have the time or the energy for one of your mindless tirades."

"Tirades, is that what they are? Tirades? That's a lovely word to describe someone talking sense to intransigence. Have you any idea how insufferably boring you are?"

"John, you're going to make me cross and that will serve no purpose."

The thin ghost sprang at him, seizing him by the lapels. "You listen to me, you self-absorbed old bastard! I'm going to make you a damn sight worse than cross. I moved heaven and earth to get Walter where we need him to be, and by God, you're going to man up and help me throw the bastard headfirst into the light and the devil take the hindmost. We're taking the afterlife by storm."

Peter's voice and face radiated calm. "John, he's there already, smoking cigarettes to his heart's content."

John paused and looked at Peter in horror. "What have you done?"

"I stepped into the light. It's not a bad thing, it's not what we thought — it's full of life and energy."

John looked at Peter's broken and diminished body and shook his head. "The poltergeist hotel called while you were out, they have a banister ready for you." John gave Peter a dismissive shove and turned to leave.

"I came back here to wise you up. But I doubt now if that's even possible. I'm going to be with Terri, and in my more reflective moments, I'm going to think about you back here, wasting every gift that God ever gave you. Life has called your bluff, John. Turn over your hole cards. Let the world see who you really are."

"Damn you, Peter!"

Chapter 55

Kaiser arrived at Toronto Police Headquarters at 8:00 p.m. with his game face on. He asked the sergeant at the desk if he could see someone regarding Reg Topping. Detective Culp was only too happy to oblige.

"I'm here to talk to you about my friend, Reg Topping."

"How do you know him?"

"We work together at Punanai."

"What do you want to tell me?"

"There's been a terrible mistake."

"That seems very unlikely. We've charged Mr. Topping with break and enter and mischief."

Kaiser's face registered concerned. "Detective Culp, this is a foolish prank gone horribly wrong. I'm the mysterious L. Edgar Demain. I orchestrated this. I wanted to get my friend's book published and get some publicity along the way by causing a hoax. This was supposed to end with all the participants laughing over a good dinner and celebrating a new friendship. But I miscalculated. When I found out what happened … well, I came over here to put things right. It never occurred to me that the Dunns would see this as anything more than a lark or involve the police."

Culp still liked Reg in the role of mastermind. "How do I know you're Mr. Demain?"

Kaiser reached into his pocket, took out the phone he'd used, and placed it on the table. "I used this phone to do everything associated with the hoax."

Detective Culp was crestfallen. "I need you to come with me and make a statement." Culp directed him toward the interview room.

"Why all the subterfuge?" asked Culp as he passed Kaiser a pad of yellow notepaper and a black pen.

"It was all in good fun. I was certain the Dunns would see the humour. You have to admit, it's intriguing."

"No, it's juvenile and stupid. Mrs. Dunn was very upset."

Kaiser actually managed to look embarrassed. "Well, let me tell you how it was supposed to happen. I gave the movers an envelope full of money and a letter addressed to the Dunns, which I can only assume they didn't notice. That's how the wheels fell off. I timed the thing in such a way that the Dunns would have fifteen minutes of empty cottage before they heard the truck coming. The note invited them to a celebration at the Wiarton Diner where they could expect to get a full explanation." Kaiser looked over at Culp as if he was still working out the implications of what he had done. "Do you see how this story would be very helpful when you're trying to market a book?"

Culp let him talk. He was preoccupied with how this was going to look to his captain.

Kaiser kept pushing, sounding like a man seeking absolution. "I planned to meet them and pitch the book at the Wiarton Diner. I waited in the restaurant for a couple of hours, but they didn't show. It's a shame. They do a terrific pot roast. I phoned them, but they didn't pick up. I was about to drive to their cottage when it occurred to me to call around. Reg had called the office and told them about his appointment with Verna. That's when I called your detachment, and they directed me here."

***

The German man was still pacing in the cell next to Reg. "Why are you disturbing us? Can't you see how well we're sleeping with the light on and no mattresses on the bunks? Send for housekeeping. We need more roaches."

Reg looked past the two burly policemen and into Kaiser's face.

"You here to spring me?"

Kaiser had planned his line. "No, we're doing Sydney Carton this evening, not Cody Jarrett."

"Kaiser, is this one of your pranks gone wrong?"

"I miscalculated. I told them what happened. They'll drive you home."

Reg lost all interest in his own discomfort and was totally focused on his friend. "Why did you do this?"

"You needed a little help to get your book published. I took a few liberties."

"How did they catch you?"

"They didn't. When I figured out what must have happened, I got on the phone and came down here."

The German in the next cell couldn't control himself. "Hey, when you're finished over there, come talk to me. I need a hit man."

"Pipe down," said the cop as he opened the cell door to let Reg out and put Kaiser in.

Reg looked at Kaiser in utter disbelief. "You did this for me?"

Kaiser looked pleased with himself. "It was worth doing."

***

Reg saw no point in hanging around the police station. He called a cab and, to his great surprise and relief, got a good night's sleep. He was back at the College Street court at 9:00 a.m.

Judge Sarah Brannon saw Kaiser at 9:15. On the recommendation of Detective Culp, he was offered the diversion program, which meant that he had the choice of a $500 donation to a registered charity or fifty hours of community service. Kaiser wrote a cheque, which he knew would never clear the bank, to the WWF in memory of L. Edgar Demain.

Reg gave Kaiser a playful punch on the shoulder as he exited the clerk's office, once again a free man.

"It was good of you to come," said Kaiser.

"I thought you might need to see a friendly face."

As Kaiser turned to walk away, Reg asked the question he had come all the way downtown on the bus to find the answer to. "Kaiser, did you really do that for me?"

Kaiser thought about the kaleidoscope of moving parts that had been set free with a single action before producing a wicked smile. "That was certainly one of the reasons."

Chapter 56

Peter got back to Flannerman's before John did, his limbs on fire. He had to lie down on the pew to rest. It was hard to focus. Every fibre of his being cried out for relief. He'd put up with pain and fear for a long time.

I could've done it for a long time to come, too, because I wanted Terri. *But that pain was all pointless. That suffering an option. Suffering can be heroic if there's only that one path open to you.*

I know now there's something better. I was only in the ballroom for a few minutes, but that changed everything. *He looked at the familiar stained-glass window and sighed.* I don't ever want to see this room or this building or this block or this city ever again.

Peter gathered his strength and struggled to sit up. He used the pew to steady himself. He paused to have one last look around as he found his feet. It was too much for him. He collapsed in the pew. He thought about what the little girl had said, taunted him with really.

John will be fine without me. Some other spook will show up — someone who hasn't heard the stories. It will be a renaissance for him.

John slunk in a few minutes after sunrise. He felt bad about where he had left things with Peter. He found him in the front pew at Flannerman's with pending poltergeist written all over him. He'd been there all night. He hadn't done any of the things he loved — no checking on his head, no newspapers. John sat with him, waiting for him to speak. Peter acknowledged him with a look, but that was all. The two old ghosts sat wordlessly through two funerals.

Not knowing how to mend their problem, and not willing to end their relationship, they simply sat and let the natural engines of healing do their work. It was a very peaceful and beautiful day.

When the sun went down, John said his goodbyes by touching Peter lightly on the shoulder. The fat ghost wasn't there the next morning. And John never saw him again.

Chapter 57

Klaus Schaller put his bags down beside the heavy oak door and walked into the living room.

"Hello, does anyone work here, or do you all just take turns sleeping on the couch?"

Daniel put down his newspaper. "The counsellors are in a meeting. Are you here for treatment?"

"Yes, my dear papa sent me here so that I can get sober for him."

Daniel smiled. "If you say that to the staff, they'll yell at you and say you have to want to get sober for yourself."

Klaus was enjoying himself. "English sometimes baffles me. What I'm trying to say is my father drinks too much and he sends me here. Do you see the joke of it?"

"I don't follow you."

"My father is the drunk, not me."

"So why are you here instead of him?"

"Money! My father is very well placed. He knows people, important people. He had me put in jail for talking back to him, and then he paid to have me put in here."

"So why don't you go home?"

"I don't want to — I'm mad at him. What kind of place is this?"

"It's not so bad. We actually have fun here."

"Any ladies?"

"Not that kind of fun."

They heard the door to the office open.

Reg and Kaiser didn't see Klaus Schaller as they exited Doug's office, but he saw them. Klaus felt a stab of recognition. He'd seen these two birds before, and together — but where?

In the low light of the living room, his initial reaction was that his eyes were playing tricks on him. Not an uncommon occurrence for an aging alcoholic. The canes that Reg was using seemed out of place to him, because the other fellow had used a walker.

Klaus's heart soared to the rooftops. He had both his exit visa and plane ticket in hand. He turned to Daniel with a look of mock horror on his face. "You say this place is good?"

"Yeah."

His voice rose half an octave and doubled in volume. "And those two characters work here?"

Daniel couldn't tell which two he was referring to. "They all work here."

Klaus got to his feet and talked loudly enough for everyone in the house to hear. "Some place you got here. Give me back my papa's money."

The counsellors looked over at the unfamiliar face kicking up a fuss.

Paul moved toward him. "Are you here for treatment?"

"Not here in gangster land."

"What does that mean?"

"Ask those two," he said pointing at Reg and Kaiser. "The two jailbirds, go ahead and ask them. What kind of place are you running here?"

Paul looked at his colleagues with a happy grin. "Kaiser, what have you been up to?"

Chapter 58

Peter knew instinctively that he had to get back to the room Lou Canon had previously occupied. Since he'd gone home, the preternatural riptides in the house had begun to ebb. Was the moon half full or half empty? When he entered the ballroom, he could see the waiters looking very tired and discouraged as they gathered up the wine-stained tablecloths and empty glasses. He went to talk to the bartender, but he couldn't get the man to look up from the glasses he was drying.

Off in the corner, he could see Walter feeding an endless stack of nickels into the cigarette machine.

A voice from a booth startled him. "It's late. Everyone wants to go home."

Peter wheeled to see who was talking. "You're still here."

"I knew you'd be back. I thought that I'd wait up for you."

Peter looked defeated.

"Sit down," said the little girl. "Let's do our nails."

Peter was too tired to argue. He took a seat. For a second, he saw a crocodile reading a newspaper across the table from him, but when he rubbed his eyes and shook his head, it was the angel of death again, all pink cheeked and lovely, intent on colouring her toenails.

"Is this how you fix things and put your affairs in order?"

Peter's brow was fearsome. His eyes blazed defiance even if his chin was resting on his chest. "I did what I needed to do. My God it felt good."

The little girl slurped the last of her drink through a brightly coloured straw before returning to her task.

"*You did what you wanted to do. There's big a difference.*"

Peter looked up at her in wonder.

The little girl held out her foot for his inspection. "Peter, for once I need you to listen. You get things wrong when you're afraid and then you run with them. I wanted you to help your friend…"

Peter pointed over at Walter. "He's here."

The little girl frowned and rubbed her temples. "Your other friend, Peter, your friend John, he's going to be alone now."

Peter had a moment. A tear slid slowly down his cheek. "I wanted to bring him, but we fight all the time, and I didn't know how. I'm sorry, he was all I had the last couple of years. I missed my chance. I did everything wrong."

He looked sadly over at the dance floor. It was dark and deserted. Not a bad match for what he was feeling.

"I even messed up my dance with Terri."

"Nonsense." The angel snapped her fingers and a single bright light illuminated the centre of the dance floor. Peter's face lit up. She nodded to an unseen ally and the jukebox began to play "Redemption Song." The air smelled faintly of cigar smoke and salt sea air. Peter saw a familiar figure emerging out of the darkness. Terri beckoned to him as she swayed to the music.

Peter took her hand and followed her into the light. Her embrace meant everything. It was different this time — he couldn't explain how or why. He shut his eyes and felt his body begin to move in harmony with the music and with something else. Something entirely new.

"Do they have crayfish in heaven, Terri?"

"I know a lovely spot."

Fin